Praise for Laurie Forest and *The Black Witch*

"I absolutely loved *The Black Witch* and will have a very hard time waiting for the second book! Maximum suspense, unusual magic—a whole new, thrilling approach to fantasy!"
—Tamora Pierce, #1 *New York Times* bestselling author

"This briskly paced, tightly plotted novel enacts the transformative power of education, creating engaging characters set in a rich alternative universe with a complicated history that can help us better understand our own. A massive page-turner that leaves readers longing for more."
—*Kirkus Reviews*, starred review

"Forest uses a richly imagined magical world to offer an uncompromising condemnation of prejudice and injustice.... With strong feminist messages, lively secondary characters, and an especially nasty rival (imagine a female Draco Malfoy), fans of Harry Potter and Tamora Pierce will gobble down the 600-plus pages and demand the sequel."
—*Booklist*, starred review

"*The Black Witch* is a refreshing, powerful young adult fantasy. This strong debut offers an uncompromising glimpse of world-altering politics amplified by a magical setting in which prejudice and discrimination cut both ways."
—Robin Hobb, *New York Times* bestselling author

"Exquisite character work, an elaborate mythology, and a spectacularly rendered universe make this a noteworthy debut, which argues passionately against fascism and xenophobia.... [The] thrilling conclusion will leave readers eager for the next book in this series."
—*Publishers Weekly*, starred review

"We fell under the spell of this rich, diverse, Potter-worthy university world! Characters that come alive off the page, tangled relationships, swoon-worthy romance! Love the fresh way this also tackles prejudice. Prepare to fangirl!"
—*Justine* magazine

LAURIE FOREST

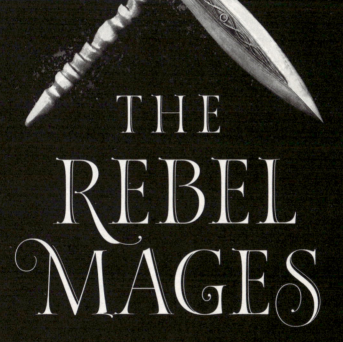

THE REBEL MAGES

ink
yard
press

Recycling programs
for this product may
not exist in your area.

ISBN-13: 978-1-335-55677-6

The Rebel Mages

Copyright © 2019 by Harlequin Books S.A.

The publisher acknowledges the copyright holder of the individual works as follows:

Wandfasted
Copyright © 2017 by Laurie Forest

Light Mage
Copyright © 2018 by Laurie Forest

This edition published by arrangement with Harlequin Books S.A.

For questions and comments about the quality of this book, please contact us at CustomerService@Harlequin.com.

® and TM are trademarks of Harlequin Enterprises Limited or its corporate affiliates. Trademarks indicated with ® are registered in the United States Patent and Trademark Office, the Canadian Intellectual Property Office and in other countries.

InkyardPress.com

Printed in U.S.A.

CONTENTS

For Diane Dexter—
tireless youth advocate, talented writer and reader, devoted mother
and my good friend.

WANDFASTED

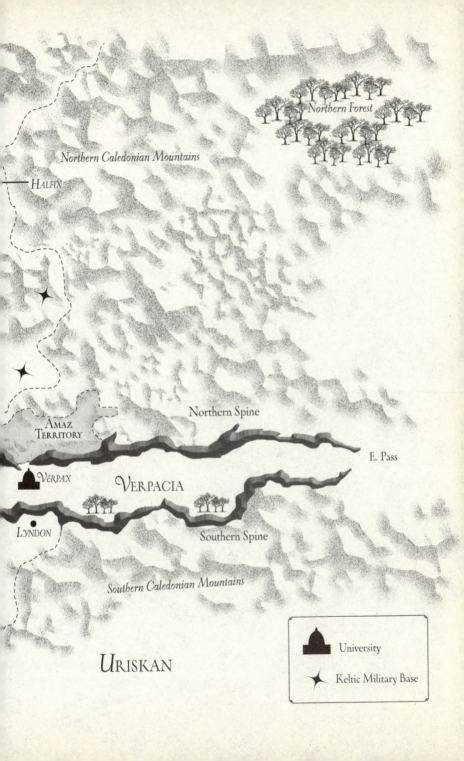

PROLOGUE

I've gotten used to the names they call us.

Crows. Roaches. Hedgewitches.

I no longer cry when I'm shoved in the market or spat on in the streets. I endure their mocking, hateful glares and the signs of protection they make against me to ward off my perceived evil.

I am Gardnerian.

As such, I'm barely tolerated here, stranded in a sea of Kelts, allowed to exist only because my aptitude for healing brews is considered useful in this tiny, remote village.

It would be easier, perhaps, if my appearance didn't set me apart so much. My forest-green eyes and dark hair might seem unremarkable, but the black tunic and long skirt I wear, paired with a silver Erthia orb necklace, mark me as one of the First Children. And the way my skin shimmers a faint emerald in the dark—perhaps the most undeniable sign of all—makes it impossible for me to hide what I am.

A Gardnerian Mage.

Hated by all but my own people.

When they painted Heretics on our barn and set fire to it, I thought that was the worst it could get.

Until they sent the dragons.

But they didn't count on us having dragons of our own. And they certainly didn't count on Her.

Our Great Mage. The Bringer of Fire. The Storm of Death. The Crow Sorceress.

Our Deliverance.

The Black Witch.

CHAPTER ONE:
Front Lines

"We're not doing business with Crows," Mistress Darrow states. "Not anymore."

She stands with one fist propped on a broad hip, her apple-cheeked face twisted up into a triumphant sneer, strands of her blond hair escaping her crimson kerchief. The flag of Keltania is pinned above her ample bosom—an iron-black X on a rectangle of bloodred linen.

Her husband, Merchant Darrow, seems embarrassed, his own Keltanian flag haphazardly pinned up near his shoulder. He looks down at the wooden counter in front of him, toying with the smooth abacus and deliberately avoiding my gaze.

Panic rears inside me. My grip tightens on the apothecary crate I've set down before them, tidy medicine bottles lined up in the segmented box. I think of the money we need for our journey east to Verpacia. Of the red tinge to the leaves, winter close on our heels. My elderly grandfather, my young brother.

Doveshire has become too dangerous for Gardnerians. It took ages for my brother, Wren, and me to convince our stubborn grandfather that we needed to leave, but now, everything is ready for our departure—the wagon is packed, the horses already hitched, the house closed up.

All we need is the money for these medicines I've spent

weeks brewing. The money we've been counting on to buy supplies—supplies we'll need to survive.

I straighten my shoulders, trying not to shrink under Mistress Darrow's glare. "I don't understand. The last time I came in, you were happy to buy my medicines."

She blows out a disgusted breath. "Dark witches with dark magic, that's what your lot is. First you twist the faith that belongs to *us*. Then you use your dark magic to steal a nice big chunk of *our* land." She gives her chin a defiant lift, her smile full of venom. "Well, the tide is turning. Your magic's *faded*."

Some of what she's saying is true, to the sadness of many Gardnerians. Most of my people have no magic or weak magic at best. And we haven't had a Great Mage in generations. But our magic isn't dark, and I've never done a thing to harm her or anyone else—though I'm sorely tempted to in this moment.

I can feel her angry gaze on me as I turn to her husband. "Please, Merchant Darrow," I plead, the forced politeness of my tone ringing false in my own ears. "I've spent weeks preparing these healing brews for your shop. My family is counting on me to sell them."

Conscience seems to get the better of Merchant Darrow, his lined face tensing in discomfort. "Just this last time, Tessla," he forces out gruffly, still not looking at me as he pulls the vials of medicines closer to inspect them.

Mistress Darrow throws him a tight look of fury before grabbing the crate and jerking it away from the both of us.

"We'll take them, then." She smiles malevolently. "Just like you Crows took our land." She sets a hard gaze on her husband. "No payment."

I'm not sure I've heard her right. "What?"

She skewers me with her glare. "Oh, we're onto the lot of you. Figuring you'll wave your wands around and take everything we've got right from under us. Well, not this time.

We're going to fight, and we'll stamp you all out before you have a chance to raise up another Dark Mage. And we're taking our land *back*."

My heart pounds like a hammer. I lunge for the crate, but she's anticipated me, pulling it quickly out of reach just as Brandon and two other burly blacksmith apprentices lumber into the Guildmarket.

"You can't," I protest, full of righteous fury and mounting desperation as she sets the crate on a high shelf behind her. "That's a whole month's work. We've nothing else to trade. You're *stealing*."

"Got a Roach in here? Causing trouble?" Brandon saunters toward me, smelling of sweat and smoke. His blond hair is greasy, and the flag of Keltania is securely pinned over his heart.

I glare up at him with undisguised loathing. Undaunted, Brandon reaches out with a broad, dirty hand to paw at my hair. I flinch away, and he laughs, a cruel gleam in his eyes. "At least she's a pretty Roach."

"Is she?" Gerrig sidles up and gives me a slow once-over, Adam's apple bobbing in his skinny, chicken-like neck. He flicks up the edge of my tunic with his finger.

"You'd never know it, with all this black fabric they wear. Could have three titties, for all we know."

I recoil and slap my tunic hem down flat, flushing with embarrassment and horror as the young men and Mistress Darrow break into laughter. I'm stunned by their brazen cruelty and find myself blinking back tears.

"We could check that," stocky Colton offers, mischief lighting his eyes.

Their chortling quickly turns to an open leer. I shrink back, my gaze darting toward the door, then desperately back to my medicines.

Merchant Darrow won't let them hurt me, I reason, trying to calm myself. *He's never been unkind. And surely he'll pay me.*

Out of the corner of my eye, through the store's large front windows, I see young Keltic men running down the street armed with bows and swords, the flag of Keltania pinned to their arms. My mind is cast into confusion and mounting alarm.

"What's happening?" I ask nervously. "Where are they going?"

Brandon leans in close and I know what his answer will be before he speaks.

"To get rid of all of you."

A Purging.

The villagers have murmured about it for months as the border hostilities heated up, hissing their threats as I passed by. Grandfather kept dismissing it all as overinflated bravado, so we stupidly remained here.

My plan for escape is a single day too late.

I back away from Brandon as my stomach gives a sickening lurch, suddenly aware of how much danger we're in. I have to get home to Grandfather and Wren. I have to get them to safety right now. And I have to get hold of Grandfather's wand so I can use what magic I have to protect them.

"Come along, Edgard," Mistress Darrow slyly purrs to her husband, a vengeful gleam in her eye. She takes in the restless crowd on the street, Brandon and his cohorts—and me, conspicuously unarmed, unprotected. "Leave the girl," she directs as Merchant Darrow hesitates, a worried expression on his face. "Let the young men take care of the Crows."

My throat goes dry and tight. "Please, Merchant Darrow," I plead. "You've always been fair to us."

Merchant Darrow glances toward the young men, then back at me, obviously torn, a hard crease between his eyes.

Another mob of men streams by the windows, brandishing

knives and swords. Some are on horseback, riding toward my home downriver.

My panic crests as I turn back to see Merchant Darrow and his wife quietly slipping into the back of the shop, a heavy curtain falling shut behind them.

Emboldened, piggish Colton licks at his lip, splotches of red coloring his cheeks as he stares at my body. "Should we find out what's under all that black?"

"Leave me alone, Colton," I demand, backing up as far as I can, my skirts pressing against a grain barrel.

"'*Leave me alone, Colton,*'" he jeers, his tone a high-pitched mockery of mine that sets Brandon laughing.

Gerrig snorts in derision, his smile excited. "Think they're holier than us. That they're the true First Children."

"You too good for us?" Brandon chides, eyeing me smugly. "That why you go 'round with your nose stuck high in the air?"

"Stop it, Brandon," I seethe, glaring at him. *If I only had a wand.*

"Or *what*?" Brandon taunts, stalking closer. "You'll wave a magic stick at us? You don't have any idea what's coming, do you?"

"That's enough," I insist, my heart pounding. "I have to leave." I step around him, but his muscular arm swings out to catch me.

"Not so fast, little witch."

Growing desperate, I slip away from his grasp and try to go around his other side.

Laughing along with his friends, Brandon grabs me and jerks me roughly backward.

Infuriated, I wrench myself around and slam the base of my palm hard up against his nose, the pain of impact knifing up my arm.

He stumbles back in surprise, his hand flying up to his nose, blood seeping through his fingers. I glare at him fiercely.

Brandon's eyes narrow, but before I can bolt for the door, he rushes forward and smacks me hard across the face.

Shocked, I stagger and lose my footing, falling to the floor. Brandon stalks toward me as I scuttle away from him, dizzy from the blow.

The door to the Guildmarket creaks open.

"Hit her again, and I will split your head, Brandon. I swear I will."

Brandon stops, his fist clenched midair.

Jules Kristian is standing in the doorway, pointing an arrow straight at Brandon's head.

Tall, skinny Jules. My Kelt neighbor. His glasses are askew, his hair is its usual brown, tousled mess and he's not wearing a flag. He looks like one of them, dressed in an earth-toned tunic and pants. But he's nothing like them—he always makes up his own mind rather than following the crowd.

And he's made the very bad decision to be friends with me.

CHAPTER TWO:
Jules Kristian

Brandon and the others stand frozen, as if stunned that book-ish Jules has it in him to defy them.

Filled with relief, I seize the chance Jules has given me. I burst through a gap between Brandon and Gerrig, dive around Jules and fly out the front door, almost losing my footing on the wooden steps.

I skid to a halt at the sight that lies before me, my stomach clenching into a tight vise.

At the center of the five-point intersection, just off to the side of the village's central, raised dais, a wagon has come to a stop. An angry mob of Kelts surrounds it, their collective voices rising. The wagon is jammed full of black-clad Gardnerians with dark hair and green eyes.

I know them all.

Before anyone in the crowd can see me, I dive behind a stack of grain barrels and peer through the gaps, my heart hammering. The streets are packed, and I can see no obvious route of escape. But if I can't get out of here, I'll end up in that the wagon with the rest of my Gardnerian neighbors.

Mage Krell, the mild-mannered cooper, stands against the wagon's edge and blinks, gazing vacantly at the crowd as the mob rocks the wagon and hurls insults. His glasses are gone, and a large bruise colors the side of his face. Years ago, he made me a small set of wooden animals that were so tiny, I could hold them all in the palm of my hand. His elderly wife clings to him, white strands of her hair flying around like unworked wool, her eyes wide and terrified. Mage Cooke, the quiet widow who scrapes by selling herbs and teas, is cowering, her arm raised protectively in front of her face. Young, sour Rolland is shaking his fist and stupidly yelling back at the crowd. He falls back as a large rock hits him square in the head. Mage Cooke ducks and cries out, her hands flying up to her face as more rocks are hurled at the wagon. When she lifts her head again, blood is streaming down her temple.

The voices swell as a young blonde Keltic woman is dragged onto the central dais by the village smith and his strapping son, Orik. Her head is shorn, and there's a sign around her neck that reads CROW WHORE. My heart lurches into my throat as I realize it's meek Daisie, the smith's own daughter. She struggles in vain as they thrust her into the wagon with the Gardnerians. A limp, black-clad Gardnerian youth is dragged up next—quiet Gramm, who's been sweet on Daisie for years, his face bloodied, his sign reading FILTHY CROW. I lose sight of him as the miller hurls him off the dais and into the blood-thirsty crowd, their voices surging.

The sea of voices is one loud blur, but some of their rage-filled words sound out clearly.

"Kill the Mages before they kill us!"

"Keltania for Kelts!"

"Smash the Roaches!"

"Kill him!"

"There's another one! Hidin' back here!"

I cry out as a large hand clamps down on my arm and I'm wrenched out into the open, the nearest edge of the crowd turning to face me in a sickening, murderous wave.

Terror stabs through me, filling me with feral desperation.

I stomp and claw at my attacker, struggling to free my arm. My other arm is grabbed tight by another man, stretching me out between them. I kick and twist wildly in a futile effort to break free.

Then an ear-shattering shriek rends the air, and the entire crowd gasps and ducks. The hands restraining me fall away, and I almost stumble to the ground.

I flinch as a mammoth black dragon bursts into view overhead and thunders across the sky.

There's another collective ducking-down as a series of shrieks echoes out from above. Two more dragons slice through the clouds, their dark wings expansive. The dragons are ghoulishly skeletal, their wings covered with sharp feathers. They push air down onto us in a heavy stream that blows my hair flat against my scalp. A foul stench washes over me, like rotted carrion set on fire.

A cheer goes up from the crowd.

My gaze is torn from the sky as another hand grabs my arm, but my panic recedes when I see Jules standing beside me, a finger to his lips. He pulls me backward into an alley, and I stumble to keep up with him as more dragons shriek by overhead.

They're all flying in same direction. North. Toward Gardneria. Toward my homeland.

Jules's pace is furious, his bow slung over his shoulder, bobbing up and down as we run. It almost slides off as we dart down the narrow alley, then take a sharp left behind the Guildmarket.

He practically hurls me behind the clutter of damaged barrels, torn jute sacks and other mercantile debris that's piled up. My elbow makes painful contact with a large crate as I duck down for cover. Then the light is snuffed out as Jules throws an old grain sack over the both of us, and not a moment too soon.

Heavy boot heels thud down the alley and across the dirt ground right in front of us. "She ran back here!" a man yells.

"Must be headed for the Roach Bank," another answers.

My breath seems outrageously loud. I cover my mouth and nose with my arm to stifle it. I start to feel faint as my pulse hammers in my ears and fear threatens to crack me into a million jagged pieces.

More boots thud by, but the voices begin to recede. "She went this way! Toward the river!"

The alley finally falls silent, and Jules peeks out. Weak twilight seeps in under the sack.

My head is spinning, my heart thundering in my chest. *My brother. My grandfather.* My entire universe constricts to one singularity: a suffocating fear for my family.

I murmur a fire spell and pull up a ball of magic from the ground.

The spell sizzles up in a buzzing thread to curl tight inside my chest. A vibrating pain grows, prickling like a rotating ball of needles in the center of me. I can't do anything with this power, not without a wand, but it emanates a steadying warmth that stays my mounting panic.

"We need to get to the top of the peak," I rasp out breathlessly to Jules, jerking my head toward the small mountain at our backs. "We can see everything up there. And it's the quickest way to my cottage." I give him a significant look. "If we can get there, I can get hold of the wand."

Jules's eyes widen, but he nods in assent. He knows I've experimented with Grandfather's wand, even though I'm not supposed to. The wand once belonged to my father, but when he died, our Mage Council gifted it to my virtually magic-free grandfather in tribute. It's ill-constructed, this wand, the laminated wood unevenly layered and of substandard wood, but we're lucky to have it. Most Gardnerians, especially poorer ones like us, don't own wands. Even a coarse wand like ours is outrageously expensive—difficult to craft and even harder to obtain.

But I know how to wield it.

Unlike most females of my race, I've some magic in me.

Every muscle tensed and on high alert, Jules quietly pulls the sack off us entirely. Hunched down, we slip into the brush behind the refuse, into the slice of forest at the edge of town that quickly slants upward to form Crykes Peak.

It's *our* small mountain, Jules's and mine—one of the only places where a Kelt and a Gardnerian can go together and not be noticed. We've whiled away more than a few summer evenings at the top, reading, laughing, talking about history and alchemy, Jules sharing stories of the University with me.

It's getting darker, and the sunset through the trees is lovely and peaceful, a mockery of the terrible chaos that's been unleashed. There's a hard chill seeping into the air, autumn beginning to dig its claws into summer.

I grasp Jules's hand as he half pulls me up the sheltered, rocky path that cuts through the trees, my heavy black skirts slowing me down. We know just where to go—we're familiar with all the footholds, and my dark clothing blends into the long shadows.

When we reach the jagged peak, my chest hurts like I've swallowed cut glass and my stomach is a painful knot.

More fiendish dragons soar overhead, racing across the sky. Jules and I flatten ourselves among the surrounding rocks to avoid being sighted. One dragon flies so close to the top of the mountain that I can make out the black scales of the creature's underbelly, its taloned feet curled up underneath, tipped with terrible claws.

Then the air around us goes quiet again, and we rise, trembling, to our feet. My heart lurches as I take in the sight before us.

There's a whole host of dragons in the air now, soldiers astride them as they wing their way north. They're like a flat, black swarm of mammoth insects, screeching at each other, wings whooshing. The brilliant orange sunset silhouettes their evil forms.

I swivel my head, following their movement. I rise a bit more and turn my gaze down toward the Wey River, toward home.

Our cottage is a single, bright flame.

All the Gardnerian homesteads up and down the river have been torched and are burning bright. The ball of steadying magic inside me is snuffed out in one painful jolt.

"*My house!*" I cry. My knees give way, and I stagger down to the rocky ground.

"*No,*" Jules gasps, his eyes fixed on my cottage, face stricken.

"Oh, Ancient One," I cry, a great sob tearing from my chest, my palms clinging to the rock behind me. "Oh, Jules, do you think they're alive?"

He falls beside me as more dragons streak by, his hands coming up to grip my arms.

"Ancient One, help me," I wail, my chest heaving, sure I'm going to retch. I look to Jules with crippling despair. "Do you think they killed them?"

He opens his mouth, but no words come out. The entire world seems to fall away, but he catches me as I crumble, his arms closing around me.

"They're dead, aren't they?" I moan into his chest, rocking my head side to side in grief.

"I don't know," he says, clutching me tight.

"My mother's gone. My father. Not Grandfather and Wren, too!" His hand comes up to cradle my hair. "Oh, Jules," I sob,

"Grandfather should have let me have the wand! He should have let us leave sooner!"

"I know. I know it, Tessla."

"I could have saved them!" I let out a low, agonized wail as he holds me.

Choking on tears, I pull away from Jules and stagger up to peer north.

The horde of dragons is a dark splotch moving relentlessly over the Caledonian Mountains toward central Gardneria. The Kelts have turned the entirety of broad Crykes Field into a military staging area. Lines of dark tents and geometric rune-marked structures have been erected and hundreds of torches are lit. Some of the dragons are being flown down onto the field.

Horrified, I turn south and spot a large mass of uniformed Keltic soldiers wearing russet military tunics over black pants. They're riding in tight formation into Doveshire via the Southern Wayroad. Urisk soldiers flank them—powerful geomancers with pointed ears and the blue hair and sky-blue skin of their military class, their cobalt-blue armor marked with glowing georunes. Some of the Urisk are riding hydreenas, the terrible, boar-shaped beasts hunched and bristling, tusks gleaming in the dying light. Some are riding in their rune-powered horse-less carriages with glowing runes for wheels.

The Western Wayroad is clogged with Keltic families fleeing toward the coast, away from the fighting, their carts piled high with people and possessions and festooned with red flags bearing black Xs.

"They've an Icaral demon!" I gasp as a black-winged soldier rides into view astride a hydreena, his eyes pinpoints of fire. He looks much like the blue Urisk soldiers, save for his glowing eyes and the feathered black wings that fan menacingly out from his back, not entirely unlike the dragons above us.

An Evil One.

I slump down, dizzy, my back to a broad rock as I teeter sideways, weeping.

Jules crouches down and takes my arm. "Come away with me." There's steel in his voice. "I'll find Keltic clothes for you. We'll escape."

I thrust my arm out at him, my skin glimmering faintly emerald in the gathering darkness. "It's no use, Jules. How could we hide *this*?"

His jaw hardens. "I'll smuggle you into Verpacia."

I'm shaking my head as the tears stream down my face. "They'll catch us. I'm sure they've closed the border."

"I go to the University," he insists. "I know people. People who could help us."

"But my family," I keen in despair, wracked by sobs.

"*I'll* be your family."

He says this with such rock-hard conviction, the tears catch in my throat. I look to him, stunned.

"I'll marry you," he insists. "Somehow, we'll get to Verpacia, and I'll marry you. We'll get a cottage there. Somewhere remote. I'll find work at the University and I'll hide you."

"Gardnerians don't marry," I remind him, my voice choked with grief for my family, my people. "We *wandfast*. Then we seal the bond." Anguish rises in me like a terrible wave. "Just leave me, Jules. I'm going to get you killed. You can't help me."

"I *can*."

I take a deep, shuddering breath. *Kind, foolish Jules.* I touch his face. His jutting cheekbone. His infinitely intelligent eyes.

"You can't marry me, Jules," I tell him, my mouth trembling. "I'm not a Kelt."

His expression turns fierce. "I don't care! When have I *ever* cared?"

"I will always be Gardnerian."

"Then be Gardnerian," he stubbornly returns. "We'll make a life in Verpacia. And when things calm down, we can wand-fast if it's possible. I don't care. I'd bind myself to you."

I've known for some time that Jules fancies me. It's been building in him over time. I've seen it in the heat lighting his gaze when he looks at me. In the new tension between us. But he's always held back, polite and unsure of my feelings. To hear him speak so boldly stuns me into silence.

"We'll go up through the mountains," he says. "You can stay here while I get a horse and supplies."

"What if they're still alive?" My voice is small and weak, clinging to senseless hope. My crippled, doddering grandfather and my sickly eight-year-old brother. What are the chances they've escaped all this?

He gives me a hard look. We both know the likely truth.

"What would they want you to do?" Jules asks, his jaw set tight.

A bitter laugh cuts through my tears. "Grandfather? He'd want me to push you clear off that cliff." I start to weep anew at the thought of my gentle, staunchly religious grandfather and his overwhelming hatred of Kelts. Grandfather would be horri-fied at the bizarre prospect of Keltic Jules trying to wandfast to his granddaughter, for the same reasons that he foolishly, blindly heeded our religion's strictures that barred women from wield-ing wands without first securing the Mage Council's approval.

"What would Wren want, then?" Jules asks, softer this time.

I think of my brother's wide, ready smile. Roughly, I wipe the tears from my eyes, steeling myself. "He'd want me to go with you."

"Will you do it?" Jules asks, his hand coming up to caress my face. "Will you come away with me?"

I nod and let him pull me into a warm embrace.

A twig snaps to my left.

"Well, isn't this touching."

Jules's whole body stiffens, and I blanch at the sound of the familiar voice.

Brandon stands just a few feet away, smiling triumphantly as three Keltic soldiers surround us and unsheathe their swords.

CHAPTER THREE:
Prisoner

"Where's my brother? And my grandfather?" My voice is coarse and low with dread as I stumble along the wooded path toward Crykes Field. I'm stealthily summoning up bits of magic from the ground as I'm herded along, storing the power inside me, though it hurts to gather so much without using it.

All I need is a wand.

Brandon laughs. "Quit your nattering, witch." He gives me a rough shove, which almost sends me hurtling to the ground. I choke back my outrage as I regain my balance.

Narrowing my eyes, I pull up another thread of magic and wind it around the others deep inside me. Gardnerian magic runs along affinity lines—fire, water, air, earth and light. I have mostly fire.

Lots of it.

Jules is being mercilessly driven ahead of me. One of the soldiers, a tall, bearded man, gives my friend's head a hard smack every now and then, laughing when Jules nearly falls sideways. Night has taken hold, the stars shining pinpricks in the sky, shadows engulfing the woods around us.

I flinch as yet another dragon flies overhead, my hidden magic sending a knifelike jab to my ribs.

So many dragons. A sickening terror tries to pull me under, but I push the magic's simmering power at it, keeping the fear at bay.

We're close to Crykes Field, and I can hear the raucous laughter of soldiers up ahead. My nerves fray as the shrieks of countless dragons echo above and across the ground in the distance. A staccato burst of orders is shouted nearby, and I can make out rough, low voices speaking the sharp language of the Urisk.

Urisk geomancers are powerful magicians from the southern lands, able to harness the latent magic of gemstones and crystals. And their military has recently formed an alliance with the Keltic forces.

Against my people.

The woods open up, and Jules is pushed into a clearing. I hesitate, heart thudding, my steps skidding to a halt.

A mammoth barn looms before me. In the darkness of the forest, I hadn't realized that we were approaching Mage Gullin's sprawling farm. That the enemy soldiers had decided to place part of their encampment *here*.

There are Keltic and Urisk soldiers standing and talking in small groups, the barn just beyond them. Torches on iron stands have been thrust into the dirt. They ring the large, circular clearing between farm buildings, the flames casting everything in a sinister, orange glow.

This flat land extends to the steep bluff that lines the entire rear boundary of the farm, offering a clear view of the full expanse of Crykes Field below. Countless campfires are scattered across the field, flickering between the rows of Keltic military tents and the georune-marked shelters of the Urisk soldiers.

My cottage and those of my neighbors are still ablaze in the far distance, just past the river, and the smell of charred wood hangs heavy in the air. Far to the north, I can just make out the dark shapes of dragons soaring across the night sky, still winging their way toward Gardneria.

"Move," Brandon orders, giving me a shove from behind.

A few Keltic soldiers turn to give me the once-over, their red uniforms the color of blood in the torchlight, their faces filling with dark interest at the sight of me.

I push waves of my fire magic against the fear that threatens to undo me, the surge of warmth bolstering my courage. As I study the scattered Urisk soldiers—whose magical talents make them far more intimidating than the Kelts—I find myself pulling up even more magic to steady my nerves. They're lethally streamlined in appearance, their scythes glimmering with inlaid gemstones and strapped to their backs. One geo-soldier rides by on a snarling hydreena, the beast's ugly, tusked head twisting from side to side against its tight reins.

There's a military sameness to most of the blue-hued Urisk soldiers, but one soldier stands boldly out. He's the most heavily rune-marked soldier here, and the dancing torchlight reflects vividly off the gemstones adorning his armor. Sapphires encircle his wrists, looped over his palms, and a string of multi-colored gemstones is thrown diagonally over his chest. An aura of glowing power surrounds him like a soft blue mist, and the sheer quantity of gems he carries marks him as a *strafeling*, one of the most powerful classes of Urisk geomancers.

The *strafeling* stands next to a Keltic commander with a neatly trimmed blond beard, the Kelt's deep red uniform trimmed with multiple black bands around his arms and edging his cloak. Beside the Kelt commander towers a huge blond ax-paladin, one of the strongest and most feared of the Keltic soldiers, a colossal ax strapped to the warrior's broad back.

All three men turn to look at Jules and me as we're pushed forward, the Kelt commander's eyes hard and steady, the *strafel-*

ing appearing curious. The ax-paladin crosses his broad arms in front of his muscular chest and regards me with an open leer.

I cling to my magic, swallowing back my terror, and force myself to hold the ax-paladin's gaze. Then my eyes alight on something thin and white tucked into the side of his weapons belt. The ball of magic churns white-hot in my chest.

A wand!

But why would a Kelt soldier be carrying a Gardnerian wand? Kelts don't possess any magic.

"Who's this?" the Kelt commander barks at Brandon, gesturing toward Jules.

Jules's fists are clenched by his sides, blood trickling down his bruised, split cheekbone. His eyes narrow in defiance and an attempt to focus, his glasses long since smashed under Brandon's boot heel.

"Jules Kristian," Brandon announces, stepping forward with bravado. He spits in Jules's direction and shoots him a look thick with disgust. "A race traitor."

"He was trying to hide the Roach girl," one of our soldier escorts explains, his lip curled with malice.

The ax-paladin lets out a low laugh and looks me over, his eyes heavy-lidded. "More than hide her, I'm sure." He smiles suggestively at Jules, then turns to me. "Do you want a wand, Roach girl?" He bares his teeth, reaches down toward his groin and hoists his member. "I've got a better wand for you than that skinny boy."

The *strafeling* shoots the ax-paladin a look of disdain, but Brandon and the Keltic soldiers laugh, savoring the idea of my humiliation. I beat back my fear and shift my attention inward, pulling two more long, crimson strands of magic up from the ground. The power pushes at my ribs with searing heat, straining toward the wand.

"Leave her alone," Jules snarls, his eyes bright with fury.

"Jules," I caution, but his eyes are locked on the ax-paladin.

"Or *what*?" Brandon jeers, shoving Jules so hard he stumbles back. "You'll split our heads? Do you *swear* you will?"

Jules launches himself at Brandon, catching him off guard, and lands a solid blow to his broad face that knocks Brandon to the ground.

Brandon's surprise morphs to rage, his expression murderous. With the surrounding Keltic soldiers cheering him on, Brandon rises to his feet and rushes at Jules. He wrestles my friend to the ground, pinning him with his superior size, and punches him hard in the face.

"*You bastard!*" I yell, moving to run toward them, only to be caught by my elbows and jerked backward by two Keltic soldiers. Furious, I struggle to wrench my arms free.

If I could only get my hands on that wand! Breathing hard, I try to focus on gathering more power as the crowd of Kelts closes in around Jules, egging Brandon on and cutting off my view of him.

The ax-paladin smiles wickedly, his large chin thrust forward. He gestures to the guards restraining me with a hard flick of his hand.

My feet skid across the damp earth as they drag me to a fenced-in livestock pen to the right of the barn. The soldiers open the gate, and I'm pushed forward, my palms slapping down onto the cold, muddied ground. It's pitch dark back here, the area devoid of torches. I blink, my eyes struggling to adjust to the dimness.

"Tessie!" A shadowy form grabs at my arm as I rise.

It's Rosebeth, my sweet Gardnerian friend from three cottages over. I cling to her, grateful to see a familiar face.

"You're alive!" she sobs, hugging me. "Thank the Ancient One, you're alive!"

"You *embrace* her?" A disgusted voice sounds from the blackness of the pen. "She ran off with a *Kelt!*"

I can just make out the young Gardnerian woman's hate-filled eyes, large and luminous in a beautiful face. Her skin, like mine, shimmers a faint emerald in the dark. She spits on the ground in my direction, then makes the sign to ward off the power of the Evil Ones. "*Staen'en*," she hisses under her breath. *Race traitor.*

I squint into the darkness. There are five other Gardnerians in the pen, all huddled in a far corner near the hateful girl—all of them elegant Upper River Gardnerians. I can just make out their dark silken clothing in the moonlight, a stark contrast to the black woolen homespun Rosebeth and I wear, like most of the impoverished Lower River Gardnerians.

In another corner of the pen, a small figure is curled in a tight ball, sobbing, and dressed in light-hued Keltic attire. Unlike us Gardnerians, there is no faint emerald shimmer to her skin, and she's been shorn bald. It's meek Keltic Daisie, the smith's daughter.

I suddenly realize that the pen holds only women. Young women. I turn my head and see the shadows of three Keltic soldiers hanging over the fence, watching us. Their eyes glitter in the moonlight.

Trying not to panic, I look back at Rosebeth. "Did you see Wren?" I whisper, taking hold of her arm as she sobs. "My grandfather?"

Weeping, she shakes her head, her face a mask of misery. She gestures toward the barn. "Wagons keep coming. Full of Gardnerians. They're forcing everyone in there. All but us." Rosebeth casts a frightened sidelong glance at the young Kelts. "What are we going to do?" she asks me imploringly, her voice quavering. She's chewing on her lip so hard, she's bloodied it.

I look toward the men. The Keltic soldiers are passing a

flask back and forth as they laugh and leer at us, but over their shoulders, I can see that the crowd around Jules has dispersed. He's been dumped by the edge of the barn, lying on his side. His face is swollen beyond recognition, one arm cradling the other as if it's broken.

Anger swells in me, and I turn, my focus honed on the ax-paladin.

"So, are you a Roach now?" The *strafeling* idly points at the wand that hangs from the ax-paladin's belt.

The ax-paladin spits on the ground. "Some Roach filth south of here got hold of it and cut down several members of our guard. I'm to bring it to the Tenhold armory."

"Why not destroy the cursed thing?" the *strafeling* asks, eyeing the wand with suspicion.

"We've tried," the paladin says. "It is surprisingly hard to break. And it's oddly powerful."

My attention lights up. I've heard tales of wands like these—wands of great power.

"What will we do?" Rosebeth asks me again in that tremulous voice, clinging to my arm and breaking my focus.

"Quiet," I order, more sternly than I'd intended, but I need to concentrate.

I'm only a Level Three Mage. Not a huge amount of power, to be sure, but I do have a unique talent. I can pull up threads of magic from the elements and knit them together, amplifying my power. I've done this on only a few occasions, experimenting with Grandfather's wand while making medicines and using the ability once to defend myself. Each time, the spell-linking gave me a fever and scoured me out, as if I'd been grievously ill. It's dangerous, what I'm doing. Magic can turn deadly when gathered like this, catching on the very life force of a Mage and choking it clear out. The last time I linked spells, I was attempting a complicated medicine to treat Wren's chronic illness. Grandfather found me passed out in the kitchen amid vials and scattered potions, and he forbade me from ever, ever using his wand again. I was feverish and bedridden for days, but more devastated over the loss of the wand than anything else.

I've never tried to pull in and link together as much power as I'm holding right now, and I know I'm playing with fire.

Deadly, raging, elemental fire.

My chest is full of burning pain, but my resolve is strengthened by it. I coldly assess our situation.

We're completely surrounded by a sea of soldiers—but the men are hardly the only threat. Several Urisk geosoldiers struggle to contain a dragon nearby, the beast's whole body undulating with rage. The dragon turns its head to look at me and bares its long fangs, pinning me with its eerie white eyes.

Terror claws at me, but I force myself to stand my ground as Rosebeth cries out and hides behind me, her slender body quivering.

A tall, winged figure steps into the clearing, and I feel my bravado slip away.

I take a frightened step back as the Icaral demon casts its glowing orange eyes around. His black wings arch threateningly, and the terrifying evil of his grinning expression is heightened by the torchlight. He balances a bright ball of flame over his palm as he slinks over to the Kelt commander, the *strafeling* and the ax-paladin.

Eyeing the Icaral demon warily, the Kelt commander unfurls a scroll and glances down to read.

"What's the word, Lucian?" the *strafeling* asks, his words elegantly accented and clipped.

"We wait. And march into Gardneria tomorrow morn," Lucian sighs, rolling up the scroll and passing it back to a young Keltic soldier.

A new wagon pulls in, filled with Gardnerians, all of them

well-to-do Upper River folk. They're roughly herded out, blinking in confusion, the children crying.

They are met by a mob of laughter.

"All hail the powerful Gardnerian Mages!"

"Where's your Great Mage now?"

A Keltic lieutenant bows toward them. "The Gardnerian Mages! Rulers of Erthia!" Two other Keltic soldiers laugh and roughly yank at the Gardnerians as they descend from the carriage, pulling one old man down so hard he tumbles to the ground and has trouble getting back up.

A young, slender Urisk geosoldier strides forward and salutes both the *strafeling* and the Kelt commander by bringing his fist to his chest. "This should be all of them, Commander Talin," he says, his accent as pronounced as the *strafeling*'s.

All of them? Could Wren and Grandfather be locked in the barn, too?

Lucian Talin makes a casual gesture toward the barn. "Get them in there with the others. We'll deal with them later." He grimaces, as if this is an unpleasant but necessary task.

My heart clenches along with my fists. I inhale sharply, pulling the power in tight.

The young Urisk geosoldier's brow tenses, and he glances briefly at the captive Gardnerians. "The children, too, Commander Talin?" I can sense his discomfort, see him swallow and blink with stunned reluctance.

The Keltic commander fixes him with a hard glare. "There's no other way, Cor'vyyn. You know that. If they raise up another Great Mage, they'll kill us all."

The young man eyes the terrified children and the elderly man as they're herded toward the barn, crying and pleading. He looks to the *strafeling*, as if silently imploring him for mercy. The *strafeling* glances briefly at the Gardnerians, then shoots the young Urisk soldier a hard, cautioning glare as he murmurs something to him in terse Uriskal.

"Don't go all sentimental on us, Cor'vyyn," Lucian says to the young geosoldier, his tone unforgiving. "Clearly you don't fully understand the threat we're under here. Any one of these Roaches, big or small, could be their next Great Mage. You've heard the diviner's prophecies from both your people's seers and ours—he's here, that Great Mage, hidden among their people somewhere."

"Do you have a problem with this, soldier?" the ax-paladin growls, his eyes glittering malevolently, the wand moon-bright at his waist.

The Urisk soldier's sapphire eyes are a storm of conflict as he glances toward the Gardnerian families. The *strafeling* snaps at him in Uriskal, and the young geosoldier bows and strides off, casting one last, troubled look behind him.

The Icaral demon is eyeing the new group of Gardnerians, still holding the ball of fire in his palm. He hisses and hurls the flames at the Mages, and they cry out, stamping the fire out of their clothing, the children shrieking in terror.

The Keltic commander scowls at the *strafeling*. "Tell your Icaral demon to *leave off.*"

"What are they going to do?" Rosebeth sobs hysterically, tugging at my sleeve. "Are they going to set fire to the barn? My family is in there! Tessie! Why won't you answer me?" She starts murmuring pleading prayers, tracing the star sign of the Ancient One's protection over and over in the air.

The Kelts unlock the barn door. In the shadows are the dark shapes of my people, pressed together tight. Right in the front stands a skinny boy, and recognition sweeps through me as torchlight illuminates his face.

My eyes fly open wide. "*Wren!*" I choke out.

He sees me and lets out an unearthly scream. "*Tessie!*"

I hurl myself at the fence and struggle to climb over it in my long skirts, a nail tearing at my ankle.

Wren bursts out of the barn and lunges toward me. He's quickly caught by one of the Keltic soldiers, jerked back by his arm.

"*Wren!*" I scream, finally hoisting myself to the top of the fence. A searing pain erupts all over my scalp as I'm yanked back by my hair, a strong arm clenching my arm and thrusting me down to the mud, a rumbling laugh emanating from my attacker's throat.

I briefly turn to find the ax-paladin looming over me, but I don't care. My magic boils bloodred as I spring up and hurl myself at the fence once more, straining toward Wren as he's desperately reaching for me. The huge Kelt laughs behind me as he grabs my upper arms, and I kick and struggle against him.

"Tessie!" Wren cries, clawing at the soldier restraining him. "Let me go! *Tessie!*"

The soldier pulls his hand back and smacks Wren hard in the face.

My world contracts, the scene before me slowing as Wren's mouth opens, his face contorted, his scream drawn out. "Tessieee!"

The image of a white bird flashes before my eyes as the soldiers drag Wren back to the barn and throw him in. Just before the door is closed and locked, I see the face of my grandfather, his expression a mask of agony.

A great tide of fiery rage wells up within me, burning away the terrible odds, the ax-paladin, the dragons and hydreenas, the Icaral demon.

I wrench myself around, tear my arm from the ax-paladin's grip and close my fist around the wand.

CHAPTER FOUR:
The White Wand

Flames shoot from the tip of the wand as soon as I grasp it.

A violent wave of magic drives the air from my lungs as fire courses out of the wand, strafing Kelt and Urisk soldiers and setting several trees alight with a crackling explosion. I round on the ax-paladin with a fierce cry, and the fire whips out toward him. He screams with pain and falls back.

Fury courses through me as I send fire out in wide, repeating arcs, driving the soldiers farther away from the barn as an arrow whirs past, barely missing me. I hold tight to my woven knot of spells, readying it as soldiers all around aim their weapons. The Urisk pull stones to their palms and the Icaral demon snarls and gathers a growing ball of flame above his hand. The Kelt commander shouts an order, and a line of archers forms, drawing their bows.

Men's voices call out, and the arrows are released in a unified *whoosh*. The Icaral's fireball is hurled straight at me, spears are launched at my head and a kaleidoscope of searing flame bursts from affinity stones.

I slap one hand over the other and grasp at the wand, fall to my knees and send my linked power up into a great dome of a shield. Weapons and flames and stone magic slam up against it with shuddering force and are knocked back.

I'm shocked by the immensity of my power, magnified by this wand. My affinity power courses out in a translucent, golden river, rising up—over me, over the livestock pen and over the barn.

Great stabs of pain smash into my shoulders and through my arms from the impact of the soldiers' relentless assault, the blows of countless weapons reverberating against my shield, nearly knocking the wand clear out of my vibrating fists.

Jules has pulled himself up to a sitting position and is propped up against the barn wall, gaping at me, the eye that's not swollen shut gone wide.

"Pry the door open!" I yell to Rosebeth and the young women in the pen, everyone lit by golden light and flashes of color as the Urisk and the Icaral demon hurl geomagic and fire at the shield.

The young women race for the barn's locked door.

The *strafeling* clenches the stones looped around his palms and sends shockwave after shockwave of sapphire fire exploding against my shield.

My arms and shoulders scream with pain, my body jerking with each blow. But I hold on, keeping the shield intact.

"Stand down!" the Keltic commander booms out.

The assault abruptly ceases.

I'm panting, drenched in sweat as I struggle to hold the dome of energy together.

The Keltic commander moves off to my right and converses in low tones with several underlings, his eyes trained on me with careful calculation.

They're waiting. Waiting for my strength to give out.

"Hurry!" I call over my shoulder to the young women, desperation on the edge of panic coursing through me.

But the barn door is refusing to give way.

The hateful Upper River girl lets out an angry snarl and

kicks the door in frustration. "Check the back," she yells to the other young women. "Search for rotted wood." She calls to the Gardnerians inside for help breaking open a passage, and they shout back to her, their voices muffled by the barn's walls. A cacophony of hammering and pounding against the barn ensues.

Smoke rises thick in the air, my fire still crackling in the surrounding woods. Soldiers watch me with dark intent and even darker smiles.

My heart thuds with a painful slowness, my pulse loud in my ears, the power a steady stream through me, flowing up from the ground. I concentrate hard and weave the shield even tighter, sending the power upward, the tips of my fingers growing numb, my arms trembling.

A gentle hand flows down over my arm and grasps my wrist to steady me. Jules pushes himself tight against my back, propping me up.

"What are you planning?" His voice is calm, the words muffled by the swelling of his mouth.

His presence helps to soothe the fear that's making a slow crawl through my belly. "I can move the shield," I tell him, my throat tight. "We get everyone out, and we leave."

"How long can you maintain it?" His voice is purposefully measured.

"I... I don't know," I admit, terror breaking through.

He gives my wrist an encouraging squeeze, his cheek pressed to mine. "I love you, Tessla." He says it with ardent certainty.

We're going to die, I realize.

"I love you, too," I tell him, knowing we don't mean this in the same way, but what does that matter now? We might all be dead soon, and Jules is nearly as dear to me as Wren.

Exhaling sharply, I murmur a spell and push a warm wave

of magic out to bolster the shield, my teeth and the muscles of my neck clenched tight.

"Fight them," he tells me, his breath warm on my face. "Fight them to the end."

Rosebeth rushes over to my side. "We can't get the door open," she relays with breathless urgency. "But they've managed to pull a board off the back of the barn. They're all back there, prying at it."

"Hurry," I tell her grimly, my feet tingling, my toes gone numb, the numbness in the tips of my fingers starting to spread.

"Are you tiring, little witch?" the Icaral demon calls to me with a sneer, his glowing eyes hot, an evil smile curling on his mouth. His voice is like a snake's hiss as he stalks around my shield. He unfurls his black wings and starts to summon another ball of flame, the fire-orb churning and growing over his palm.

The huge ax-paladin is pacing like a giant wildcat in front of me, scarlet burns streaked across his face, charred black lines across his uniform. "You will tire eventually, Roach," he snarls, "and then we will break through your shield and take you apart, piece by piece."

"Don't listen to them," Jules urges, tightening his grip on my wrist. "Listen to me. You can hold the shield. I know you can."

Somewhere behind me, my brother and grandfather are waiting to escape from the barn.

Wren. I can't let them have Wren.

"Your strength will run out at some point, witch," the Icaral crows darkly, his fireball grown large, his wings fanning out. He rears back and throws the fireball straight at me, punching the shield's side with a shower of sparks. The shield gives way, pushing in and snapping back out. Tearing.

A hole!

The hole whips around the shield-dome like a leaf caught on a turbulent river, small, but there.

I can't feel my lower legs.

Soldiers call out and point at the hole in the shield as it swirls around the changeable vortex of the dome's surface. They send up a triumphant cheer.

The ax-paladin strides toward me, his muscles rippling, his burned face as close as he can get it without touching the scorching shield, teeth bared. "I will pull your people out one by one and flay them in front of you."

The other soldiers are scrambling about, yelling to each other. I realize they're inexplicably moving back, giving the shield a wide berth. The ax-paladin grins at something over my head and lumbers backward, as well.

"Why are they retreating?" I croak out to Jules, desperation clawing at me.

I feel his head tilt up, his hand going tight over mine.

An unearthly shriek tears through the sky above, and I look up to see a massive dragon flying in impossibly fast.

Hurtling straight for my shield.

CHAPTER FIVE:
Wandshield

The dragon crashes into my glowing shield, claws out, a Keltic soldier astride its back, and I gasp as the shield buckles toward me, stopping just a hand span from my face. I struggle to hold on to it, but the force of the attack reverberates with crippling pain around my shoulders.

The muscular animal slides to the ground, landing on its haunches with a heavy thump. The creature sets its soulless white eyes on me, growling as it backs up, then throws its full weight at the shield again.

I grit my teeth and grasp the wand more firmly in my hands, wrenching magic up from the ground. My lungs are close to bursting, and my ribs are on fire as I struggle to repel the dragon's strength. I'm hunkered down, breathing hard, the magic shooting through me in a fiery line.

"I can't hold it much longer," I force out to Jules, teeth clenched, despair taking hold. "I'm sorry, Jules. I can't."

Jules's hand tightens around my wrist again, offering support. "You *can*. I know you can."

The Icaral, dark wings flapping, hurls a fireball at me. It smashes against the shield to my right. The impact throws me back against Jules and jars my wrists to the bones, the shield nearly collapsing from the concussive blow. The glowing bubble springs back into place, but I can sense a weak spot where the fireball hit, and flames cling to the shield's surface in a blazing circle that moves around the dome in chaotic arcs, joining the hole made by the Icaral's fire.

"She's weakening," Lucian observes dispassionately to the *strafeling*. The dragon releases a grating shriek that scrapes painfully inside my head. The creature rises up and swipes its claws at the shield, the soldier astride it pulling the reins in tight. A great ripping sound, like canvas tearing, rends the air as the dragon hooks its claws into the shield and mauls it, creating three gaping slashes.

Hooks of magic catch inside me, burning hotter, and sweat cloaks my back. I cry out, struggling to pull in enough tendrils of power to close the holes, but my magic is dissipating to a papery wisp of energy.

The Keltic soldiers call to each other jovially as they drop down into a line and nock flaming arrows to bows. They wait, their eyes trained on me with bright, predatory interest.

"Fire!" Lucian commands.

A flaming barrage assaults the shield. They aim for the holes, but the holes are swirling around too fast, and the arrows just glance off the glowing surface. The dragon takes another swipe at the shield, tearing at it, the dome quickly rendered a flimsy net with ever-widening gaps.

"Here's a new sport," one of the Kelt soldiers jests as he lets loose another flaming arrow. "Roach fry!"

His arrow flies straight through a hole and lands on the barn's roof.

"*No!*" I scream as the roof catches fire. I fumble and try to keep hold of the wand, almost dropping it.

Jules's hand moves to clasp tight over my fingers, but my magic is depleted, my fire diminished to flickering embers.

The numbness of my feet and lower legs spreads toward my knees as the shield-strands begin to cave in.

Stars prick at my vision, my sight blurring at the edges, my body trembling. I want to run into the barn. Jump into the flames to rescue my family. But I can't move. The numbness has spread over my knees, and I've broken out in a feverish, light-headed sweat.

"*Wren!*" I cry out, choked by tears, my vision growing mottled and hazy.

Jules's arm comes tight around me in a fiercely protective embrace. I can't move my limbs. The magic is burning me out from the inside. Consuming me.

The white wand falls from my hands to the ground.

The remnants of the shield collapse and dissolve into the dirt with a steaming hiss.

"Stand back!" Lucian orders.

The soldier astride the dragon dismounts and pulls the creature back as it bares its hideous teeth at me. The Icaral is right beside the dragon, growing a tight fireball that rotates above his palm. He glances pointedly at the barn, then grins maniacally at me.

"*Blessed Mages*, cowering in the dirt," the demon hisses mockingly. "The Wingeds are triumphant. We have kept our wings. *And* our power. And now you will *burn*."

He flings the fireball, and it collides with the barn's roof, exploding the entire top half of the structure into churning flames.

A raucous cheer erupts.

A wail of despair escapes me as I'm jerked backward, rough hands pulling me away from the barn as Jules fights to cling to me. Brandon comes up behind him and wrenches his broken arm backward. Jules cries out, wild with pain as he's pulled free of me and dragged off.

I hunch forward, weeping as a pair of Kelt soldiers drag me back from the inferno. Jules calls my name, but I can't bring myself to move, to fight. The world seems to tilt, everything going in and out of focus.

Wren. He's just a child. Oh, Ancient One… Wren!

"The Roach bitch is *mine!*"

Through a veil of tears, I see the ax-paladin stalking toward me, a triumphant snarl on his face.

I let out a strangled, high-pitched cry as he grabs my hair and yanks me up. I dangle in the air, helpless, pain spearing my scalp.

Then a giant explosion thunders around us, and the ax-paladin's head snaps up. The shockwaves pulse straight through me, the very ground shaking, the world lit up by powerful orange lightning. The soldiers flinch away, instinctively shielding themselves with hands and arms. All heads turn to the mountains and stare, slack-jawed and silent.

"What in the Ancient One's name…?" a young soldier croaks out.

Another deafening explosion sounds, this one closer. Soldiers shield their eyes, blinking toward the mountains in confusion as the barn fire flares and spreads, flames licking at the door, beams cracking and falling to the ground.

My eyes water with pain as I'm wrenched farther up, forced to look right into the murderous eyes of the ax-paladin.

"What. Is. This?" he grinds out, low and fierce, but I can sense a sliver of desperation clawing around the edges of his words.

Another flash of orange just past the mountains. Alarm horns sound.

Commander Lucian barks out commands, then glances up at the flames rapidly consuming the barn, his jaw set tight. "Karver," he orders the soldier restraining the dragon. "Guard the barn. Set your dragon on any Gardnerians who live." He turns toward the remaining troops. "Take the men down to Crykes Field. We have to get off this high ground. Now!" The *strafeling* echoes the command in Uriskal.

An organized formation of dragons rises up from the central field, soldiers astride. The riders are mere silhouettes from this distance, flying toward the mountains and the orange explosions beyond.

Thunder shakes the ground as soldiers scramble toward the field. Lucian mounts his horse and the *strafeling* leaps astride his hydreena, both leaders taking off after their men at a furious pace.

The ax-paladin jostles my head, sending waves of agony down my spine. "Answer, witch! What dark magic is this?"

A black flood of rage and despair crashes through me.

I don't care what's coming for you. Wren is dead. Burned in your fire.

I suck in a breath and use my last shred of energy to spit in his face.

He snarls and grabs up his ax with lethal ease.

My heart falls straight through my feet as the world slows around me. My mouth falls open, and a low moan escapes my lungs. He pulls back his muscular arm, ax in hand, ready to impale me on its curved edge.

A streak of crackling, blue lightning hurtles in from my right and slams into his chest.

His body bucks from the impact, eyes bulging, ax falling. His hand releases my hair, and we fall hard to the ground—me, crumpling into a useless bundle, and him...

Dead.

I gape at his body, stunned.

Brandon's eyes fix on mine, enraged. He lets go of Jules and stalks toward me, shoving aside the fleeing Kelt soldiers.

But before he can take more than a few steps, another streak of blue lightning hits him in the chest, killing him instantly before it lashes sideways to take out a whole row of Kelts and the soldier restraining the dragon.

I lie on the ground and blink in disbelief, trying to clear my unstable vision.

A Mage strides into the clearing, slashing blue lightning from the tip of his wand. He's young, with severely angular features and black hair, his expression fierce. His uniform is dark and marked with a single silver sphere. A black cloak edged with five silver lines flows out behind him like dark water.

The uniform of a powerful Gardnerian Mage.

One of ours.

My hazy, magic-battered mind sharpens and focuses in tight on him. His presence is overwhelming. I can almost feel the lightning burst from his wand, like thunder resonating through the ground, through my body. Straight to my core.

Another young, black-cloaked Mage appears, trailing the lightning-wielder. I flinch back as the unrestrained dragon roars, exposing long, sharp teeth, and lunges for him.

"Hit him at the base of the neck, Fain," the first Mage calls back over his shoulder as he smashes blue lightning into two geosoldiers who've just emerged from the woods.

Fain points his wand at the dragon, his spell streaming out, translucent and flowing like a spring current, to collide with the dragon. The creature stops midlunge, its head jerking back, steam hissing from its nose, then its mouth. Its hide seems to shrink, as if the beast is growing emaciated before my eyes. I can see its ribs, then the outline of its skeleton as the beast's entire body releases steam, its very life essence ripped away. Its scaled skin withers to the ground like a discarded coat.

"Help," I try to cry out, but my voice is a ragged whisper,

my shoulders uselessly slumped, my feverish cheek pressed hard into the dirt.

Fain turns, his eyes lighting on mine as my head lolls weakly against the ground. He runs to me and falls to his knees by my side, his hand coming up to rest gently on my head. His eyes flick toward the white wand, abandoned on the ground. He sheathes his own wand and picks up the powerful wand, rolling it in his hand, as if gauging the strength of it. He's young and elegantly handsome, with aquiline features, a long, graceful neck and bright green eyes. A few curls of dark hair fall over his forehead as he quickly takes me in from head to toe.

He smiles and cocks his head, like the world isn't falling apart around us. "I saw your shield work, Lower River Girl," he says teasingly, his voice velvety smooth. "*Nicely* woven."

"They're in the barn," I rasp out, desperate. "*Please*, my brother…"

"Shhh." His hand goes to my limp wrist, holding it, brow furrowed with concentration as he checks my pulse, then slowly feels along my arm as if he's reading a complicated book. "They're out," he tells me absently, his brow cinching tighter. "We pulled them out the back. They're fine. And shielded. Can you feel my hand at all?"

I shake my head. My throat begins to close. I can only force out a constricted whisper. "I can't feel my arms. Or my legs," I tell him with mounting panic. "I… I can't take a deep breath."

"Tell me what you did." His words are slow and carefully calm.

"I gathered the magic," I rasp out, struggling for breath as the magic burns and pushes against my lungs. "As much of it as I could pull up."

"Vale," he calls out in the direction of the other Mage, his voice now serious and urgent, his hand tight around my wrist. "I found the shield Mage."

Vale turns and spots me, then Jules, crumpled up in the flickering firelight cast by the disintegrating barn. Vale's eyes go wide as his head whips back to me, a shock of recognition lighting his face.

Vale starts toward us just as the Icaral slides out from behind an untethered wagon. The demon stalks forward, balancing a ball of flame over each of his palms. His glowing eyes are set hard on Vale, his black wings flapping.

I open my mouth to warn him, but can't speak above a whisper.

The demon growls and hurls the fireballs straight at Vale.

CHAPTER SIX:
Lightning Mage

Vale whips around in a graceful arc and slashes out with his wand.

A forked tongue of blue lighting smashes into the fireballs and sends up a crackling, spitting wall of blue that hurtles toward the Icaral.

Snarling, the demon sends a line of fire out toward the lightning wall, coating the Icaral's side of it with yellow flames.

Their heels digging into the ground, both Vale and the Icaral furiously push their magic against the wall, which is now a glowing and sparking green. It grows taller than their heads and widens, setting the ground aflame.

"Do you need assistance?" Fain calls to Vale, worry lacing his tone.

"No," Vale grinds out, pushing the shield forward. "It's got to be fire. I've got him."

Fain sends up a watery shield-dome over us, its translucent ripples limned with glowing orange light reflected from the torches. He must have a water affinity, whereas Vale's is clearly fire, like mine.

Though my body is still wracked with burning waves of pain, I can still see the Icaral demon through Fain's shield, the creature's eyes flaming white-hot. The demon grins, pushes his palms out and forces the fiery wall toward Vale. The lines of Vale's lightning fan out in response, and a stray bolt slams into the ground beside us, just past our shield, sending up a smoking hiss.

A Keltic soldier bursts from the forest far to our left, his ax raised. Ignoring us, he runs past the livestock pen toward the distant side of the barn.

Giant icicles, like clear javelins, shoot from behind the barn and slam into the mammoth Kelt, knocking him down, instantly freezing him. Wide-eyed and rigid as stone, he lies immobilized, ice spreading out from his body in a frosty haze.

Another cloaked, black-haired Mage strides into view, his eyes set tight on the frozen Kelt. He's tall and broad-shouldered, this ice-wielding Mage, descending like a winter storm. Flanking him is the hateful Upper River girl—the young woman who named me a race traitor.

"Over there!" she says. "Another Kelt! A *staen'en* whore!" She points into the shadows of the livestock pen, where a small, dark ball huddles between the feeding trough and the water pail.

Daisie!

"Please," I hear Daisie plead as the Mage's eyes fix tightly on her.

Without even a flicker of pity, the Mage raises his wand and sends an ice javelin straight into Daisie's chest with a sickening thump.

My body trembles with shock and horror.

"Gods, Malkyn!" Fury flashes in Fain's eyes. But the Icaral's shrieking hiss and Vale's grunting cry divert his attention back to maintaining our watery shield.

"There's another one, there!" the girl cries.

I follow the point of her finger, which leads straight to Jules. I look to Fain and our eyes lock. I try to speak, but my lungs are still burning with the magic I gathered, and I'm unable to utter a single word to save my best friend.

Behind Fain, Vale utters a final spell, slamming his ward arm down. The whole shield, both fire and lightning, goes down with it. He gracefully flips his wand back and then straight out, sending a bolt of lightning through the Icaral's chest.

The demon lets out an unearthly howl, his whole body arcing back into a taut bow. He falls limply to the ground, and Fain's watery shield follows suit.

Vale runs toward us.

"That Kelt, there! He's *her* Kelt," the girl cries to Malkyn, pointing first at Jules, then at me. Her beautiful green eyes are red with tears, her mouth pulled down and trembling with disgust. She jabs her finger at Jules, her tone venomous. "He goes after our women!"

I struggle to tell them how Jules saved me, how he helped me stay strong enough to protect everyone. But my voice is gone. All I can do is gasp for air.

Vale throws the young woman a knife-sharp look of cold appraisal just as Malkyn flicks his wand toward Jules.

Fast as a cobra, Vale hurls a bolt of lightning that knocks Malkyn's ice javelin into the rapidly disintegrating barn. The javelin explodes into a shower of ice, then instantly turns to steam.

"What are you doing?" Malkyn's voice is calm enough, but there's rage just beneath the surface. I shrivel at the sound of his deep, resonant voice, the image of him murdering gentle Daisie vivid in my mind.

"He's *mine*," Vale states coldly.

"You seem to be forgetting that I outrank you, *Vale*," Malkyn states slowly and coolly. I notice Malkyn's uniform has two silver bars on his chest to Vale's one.

Vale bares his teeth at Malkyn, his eyes glittering dangerously. "Does your magic outrank mine, *Malkyn*?"

Malkyn sighs, his expression relaxing to one of bored resignation. He languidly turns away from Vale and then, whip-fast, slices his wand out.

Vale flicks his wrist and catches Malkyn's javelin with a small strike of lightning, exploding it into a puff of snow that falls harmlessly at Vale's feet.

"Ah," Vale says, giving Malkyn a nod of mock encouragement. "You're improving." He strides toward Jules, wand out, lips moving. Black vines fly out from the wand to encircle Jules's upper body. Jules groans in agony as the vines cinch tight.

Vale grabs Jules's good arm and roughly hoists him up. Jules looks dazed, his eyes barely focused, his face a bloody mess.

"I know this one," Vale states coldly. "We've a score to settle." Not waiting for a response, Vale drags a shambling, half-conscious Jules off toward the woods.

"Where are you taking him?" Malkyn asks as he inspects his wand, flicking frost off the end it.

Vale doesn't bother to turn around. "Somewhere no one will witness what I'm about to do."

Tears roll down my face as I struggle to breathe, to summon enough air to utter a protest. I try to shake loose from Fain's grip, thrashing my upper body, but Fain holds tight as spears of fiery magic lash against my insides.

Another orange explosion lights up the horizon. Fain, Malkyn and the Upper River girl look toward the mountains.

"I'll need you for the shield," Malkyn tells Fain, his voice low and level. He sets his dark gaze on me. Gasping, I still manage to send him a glare of red-hot defiance.

"Go," Fain says to Malkyn with a flick of his chin toward the barn. "I'll be right there."

A scream of agony tears through the air.

Jules!

Malkyn pauses, his face taking on a fleeting look of half-lidded rapture. The Upper River girl fixes me with a hateful look before Malkyn leads her away, the two of them disappearing behind the burning barn.

Images of Jules being tortured flash through my mind, and a shuddering sob overtakes me, my chest heaving, the fire whipping my insides in relentless slashes. I throw my head from side to side, fighting against Fain, fighting to breathe, barely hearing him as he urges me to slow my breaths.

Another explosion sounds, closer this time. My lungs heave, burning, then constrict tight.

I've lost the ability to breathe.

CHAPTER SEVEN:
Affinity

Fain rips open my clothing and pushes his hands hard against my chest as I thrash my head back and forth, desperate for air, my eyes bulging out, straining. Teeth gritted, he increases the pressure and murmurs a spell. A cool current of his water magic flows through me, loosening the net of fire, briefly opening up my lungs.

I greedily breathe in what air I can, panting shallowly in desperation, wondering if Jules is still alive. Anguish rips through me at the thought of him dying, and the fiery net takes hold once more.

Fain leans in close as I fight for breath, terrified.

"What's your name, love?"

"Tessla," I rasp out. "Tessla Harrow."

"Your brother," he asks me, deadly serious. "How old is he?"

"*Eight*," I mouth as my chest heaves and hot tears course down my trembling, fevered face.

"He needs you alive, hmm?" His voice is calm and controlled, his eyes locked hard on mine.

I gasp and nod, my eyes fixed on him.

"Don't think of anything but him," he orders. "Can you do that?"

I nod again.

Fain pushes his full weight down onto me as he hisses out the spell through clenched teeth, flowing more of his cooling water magic around my scorched lungs.

Vale runs out of the woods down toward us, his boot heels thudding hard. His expression is one of deep urgency.

I can feel his fire the minute he gets close, and my magic responds with a mind of its own. All the tendrils of power within me orient themselves toward him like a flock of birds, then rush out in a wave of heat.

I cry out as a searing pain scorches the side of my ribs closest to Vale.

Fain holds his palm out stridently. "Stay back! Your affinities *match*."

Vale halts, his eyes gone wide, his gaze fixed on me. He swallows, looking rattled. "I know. I can *feel* it."

Sweet Ancient One, such fire in him!

His cold visage is a lie. I'm clear now on what lies underneath it—the same molten landscape that lives under my skin.

"She's Magedrunk," Fain observes, shooting Vale a grave look. "I don't know how she's done it, but she's layered spells. There's a river of fire trapped in her. I've got to purge her. *Now*."

I'm suddenly all too aware of my exposed chest, and a hot, nauseating shame washes over me. As if sensing my discomfort, Vale whips off his cloak and thrusts it toward Fain.

"You care about *modesty*?" Fain gapes. "Right *now*?"

"Get it on her," Vale orders. "I can restrain her then, without inadvertently killing her."

Fain pulls his hands off me, and my lungs immediately begin to heat and seize up again. I throw my head back, gasping, painfully jostled as Fain hoists me up to slide the cloak around my body. I look at him in desperation, able to pull in only a thin sliver of air, as if from an impossibly narrow straw.

"*Vyyn'ys'en'ar,*" Vale says, teeth clenched, pointing his wand at me.

Black vines—the same he bound Jules with—flow from his wand and cinch tight around my upper body, holding the cloak in place and restraining my numbed arms as my rearing affinity fire drives the air from my lungs. Fuzzy black circles explode chaotically in my vision as Fain settles my weight against him, pressing his wand into my limp hand, his own hand coming around mine to point the wand toward the woods.

"*Scyy'yl'ar,*" Fain grinds out, his cheekbone pressed tight against my shuddering face.

Sensation blasts violently through my wand arm as a torrent of flames bursts from the wand's tip. With a turbulent roar, the fire slams into the edge of the forest, shattering the trunks of two trees, which crash to the ground with the snapping of a thousand branches.

"Sweet Ancient One's bollocks!" Fain gasps.

Air rushes into my lungs. Steam follows the fire and chugs out of the wand like a kettle at a furious boil. I take in great gulps of air and flex my hand around Fain's wand as the steam lessens. My vision clears for a moment, but searing heat advances on my lungs again, like a thousand small battering rams, spearing me, straining to destroy me.

Fain clasps his hand around mine and points the wand once more toward the crackling trees.

"Again?" I force out, my voice a scraping, frightened hiss.

"I'm sorry, but yes," he replies, his voice steely. "I need to force out the rest of the trapped fire with *quite* a bit of water." His voice turns grim, his head turning toward mine. "Are you ready?"

I grow afraid at the question. "It hurts," I tell him, my mouth a trembling grimace.

Another orange explosion from the mountains shatters the

air, and I recoil against Fain, a terrified whimper escaping my lips.

"Do you like chocolate?" Fain asks me, his voice gone suddenly gentle.

Vale whips his head toward us to gape at Fain, his face incredulous. "Have you lost your mind?"

"Look at me, sweetling," Fain says, leaning to the side and locking his eyes on to mine. "I have some lovely chocolate. With cardamom and Ishkart cinnamon. I will make it for you and for your brother. We will sit under the stars and sip it. I *promise* you. Can you think on that and *only* that?"

I know how badly this is going to hurt, but I find myself nodding in assent. Fain smiles faintly, then grips my hand like a vise and repeats the spell.

There's a rumbling *whoosh* deep in my core. Like a blockage about to be released.

The breathless moment just before an avalanche.

A flood of fire rips through me, and I scream, my body convulsing. A stream of white-hot flame explodes through the wand and ignites several more trees, destroying them. I cry out again as a thousand red-hot swords stab into me, hot knives slashing at my legs.

And then it dissipates, the heat rapidly fleeing. Cool water comes in on its heels. Then colder water. Winter cold. I start to shiver.

"I can move my other arm," I marvel, pressing it tight against the vines, then shaking out my legs as Fain guides me up, the vines still tight around my torso. "And my legs. I can feel my legs." I'm dazed by the throbbing echo of pain and the rising cold, hollowing me out. "But I'm getting so cold."

Fain shoots Vale a worried look.

"Go," Vale tells him with a glance toward the mountains. "They'll need help reinforcing the shield."

"Don't touch her skin," Fain warns Vale as he gets up. "And keep her bound. If she reaches your fire, her affinity lines will devour it and she'll burn out from overexposure. It could kill her."

"*Thank you*, Fain," Vale snipes. "For stating the patently obvious."

And then Vale lifts me clear off the ground and starts around the left side of the barn at a fast clip, Fain striding off in the opposite direction.

CHAPTER EIGHT:
Vale Gardner

Vale carries me into the shadow of the woods that bracket the fiery barn. I struggle against his firm grip, desperate to escape the Mage who hurt—possibly killed—my best friend.

"Jules saved me," I tell him, my voice choked with grief. "That Kelt you dragged away—"

"I know he tried to help you," Vale cuts me off sharply as he runs through the trees. His voice lowers to a whisper. "I didn't kill him. So be *quiet*. I'm trying to save your *life*."

Sweet Ancient One, Jules is alive!

We burst from the woods at the edge of the rocky embankment, and Vale's boot heels skid as he tries to slow his pace. Our descent down the sharp slope to Crykes Field becomes more of a slide than a run. Vale's feet kick up dust and send a waterfall of dry gravel toward the ground below.

When we reach the bottom, he pulls me backward and down toward the ground with him. His arms are tight around me, holding me close against his chest as he leans into the slope of the bluff. Then Vale throws out his wand, murmurs a spell and creates a tight, translucent shield over us. The wavering shield is webbed with turbulent blue lines of lightning that send sparking static buzzing through my head.

His fire leaps inside him, toward me. It suffuses my back

with warmth, the fabric of his clothing and the cloak wrapped around me a barrier keeping his fire at bay. Keeping it from my skin.

My arms instinctively pull at the vines restraining me, yearning to touch him, to absorb the fire in his shield. I'm desperate to melt the block of ice that's slowly forming in my core. What began as a mere pebble after Fain's purge has become a large, freezing stone. I know Fain was trying to help me, but my core of fire is all but extinguished, my affinity crushed beneath his torrent of water.

Heart thumping, shivering from cold, I glance back up the embankment, toward the burning barn, and see the irregular exit hacked through its rear.

Escape.

My gaze swerves down to my far left, down the long ditch that turns like a serpent to flow across the back of Crykes Field. There's a long, glowing shield set snug against the long bluff like a cocoon. It's surrounded by Kelt and Urisk soldiers shooting a series of flaming arrows and glowing blue streams of geo-fire at it. Two dragons are snarling and clawing at the shield, and I can just make out the mass of black-clad Gardnerians huddled together beneath it.

A cacophony of shrieks sound from above, and I crane my neck, the back of my head sliding against Vale's chest. A huge horde of dragons soars above us, circling over Crykes Field like a flock of death. Neat rows of mounted soldiers are assembling throughout the field for the march toward Gardneria. Torch-bearing sentries flank the rigid formations, and sapphire geo-shields appear above the company of soldiers, cast by Urisk geomancers astride hydreenas.

A flaming arrow smacks into the side of Vale's shield and is instantly incinerated in a crackling, spitting ball of blue lightning.

"*Ruus'fayn*," Vale curses in Alfsigr, one arm wrapped around my bound body, pulling me tight against the side of his chest. With the other arm he points his wand straight out, a stream of glowing blue feeding the shield.

"We're outnumbered," I tell him, my teeth chattering dully. My fingers and toes are starting to feel numb again. I look toward the distant Mage-shield, knowing that my brother and grandfather are likely inside it—but how long will it hold up under such a fierce attack? "They'll kill us all."

"Oh, you think so, do you?" Vale states drily.

I huff out a small sound of despair, tears stinging my dust-caked eyes.

Another arrow smashes into our shield, and I flinch back.

"How long can you maintain this shield?" I challenge him, my voice rough with tears.

"About one hour," he replies, each word succinct and calm.

Anger rises in me. How can he be so unconcerned?

Three explosions of orange illuminate the tops of the mountains. The mammoth, circular puffs of light cast a sputtering amber glow over the entire field.

"What's coming?" I demand roughly. "What can *possibly* save us from *them*?" I jerk my chin hard toward the Kelt-Urisk army.

"Their worst nightmare," Vale says. He spits out a short, jaded laugh. "A force much stronger than their dragons and their demons and their flimsy arrows."

"More Mages?" I croak out, disbelieving. We already have at least three high-level Mages trying to help our people, and yet here we are, cowering in a ditch with decaying shields.

Vale spits out an incredulous laugh. "No. Not more of *us*. We're child's play compared to *her*."

Her?

He's mad. He must be mad. There's never been a powerful female Mage.

Despairing, I glare at him. "What do you mean, 'her'?"

He cocks an eyebrow and sets his fierce eyes on me. His voice, when he speaks, is dangerously calm.

"You're about to meet my mother."

CHAPTER NINE:
The Black Witch

Alarm horns trumpet, echoing over the valley. Another round of orange explosions erupts just past the mountains, then fades to nothing.

The mountains fall eerily quiet, the sound of the alarm horns fading.

I crane my neck to look at Vale, but his eyes are fixed north.

A loud bang ruptures the air, and I flinch back against the hard length of him. Light bursts into being, the entire mountain ridge suddenly limned gold, bright as Yule candles.

The alarm horns blare again as the center of the mountain's glow flares brighter. A thin, golden line scythes out from it, straight across the sky. It slams into an advancing dragon, exploding the beast into a churning ball of flame that writhes and plummets toward the earth.

Cries sound from the ground below the beast, and the Urisk geomancers send up streaks of sapphire, catching the hurtling creature in an intricate web. The flaming dragon hangs suspended just above a battalion of soldiers. The men scatter away in panic, a spot of budding chaos on the orderly field.

The other dragons circling overhead turn and arrow toward the north. Toward the strange glow.

Golden lines strike out again from the mountain's center,

spearing the night air in regular bursts, left to right and back again, fast as the beat of a hummingbird's wing. Dragons all across the sky burst into flame, and the night lights up orange.

Full-blown chaos erupts as flaming dragons rain down from the sky, one pinwheeling diagonally above us.

"Great gods," Vale exclaims, teeth gritted, his arm extended and braced by his other hand as he forces more power into our shield.

The gargantuan dragon crashes down next to us, the ground shaking, painfully jarring my tailbone against Vale's hip. Stones and dust and flame course over Vale's shield, briefly casting us into foggy darkness.

When the air around us clears, I look toward the Mage-shield across the field, where my family is most likely to be. Two dragons crash to the ground near their shield, and a third rolls down the remaining bluff to collide with a group of screaming soldiers.

And then there are no more dragons in the sky.

Men yell orders, cry out and run aimlessly in all directions. There are tents on fire all over the field, everything lit up orange and yellow. Smoke rises in an amber fog, filling the valley.

The line of gold along the mountaintop constricts toward the center, the glow becoming fuzzy and muted. A black mass levitates inside the golden cloud, like a cobra raising its head, highlighted by the ethereal glow.

Tight lines of glowing orange flash from the black mass and strafe down the mountain in a series of flaming spears.

The black mass swoops higher, then down, over the avalanche of fire. As it moves ever closer, advancing straight toward us, I suddenly realize what I'm seeing.

Gardnerian soldiers in dark uniforms. On dragons. *Our* dragons.

Like a flock of geese, they're arranged in a V. Fire rains down from the V's lead point. A shield courses back from this point over the rest of the V like a flowing, golden current.

"*Ancient One*," I gasp.

Order breaks down completely in the face of enemy dragons and the advancing Magefire. A young Kelt clambers up the bluff nearby, his eyes wide and terrified, his face streaked with sweat and soot. Kelt and Urisk soldiers are running south, fleeing, climbing up the bluff we slid down, scrambling for safety. Trying to escape the murderous flock now coursing over the field.

And the advancing riv⁓⁓⁓e.

A Kelt clips our ⁓⁓⁓ owls in agony and falls to the ground, hi⁓⁓⁓ ⁓⁓ sparking blue flame. Haphazar⁓⁓⁓ ⁓⁓ spear out from all over Crykes Field ⁓⁓⁓s of color exploding in a harmless kaleidoscope of puffs against the shield surrounding our dragons.

They're flying low now. Low enough for me to see *her*.

She's astride the lead dragon, wand raised and throwing down fireballs with a passionate vengeance. A golden shield flows from the palm of her other hand and streams backward over the other dragons like a flaming current of air. Her face is twisted into a bloodthirsty war cry.

The fire of her bloodlust rocks through my magic-stripped body.

Like a dark flame, her long black hair flickers behind her as she swoops in close and fills the valley with fire.

Through a break in the smoke, I can see her face clearly, and our eyes meet. Her face is so much like Vale's—sharp lines, glittering Mage skin, fierce eyes.

Vale's mother.

She swoops up, the line of Mages sweeping up with her, following the curve of the bluff, rising over our ditch, her dragon's belly momentarily so close I can make out individual shard-like scales. Her fierce wave of fire crashes into our shield and crests over us, the flames overtaking our shield with a deafening roar.

Heat radiates through me. I'm so empty of fire, so painfully cold, and I cry out, unable to control my fire-lust, desperate to merge with the fire magic I'm stripped clean of. I strain toward the shield, toward the fiery river, struggling to pull my arms free of my bindings.

Vale's arm is tight around me, restraining me as I struggle for release. I'm dizzy with desire for the flames, light-headed, disembodied. Vale's arm trembles against mine as he fights to both hold the shield and keep me away from it as fire engulfs the world.

The world blazes orange, then yellow. Then searing white. Then black.

CHAPTER TEN:
The Dryad

The entire world is altered.

A bleak landscape surrounds us—scorched earth as far as the eye can see, smoke turning the dawn light a sickly yellow. Everything lifeless. Barren.

Scorched by *her*.

I'm on a horse, slipping in and out of consciousness, and a strong arm wrapped around my waist is the only thing keeping me upright. My head hangs, limp as a rag doll's, and my body feels cold and scoured out, my affinity stripped bare. The only comfort is a radiating warmth at my back that tells me it must be Vale in the saddle behind me.

A large number of Gardnerian soldiers ride around us at an unhurried pace. Fain's horse plods alongside ours. His chest is bare, and as he rides past, I see that pale, raised lash scars cover his entire back.

I glance down, my head lolling in time with the horse's slow trot. I'm in a sooty soldier's tunic, a rumpled silver sphere over my chest.

Fain's tunic.

He gave me his clothing. A wave of gratitude washes over me.

A wagon rattles by beside us, and I turn my head, the world swaying and tilting as I do.

"Tessieee." The sound is muffled and low, as if slowed down and stretched out. I numbly register that my brother is in there, restrained by the Gardnerian adults who surround him and keep him from launching himself clear off the wagon and onto me.

My grandfather is just behind Wren, looking at me in shock, tears coursing down his haggard, lined face. He's bobbing his praying hands up and down as he cries, then makes the star sign of holy blessing on his chest over and over and over.

I list to the side as the wagon passes, and the arm tightens around me.

Vale.

His cloak is wrapped around me over Fain's tunic, another barrier between us, but I can still feel the heat of him—just enough heat to keep me from slipping away.

That fire. Like his mother's. I remember her fire, coursing over the entire world.

I'm hungry for it.

But not just hungry for the fire. Hungry for how Vale and I match, our affinity lines in perfect symmetry.

Except mine are now empty of magic.

"Vale…" My head lolls, my teeth chattering lightly, the edges of my molars tapping out a choppy, uneven rhythm.

I'm so cold.

I push back against him with what little strength I have, easing into the shape of him, reveling in how well I fit against his hard chest.

I forget to be shy. To be proper. My mind is clouded, and I forget that Gardnerian women don't press themselves against unfasted men, even if they're desperate for warmth. Desperate for fire.

I'm listing in and out of consciousness, and he's so *warm*. My hand slides down to grasp at his thigh. His leg is warm, his fire affinity coursing through it. I sigh and pull at his warmth, my fingers grasping tighter, tendrils of his fire straining toward my hand, warmth flowing up my arm, muting the cold.

"Tessla," he says, in gentle but firm censure. He slides his hand down to grasp mine, to pull it away from his leg.

The minute the skin of his hand touches mine, my affinity lines shudder. Vale's breath hitches, and I melt into him, like seeking like, my affinity in perfect proportion to his. So perfectly aligned. I give out a long, chattering sigh as my hand warms. The magical void in me is like a bottomless chasm, ready for him to pour himself into me.

"Ancient One, your fire…" He's like a dream. The void in me is so great, it's overwhelming. I breathe in, grasp at his hand and pull.

A strong, long tendril of Vale's fire floods into me, through my hand, up my arm, into my chest. I groan and throw my head back, meeting his hard shoulder. My cheek slides against his hot neck.

More skin.

"No, Tessla," Vale cautions, but I barely hear him.

I press my forehead to his neck and pull, this time harder, inhaling deeply as I drag a strong edge of his fire, his complete affinity, toward me.

Vale flinches away, jerking his hand from mine and wrenching me away from the skin of his neck. Breaking all contact.

"Stop," he snaps sharply. "It's *too much*." His tone is coarse with shock.

I'm breathing heavily now, and so is he. My teeth are no longer chattering, but the world is spinning. The stolen fire kindles inside me in uneven fits and starts, exposing new pain where it flares, but melting the ice.

"We match," I slur, in a heated fog. "I fall right into you."

"You *can't* make a…" His words are seethingly tight. He breaks off, as if deeply angered and reining it in. "You cannot *ransack* my power. You'll throw yourself even further out of balance and drag me there with you."

"I'm sorry," I say weakly, catching my breath. Too Mage-drunk and disoriented to be fully ashamed of my brazen grasping of his magic. It's an intimate thing I've done, like stealing a deep-seated, secret emotion. The very essence of a Mage.

He's stiff and uneasy now. I can feel how tense he is, recoiling from me.

A small part of my brain, some part of me far away on a distant shore, feels chastened and small. Fearful that I've angered him so intensely, that he finds me to be a grasping, repulsive parasite of a thing.

But there's a kinship in this affinity match—something I've never felt before. It makes me want to cling to this stranger Mage, because he doesn't feel like a stranger at all. I feel, instinctively, like I understand him better than anyone on Erthia ever could. And his sharp rejection hurts with a spearing pain that rivals the agony of Fain's purging.

The regular rhythm of the horse lulls me into dulled, shamed oblivion. Vale is balancing me carefully at the far end of his shoulder, his fire closed off now, tightly banked to keep me out.

A chaotic tendril of green forest winds out toward us from the mountains where an expansive forest once stood, the rest of the central mountains charred to soot. The remaining forest winds out to a point, the tip of it almost reaching the road.

I look into the trees, and that's when I see it.

A Dryad.

The Forest Fae is camouflaged by the leaves, blending in perfectly with the last stand of brush and trees. Its skin is a pale, glimmering emerald, accenting its piercing forest-green eyes. Its black hair is tied back, revealing pointed ears, and it's clad in armor made of leaves.

They're supposed to be extinct, wiped out years ago by the

Kelts. But the figure before me is starkly real, looking just like a picture I once saw in one of Jules's books. Except this Dryad is staring out at the charred landscape and weeping.

Then it meets my gaze and narrows its eyes. Its hatred rocks through me, like venom coursing through my veins.

I lift a weak, trembling finger toward the tendril of forest as we ride close.

"A Dryad," I weakly rasp out as the creature's anger pounds against me. Then I blink, and the face is gone.

But the echo of the Dryad's fury remains.

CHAPTER ELEVEN:
Untethered

I am unconscious and untethered, grasping in the black. Flailing, my center gone, the drawn-out lines of my affinity shattered.

Stripped bare.

I'm spiraling down into a bottomless void. Crying out into the nothing.

Vale's fire firmly grasps hold of me, and I hang on for dear life. His flames are tentative at first, then flare as he finds me, his heat burning hot and steady.

I hang on, as if dangling off a cliff. Desperation courses through me.

I hang on for Wren. For my grandfather. For Jules.

I can't die.

Vale holds tight, his fire looped like a burning crown around my wrist.

I'm no longer falling. I'm lying down, suspended in the darkness. Vale's fire is still tightly wreathed around my wrist, his heat rising through my arm.

My lifeline.

But it's not enough to hold on to. Not enough to bring back my core. My own fire.

The cold, black void pulls at me, my balance destroyed. I'm a broken scale, listing, tilting this way and that.

Without a center.

I don't know how long I lie there, tethered by the arm to his fire.

Slowly, I become aware again that I'm more than just a wrist, an arm, a shoulder. His warmth courses through me, warming my heart, strengthening my heartbeat as the heat spreads.

But it's his heat. Only his. If he withdraws it, I will spiral down into the void. I have no more power of my own. No affinity strength to anchor me.

And then his fire is at the base of my neck, close to my pulse. The heat flares, radiating with each beat of my heart, pulsating up and down my neck, down through my chest. It floods through me in a shuddering blaze, lighting me up, hurtling straight down my limbs.

There's pain, just on the edge of a burn. Another great flare radiates from my neck, echoing deep in my center—and then a throbbing explosion, igniting in a fierce rush, catching fire.

Suddenly, it's there.

Small, but there. In the core of me—a circle of fire. Light and wood and air swirling in a thin layer around the edges. And over that, a trace of water. All five affinities, but fire at the core. Small and strong and hot.

My fire. There again, but perilously fragile.

The darkness swirls around me, like I'm caught up in a huge vortex of black smoke. Then it abruptly flows to the background, and Vale is before me, his form made of shadow and limned in an outline of flickering fire. One of his hands presses his wand against the side of my neck, the other steadies my head. His face and neck are slick with sweat, his expression rattled, his breathing labored and uneven. His fierce eyes glow orange with flame.

"Tessla," he says, his voice rough, surprise in his tone.

"I can see you," I tell him weakly, my head clearing. "You're outlined in fire, but I can see you."

His intense stare doesn't waver. There's an urgency there. "I've pushed as much fire into you as I can summon," he says, "but…it's not enough. I… I'd like to try one more thing. It's… unorthodox."

"What?" I force out, weak but fully aware.

He hesitates, eyes searing. "A kiss."

I'm barely tethered to my small circle of affinity fire, but still, the tiny flame gives a leap as surprise flashes through me, the flame straining toward Vale.

"Kiss me, then," I tell him, tilting my chin slightly up, wanting his fire. Wanting to live.

Vale hesitates for a split second, the glow of his eyes heightening. He leans in and brings his lips to mine, his mouth gentle and warm. A stream of his fire flows in with the kiss, straight to my core, merging with my affinity lines. My whole body arches toward him.

"Yes," I murmur, my own voice strange and low. "That's it. Do that." I pull him close.

He brings his lips back to mine, his kiss more insistent this time. The stream of fire he's pushing into me ignites all over my body, scorching through me.

We both gasp into each other's mouths as our affinities merge tight.

Our kiss turns hard and hot as we grasp at each other's magic lines, a torrent of fire coursing down my throat, shattering through my body. His fire is hungry and seeking, pressing down through my mouth, on the edge of scalding.

The core of me is hot and strong now, my center fully returning as his heat burns hot on my lips, pouring into me, blazingly strong.

I can feel my whole body now—battered, exhausted, weak and ragged.

But whole.

Whole, and with a precarious balance restored.

Vale's heat draws off my mouth. But I don't fall.

It's back. My own fire. My own affinity. Solid and sure.

The shadows pull in from the edges of the room, and Vale's form recedes into the dark.

After what seems like an eternity, flowing magic slides around my wrist, cool like a spring river—tentative, searching.

Water magic.

My eyes flutter open a sliver.

Fain.

"Vale," I rasp out, still barely able to speak. "Where's Vale?"

"He'll be back," Fain reassures me, his voice a warm lull. "Don't fret, love. You're going to be fine."

"What happened to me?" My mouth is dry and hot, my body slick with sweat.

"You're Magedrunk, sweetling." He props me up and presses a small cup to my lips. "Here, drink this," he says, his arm tight around me, keeping me from tilting as the room spins.

It's warm and pine-bitter, with an undercurrent of sweet.

"*Beeswellin,*" I murmur, sloppily running my tongue over the edge of my upper lip. "And *arniss* root. And *honeythistle.*"

"Very good, my little apothecary," Fain says approvingly, guiding me back down onto the pillow.

I half smile at his affectionate tone and kind touch. "When can I see my brother? And my grandfather...?" My head feels strange, lolling about, as if it's disconnected from my body.

"Soon," he gently croons. He brushes a tendril of damp hair off my face. "But first you need to sleep this off, Tessla. Let your affinity fully restore itself..."

His voice fades far away, the scene blurring...

To nothing.

CHAPTER TWELVE:
Wandfasting

I'm awakened by the sound of Fain's voice. My eyes are sticky, the lids unnaturally heavy, and I can manage to open them only a sliver.

I'm leaden with exhaustion, half sleeping, but I can breathe normally now, and I feel only slightly hot with fever, not trembling and burning up like before. Still, the images before me seem ephemeral, the colors deepened and heightened.

"She fought off an ax-paladin, apparently." Fain's reclining against a silk-cushioned divan, sumptuous red tapestries lining the walls and ceiling of the immense tent, a deep crimson rug on the floor patterned with sweeping gold and violet inlay.

I blink, confused.

Am I dreaming?

My mind is as sluggish as my leaden body, but I know we're supposed to be at the nearest military base. Instead, I'm surrounded by luxury.

An exquisitely carved bookcase lines the wall directly in front of me. It's filled with leather-bound volumes with gilded lettering, some written in Alfsigr. Gleaming brass nautical equipment lines the top shelf—compact telescopes, a complicated sextant. An iron woodstove engraved with a branching

River Maple design pumps out warmth, the tent toasty even though its flap is tied open.

A cook fire blazes just outside the tent, and a young, bespectacled Gardnerian sits by it, tuning a violin. He's stocky, his hair mussed, his civilian's tunic finely made but wrinkled and haphazardly belted.

It's twilight, the sky a deep blue fading to sapphire and hung with a waxing moon.

Vale is seated near the tent's entrance, holding a glass of deep green liquid, unlike the crimson drink Fain is balancing on his knee. Their crystalline glasses glint in the amber light of a hanging lantern and the golden firelight emanating from the woodstove.

Heat stabs and twists deep in my core at the sight of Vale, and I'm thrust into unsettled confusion. I can still feel his fire on my mouth like a ghostly brand, still resonating, still flushed warm.

Vale and Fain are both clean and pressed, not sooty and worn like they were after rescuing me. The silk of their black uniforms is smooth and new, the silver spheres on their chests bright and unmarked. Their Mage cloaks are thrown casually over the backs of their satin-cushioned chairs.

"Seems the ax-paladin was rough with her," Fain tells Vale, his tone flat.

I internally wince at the memory. The huge Kelt laughing as he dragged me away from my brother.

"So she stole his wand and hurled fire at him." Fain sips from his glass, his eyes tight on Vale. "Well done, I say."

Vale's eyes flash. "Yes, well, she almost killed herself in the process. Mage Aniliese said this is the worst case she's ever seen." Vale looks around. "Where *is* the apothecary?"

"She'll be back in a few hours," Fain responds. "She's prepping more tonic. But Priest Alfex has been here. He performed the healing ablutions."

Vale's gaze turns cynically cool. "Oh, thank the Ancient One for that. She'll have no need for me, then. Or the apothecary. She can be healed with *prayer*."

Shock cuts through my haze, anger riding swiftly on its heels.

How can he talk like this? He sounds like one of the bullying Kelts, sneering at our religious beliefs. First comes the sneering, then the vandalizing of our churches, then we're being rounded up in barns...

Fain sets his drink down with a sharp clink. "I accept that you're a complete heathen. But I would ask that you refrain from mocking our faith." His tone is biting.

Vale stares at him for a long moment. Then his expression hardens, and he shakes his head. "No. I absolutely cannot do that. My mother has turned into a complete zealot, and frankly, so has Vyvian. You're one of the only people I can speak freely with. I respect *you*. Can't that be enough?"

Fain is silent, his eyes hot with offense.

"It was kind of you to let us use your tent," Vale offers, his tone conciliatory.

Fain lets out a long, angry sigh and shoots him a sarcastic look. "It wasn't kind. I *hate* staying in your tent. Priests have more flair for decorating than you do."

Vale's mouth lifts in a crooked grin, the tension dissipating. "I prefer minimalism." He looks around and shakes his head. "Unlike you. It's like an Ishkart market exploded in here."

Fain's expression goes sly. "Spoils of war, sweet Vale."

"It's not really Gardnerian, your aesthetic."

"I have exotic tendencies." Fain's eyes dance as he sips his drink, as if holding on to a delicious secret. He reclines back and sends Vale a critical glance. "You seem spent. How long did it take to revive her?"

There are dark circles under Vale's eyes, the angularity of his face seeming heightened by fatigue. "Almost the entire night."

That unsettling warmth rises in me.

Vale revived me. Stayed with me the whole night.

Kissed me.

"Drink." Fain motions toward Vale's glass. "You need it. I could barely sense your fire affinity earlier—it was like she stripped you bare." Fain's mouth turns up at this, as if he's amused by his own words. "Really, though," he continues, his tone now laced with concern, "you look truly awful. How much of your fire did she pull?"

Vale lets out a long sigh and throws back a good portion of his drink, grimacing. His expression darkens. "Fain, she basically tried to *devour* my affinity on the way here. And it took—" he pauses, clearly uncomfortable "—a *great deal* of fire to restore her." His brow tenses, and I have the strange sensation that he's struggling not to look at me, holding himself tightly removed.

But I remember how he kissed me. The feel of his fire against my lips.

As I watch them, I realize that Fain and Vale are both incredibly striking, with their angular features, aristocratic cheekbones and dark hair. Even their postures are similar—they're both reclining with natural grace and elegance, like people used to luxury and money.

But in other ways, they're complete opposites, much like their affinities. Vale sits still enough, but a simmering, almost vibrating tension seems to emanate from him, his eyes razor-sharp. Fain, in contrast, seems all cool, unflappable grace, a fey light dancing in his gaze. There's an artistic grace about him.

I study their uniforms, all black silk and silver embroidery, each with five lines on their sleeves to mark them as Level Five Mages, and part of me is stunned by this turn of events.

Our uniforms. *Our* soldiers. Powerful, Level Five *Gardnerian* soldiers. Ready to take on Kelts and Urisk and anyone else who could come after us.

The burning barn flashes through my mind. Fear grips me, pulling my gut tight. I focus on their uniforms, trying to stave off the terror. The silk of Vale's uniform lies smooth on his chest, his wand tucked into his wandbelt. He carried me easily, back in Doveshire, all sinuous muscle and strength. Struck down the paladin and the Icaral. And others. Shielded me against his mother's fire.

They're both dangerous. And I'm safe. My family is safe.

I breathe in deep. A blessed feeling of protection washes over me and beats back the lingering terror.

"The grandfather says she's a Level Three Mage," Fain tells Vale.

Fire flashes in Vale's eyes, and he shoots Fain a scathing look. "The same fool of a grandfather who wouldn't let her have a wand?"

Warmth floods through me at his show of support. I've been so long without the support of anyone, save Jules. None of my people have ever been willing to go against the grain to support me in my quest for a wand.

Fain presses his mouth into a thin line. "The grandfather's traditional."

Vale spits out a sound of disdain and glares at Fain. "Isn't everyone these days?"

"You know, you might try being positive once in a while."

Vale's eyes flare. "I'm too educated to be positive."

Fain lets out a long sigh and grimaces at Vale. "As I was *saying*, the 'fool of a grandfather' informed me that our Tessla only knows about five spells. *Five*." He glances toward me, and his gaze takes on a look of rapturous admiration. "The way she gathered the spells and layered them…" He pauses and shakes his head. "Extraordinary, really."

Vale's eyes glitter coldly in the firelight. "One more spell, and she would have essentially exploded her own body."

Fain glowers theatrically at Vale. "Does the sheer artistry of this fail to reach you?" His lip quirks up, and he gestures toward me with his chin, his eyes filling with mischief. "She's quite pretty. You should fast to her, Vale."

Vale's throws him a look of sharp censure. "Yes, I'm sure we'd hit it off famously."

Fain laughs into his glass. "You do have quite the way with women."

"A Lower River girl. And me." His tone is flat. "You're quite the matchmaker, Fain."

"You're a fool."

"She is a Lower River girl," Vale counters, irritated.

Hurt slices through me like jagged glass at the implied insult.

Fain gapes at him, his brow tensing with disbelief. "You can't be serious."

"What?" Vale snipes at Fain. "Did you imagine we'd enjoy the symphony together?" Biting sarcasm twists his tone. "Meander through the Verpacian archives? Discuss literature? *If* she even knows how to read."

"She's an apothecary," Fain snipes back, annoyance darkening his gaze. "*Clearly* she knows how to read."

"You know what most Lower River Gardnerians are like," Vale scoffs. "They're practically Keltic peasants."

Fain's eyes have narrowed to slits. "Well, she could teach you a thing or two about layering spells."

"And carding wool, I'd imagine."

Fain's expression turns cold. "So, she's a peasant, and you're royalty. She's still a peasant who faced down an ax-paladin, a large section of the Keltic and Urisk armies, an Icaral demon *and* a dragon attack. Surely that counts in her favor."

Vale glares at him, unmoved.

Fain's lip turns up in a taunting sneer. "Admit it. She's pretty."

Vale swirls his glass and eyes Fain cagily. "She's...tolerable. In a rustic sort of way."

Rustic? My profound hurt swells to a burgeoning, blood-simmering anger.

"Who's wandtesting her?" Fain asks, undaunted. "Surely they'll want her tested."

"I have that unpleasant task."

Fain shakes his head and pours himself another glass of crimson liquid from a gilded carafe decorated with red glass in the shape of diamonds. "Vale, you are my best friend. But right now, I think you are being a complete and utter ass."

"I have no desire to wandfast. You know that," Vale counters. "And certainly not to...*her*. Besides, she'll soon be swooning over Nils and his ilk, like the lot of them."

"Ah," Fain gloats, grinning. *"Jealousy.* You know, Vale, if you tried to be just a *little* bit friendly, they'd swoon over you, too."

Vale throws him a look of downright indifference. "I'll never rate high as anyone's romantic obsession. I'm resigned to it."

Fain laughs. "That's because you scare people, what with your cheerful personality and all."

I bite back the desire to curse. I stare at Vale, inwardly seething. I struggle against the impossible, exhausted heaviness of my frame, like I'm a great hunk of iron fused to the cot beneath me. It takes great effort to even lift my tongue.

Vale is staring into the middle distance, the flash of a storm in his eyes, and I get the strong sensation once again that he's fighting the urge to stare at me. That he's fighting my pull, like a ship struggling against a strong current.

"Vale," Fain says, his voice now stripped of its edge. "You should fast to her. There's more to that girl than homespun wool and calloused hands. And..." He stiffens, blinking, looking momentarily toward the floor. "It would squelch the rumors about us." When Fain looks back up at Vale, there's vulnerability there. And an edge of fear.

Vale's expression turns hard. "I don't care what they say. I despise almost all of them. Except for you, and my siblings. Though Vyvian is growing more intolerable by the day."

"They're going to fast them all, in two days' time—you know that, don't you?"

What? No. Not me!

Vale sits dangerously still, tension simmering off him. If I touched a flint to him, I imagine he'd ignite. "No," Vale says, his voice firm, his expression bitter. "I'll not wandfast to anyone. Ever."

Wandfasting.

My mind is thrown back to only days ago. Jules and I were sitting high up on Crykes Peak, side by side, our legs kicking over the edge. Jules's thigh briefly touched mine, and he was careful to edge himself slightly away, keeping a discreet and purposeful distance.

"I suppose someday you'll be wandfasted," Jules said off-handedly, but his brown eyes were fixed tight on me with unwavering intensity.

The strong undercurrent of dissatisfaction in his tone unsettled me. "All Gardnerians wandfast," I replied, more defensive than I'd intended.

He'd nodded, jaw stiff, then stared down at my hand, the subtle shimmer of my skin apparent in the dark.

Jules's expression softened, became almost entranced.

"You've emerald dust on your skin." A dazed smile lifted his lips. "It's so lovely."

The heat of an uncomfortable flush bloomed on my cheeks.

"They'll mark your hands, won't they?" he asked softly, trailing his finger lightly over the side of my hand. I could tell he meant it as a casual gesture, but his touch lingered, trailing gently on the skin of my little finger. There was a prickling heat in it that made my breath catch.

Heart hammering, I'd moved my hand a fraction away, enough to break the contact, my cheeks burning.

Perhaps sensing my discomfort, Jules had pulled his hand clear away until it was tight in his lap, restrained in a fist. He looked toward the horizon, stiff as a post, as if holding himself in censure. He swallowed audibly and looked sidelong at me.

It became clear to me in that moment that he'd thought on this quite a bit. Wanting to touch me. At war with himself over it. There was an apology in his eyes, mixed with fierce sadness.

I took a deep breath and gave him a brief, encouraging half smile, which he tried to return. But it didn't reach his eyes.

We couldn't touch each other.

We were both clear on the rules, both our cultures settled on this matter.

He was quiet for a long time, his jaw set. "It's for life then, wandfasting."

I nodded.

He turned a fraction, looked at me out of the corner of his eye. "How do they do it?" His voice was laced with dread, like I was headed for the gallows and he wanted to know exactly how I would be executed.

"Well," I said uncomfortably, "a Priest Mage does it. The couple clasps their hands over each other's—" I demonstrated with my own hands, drawing them into my lap, moving one over the other "—and he recites the spell over their hands and… the lines appear. And they're bound. For life."

"And that's it, then?"

I shook my head. "That's just to bind the couple. It's like your engagement ceremony. There's a separate ceremony to seal the fasting. Like Kelt weddings. The wandfasting lines darken when the couple is sealed. And after..." I reddened. "After they consummate the sealing, the lines spread up their wrists as a mark of their union."

Jules considered that, his face tense. He looked at me sidelong. "So, once you're wandfasted...you can't be with anyone else?"

I nodded. "Or the marks turn painful. For women. Only the women's lines turn into burns if they break their wandfasting vows."

"But not the men?" He spat out a sharp sound of derision. "That's hardly fair."

"It's to keep our bloodlines intact," I said defensively. "We were almost wiped out, Jules. It's still going on..."

"I know," he interrupted, but there was understanding there. Along with his frustration.

The scourge of prejudice. We Gardnerians never seemed to get a moment's peace from it, especially those of us in border towns. An ever-shrinking border. Our Mage soldiers were no match for the combined Kelt and Urisk forces.

Jules gave me a wry smile. "If I were Gardnerian, do you think your grandfather would have us fasted?" He clearly meant to toss it out as a flippant jest, but there was too much heat flaring in his eyes.

My flush deepened. "Perhaps."

I can't tell him of my private, romantic longings. The things I think about only deep in the night. My dreams aren't of him—I dream of going to the University in Verpacia. Apprenticing to an apothecary there, and someday meeting a Gardnerian scholar. He'd be tall, his hair raven black. His eyes piercing green. He'd have a ready smile that would light up his angular face. Kind, courteous and bookish, he'd be privately affectionate and publicly reserved.

But when he looked at me, there would be heat in his gaze.

In my imaginings, my Gardnerian would see me one fall day, leaves ablaze as I walked from a University hall to the apothecary laboratory. He'd be immediately entranced. Court me. Leave me a single red rose and his favorite book, bound in black leather with gilded lettering along its side. He'd kiss me in a garden at night, lit by the blue glow of Ironflowers. Then he'd fast to me, as quickly as he possibly could, the lines on our hands now matching—thin, delicate black swirls.

We'd kiss in every secret alcove we could find.

And there'd be fire in those stolen kisses.

Then we'd seal our fasting, our fastlines darkening. And that night we'd consummate the sealing, the fasting lines flowing down our wrists, made intricate by the consummation, twining around our skin the way our bodies would twine around each other...

"Does it have to be to a Gardnerian?" Jules asked, shattering my breathless reverie. His gaze is fraught with longing. "Just curious," he quickly amended.

I'm momentarily concerned that it might show in my face—my secret, passionate longings. Longings that aren't for him, my kind, beloved friend.

Jules's question hangs in the air, silent and still. Full of meaning. The summer breeze holding it.

"Yes," I told him, treading lightly, not wanting to hurt sweet Jules.

The hope in his eyes morphed to dismay, and his eyes lingered on mine the way his fingers lingered on my skin. Warmth rippled through me, and I was momentarily thrust into a new confusion.

I realized, in that moment, that I liked Jules's brief touch. It was pleasant and thrilling to be touched by a young man. And then the thought came, unbidden—

What would it be like to kiss Jules?

Alarmed, I shook the thought away. Such thoughts were too dangerous, straying clear past the rigid, fiercely protected and imposed boundaries between our two peoples. Those lines were the whole reason we weren't supposed to sneak up here alone.

"The fasting spell doesn't work unless the woman is pure, and both people have to be Gardnerian, or the priest won't fast them," I clarified, the words coming out harsher and firmer than I intended.

He stiffened, seeing the barrier I'd set up. The barrier I was going to hold.

"I wish there were no races," he ground out, glowering at the horizon, his voice low with frustration. "Just all of us the same." He let out a harsh, troubled breath, his jaw tensing. Finally, he sighed deeply, appearing resigned. "I'm sorry, Tessla. I just… I feel like once you fast…" He turned toward me, his eyes intent. "I don't want to lose your friendship."

"You'll never lose my friendship," I told him with fierce assurance. "I don't care if you're a Kelt. You'll always be like a brother to me."

He winced, and I felt a pang in my heart for hurting him. But the boundaries between us needed to stand.

Or I would lead this friend I loved headfirst into disaster.

"She's awake."

Vale's sour tone intrudes on my memories. His eyes are honed tight on me, and I feel his fire briefly shudder through me before he looks away.

Fain scoffs at this. "She's delirious, is what she is. She'll be in and out for a good while yet. Mage Aniliese says she should come around sometime tomorrow morning." Fain's tone softens, and his eyes are gentle as he sets them on me. "I do hope they find someone worthy of her."

Vale huffs impatiently at this. "Why don't you fast to her, Fain, if you're so taken with her?"

"Who might Fain be fasting to?" a woman's voice asks. The voice is soft and melodious, like the trickle of water. A young woman pushes the tent flap back and sweeps inside, smiling at Fain and Vale.

She's impossibly lovely, absolutely dimming the beauty of the Upper River girls in both appearance and dress. A perfect, oval face with full lips and riveting emerald-green eyes, her black hair cascading over her shoulders and down her back. Rubies hang from her perfect ears, and her black tunic and long underskirt are exquisite, the silk embroidered with threads of a deeper black than the silk, covering her garb in repeating designs of branching trees.

"Vyvian! You glorious creature!" Fain gets up and warmly kisses her on both cheeks, beaming. She beams back at him.

She pulls off her black silk gloves and folds them neatly with slender, graceful hands, swirling wandfasting marks decorating them.

"Vyvian." Vale's greeting is guarded, but there's a trace of amusement there.

"No, really, Vale. Don't get up on my account," she teases snarkily. She turns back toward Fain. "My brother overwhelms me with his affection."

Violin music lifts into the night air, winding into the tent. A heartbreakingly mournful, yet lovely song.

"To what do we owe this immense pleasure?" Vale inquires, though with considerable disinterest.

Vyvian takes the seat Fain offers her and settles in. "I'm here to see Mother, of course."

"You may have to wait a day or two," Vale idly comments. "She's busy laying waste to the world."

I remember the dragons. The terrible fear. The river of fire.

How can Vale sound so blasé? How can he remember that night and speak of it with such cool composure?

Fain fusses over Vyvian, pouring her a drink, then takes a seat once more. He raises his glass in a toast. "To our beloved Great Mage."

Vyvian lifts her own glass, her eyes misting over. "Yes. To Mother." She takes a sip, contemplative for a moment, then gives Fain a look heavy with import. "The Kelts just ceded their entire northwestern territory to us. The border war is essentially over."

Fain nods, a calculating glint in his gaze. "She's taken out their entire dragon horde, then?"

Vyvian huffs a sound of contempt. "Their entire horde, or at least most of it. Any surviving dragons won't be in their hands for long." Vyvian smiles. "They're calling Mother the 'Black Witch.' Did you know that?"

Fain smirks, lounging back. "I rather like that! Your dear mother has a flair for the dramatic, I'll give her that. She certainly deserves an equally dramatic name. Her attack..." He pauses, shaking his head as if momentarily overcome. "Well timed, I say. And well played."

Vyvian gives Fain a significant look. "By the Ancient One's power, Fain."

Fain dips his head in assent. "By the Ancient One's power, indeed."

Vale rolls his eyes at the two of them and gives a disdainful sigh.

Vyvian swivels her head and narrows her eyes to peer closely at her brother. "You look dreadful, Vale."

"He was saving a damsel in distress," Fain informs her, giving Vyvian a look ripe with suggestion.

Vyvian glances sidelong toward me with obvious distaste. Then she looks to Fain and her expression lightens, her drink resting prettily in her lap. "Enough talk of war. Who is it you're fasting to, Fain?" She's delighted by the prospect. I can see it.

Vale is studying his sister, his expression wary and unreadable, one eyebrow slightly cocked. They don't resemble each other much, except, perhaps, in their aristocratic features. But it's Vale who looks more like his powerful mother.

"To absolutely no one," Fain insists, stressing each word, looking to Vyvian with theatrical devotion. "You know my heart belongs to you, Vyvian. And that you broke it when you so callously fasted to that glorious clod you're so enamored of." He gestures toward me with his glass. "We were speaking of Vale and Mage Tessla Harrow. Don't you think she deserves a Level Five Mage for all her trouble?"

Vyvian gapes at Fain. "Fast *her*? To... *Vale*? To the son of the Black Witch?" Her voice has gone shrill. "As a *reward*? Is that what you're suggesting?" She shakes her head decidedly. "Absolutely not. The girl's brave, to be sure, but there's talk she ran off with a Kelt." Vyvian takes a sip of her drink and shoots Fain a poignant look, full of dark meaning. She leans in toward him. "She might not be able to fast at all."

Fain gapes at Vyvian, his face a mask of bewilderment. "They're spreading rumors about her? *Already*?"

Vyvian purses her lips at him. "It's more than a rumor."

"I'm astonished. Truly." Fain jabs his finger at me. "*This* girl should be given a parade through the streets of Valgard. With *roses* thrown at her feet. *A lot* of roses." He shakes his head and crosses his legs gracefully, then lets out a long sigh. "But if you *truly* want to punish her, then by all means, fast her to Vale. With his legendary charm and extraordinary tact..."

Vale's head gives a slight bob of amusement, his mouth tilting into a grin.

Vyvian eyes Fain with shock. "Vale has a *legion* of young women champing at the bit to fast to him."

Vale gives her an arch look. "True love, all of it, I'm sure."

She rounds on him. "You could put in some small effort to be pleasant."

They spar for a while longer, and I grow weary, their voices harder and harder to follow.

The violin music turns to a piece I know. "Winter's Dark." It's achingly beautiful. Played masterfully.

Fain is lost in the music as well, his glass tipped precariously to one side, tears filling his eyes.

"Ancient One, Edwin," Fain calls outside, his mouth lifting into a wavering, melancholy smile. "If you keep playing like that, I'll fast to *you*."

It's the last thing I remember before the fatigue pulls me under.

It's fully dark outside when I wake again.

Vyvian and Edwin are gone. Vale's and Fain's low voices rouse me from a deep, heavy slumber.

"The way Malkyn killed that Kelt girl. I can't get it out of my mind." Fain's expression is dark and troubled. "I dreamed of it. A terrible nightmare." He shakes his head, as if trying to clear the memory. "That poor girl, huddled in the dirt. I didn't see her until…" Fain takes a deep breath, collecting himself. "It's like he goes out of his way to be just like the Urisk. The Kelts. It's…it's not right. We're supposed to be the Righteous Ones. The Beacon of Hope for a dark world."

"Spoken with the idealism of a man who has studied far too much scripture and exactly *no* history whatsoever," Vale says, leveling a piercing gaze at Fain. "Gardnerians with over-whelming power will do exactly what any race does with over-whelming power. *Abuse it.*"

Fain narrows his eyes at Vale. "Your cynicism borders on blasphemy."

Vale drops his forehead in his hand and massages it, shaking his head. "For the life of me, Fain, I cannot understand your attachment to this inflexible religion of ours. Frankly, it makes me question your intelligence." He straightens and gestures toward Fain's drink, perched neatly in his elegant fingers. "You're a walking contradiction."

"A reclining contradiction," Fain tartly replies.

"Waxing poetic about being the Righteous Ones with a glass of illegal Keltic spirits perched on your knee." He shoots him a significant, knowing look. "I *could* go on."

"I'm complicated," Fain snipes back.

"You're intellectually deluded," Vale puts in flatly.

Fain waves him away. "Your disdain won't work on me, Vale. I actually enjoy your unabashed elitism."

Vale is implacable. "I do *not* enjoy your romanticized ignorance."

Fain laughs. "You know, Vale, your absolute conviction that you are superior to me is sometimes…overwhelming. Contrary to what you think, I best you in many areas."

"And they would be?"

"Hospitality. Charm. Water Magic." Fain shoots him a meaningful look. "Tact."

Vale eyes him slyly. "Don't forget historical delusions."

Fain glowers at him. "Don't meddle with my fantasies of reality. Your strident cynicism is one of your worst traits."

"So I should join the ignorant, deluded and falsely pious masses, according to you?"

Fain laughs and mock-toasts him. "You'd be much happier."

"Would I be, Fain?" Vale sweeps his drink in an all-encompassing gesture. "Does all this lead to a happy ending?"

A shadow passes over Fain's expression. Then his face lightens with resignation. He holds his glass high. "For tonight, we will pretend that it will, and we will toast to our new champion, the exquisite Tessla Harrow."

Vale considers this with a tilt of his head, then nods, raising his glass a fraction, his eyes calmly taking me in, but I can feel the wild heat simmering beneath the calm.

"To Mage Tessla Harrow," Fain declares, chin high. "Champion of the unappreciative, deluded masses." Fain downs his glass, takes a deep, satisfied breath and lets it out. "Fast to her, Vale. And quickly. Before you lose your chance."

CHAPTER THIRTEEN:
Lower River Girl

The next morning, I'm awake before everyone else in the tent. A plump, gray-haired woman, who I assume is the apothecary, slumbers in the chair next to my cot, her breath a rhythmic whisper, and Fain is nowhere in sight. Vale is sprawled out on a floor cushion, a thin blanket fitfully wrapped around him like a messy binding.

My blood turns hot at the sight of him, a black hurt mingling with the fire inside me, fierce as a lowering thundercloud.

Lower River Girl.

He spat it like I'm nothing but silt beneath his feet.

Vale tosses and turns, his dreams seemingly troubled, his brow tensed tight as he murmurs to himself unintelligibly. A few times his face loses its angry sharpness and softens, his lips slightly parted as if he's about to speak, his expression becoming vulnerable and edged with sorrow.

It twists something deep inside me and I rail against it, tears biting at my eyes. Seeing him like this, I feel unguarded and exposed—and deeply rattled.

But his hurtful dismissal of me echoes through my mind, spearing through me like ice.

★ ★ ★

By the time the gray light of an overcast dawn filters through the gap in the tent flap, I'm utterly furious. Inwardly seething as Mage Aniliese methodically tends to me with practiced hands, checking my pulse and reflexes, rubbing salve into my hands and feet. She places a warm mug of tonic into my hands, the steam wafting up to moisten my chin and my nose with its minty, metallic scent.

I glare at Vale, resentful of the sight of his sharp shoulder blade jutting out against the disheveled silk of his tunic. His back to me, he's still asleep on the rolled out floor mat. There all night long in case his fire was needed—to help me.

I should be thankful.

His warm fire restarted my affinity, gave it fully back to me.

But I'm not thankful. I'm lost in a wilderness of intense emotion.

I hate that I feel this intense pull toward him. That our affinities line up so exactly. That I can't forget the feel of his lips on mine.

She's a Lower River Girl.

She's tolerable. In a rustic sort of way.

Hurt pierces through me, then an anger so raw I could spit fire right into his intimidating face.

"There, good. Rest a bit more."

Mage Aniliese is oblivious to my dark thoughts, smiling to herself as she pats my arm with an efficient hand, her silver Erthia orb bobbing restlessly on its chain alongside her golden apothecary guildmaster pendant.

I'm weak, but whole.

And so upset I don't want to spend another minute here.

And I feel humiliated. Humiliated that both Vale and Fain saw me half-naked. At the time, I was so desperate to breathe, so sickened with my own magic that I barely noticed my nudity. But now, my health returning, I'm completely aware of what happened. How exposed I was.

And I don't want to see Vale Gardner or Fain Quillen ever again. I want to forget that any of this ever happened.

Vale is sipping some tea, both hands tight around the mug. His uniform is wrinkled and disheveled, and the shadow of a sparse beard edges his chin. The dark circles under his eyes have deepened, and his hair is uncombed. I can sense his heated awareness of me, his brow drawn tight, but he keeps his gaze resolutely fixed on his tea.

The tent flap pulls back, the gray light momentarily washing out the riot of tapestry color surrounding us. Fain sails in, whistling to himself, looking well rested and polished as a shiny guilder. His uniform is clean and pressed, with his cloak jauntily flowing out behind him and his exquisitely carved wand resting in his wandbelt at a rakish angle.

He's the epitome of a handsome, well-to-do, elegant Gardnerian.

And this makes me angry, too.

Fain beams a dazzling smile at me as he enters. "Ah, the lovely Mage Harrow awakens." He reaches into his cloak pocket and pulls out a scarlet pomegranate and a small, fat coin purse, setting them down on the table beside me.

Mage Aniliese quirks a smile and cocks one eyebrow at him. She flicks her finger toward the pomegranate. "And where ever did you find this, Mage Quillen? At this time of ration and communal sacrifice?"

He kisses her on the top of her head, and she bats him away with mock annoyance. "Where I found it does not matter," he says, with great import. "What does matter is that you are brilliant and should be given a lake full of gems for everything you do for us."

Mage Aniliese chuckles, her moss-green eyes dancing merrily. She scoops up the pomegranate and the coin purse and drops them both into her tunic pocket, then gathers up her supplies—stoppered vials, small sacks of dried herbs, a stone mortar and pestle.

"Well," she says to Fain as she stows her tools, "Ancient One knows I've pulled you out of a scrape or two." She shoots him a poignant, amused glance. "How many times have you been Magedrunk?"

Fain thrusts his lip out, thinking. "Oh…a few." He smiles mischievously at her.

"Hmm," she says, nodding at him with jaded good humor. "Never like this, though." She turns to me. "Young lady, repeat after me. I will not layer spells."

I'll do whatever I need to do to protect and take care of my family.

"I will be careful," I tell her flatly, meeting her level gaze with my own restored wall of fire.

"Hmm," she repeats, frowning as if she sees me more clearly now and doesn't quite approve. "Well then," she says, taking a deep, resigned breath. "I'll be off."

I attempt a polite smile at Mage Aniliese, but I know my anger makes it appear strained. "Thank you," I tell her tightly. "I am in your debt."

Mage Aniliese nods at this, then gives Fain an affectionate pat on the arm and takes her leave.

"Well," Fain says pleasantly, turning to me. "I want you, Mage Harrow, to rest here as long as you like. My home is your home." He gracefully places one arm over his chest and gives me a slight deferential bow.

My irrational anger rises even higher along with the irrational urge to smack both Fain and Vale, so insulated by their money and their fancy cloaks and their fine wands.

Panic rears its ugly head.

Where will my family and I go? What are we going to do?

I might be able to find an apprenticeship in Verpacia, but I have no way to get there. No money. No horses. *Nothing.*

We're all alone.

Lower River, low-class peasants.

Fain is still smiling wide at me, smug as a contented cat. There's an anticipatory gleam in his eye, and I realize that he's waiting for my thanks.

"I'm leaving," I tell him succinctly. "Thank you for your assistance, but I need to find my family." I pin Fain with a polite but level stare, my heart pounding out my hurt. "And I wouldn't want to sully your tent further with my rustic, peasant ways."

Fain steps back in surprise, like he's been slapped, then swallows audibly.

"You were awake."

"Yes." I bite off the word, my tone gone hard. "I heard quite a bit of what you said. You and...*him.*" I turn and spear Vale with my stare.

Vale's eyes have gone a fraction too wide, his intense gaze locked on to mine. I can't decide if he looks troubled or filled with furious contempt, which only makes my anger burn hotter.

Fain's voice is tremulous. "Tessla, I *never...*"

"Stop." I cut Fain off, my cursed voice wavering. "I know how it is. My family and I were low-class and looked down on in Doveshire, and we'll be low-class and looked down on in Gardneria. Because I didn't grow up with money like you." I glare at Vale. "Or *you.*" I turn back to Fain. "We were so poor that we usually didn't have decent food. That's how *rustic* we are. Lower than peasants, actually." I shrug with feigned nonchalance, fiercely willing back the tears. "The farmers ate better than us most of the time."

Fain looks distraught. "Tessla, *please*."

"No. Really. Stop." I thrust my palm out at him emphatically. "I'm thankful to you, Mage Quillen. Truly I am." Tears sting at my eyes, and I blink them back. "You both saved me and my family. And I will *never* forget it. But there are a few things you should know before I leave." My heart hammers hot and hard. I turn to Vale and lock my gaze on to his. "Like the fact that Jules Kristian, the Kelt I was with…he's my closest friend."

"You might want to keep that bit of information to yourself," Fain cautions, his voice gone low.

I stare him down. "Jules saved my life and was going to smuggle me into Verpacia."

Fain shakes his head, his expression now troubled and uneasy. "It's often best to pick and choose which people might know of these private sorts of…"

"No," I put in, my tone firm. "I'm not ashamed of it. And I'm glad you brought the priest in to bless me. I was glad for the ablutions." I glance at Vale again. "My grandfather prayed for our safety day and night. Maybe you think that's superstitious nonsense. Maybe you've never had anything you needed to pray for." I'm reminded of the white bird briefly appearing that night, the image flashing in the back of my mind. "But against all the odds, we're all here. What's left of my family. Alive. So…perhaps Grandfather's prayers were answered. By the *Ancient One's power.*" I pointedly make the symbol of self-blessing and self-protection toward Vale.

Vale's jaw goes tight. He looks away, as if angered by my show of faith, and stares hatefully at the tapestried tent wall.

"And I do, in fact, know how to read." I look to Fain. "Are you familiar with *The Realm Apothecarium*?"

"Y-yes, of course," Fain stammers, nodding disjointedly. "That's the premier guild text." He gives a nervous titter and shakes his head. "I've a hard time making heads or tails of the bulk of it."

"I've worked every tonic in there to at least one-eighth capacity using substandard, cheap ingredients," I state flatly.

Fain blinks at me. "That's, er, impressive."

"And *Principia Mathematica*. Have you studied that?"

Fain laughs. "Of course I've worked out most of the sets. Almost to the end…"

"I finished it two years ago."

Fain stares at me, silent.

I turn to face Vale. He's gone very quiet and still, but I can sense the unsettled heat churning behind his fiery gaze. "How about you, Vale? Have you worked through it?" I purposely address him informally, even though it's considered disrespectful.

I mean to insult him, and he knows it.

He narrows white-hot eyes on me, his words clipped. "It was a bit beyond me."

Fain blows out a deep breath and shakes his head.

I turn back to Fain. "Vale and his sister think that because I'm poor, I can't appreciate fine things. That I'm illiterate." I pause, looking them both over boldly. "I can see that things won't be that different here in some ways. My family and I are still poor. Still viewed as lower class. But that's fine. No one is trying to kill us, and I can make a better life for us. I'm an apothecary. A good one. We'll find our way among the lower classes." My eyes flick toward Vale, whose storming gaze is hot on mine, and I hold his gaze with searing defiance before returning to Fain. "I won't ask you to suffer my presence any longer than is necessary, Mage Quillen. I've polluted your dwelling long enough."

I rise and ignore the hand Fain holds out to me, even though the room spins. I close my eyes for a brief second to steady myself, then make my way toward the exit.

I pause, tent flap in hand, and turn back to them. "And just so you both know, I've read Aughnot and Ellerson and studied a fair bit of the history of the Realm. And I can read simple Alfsigr. All self-taught."

Fain stares at me in rapt amazement. His eyes flick toward Vale. "I told you, you should fast to her," he murmurs.

I blow out a contemptuous breath and eye Vale with disgust. "You must be joking," I tell Fain. "Vale can't even manage advanced mathematics. I'd never fast to him. He's *far* too ignorant."

I turn on unsteady legs, push the tent flap open and leave.

CHAPTER FOURTEEN:
Level Five Mage

The air is damp and cool outside the tent, a gauzy fog veiling the base. Fain's tent is perched high on an outcropping of rock, and I follow the sole meandering path sharply downhill, my body stiff as I scuff along the wet dirt. My thoughts are turbulent, but I have one goal in mind—to find my family.

Soon the shadowy forms of black Gardnerian military tents emerge from the fog. The sounds of early morning conversations echo in the air as cook fires are stoked, and small knots of soldiers mill about, some at ease, some on duty and purposeful in their movements.

Two young soldiers are sitting on a large rock that hugs my path, their conversation low and congenial.

One of the young men turns, catching sight of me as I near. He shoots me a dazzling smile. He's breezily handsome, his cloak finely made, three silver lines hemming its edge.

A Level Three Mage.

I stop in front of them. "Please," I say imploringly. "I need to find my family."

"Of course," the Mage says, sliding down off the rock. "We can help you. I'm sure they're more than fine. They're being very well cared for, all the refugees." He looks me over closely and glances in the direction of Fain's tent. "You must be Mage

Tessla Harrow. I'm Nils Arden." He gestures toward his companion with his chin. "And this is Myles Richard. We've heard tales of your creative shielding, and what I think must be a stunning level of bravery."

He holds out his hand to me. He's beautiful, Nils, his vivid green eyes lit with intelligence and curiosity, and my heart picks up speed as I give him my hand. He lifts it to his lips and plants a gentle kiss on the back of it.

I gulp. He's got fire in his affinity lines. Not like Vale, but a steady line of it, simmering in flares, artfully woven. The way he has his fire magic so firmly tamped down feels dangerous, like an unsettling mystery. This secret knowledge sends a delicious shiver through me—it's so at odds with his open, unguarded expression.

I'm suddenly aware of the fact that I'm still wearing Fain's rumpled military tunic over my long skirt, and that my hair must be a tangled mess.

"You're even more lovely than they said," Nils tells me. I blush and look down, my eyes wandering to his hands. They're unmarked.

He's unfasted.

He gives me a brief, knowing glance before he releases my hand, his eyes liquid with warmth, as if we've shared a private joke. Like he knows some delicious, decadent secret about me.

His companion, Myles, is not nearly as handsome. His eyes are too closely set, his nose large and long. He's also reed-skinny and hunched awkwardly down, as if he's slightly put off by his own height. But his expression is open and well meaning, and there's kindness in his eyes. He lurches forward, as if overcome, and takes both my hands in his.

Earth magic. Not a lot, but what little there is runs strong and deep.

My eyes flit to the two silver lines that hem his cheaply made cloak.

"Thank you," Myles says with deep feeling. "Thank you for what you did. You saved my family. They were there, in the barn. I was stationed on the southern border when the Keltic and Urisk armies advanced. They moved more quickly than we anticipated. When my family was locked in that barn…you bought them those few seconds. If you hadn't…" His eyes are overflowing with gratitude, filling with tears. "Just…thank you, Miss Harrow."

My eyes flit to Nils, who's smirking at him good-naturedly. "Speaking like a Kelt again, Myles?" Nils teases.

Myles winces and drops my hands, spots of red lighting both his pale cheeks. "I'm so sorry. I mean *Mage* Harrow." He shakes his head in self-censure. "I… I grew up in a border town. Along the river." He shrugs. "Bad habits of speech. And quite a bit else. Too many Keltic ways…" He trails off.

A Lower River Gardnerian, like me.

Nils hangs his arm around Myles's shoulders and grins at me. "Myles here is just overcome, Mage Harrow. It's not every day he holds the hand of such a beautiful woman."

The skin on my back prickles with a sweeping heat, and I notice Nils and Myles looking past me. Their eyes go wide, and they immediately straighten to military attention, stiff as posts. They slam their fists with a thump over the Erthia orbs on their chests in a formal salute.

I turn. There's a Mage coming through mist, his cloak flapping behind him.

Vale.

His scorching eyes are the first thing to cut through fog. He shoots Nils a brief, deadly, piercing glare as he stalks swiftly past, pointedly ignoring Myles and me.

I cross my arms protectively in front of myself, and my eyes narrow to angry slits. I can sense Vale's heat trailing behind him in a furious flare. He's all askew—his hair mussed into

uneven spikes, his clothing wrinkled, his affinity lines turbulent as a wild storm.

His residual trail of angry fire lashes out at me in whipping
tendrils, gradually losing force as both Vale and his fire are
swallowed up by the steamy fog.

"Where's he going, do you think?" I ask.

"Probably to Morning Report," Nils says, his posture relaxing.

"That's Vale Gardner," Myles puts in helpfully, and with
more than a little awe. "The son of the Black Witch herself."

"I know," I tell them distractedly, staring off into the fog
where Vale disappeared.

Myles looks down the path, his expression tightening. "He's
the strongest one of all the Level Fives. He's got her fire. That's
what they say, Miss."

Nils raises his brow at Myles.

Myles winces. "I mean, *Mage* Harrow, Miss."

Nils laughs and pats Myles on the back. "You, my friend,
are a hopeless case."

Myles shoots Nils a rueful smile. "No one forces you to
mingle with the lower class."

Nils expression turns serious. "No one here is lower class,"
he says, his tone emphatic. "We're *all* Gardnerians."

A tingle of warmth courses through me.

"It's hard to get used to," I reassure Myles, heartened by
Nils's startling, broad-minded acceptance. "I'm Lower River,
too." I look to Nils. "*Mage* was a slur there. Always an insult.
The Kelts would even use it against each other."

"Well, it's no longer an insult," Nils says, his hidden fire
breaking through heatedly. "And we'll cure them of their penchant for using it as such."

I find myself marveling over how different Nils is from

Vale. There's no sense of elitism, no contempt in his eyes. It's deeply refreshing.

A vision from a storybook cuts through the fog before us, running toward me. I realize it's Rosebeth, and relief washes over me like cool water.

She's dressed like a Gardnerian princess. No more ill-fitting black wool—her dark silken tunic fits like a glove over her lovely figure, shimmering even in this dim light, her skirts swishing. Blue Ironflowers are delicately embroidered along the collar and edging of her tunic. Her long black hair is beautifully styled, with small looping braids decorating her wavy black locks.

"Tessie!" she tearfully cries, falling into my arms, her fine silks slick against my palms. Her magic is as weak as ever—a small trickle of water, so faint I can barely read it.

"I'm so glad you're safe," I say, embracing her. "Have you seen my family? I need to find out where they are."

"They're fine and safe," she breathlessly assures me. "I'll take you to them. Oh, Tessie, I thought you were *dead*!"

She hugs me again, and tears sting my eyes. I'm so glad to be safe and in the company of friends. I look to Nils and see him beaming at us, respect lighting his eyes.

Not everyone here is like Vale Gardner, I realize with immeasurable relief, and no small amount of spite.

Then I look to Myles and am momentarily caught off guard by his expression. It's like a thousand stars have burst into view before his eyes, and his mouth hangs open as he gazes at Rosebeth.

I turn back to my friend, searching for what's inspired Myles's unbridled awe.

Rosebeth is running her silk-covered forearm artlessly across her eyes to wipe away her tears, giving a loud sniff that's almost a full-blown snort. But this does nothing to diminish Myles's mesmerized stupor.

"Oh, I'm so sorry," she says, looking toward the young soldiers as if noticing them for the first time. "Where are my manners?"

Her eyes lock on to Myles, instantly as riveted by him as he is by her—as if he's not some plain Lower River lad, but a prince stepping through the mist of her most cherished dream.

Incredulous, I glance up to find Nils eyeing them, then me with dancing amusement, clearly struggling not to burst into outright laughter.

And in spite of everything—my family's homelessness, our extreme poverty, my scrape with violent death—I momentarily rally. Perhaps we have a chance for a good life among our own people in Gardneria. A future of happiness for us all.

Nils glances at his pocket watch. "Myles, we've got to report." He smiles at Rosebeth and me. "We're free again at midday. Perhaps you lovely Mages would care to meet us at the dining tent? We could take our food together at the central fires."

"Oh, yes," Rosebeth breathes, her eyes still stuck on awkward Myles. "I'd like that a great deal." She looks to me hopefully.

We're all Gardnerians. Nils's beautiful words hang bright in my mind.

"I'd like that, too," I tell Nils with a heartfelt smile.

They take their leave, Rosebeth glancing prettily after them, her lashes shyly fluttering.

"You look like an Upper River girl," I tell her, grinning affectionately at my childhood friend. I momentarily wonder what it would feel like to wear such fine things.

"Genna's helping me!" she says brightly. "She's made me her pet—that's what she calls me, anyway. She's ever so wonderful, Tessie." Then Rosebeth bites worriedly at her lip, her expression darkening. "You've met her, Tessie. She was rather unkind to you that horrible night. She called you names, but you shouldn't judge her for it. You confused us all so, clinging like you did to Jules Kristian."

Memories of that night slam through me. Genna. That horrid Upper River girl, calling me a race traitor. Encouraging that terrifying Mage to strike down poor Daisie.

"She's just so beautiful," Rosebeth enthuses, shaking off the darkness, and I feel a flash of bitter, fleeting jealously that she can shed the trauma of it all so easily. "*And* Genna's going to fast to one of the Level Five Mages. *Everyone* wants them, Tessie. They have the most power. And the most money. Most of them are quite young and quite a few unfasted." I can barely keep up with her, she's talking so excitedly. "They have their own *houses*! Mage Vale Gardner has *two*!"

"Two?" I'm disgusted by such unnecessary luxury. I think about our cottage. Momma's quilts. Poppa's things. Wren's toys. All my apothecary tools.

Our cat, Patches.

Pain twists at my insides, and my stomach tightens with grief.

Rosebeth glances around, biting her lip again, as if searching for the right way to tell me something troubling. "Take care around Vale Gardner and Fain Quillen," she warns me, her tone low. "I know they helped you, but…you should know that there are disturbing rumors about them."

I quirk my brow in question.

"I heard," she whispers, shielding her mouth, "that they might have…*evil tendencies*." She shoots me a serious, scandal-fraught look. "Like, they might fancy each other. Someone actually asked Vale Gardner about it, and…" She trails off, clearly too nervous to continue.

"What? What did they say to him?" It's always irritated me, her tendency to be hesitant and trail off like this.

She takes a break from chewing her lip. "It might have been

in jest. It probably was. They asked him if he wants to fast to Fain Quillen. And do you know what he said?"

I shake my head.

"He said, 'And what if I did?' Can you imagine, Tessie? He only gets away with such things because he's Carnissa Gardner's son. He shouldn't speak so, even if it's in jest. It makes people think he's engaging in…" She goes back to gnawing at her lip, rendered mute by her own sordid imaginings.

I take in a deep breath, remembering how I overheard Fain's mention of rumors about him and Vale. I've heard whispers of such forbidden relationships—and know what cruel things can happen if the couple is discovered. A couple of years ago, the cooper's son, Flynn, and the young farrier, Nick, were beaten senseless in Doveshire's town square as a warning. I found the story to be deeply troubling, but unfortunately not surprising. I'm clear on what mobs are capable of and that relationships like these are not tolerated by Kelts or Gardnerians—or really anyone else in the Western Realm.

Can the rumors be true? I'm suddenly filled with worry for both Vale and Fain.

Vale is insufferably arrogant, but he saved my life—and Jules's. And Fain has been nothing but kind to me.

But what of Vale's kiss? I wonder, confused. *There was so much fire in it.* "You've got to wash yourself up, Tessie," Rosebeth says with nervous urgency, interrupting my thoughts. "There's not much time."

"Time for what?"

"Didn't you hear? They're fasting all of us. Tonight. We've today to choose partners, or they're choosing them for us."

I can feel myself blanch, shock coursing through me. "No." I shake my head emphatically. "That's…that's just not possible. I'm not fasting to anyone. Certainly not tonight."

"We have to, Tessie. Don't you see? That way we'll all have

family here. People to take us in. You have to do it, Tess. For your family." Her eyes take on a dreamy quality. "And all the young men—they're so dashing and handsome."

The image of Nils's easy grin flits into my mind. Would it be so bad, fasting to someone like him? He seems kind and smart and good-humored. And not pretentious at all. He's nothing like pompous Vale Gardner. And fasting to Nils would give my family connections. And safety.

No, I think to myself. It's too quick. How could I fast to a young man I barely know?

But then I fully realize what Rosebeth just said. I have to choose—or someone else will choose for me. Though I'm deeply troubled by this, I try to push all the fasting worries to the back of my mind. *After all*, I reassure myself, *surely no one would force me to fast against my will.*

No, there's only one thing that's important right now.

"Rosie, please... I need you to take me to my family."

CHAPTER FIFTEEN:
Rigid Lines

The first thing I see as I near the tent that's been assigned to my family is Wren, sitting on the ground in front of it, looking desolate. As soon as he sees me, he bursts up and runs to me on his skinny eight-year-old legs, his arms outstretched as he dissolves into tears.

"Tessie," he sobs, clinging to me, "I thought you died! No one would tell us where you were!"

"Shhh, I'm fine," I tell him, my own tears running down my face as I pat his unwashed, knotted hair. "Oh, Wren, I'm so happy to see you." I pull back and smile at him, forcing a look of untroubled reassurance. But even my false smile almost dissolves as I take in the sight of him.

He's even sicker than he was. The chronic Red Grippe he's been fighting off for years is slowly pulling him under. His voice is wheezier, his eyes rimmed red, and more of the small crimson spots ring his mouth.

I have to get him medicine, and soon, I agonize. *Medicine we'll never be able to afford. Medicine you have to be a Level Five Mage to afford.*

Wren coughs, deep and rattling, and I smooth back his stringy hair. "Everything's going to be fine now," I tell him.

But we need money. And we have none. And you need medicine.

"Where will we live, Tessie?"

I don't know. I don't know. We're on the poorest end of a sea of refugees.

I keep my smile bright. "I'll find us a nice little cottage. Warm and dry. Don't you worry yourself."

We've no money. We've nothing. We've nowhere to live. I'm scared, Wren.

I kiss his head, wanting him to believe the fairy tale I'm spinning. Wanting to believe it myself. But I feel lost and desperate and afraid.

"What happened to Patches, Tessie?"

The question hangs in the air between us, dark and terrible. Our cat. Our lovely calico cat. Probably dead in the fire.

"I'm sure she got away," I tell him, my voice breaking. "She's smart. She can make her own way."

Wren pulls back and looks at me with level grief. "I don't think so, Tessie. I think she's dead."

We stare at each other for one intolerable, horribly honest moment.

"I'm sorry, Wren," I choke out, my voice ragged with tears, their salt on my lips. "I'm so sorry."

"I hate them," he says with a grimace, his eyes hard and fierce with pain. "I hope our Mages kill them all. All those Kelts and Urisk."

"No, Wren," I say, trying to soothe him. "The bad ones, maybe. But not all of them."

"They're all bad," he cries, hiccupping from his sobbing.

His words send a chill through me. "Not all of them, Wren. Jules isn't."

If he's still alive.

But Wren is unmoved.

"Jules is our friend," I remind him. "He tried to help us."

"I don't care," Wren says, pulling out of my embrace, his

expression gone hard as stone. "He didn't save us. Our Black Witch and the Mages did. The Kelts and the Urisk tried to kill us. But they lost, and now we're going to kill *them*."

Uneasy concern pricks at me. I'm thrown by the sharpness of my little brother's newfound hatred—hatred with such savagely drawn lines.

CHAPTER SIXTEEN:
Staen'en

"No, Grandfather," I adamantly insist, my fire rising. "I'm not fasting tonight."

He's staring at me with his usual daft, head-in-the-clouds benevolence, which was very endearing when my father was alive. But ever since my grandfather became my official guardian, I've found his well-meaning incompetence to be a source of endless trouble.

We almost died because of it. Because he wouldn't let me use his wand.

"Of course you'll fast, child," he reassures me with a condescending pat on my arm.

Frustrated, I glance around our temporary home—a plain military tent, but it's well-appointed with three sturdy cots, warm bedding, a woodstove that's keeping out the rainy chill and lanterns to light the gloom.

Warm, safe and dry.

And we're well fed, too. The fare here is simple, but readily available. The Upper River folk are turning their noses up at it, but I'm thrilled to see the huge bowl of barley soup thick with carrots that Wren's rapidly consuming, a hefty chunk of buttered brown bread on the small table beside him.

Better food than we've had in a long time.

But what happens when we leave here? Where will our meals come from then? Will we be beggars on the streets of Valgard?

Maybe there's no choice but to wandfast.

No, I'll find a way, I stubbornly vow. I could go to Mage Aniliese and beg her for a job. I'm a good apothecary already, clever and well-practiced. I could do prep work for her if she's hiring. The pay probably won't be much, but we could rent a room until I secure an apprenticeship in Verpacia. And if I can't work for her, maybe she'll know someone else who will give me a job.

But Grandfather is insistent. "The Ancient One will send you the right young man tonight, just like He sent our blessed Black Witch to liberate us," he says with a reverent smile. "If He can do all that, He can certainly provide a fastmate for you. Have faith, Tessla. I'm praying on it."

My hackles rise. Grandfather's prayers again. Prayers while he passively waits. I prefer my own prayers to the Ancient One for strength while I actually *do* things, like keep us fed.

"I need to get myself cleaned up," I tell Grandfather. "Where is there water enough for bathing? And fresh clothes?"

"Ah," he tells me with a hopeful smile, "soon. Tomorrow. At the very latest, the day after that. They didn't expect so many of us. But it's no matter, waiting one more day."

At midday, I go to join Nils and Myles and Rosebeth, resigned to my wretched appearance.

Despite my resolve not to be wandfasted, I'm thrilled to spot Nils again.

I find them all just past the long dining tent, gathered around one of the central fires, benches set around the small bonfires in compact rows. Mostly young people are gathered there, soldiers and refugees alike, the mood one of giddy excitement.

Raucous cheers go up every time a grouping of our military dragons flies overhead, heading south to the front lines.

They're all bright-eyed, and many have managed to wash up and obtain decent clothing. Only some of the Lower River cook boys in the dining tent still look as bedraggled as I do.

Rosebeth is sitting close to the fire next to Myles, the two of them lost in their own happy bubble. Nils stands nearby with Genna and her Upper River friends, the young women laughing and chatting animatedly.

The girls from that night.

I'm rocked by a powerful flashback. *The white wand. The children screaming and crying. Being dragged away from Wren. The dragon snarling. The fire balled up inside me. Then the terrible cold.*

Heart racing, I force myself to breathe deep, struggling to calm down and push the terrible memory away.

Genna's eyes meet mine and narrow as her smile turns calculating. She leans in and whispers something to Nils.

Nils turns to looks at me and visibly stiffens, his face hardening into a grimace.

I tilt my head in confusion, my stomach clenching into a tight knot.

Why does he look so...hateful?

Nils breaks away from the crowd and strides quickly toward me.

"Is it true?" he demands as he nears. "That you embraced a Kelt?"

Hope drains away and despair rises like black waters.

"Yes," I say, fighting back a swelling dread. "My friend, Jules Kristian. But it isn't what you think. He tried to save me—"

Nils's frown grows furious and he spits at me, the spittle landing on my borrowed tunic. My words catch tight in my throat.

"*Staen'en,*" he hisses, then turns on his heel to rejoin Genna and her friends.

It's such an unexpected blow that I can't move. I can't breathe.

I look pleadingly at Rosebeth. My shy friend's lips tremble, her eyes full of momentary conflict. Then she averts her gaze and leans into Myles, making her alliance painfully known. Myles shoots me a brief look of outraged betrayal, then puts his arm around Rosebeth and pulls her to him protectively.

And then there's Genna. The cruel, gloating look in her eyes knifes clear through me before she turns back to Nils with a flirtatious smile.

I slump down onto a bench, watching all my hopes flit away into a dark abyss.

We'll be worse than poor, I realize with an incapacitating terror. *Worse than Lower River Gardnerians. We'll be the beggars no one will help.*

I don't know how long I sit there, the silent pariah in their midst, the object of dark whispering and barely concealed pointing. Sinking deeper and deeper into misery.

Wren. What will happen to Wren?

I know the answer to this full well. I know exactly what's going to happen to us. It's like a nightmare about to consume us whole.

Abruptly, everyone seated around me stands, all the soldiers coming to swift attention.

I look up the path and see a large grouping of Level Five Mages, wildly impressive with their silver-striped cloaks, fine uniforms and powerful, confident strides. Including Vale and Fain.

The lower-ranking soldiers around the fire and by the path throw their fists over the silver Erthia orbs that mark their chests. The civilians bring fists over hearts in their own salute as the Mages near, the outpouring of fierce respect palpable on the cool air.

Our most powerful Mages—the Mages who helped the Black Witch liberate all of us.

I slowly rise to my feet and join the standing crowd, my mind a tumult.

Vale's fiery eyes flare with intensity as he spots me.

Fain is beside him, and his eyes follow the trajectory of Vale's gaze. He immediately breaks from the ranks of the Level Five Mages and makes for me, like a defiant bird leaving his flock. His expression is congenial, but his eyes blaze with determination.

The other Level Five Mages stop, and the whole crowd turns to watch Fain.

My head jerks back in surprise as Fain falls to one knee in front of me with theatric grace. He drops his head, his forearm coming up before him, fist clenched, in the posture of formal supplication.

Nils and the others are gaping at us, silent and stunned.

Fain's voice sounds out clear as a bell. "Dearest, loveliest Mage Tessla Harrow. I beseech you for your forgiveness. I, Mage Fain Quillen, am an ignorant fool who is not fit to kiss your shoes. *I* am the peasant, clearly, not you."

He lifts his head to shoot Vale a quelling look. "Are you watching, Vale?" he asks. "*This* is how it's done." Then he looks to me and waits, a slight smile tilting his mouth, but genuine apology in his eyes.

I blink at him, stunned and completely dumbstruck for one long moment. Finally, I find my voice. "I forgive you, Mage Quillen," I reply, overwhelmed and deeply touched by his unexpected and decidedly public support. "Please, Mage. You may rise."

"May the Ancient One bless you for your graceful forbearance, my sweet lady," he says as he stands and takes my hand, kissing it with dramatic flair. He lifts his gaze and smiles slyly at me, but there's something deeper there and unflinchingly serious.

Respect.

Vale is watching us, one eyebrow cocked, his lips tightly pursed, his eyes gone dark and guarded.

With a graceful swirl of his cloak, Fain rejoins the Level Five ranks and gives me an impish wink as they continue on.

Vale determinedly does not glance in my direction, though a ripple of his fire sears over me as he passes.

CHAPTER SEVENTEEN:
Ironflowers

"Tessie…can I talk to you?"

I let out a long sigh, then stop and turn around to find Rosebeth hanging shyly back. She's biting nervously at her lip, her doll-like beauty and floral-trimmed garments so pretty and fresh, so out of place amid the lengthening shadows and the thunder rumbling in the distance under a darkening sky.

Fain's public show of support and affection has thrown them all into confusion, everyone around the bonfire visibly re-evaluating whether or not I should be shunned now that I've made very public inroads into the most exclusive Gardnerian club of all—the Level Five Mages.

One step removed from the Black Witch herself.

Rosebeth pulls nervously at her lovely silk skirt, the little Ironflowers at the hem fidgeting along with her.

"I'm sorry things are going so badly for you, Tessie," she tells me. "It's just… Genna's been so good to me. And Myles… he wants to fast to me." Her rose petal mouth pulls up in a wavering smile, begging for my approval. Like a timid lamb. "And I so want us to be friends, but…" Her smile trembles away.

"You have to keep your distance from me," I fill in for her

bluntly, but not unkindly. Nonetheless, Rosebeth wilts under my steady gaze.

"There's nothing I can do, Tessie. Genna hates you so. I wish…" She trails off, unsure.

I narrow my eyes at her. "I saved those girls," I remind her. "Genna and the rest of them."

Rosebeth averts her eyes, chewing more frantically on her lip, unable to meet my gaze. "Well, that's not what *they* say, Tessie." She shrugs, hunching down. "Everyone says you stole a wand that you had no business using, and that you could have gotten *everyone* killed. That you only did it to shield yourself and Jules Kristian, and that the Mages were about to save us and you *interfered*."

Anger and hurt roil through me. "Is that what they say?"

She nods, her eyes venturing toward mine, skittish and innocent.

I sigh, my temper dampening, then relent and reach out to touch my friend's arm. "It's all right, Rosie." I give her an encouraging smile that feels thin and false. "Don't trouble yourself. I'll be okay, regardless of what they say."

No, you won't, I inwardly scoff at myself. *You have nowhere to go. No help. No fastmate to save you. No money. No home. No prospects.*

Pain twists at my insides. But there's no sense in hurting my gentle friend. I want her to be happy and protected, the way I'd want a child protected. I want her to be safe.

"I think you and Myles will be very happy together." I give her arm a gentle squeeze. "I'm glad you're fasting to him."

Rosie brightens, shedding her momentary sadness like a child given a sweet. "Isn't Myles so lovely?" Then she wavers, growing momentarily subdued. "It's too bad no one will have you now, Tessie. Because of… Jules Kristian. But…" She smiles uncertainly at me. "Maybe there's still some hope. There's still

Mage Quillen. Perhaps all the rumors about him aren't true. Maybe he's sweet on you, Tessie."

I think of the troubled look in Fain's eyes when he brought up the rumors to Vale.

No, I realize. All the rumors about Fain are absolutely true.

I smile at her and nod, biting back all the things I really want to say. Bitter, troubled things that would just thrust her into confusion and destroy our tenuous bond.

"You can come in if you want," I tell her, turning to untie the flap to my family's tent, knowing I'll find it empty. Grandfather took Wren to be blessed by one of the base's priests and sanctified with healing ablutions.

He needs expensive medicine, not just prayer, I sourly reflect.

I pull the tent flap open and my eyes widen in surprise.

"Oh, Tessie," Rosebeth enthuses from behind me. "Someone sent you *flowers.* And...and, oh, there's a *present!*"

There's a large package on my cot, wrapped in parchment and tied with ribbon. A beautiful bouquet of Ironflowers graces the top, the flowers glowing a deep blue in the dim light of the tent. A small envelope lies beside them.

Rosebeth watches with dancing anticipation as I cross the tent's length, light a lantern and kneel by my cot. I can hear her excited breathing just over my shoulder.

I untie the ribbon on the package and gasp as the parchment falls away.

Inside is a wildly beautiful tunic and long skirt made of outrageously expensive Ishkartan goldweave. The black silk shimmers gold and red along the folds as the lantern light hits it. Small rubies grace the neckline and hem.

It's the most exquisite clothing I have ever seen.

"Oh, Tessie," Rosebeth gushes. "You'll be the prettiest one at the fasting. Who sent it? Open the card!"

With shaking hands, I open the small envelope.

Dearest, Loveliest Mage Tessla Harrow,
Please accept this token of my deep and unwavering affection.
Your Ignorant, Unworthy Servant,
Mage Fain Quillen

"Oh, you're being *courted*!" Rosebeth cries with delight, clapping her hands and bouncing on her heels. "By a *Level Five Mage*! Oh, Tessie! Think of the parties! And the fancy things you'll have! Oh, how *lucky* you are!"

No, not courting, I realize with warm certainty. *Just unabashed, overwhelming kindness.*

Tears sting at my eyes, and I blink them back.

"He's so handsome and dashing!" Rosebeth says happily. "Genna was wrong about him after all!"

No, my thoughts counter with decided firmness. *Genna's not wrong. But it doesn't matter, not a bit.*

I cradle the exquisite tunic in my hands, the silk as light as a feather. A tear streaks down my face, and I wipe it back. A fierce wave of gratitude washes over me, followed by an equally fierce desire to protect Fain.

I don't care what people say he is. I don't care who he loves. He saved me and my entire family, along with Vale. He literally gave me the shirt off his back. He saw me nursed back to health, saved me from being humiliated by all the other Gardnerians.

And now this.

I hug the tunic to my chest, bringing my hand up to cover my eyes and catch my tears.

CHAPTER EIGHTEEN:
Embroidery

I'm still hugging the beautiful clothing to my chest as I hover at the entrance to Fain's tent. Twilight darkens the sky, the thunder in the distance growing more insistent.

I take in the enormity of the base from this elevated height, the fog having lifted, a multitude of torches springing to life. There are long rows of tents and scattered campfires covering the entire valley, right up to the surrounding mountains. A small flock of our dragons makes their way across the sky in the distance, headed south.

I peek inside, the tent flap tied back a fraction. Fain is reclining on his plush, tapestry-covered divan, a drink in one hand, a thick book open on his lap. He beams as he catches sight of me, his eyes dancing with amusement.

"Ah, the fair warrior, Tessla. Come in. I've been expecting you."

Awkwardly, I enter and pull the tent flap closed as I hug the beautiful dress, the warmth from his expensive stove instantly enveloping me. I stand before him, my back ramrod stiff as he lounges back and waits.

"Mage Quillen," I say with heartfelt emotion, "I've come to thank you for your great kindness."

"Oh, please, Tessla," he scoffs good-naturedly. "Surely we're on a first-name basis by now?" He sets down his drink and book and gestures toward the other chair. "Sit. Please. My home is your home."

He gets up, takes the clothing from my hands and puts it aside, then fusses with a pot that's placed over a small burner. He pours a steaming drink from it and hands it to me.

It smells rich and delicious, and there's powdery cinnamon skimming the top.

"What is it?" I ask, settling back into the cushioned chair, testing the heat of the rich drink against my lips.

Fain sits and picks up his own cup, smiling his catlike grin at me. "Ishkartan cocoa. I did promise you some. It's so good, you'll want to fast to it and have its babies."

I cough out a laugh at his outrageous comment. Gratified, Fain takes a sip, eyeing me with mischief.

I taste the cocoa and am momentarily overcome with bliss. The rich, sensual sweetness of the creamy drink explodes in my mouth, delighting every sense.

"Oh, Fain," I enthuse, forgetting to be awkward about using his first name. "It's so good."

He smiles contentedly at me, licking away the half-moon of cocoa coating his upper lip.

Heartened, I return his smile.

"It's nice to see you smile, Tessla," he tells me, his voice gentle. "You've a lovely smile."

I look down at the cocoa, blushing. "I don't know where you found such a stunning dress—"

"Ah," he cuts in, eyes twinkling. "You will find that I am delightfully resourceful."

I nod at this, amused, then take a deep breath, growing more serious. "Fain, what's going on tonight? They don't force fasting, do they?"

His levity disappears. "Is your grandfather likely to force you, Tessla?"

"No," I say with a shake of my head. "No, he wouldn't. And no one would fast to me now, anyway." I throw him a level look, bitterness seeping through. "I think Nils Arden briefly fancied me. But now he hates me. Because of my friendship with Jules."

Fain gives a short laugh and nods with understanding. "Ah, yes. Mage Nils Arden." He shoots me knowing glance. "He's quite lovely. But…a tad inflexible in his views. Life doesn't flow in such rigid lines, my dear, as much as we might like it to." He shoots me a poignant look.

"The rumors about me aren't true," I tell him flatly.

Fain smiles benignly. "Rumors are like chaff, my love. Don't give them anything rough to hook on to, and they float away on the wind."

"But they're complete lies. Jules and I…we were never… intimate."

Fain waves his hand, as if clearing my words from the air. "Whatever he is to you, Tessla, I've no judgment on it." His eyes darken, his expression growing insistent. "He's a Kelt. I'd speak of him no more."

I bristle at this. "Kelt or not, Jules is my friend. I'm not ashamed of him."

"Nor should you be, sweet Tessla," Fain agrees with a calm nod. "But there's nothing wrong with you being unashamed *privately.*"

"I won't deny my friends," I staunchly insist.

"And that is absolutely commendable, my dear, but also potentially tragic." Fain lets out a deep sigh, shakes his head and looks to the ceiling. "I keep surrounding myself with such stubborn idealists." He closes his eyes, shakes his head again, then picks up a plate full of biscuits with purple candied flowers gracing their tops. "Here, have a lavender biscuit," he says lightly, holding the plate out to me. "They're lovely. Flavored with vanilla and cardamom."

Though I'm still unsettled, I take a biscuit and bite into it. The flavors of the buttery, spiced biscuit perfectly complement the cocoa. Slightly mollified by the amazing food, I look to Fain.

"Patriotic fervor is running high," Fain cautions me, all amusement gone. "One can speak more freely in Verpacia, especially at the University. But not *here*, Tessla. Not two steps away from the front lines." He pours himself more cocoa, his expression turning untroubled once more. He smiles at me. "One must be smart in this world, sweet one."

I bristle at his lecturing me about the world.

What does he know of the world? He's kind, to be sure. And I like Fain a great deal. But he's pampered and privileged. With his lavender biscuits and his spiced cocoa, his fancy embroidered tapestries and his luxurious tent and all his money.

A rich, entitled Mage barely out of his teens, if I had to guess.

"How did you and Vale become friends?" I ask, an edge of cynical challenge creeping into my tone. "Do all the rich people congregate together?"

A laugh bursts from Fain's mouth, and he looks me over with narrow-eyed incredulity. "My people weren't moneyed. I grew up in Graveshire, further down the river than you, my dear."

Shock courses through me, disbelief riding close on its heels. I eye him with skepticism. "You're…a Lower River Gardnerian?"

Fain narrows his eyes further, his mouth lifting into a sly, feline smile. "So you think Lower River Gardnerians can't be cultured and refined?"

I flush. "No. No, of course not," I stammer, immediately chastened.

"My father was an illiterate pig farmer," Fain tells me, a hard gleam lighting his gaze. "Horrible man. We did not get on. I was never his vision of what his only son should be. I've a penchant for learning. For elegant things. I have—" he pauses, his lip curling with cool defiance "—artistic fancies. He caught me embroidering with my sisters when I was ten." His expression darkens. "You've seen the scars on my back."

I suck in a quick breath of air. I was barely conscious on our way here, Magedrunk beyond belief, but I remember the pale lines crisscrossing the skin of Fain's entire back.

"He beat me senseless." Fain bites out the words with a cold smile. "But then, I was beaten by so many. Until I turned fourteen and came into my power." His eyes grow fierce, full of glittering pain and simmering anger.

For a brief moment, it's as if the tent's interior shimmers and darkens and we're cast into the ocean's great depths. I have the strong sense of devastating water power gathering on all sides and am struck by how overwhelmingly dangerous Fain is.

"What happened?" I ask, my voice almost a whisper.

The tent brightens as Fain's pain and anger fall away, his staggering power abruptly subdued, as if brushed behind a curtain. "No one ever beat me again," he says lightly with a shrug. "I left soon after. Went to sea. Gained employment as a Water and Wind Mage on merchant vessels and became quite rich."

"Did you ever see your family again?" I venture.

Fain's head bobs in a suppressed laugh, and then his gaze hardens. "I went back home once," he tells me with a chilly grin. "As soon as I came into money. I gathered my sisters and took them to Valgard with me."

My eyes widen. "And…your father let you?"

Fain's smile turns dangerous. "He took some convincing. Privately. With my wand jabbed into his vile throat."

The color in the tent darkens and ripples once again, and

I feel a heavy pressure, as if leagues of water are surrounding us. Then Fain's power withdraws, flowing back into him, the colors of the room vivid once more.

Fain settles back in his chair, his expression warming. "I met Vale about a year later, en route to the Salishen Isles. We've been friends ever since." He grins. "We've had more than a few adventures together. And though our affinity lines are complete opposites, we fit together, Vale and I. Like two pieces of a puzzle."

I ponder this for a moment, trying to decide if there's a deeper meaning behind Fain's words. If that means the two of them really are together…as more than just friends.

An acute sense of my isolation washes over me, filling me with sadness, and a bit of envy. At least they have each other—they're not alone, like me.

I clear my throat, dismissing my feelings of self-pity, and say lightly, "I'm surprised Vale will suffer your company. You're even more Lower River than I am."

His eyes dance at this. "Don't let Vale upset you, sweetling. He doesn't do tactful."

I purse my lips at him. "So I've noticed."

He laughs and holds the plate out to me again. "Here, have another biscuit."

I take one as he watches me, his expression growing thoughtful. "You know, Tessla," he says, his voice kind, "I have friends on the other side, too."

I nod, suddenly drawn in by his openness and our growing kinship. Tears prick at my eyes as I think of Jules, and my lips begin to tremble.

Jules. Where are you, Jules?

I look down at my gleaming cocoa cup in one hand and the biscuit in the other, the images growing liquid and wavy through the veil of my tears. The feeling of sadness overwhelms me, and I begin to sob.

After a moment, I hear Fain get up and kneel down before me. He rests his hand on my arm.

"It's hard, isn't it?" he asks, his own voice breaking. "To have a mind that strays outside the lines?"

I nod jerkily, my chest heaving.

Fain grips my arm gently, and his cool water magic flows into me, quickly dampening my unsettled fire, slightly calming the storm that's roiling inside me. Some of the tension released, I let the tears flow freely, and he holds on, his magic a soothing comfort. There's no attraction in it, just friendship and understanding.

"Take heart, my love," he tells me. "We've both moved through insurmountable odds, and yet here we are, improbably alive. Sipping cocoa."

The sheer outrageousness of this catches me off guard, and I cough out a tear-soaked laugh.

"We're sipping cocoa," I tell him, sniffling, "in an Ishkart tent."

"That belongs to a devastatingly handsome Level Five Gardnerian Mage of considerable influence," he puts in helpfully.

I laugh, my voice stuffy from the tears, and smile at him with deep affection. "Do you need a fastmate, Fain?" I ask teasingly.

Fain gives a hearty laugh and tilts his head to the side, a rueful look in his eyes. "Oh, honey, you wish."

Our eyes meet, momentarily aligned in perfect understanding and acceptance.

He sits back on his heels and grins at me. "I will not fast to you, Tessla Harrow. But I like you. We understand each other, I think. In ways unique to the lowly folk."

"No one will ever fast to me," I tell him. "Not with all the rumors."

Fain considers this. "Perhaps not, sweetling, but you're clever. You'll find your way. I'd wager on it." He pats my arm and rises, holding out his hand to me. "Come, sweet Tessla. I'm a Water Mage. I'll draw a nice bath for you, and you can get yourself properly cleaned up. And then we'll turn you into a creature ten million times more enchanting than all those Upper River girls combined."

CHAPTER NINETEEN:
Predator

I am transformed.

My body scrubbed clean and smelling of vanilla and jasmine soap. My hair blessedly washed, combed out and styled similarly to Rosebeth's in long, flowing locks with tiny interwoven braids created by Fain's nimble fingers.

And I've never been garbed so richly. The entire tunic and underskirt catch the light of every torch or lantern I pass, the black silk shimmering gold and red as I move, and the rubies reflect golden stars of light.

A threatening storm hangs over the west, thunder steadily rumbling, puffs of lightning periodically flashing, the very air charged with electricity.

Fain walks through the base with me, my arm threaded through his. He's handsome as sin, with his silks perfectly pressed and a rakish smile on his face. We must be quite the impressive-looking pair, judging by all the eyes turning toward us as we pass. I flush, noticing more than a few appreciative glances from young men.

"I will find you later, my dear lady," Fain tells me with a mischievous smile, leaning to kiss the back of my hand.

He's to meet up with the other Level Five Mages before this evening's gathering, and I'm to find my grandfather. There's a bustle of activity around us. Torches being lit. Couples chatting animatedly and often ardently, while the singles in the crowd seek to secure fasting partners for the mass fasting that's planned.

Fain strides confidently away with effortless grace. I turn and begin to weave my way through the rows of tents toward the base's mammoth Command Tent. It's the only tent large enough to hold both the unfasted soldiers and most of the fasting-age refugees and their families.

I haven't walked but a few steps when I see Genna and her lovely Upper River friends laughing and chatting up ahead. Getting ready to fast to Level Five Mages, I imagine sourly. To continue their easy, charmed, elitist lives.

No matter, I remind myself. *You'll find work as an apothecary apprentice. Fain can help you. And you'll eventually get your small, warm cottage in Verpacia. Things will be okay.*

But I'm tired. Too tired to endure Genna's mocking ways. I don't feel equal to it. So I quickly dip between tents, watching Genna, waiting for her and her cruel friends to turn and make their way toward the Command Tent.

Genna catches sight of something and gestures for her friends to continue on without her. They smile and set off, looking backward a few times to shoot her admiring smiles.

I feel Vale's heat just before he strides into view and I quickly lean back against a tent wall, taking shelter in the shadows. My heart is suddenly racing in my chest, my fire reaching for him against my will. I try to quell the flames, hoping he doesn't notice me.

Genna's face has gone all doe-eyed and bashful. I watch as she moves to intercept Vale, her voice sweet and sultry.

"Mage Gardner."

Vale slows and turns to look at her, his movements full of lithe grace, his hand stiff on his wand. There's such power in the way he holds himself, coiled and seething. He eyes her coldly, but I can sense the edges of his fire, tightly held in check.

"I… I was there that night. Perhaps you remember," she tells him, moving in close, feigning an enchanting hesitancy. "In Doveshire. I saw what you did for us. You were so…so *powerful*. I had to speak to you. To…to thank you." She looks away momentarily, as if overcome by his magnificence, demure and lovely. She brings her heavily lashed eyes back up toward his stern face. "Thank you, Mage Gardner. May I…may I have the honor of sitting with you this eve?"

Vale's wintry stare doesn't budge, but his controlled fire lashes out at the edges. He looks at her probingly, his lips turning up in an icy smile. When he speaks, he bites out each word. "Your ambitions far outweigh both your beauty and your charm. Please, let me pass."

Genna's eyes catch fire, her mouth falling open. "You…you are not kind!" she sputters.

Vale makes a sound of disdain. "And you are absolutely predatory." He starts to walk away from her, then briefly turns around and sets his intense eyes on her. "There are a number of Level Five Mages who are unfasted and far more gullible than I. Go flirt with them."

Vale turns on his heel and strides away from her, his silver-striped cloak flapping behind him, tendrils of angry fire lashing back, stinging at my affinity lines.

Genna turns away in a huff, her eyes storming with outrage, her hands in tight fists, looking as if she'd run after him and strike him down if she could.

Another group of Genna's friends approaches, and she immediately falls in with them, making her own way to the Command Tent.

I blink after them, Vale still visible far down the path, like a dark specter moving alone through the night.

"Mage Tessla Harrow."

I flinch in surprise at the low, mocking voice emanating from the shadows to my right. I turn and see his eyes before I make out the rest of him. It's dark here, between such a long line of tent walls, away from the main routes. No torches.

His eyes are large and frigid green, every color of green in pale alternating lines, like ice picks. The savagely cold lines of his affinity crawl over me like a creeping frost.

Mage Malkyn Bane.

The Level Five Mage who killed Daisie that horrible night as she huddled in the shadows of the livestock pen. He killed her without a moment of hesitation.

And he enjoyed it.

I'm suddenly aware of how isolated we are here, all alone, the closest people still quite a distance away.

His icy eyes flick over me, making my skin crawl, his chill seeping further into me. "So this is what was hidden under all the filth."

My heart picks up speed. I'm frightened of him, and he knows it.

He unhitches himself from the tent pole he's leaning on and moves toward me, his hands hidden casually in his tunic's pockets.

"Did you whore yourself out to that Kelt?" He asks the question so lightly that at first, I'm sure I must have misheard him.

But his smile grows lascivious, and I realize I did not mishear. My shoulders go tense with offense. "Excuse me?" I sputter, taking a step back.

He laughs and moves closer. "The Kelt," he clarifies. "Were you his little whore? I think you were."

A flicker of terror flashes up my spine, and I open my mouth to protest. But before I can respond, his hand flashes out and grabs my arm. Ice sears through me, knifing, twisting, a sly

affinity wind coming in close on its heels—invading, probing, hurting.

"Leave me alone!" I cry out, wrenching away from him, the
harsh sting of his ice still painfully encircling my arm. I turn
and run for the crowds, for the warm torchlight.

For safety.

His cruel laugh sounds out behind me. "We'll find out," he
calls after me. "We'll find out soon enough, Tessla Harrow."

Heart thudding, I finally reach the Command Tent. I spot
my grandfather up ahead, tottering on his knobby cane, just
one more Mage in a sea of refugees.

"What's the matter, child?" he asks as I hastily approach.
"You look as if you've seen an Icaral demon." He eyes me with
paternal concern.

"I'm fine," I tell him, my voice hoarse. I glance over my
shoulder worriedly, terrified Malkyn Bane might be trailing
after me. "It's nothing. I just…it's just that…" I'm unable to
speak for a long moment as I look into my grandfather's kind,
watery eyes, deeply spooked by Malkyn's icy grip, his open
leer. "Things have been hard, that's all."

I can't share this with Grandfather. He'd assure me I misheard Malkyn, never able to believe anything ill of one of our
blessed Mages—believing that all of us First Children are pure
and blameless in a sea of Evil Ones.

I look around nervously once more, scanning the vast crowd
for Malkyn Bane.

Is he fasting tonight?

I pity the poor young woman chosen for such a cruel monster.

Grandfather reaches out and places a quivering hand on my
shoulder. "You've nothing to fear, my dear. We're among our
own people now." He glances toward the sky and smiles at me

benevolently. "The Ancient One will protect us and provide for us." He looks at my tunic and skirt, as if noticing them for the first time. "And don't you look lovely!" He beams at me, tears coming to his eyes. "See how well they provide for us here? Simple Lower River Folk, and they dress you in rubies!"

No, Grandfather, I want to tell him, wanting to shake his delusions clear away. *They despise me and call me names. This dress is Fain's doing. And you'd despise and shun him if you knew half the truth of his life.*

Grandfather pulls me into a bony hug that's full of genuine warmth, and I lean into him, letting him offer what comfort he can. It's parchment-thin, this sense of protection, the momentary feeling of being taken care of, but I cling to it, fighting the urge to burst into tears. And I suddenly wish I could confide in my grandfather—talk honestly with him for once and have him truly hear.

I'm tired, Grandfather, I yearn to tell him. *Tired of struggling. Tired of never knowing where our next meal will come from. Of fighting and never having enough of anything. I wish someone else would take the reins for a while and let me rest. Just for a little while. Why does it always have to be so hard?*

I'll talk to Fain, I reassure myself. *He'll understand. He knows what it's like to struggle and not fit in. To be attacked and misunderstood and thought to be morally unclean.*

He knows what it's like to feel completely alone.

He said he'd look for me after the fasting, I remember. Comfort washes over me at the thought of at least one true friend. *And he'll believe me when I tell him about Malkyn Bane.*

"Tessie!"

Rosebeth's high-pitched, little-girl voice sounds over the jovial murmur of the crowd. She rushes toward us, her pretty skirts swishing, and my grandfather beams at her.

"She's coming!" Rosebeth squeals, full of bouncing energy.

A long line of military men with grim expressions march in, parting the crowd. Some stream into the Command Tent, while others position themselves along the length of the path.

"Who's coming, dear?" my grandfather gently asks her, his hand resting on her agitated shoulder.

"She's come back from the front!" Rosebeth says breathlessly. "And she's going to meet with us! Can you believe it?"

"Who is?" I ask her, realization starting to dawn, but I can't quite bring myself to believe it.

"Mage Carnissa Gardner!" she cries, overjoyed, tears brimming in her eyes. "Mage Vale Gardner's mother! Oh, Tessie, can you believe it? We're going to be fasted by the Black Witch herself!"

CHAPTER TWENTY:
Mages

There are flags everywhere. Hanging from the tent's colossal support beams, streaming from the rafters. I take in the sight of the black fabric marked with silver Erthia spheres. I'm used to the red Keltic flag with its iron-black X. It was a crime to hoist our flag on Keltic territory, punishable by death. And now, here they are, everywhere.

Our flag. The flag of Gardneria.

Grandfather and I follow the flow of the crowd. We're ushered onto a long bench by a gray-haired woman wearing a white armband, who throws me a look rife with suspicion. Have Genna's rumors about Jules and me reached *everyone* here?

The tent is being filled from front to back with orderly rows of refugees, a broad aisle cutting through its center. Young soldiers line the tent's edges, some holding torches. Our uniformly dark garb and the wavering torchlight lend a sobering air to the growing gathering, but there's a heady excitement in the air. Murmurs of anticipation ripple through the crowd, and heads repeatedly turn back to search past the open entrance flaps.

We're all on the edge of our seats, waiting to meet *her*.

The Black Witch.

All twelve of the base's Level Five Mages stand in an arc around the back of the dais. My eyes immediately light on Vale.

He's standing next to Fain, the two of them speaking to each other, their faces grim. I recoil as I spot Malkyn Bane there, too, off to the right, near a knot of priests. I shrink down at the sight of him, heart hammering, hoping to hide from his icy gaze.

I peek through the crowd and spot Vale's sister, Vyvian Gardner, and his bespectacled brother, Edwin Gardner, standing near Vale and Fain. Vyvian's clothing is appropriately somber, but still devastatingly elegant. Her tunic rises high at the neck, and gleaming gems are loosely scattered all over the dark silk.

Rosebeth is seated across the aisle from me, overflowing with joy, color high on her dimpled cheeks. She's seated by Myles and is surrounded by her brothers, her parents and Myles's entire family. Elated by the sudden turn of their fortunes, they're all smiling, an ecstatic mood in the air.

A parcel of farmland has been offered to every newly fasted Gardnerian couple, portioned out from the recently annexed Keltic territory. There's also the possibility of more land and money for every Gardnerian child born.

All the couples who are about to be fasted have bright futures ahead of them.

But not me, I dispassionately observe. *No one here would fast to me.*

Genna and her friends sweep in and settle near Rosebeth. After Vyvian, Genna's easily the most beautiful woman here. The dark silk she wears shimmers silver along the folds, and pearls edge her sleeves and collar.

Genna spots me and looks me over from head to toe, obviously surprised to see me clean and dressed in such elegant clothing. She shoots me a malicious look, then leans over to whisper to the young woman standing next to her. They both narrow their eyes at me, and there's a knowing smirk on Genna's face. As if she's certain my pariah status is cemented in stone.

I remember Vale's surprising rejection of beautiful Genna

and look toward him. I feel a jolt when his eyes lock on to mine at the exact same moment. I can feel the sting of his fiery surprise from clear across the room, and he looks sharply away.

I turn to Fain, and his head jerks up slightly as he catches my eye, warm recognition lighting his expression. Fain's mouth turns up into his usual impish smile, and he throws a line of cool water out to me from across the room. The affinity water flows in to meet my unsettled fire, momentarily tamping it down and soothing me.

He knows, I realize. *Fain knows I can read affinity lines*. It's a rare skill, and usually held only by Level Five Mages.

Breathing in deep and feeling bolstered by his show of support, I smile back at Fain gratefully.

Vale's attention is still on me, even though he's keeping his eyes averted from mine. Lines of his fire occasionally whip out to meet with my own affinity lines.

Then a sharp, painful prod of ice cuts through Vale's fire and Fain's water. It tears at my fire like a cruel taunt.

Startled, I look to the right to find Malkyn Bane staring at me, a disturbingly malicious grin on his face.

I glance away and slump down further. Ice jabs at me again, and again. Angered, I send up an internal wall of fire against it, pushing my lines out with as much force as I can summon. Laughing, Malkyn turns away, his ice retreating.

He knows, too, I realize. *He knows I can sense affinities. Or at least, he knows now.*

I turn and see Fain eyeing me quizzically, his head tilted with concern.

Small dots of ice probe at my fire, featherlight. Horrified, I realize Malkyn's testing my wall. Testing for a weak spot.

I'm not only a pariah, I realize with icy clarity. I've become prey for both Genna and Malkyn Bane.

I grit my teeth, link air to my fire lines and send up a stronger wall of fire that shatters Malkyn's icy probe, driving it back with gale force. His eyes light with surprise.

Deeply rattled, I wind more wind around my fire lines, securing my wall. Bolstering it with a long line of wood.

Just try it, I seethe at Malkyn Bane. *Try to torment me now.*

Suddenly, everyone around me rises. A murmur of anticipation ripples through the massive crowd as every head in the room turns toward the entrance of the tent.

I rise along with the crowd as a new contingent of soldiers march in. Voices swell with excitement all around me, and I'm instantly swept up in it.

She's coming. The Black Witch is coming.

My memory of her is crystal clear. Our valiant destroyer, riding in on a dragon that fearsome night, raining fire down on our enemies.

Saving us all.

Soldiers fan out as they enter, everyone's fists going hard over their hearts with a communal thump, and I join them. Grandfather is weeping beside me.

I can feel the Black Witch's rush of fire power before I see her.

The soldiers part, and she enters, her forest-green eyes dazzling with ferocity.

The crowd whips into a frenzy at the sight of her, roaring their support. People burst into tears and thrust their hands out toward her as she passes, her stride powerful and controlled, like a wildcat's.

Her black hair is long and streaming over her shoulders, the lines of her face severe and beautiful. Carnissa Gardner's affinity lines are so strong, her power so immense, that magic courses off her body in visible waves. Tendrils of black mist flow from her like a terrible mane.

A rush of her affinity fire slams into me and nearly drives

all the breath from my lungs. My throat goes scorching hot, so intense is the power of her fire as it whips out in a turbulent frenzy.

I feel almost Magedrunk again from the effects of Carnissa Gardner's power, her fire flowing into me, coursing around the wall I've sent up. Her affinity dwarfs every other affinity in the room, and I'm momentarily unable to sense a single other line of magic.

As she ascends the dais, the roaring outpour of support takes some time to settle down. She holds up her hands, awe-inducing lines of power streaming off them. The room silences, save for the occasional quiet sob of joy.

"Mages."

It's just one, simple word, but the crowd catches fire. Cheers erupt, near deafening, my own heart swept up along with it.

Tears sting at my own eyes as my grandfather continues to weep.

Mage.

It used to be a slur. But on her lips, it's become a mighty word of power.

This is a new world for us. A Gardnerian world.

She waits, and slowly the crowd quiets.

"For too long," she booms out, "we Mages have been crushed down. Enslaved. Abused. Mocked. They thought they could push back our borders until we were left with no ground to stand on. They thought they could steal our homes and every meager possession we owned." Her tone grows fierce. "They thought they could wipe us off the face of Erthia."

The crowd briefly erupts, yelling out their protest. A maternal smile comes to Carnissa Gardner's lips, and she raises her arms, as if she's embracing all of us. "My beloved First Children, you have waited so long. Waited for the age of the Evil Ones to draw to a close. I tell you this, Mages." She pauses, and her eyes seem to catch fire. "The Ancient One has a *mighty fist*, and the Reaping Times have come."

The crowd goes wild—Mages shouting with defiant joy, slamming their fists to their chests. People are calling her *May'im—revered mother* in the Ancient Tongue.

When the Mages finally quiet again, Carnissa Gardner looks toward a knot of priests. "Bring the children forward."

The priests and a group of elderly women usher a group of about twenty young children forward onto the dais, white bands around the women's arms. Volunteers from inland, here to help all of us refugees.

There's a boy of about two with pudgy cheeks, his wide eyes looking out over the crowd in terror, his mouth set in a wide, trembling grimace. A little girl of about four years old whimpers as she grasps at a worn blanket, her eyes tightly shut. There are two babies being gently rocked by volunteers.

So many children. Looking so lost.

Orphans, I realize with a sharp pang of grief.

"Mages," the Black Witch calls out, looking over the crowd. "The Evil Ones think they can make orphans of our children. They want to see Mage children begging in the streets and cowering in the shadows." Her eyes burn with outrage. "But they do not know who we are. They do not know that every Mage child is the Ancient One's beloved." A righteous challenge lights her eyes, tendrils of power circling around her. "Who will take in our blessed children? To raise as your own, giving them the protection of your name?"

Hands shoot up, Mages calling out, "We will!" and "We'll take a child!" A husband and wife seated near me give each other quick glances and volunteer as well.

Couples and their relatives go to the dais. The children are given out to their new families. The terror-stricken little boy is lifted into the arms of a young couple, his terror dampening to confusion as he's surrounded by encouraging smiles. The little girl with the blanket is the last to leave the dais, surrounded by adults kneeling down to her level, her new father talking to her in hushed tones. Eventually she stops crying and lets herself be led away by her new family.

Practically everyone in the room is blinking back tears. I look to the Black Witch, my own eyes burning with emotion. A great love for her washes over me. She's created a new world for us, made sure our most vulnerable are now cherished and cared for.

The Black Witch bows her head and draws her fist over her heart as the crowd stills. "Pray with me, blessed Mages."

A tall, bald priest raises his hands above the crowd, and the entire room places fists over hearts once again, bowing their heads.

Everyone except for Vale.

I'm shocked to find him standing straight and stiff, his eyes burning with defiance as his siblings take on the posture of prayer beside him.

How can he refuse to pray with all of us at this moment? How can he fail to be moved? A hot flame of censure flares inside me, and I press my fist to my chest, bowing my head in defiance.

"Oh, most holy Ancient One," I intone with the others. "Purify our minds, purify our hearts, purify Erthia. Protect us from the stain of the Evil Ones."

Our prayer ends, but this time there are no cheers. Most of the room is crying. And now I'm crying, too, along with Grandfather.

Allowed to pray together without being dragged out and beaten. Without being thrown in prison. Flogged. Killed.

"Mages," the Black Witch tells us, her voice thick with emotion, "we must increase our numbers and fill *all* the corners of

Erthia. Tonight is a night of new beginnings." She looks out over the crowd. "Who here is ready to be fasted? To join with me in building our blessed Magedom?"

Cries rise in a cacophony throughout the room. Young couples' hands thrust up into the air.

The priest gestures solemnly toward the center of the crowd. Rosebeth and Myles get up and walk to the dais.

The crowd bursts into a frenzy of jubilation. Women pull Ironflowers from their hair and pockets and throw them into the air. The glowing flowers soon carpet the central aisle, and the blue petals cling to Rosebeth's and Myles's hair.

They're guided onto the dais by the priests as everyone beams at them. They move to stand on either side of a small altar, then clasp their hands over it. Another priest guides their families forward to stand around them.

The Black Witch holds her wand over the couple's clasped hands as a hush falls over the room. The head priest opens our holy book, *The Book of the Ancients*, and reads the fasting prayer.

Tears stream down my cheeks as I watch them, overcome. Though Rosebeth hasn't been the most loyal friend since we arrived here, I've known her since we were small children, and I'm beside myself with relief to see her so happy and cared for.

The Black Witch murmurs the fasting spell, and her dark lines of power whip about the couple, whirling around their hands.

And then it's over, the dark lines of magic abruptly pulled into both Rosebeth's and Myles's hands.

With ecstatic smiles, they lift their fast-marked hands to the crowd. The permanent black fastlines now swirl in a dancing pattern over their glittering skin.

Everyone applauds and cheers. The couple's families envelop them in an embrace, their collective happiness bubbling over as they all make their way off the dais and into a bright future.

Couple after couple follow their lead, bounding up to be fasted to wild cheers. Each couple's eldest male guardian makes a tearful, earnest speech of gratitude to the Ancient One, to our Black Witch and to Gardnerians everywhere.

All of Genna's Upper River friends rise to fast, three of them to Level Five Mages. Genna looks on, beaming, but she remains curiously seated.

It goes on for some time, and my elation for my long-beleaguered people slowly starts to chip away.

I'm standing on the fringes of all of it. Dressed up for a party where no one would ever want me. Not if they all knew about my friendship with Jules.

I'm an outcast, like Fain. And not just because of Jules. The list of my oddities is far longer than just that. I can read affinities. I'm one of those rare females with magic, and I've used it without Mage Council approval.

Nils ascends the dais, his military cloak swishing, one of Genna's pretty friends on his arm. I can feel Genna's triumphant glare as my heart sinks low as a stone in a well.

I watch the shy way the pretty young woman looks at Nils, their eyes gleaming with hope and the promise of sweet romance. The whole atmosphere of the hall is vibrating with such emotions, the results of rampant matchmaking everywhere I look. Couple after couple cling to each other.

I'm filled with a sudden longing for a fastmate of my own. Someone handsome and kind, someone who would help me look after Grandfather and Wren. Someone who wouldn't think I was strange to be friends with a Kelt.

"Mage Bartholomew Harrow, please approach with your granddaughter."

The sound of the priest calling out Grandfather's name jolts through me. I look to Grandfather in confusion, but he simply pats my hand and smiles at me with gentle reassurance.

I take a steadying breath to calm myself.

The fastings are finished. The priests are stepping back from the altar.

I know Grandfather has spent most of our brief time here with the priests—going to service, praying, even leading an informal prayer circle. And the priests have been kind to us, praying over Wren, sending over their own apothecary. And it's been a blessing to see Grandfather treated with reverence and respect, instead of targeted with cruel taunts.

Perhaps the priests seek to honor Grandfather in some way for his deep faith.

I help him toward the dais, the two of us soon joined by the head priest, who smiles at me benevolently and helps me support Grandfather the rest of the way.

I bolster my protective wall of fire as we climb the stairs of the raised platform. The combined affinities of so many Level Five Mages as well as the overwhelming affinity power of the Black Witch are like a barrage of magical spears. Fire, earth, air, light, water—a cacophony of elemental magic courses through the air and against my wall of fire.

We approach the Black Witch, and I struggle to maintain my balance. The black tendrils of her power circle around her, waves of fire emanating out with insatiable heat.

Breathless, I hold on to Grandfather's arm and struggle to maintain my protective wall. Her eyes are deep green, just like Vale's, and the same fiery heat simmers behind them—except her heat is multiplied a thousandfold.

"Mage Harrow, I have heard tales of you."

I'm astonished—and a little panicked—to have her attention directed so singularly toward me.

"All conflicting," she continues. She motions toward Vale, who seems as thrown as I am by this turn of conversation. "But my son, Vale, assures me that you did, in fact, save a considerable number of your brethren through bravery and magic."

My heart races. Her magic. It's so strong I can barely think around it.

"I believe him," she says, a slight smile forming on her lips. "Which is why I have decided to allow a test of purity."

"What?" I look to Grandfather in confused desperation, but he's smiling at the priests, and they're eyeing him knowingly in turn, their expressions filled with paternal solidarity.

They're allied in this, I realize with spiking alarm. *Whatever this is.*

I catch Fain's look of confusion and apprehension. His disorientation is mirrored in Vale's storming eyes.

I'm suddenly on high alert, my heart thudding against my chest.

"Mage Harrow," the Black Witch says, her tone gone hard. "There have been charges of *staen'en* raised against you. With a Kelt."

A shocked wave of sound flashes through the crowd. I shrink back, blinking out at them all, intimidated by the sheer force of the dark censure pressing in all around me.

"It's not true," I defend myself, my voice shrill. "Jules and I...we were never..."

I'm drowned out by a swell of outraged murmuring in response to the sound of Jules's Keltic name, overlaid with shouts of outright condemnation.

"You will be fasted this very night, Mage Harrow," the Black Witch commands, her fire coursing around me. "And if you are not pure, it will be revealed to all."

"Fast?" I cry out. "To whom?" I look to Grandfather, who pats me on the shoulder. His eyes aren't on me. They're on Priest Alfex, who nods at him approvingly, all of them humoring my anguish.

"Tessie, calm yourself," he tells me in a stern tone I've never heard him use before. "I prayed on this, and the Ancient One led me to the right young man for you. It's high time you were fasted. You must trust me in this."

My grandfather and the priests turn and look toward the line of Level Five Mages, past Vale and Fain, clear across the dais.

Malkyn Bane strides forward, smooth as a serpent, a cold, cruel gleam in his eyes.

"No," I gasp, blanching, staggering back. I look to Grandfather, pleading. "I can't fast to him, Grandfather. Please, don't make me do this. Not to him. *Anyone* but him."

"Tessla!" he admonishes me. "Be calm. I… I *demand* it." He looks to the head priest for reassurance, and the tall man nods at him. "I am your guardian," Grandfather says with a pious authority at odds with his reedy, quavering voice. "I must be obeyed as such. This is for your own good, Tessla. You will see, in time—"

"No." I step away from his hand, panic rising. "I *won't*."

Grandfather looks to the Black Witch and holds his hands out to her in a pleading gesture. "It is completely natural for an innocent girl to have some hesitation."

A nasty smirk spreads across Malkyn's face. I suddenly know exactly what this is.

He's agreed to this in the hope of seeing me disgraced. He believes Jules is my lover, and that I can't be fasted. He wants to reveal me as a *staen'en* and watch the mob consume me.

Instead, I'm about to be permanently bound to a monster.

I send an imploring glance toward Fain, but he's not looking at me. His eyes are locked on Vale's, as if they're relaying information to each other through the very air.

"I won't!" I snarl at them all, glaring at Malkyn Bane. "I won't fast to him!" I move to flee and cry out as firm hands grip both my arms.

"Stop!" Vale's voice rings out clear as he strides forward. He looks grim and calm, but I can feel his fire raging, so strong it cuts through his mother's affinity. "She can't fast to him," Vale states coldly, addressing his mother.

The Black Witch looks at her son, fire meeting fire. "And why is that?"

"She's promised to *me*."

A gasp ripples through the crowd.

"You've finally agreed to fast?" Carnissa Gardner asks, clearly startled.

"We're a perfect match, Mother," he says, as if only mildly interested in the proceedings, but his fire is burning violently hot. He gestures idly toward me. "Read her affinity lines."

The head priest pulls up my sleeve. I defiantly struggle against the hands restraining me as the Black Witch's fingers clench down around my forearm, tendrils of her dark power curling around my skin.

My wall of fire implodes the second she touches me, my affinity instantly laid bare. I'm vulnerable, splayed out like an open book, at the complete mercy of her fire.

"Incredible," she says as I tremble beneath her touch, her terrible heat searing through me. She glances at Vale, astonishment in her eyes. "You're a perfect match. Line for line. Amazing." She looks toward the head priest with excitement. "Imagine the Great Mages a union like this could bring forth."

"The Ancient One works in surprising ways," the priest responds with a reverent dip of his head.

"Thank you, Mage Bane," the Black Witch tells Malkyn as she releases me. I gasp and almost stumble backward, abruptly freed from the weight of her magic. "But if they are promised, then they must be fasted."

Malkyn nods, shooting me a dark look, and steps back into the line of Level Five Mages. Vale takes his place across from me.

"Grasp hands and place them before our Great Mage," the priest intones. He opens *The Book of the Ancients* to a passage marked with a crimson silk bookmark.

I look to Vale, a desperate plea in my eyes, and I can see my own urgency mirrored in his gaze. I can feel how high the stakes are in how hot Vale's fire is running.

I've no choice, I realize with crushing certainty. *It's Vale Gardner or Malkyn Bane. And Vale's trying to help me. He's trying to save me.*

Choking back a sob, I hold my hands out stiffly. My fire is whipping out of control, my protective wall of magic shattered.

Vale grasps my hands firmly in his, and our fires fall into each other, flame crashing through flame.

The Black Witch holds her wand over our clasped hands. Her power curls over us, cinching tightly around our hands. She murmurs the spell, and the priest begins the droning prayer. I can barely hear it as hot tears stream down my cheeks.

I cry harder as the lines appear, snaking around my hands, around Vale's.

The lines curl and creep and then settle, the Black Witch's tendrils of power pulling back and releasing.

I try to pull away, but Vale holds on tight.

"*Seal it,*" he says, the words hard and clipped. Like the final blow of an ax.

I gape at him with sudden fury. I try to pull my hands away, but his clutch is relentless, and suddenly her power is cinching our hands together once more. I glare at Vale, wide-eyed, shocked and thrust into a wild confusion by his betrayal.

By insisting on the sealing ceremony, Vale is ensuring that the consummation of our fasting occur this very night.

But why? Why would Vale want to be sealed?

The fasting lines grow darker, more intricately etched.

The final bond of a Gardnerian couple. With the inevitable public showing of intimacy, the dark lines ready to spread down our wrists after our union is consummated.

I wrench away from Vale, my mouth open in horror. His eyes are on me, white-hot, his fire coursing higher.

"How could you?" I rasp out.

I push through the wall of priests behind me and flee.

CHAPTER TWENTY-ONE:
Sanguin'in

"Tessla!" I hear my Grandfather's heartbreaking, pathetic plea.

I ignore him as I bound down the dais steps and erupt into hot, angry tears. *I hate you! I hate you! I hate you all!*

"Let her go," I hear Vale call out as I run down the aisle, my fire lashing.

There are sounds of shock as I pass. A soldier laughs and yells out, "*Sanguin'in!*" The word is taken up by more soldiers and echoes after me as I flee. "Bloody the sheets!" in the Ancient Tongue, the traditional and awful sealing cheer.

I stumble through the doors, past the rows of military guards, confusion etched on their faces.

I run and run, past tents, down deserted paths, until my lungs feel full of jagged glass. Until I reach a dark area just past a long line of tents, past the edge of the base, a dark field before me, a darker forest beyond that.

Thunder rumbles. Lightning cracks in the distance.

I fall to my knees, my palms in the dry dirt. Sobbing uncontrollably.

With each flash of lightning, I can see the black lines snaking around my hands like a cage.

An unstoppable wave of grief swamps over me.

Wandfasted.
Forever. Final as death.

I feel his fire before I see him or hear his steps.

"Tessla."

My fire explodes. I wheel around, my knees scraping on the rocky dirt.

"I don't want to be *fasted!*" I snarl at him, my hands clenched into fists. I want to rip off my own skin, rip off the lines. "I don't *want* this!"

"I know," he says calmly, but I can feel the full heat of his fire battering against mine.

"Are they happy *now?*" I cry at him, throwing as much affinity fire as I can toward him. I splay out my cursed hands. "Here it is! *Proof* that I'm pure!"

I drop my forehead in my hands and clutch at my hair, furious tears coursing down my face.

I'm bound. Forever.

Vale doesn't move, and his fire doesn't diminish. It's burning hot as mine, barely contained. But he stays where he is, silently watching me.

Fasted. Forever. To him.

But it could have been Malkyn Bane, a small voice reminds me, cutting through the angry fire. *It could be much worse.*

I draw in a shuddering breath, trying to take full stock of the situation.

"You helped me," I state flatly.

He doesn't answer, his fire churning.

Defeated, I slump down to sit on the dirt path, our fires meeting, his outrage surprisingly as scorching as mine.

"We're fasted," I say miserably, my hands going limp in my lap, fire sparking hot in fits and starts all over my affinity lines.

"We are," he affirms, his mouth a tight line.

I take a shuddering breath, wipe away my tears and look up at him.

"I didn't want this, either," he tells me, his voice suddenly hard. "A fastmate, fleeing from her own fasting."

His rebuke stings like the point of a knife. "I know that," I relent. "But you did it, anyway. And you saved me. You saved me from *him*."

Vale nods, as if darkly resigned. Then his mouth turns up in a cold smirk. "You're perhaps the only woman in Gardneria who would be this furious over having to fast to me."

My fire flares, and I glower at him. "I'm sorry for not slavering over you sufficiently, Vale."

"Don't apologize," he counters tightly. "I rather enjoy your straightforward displeasure."

"Hostility," I scathingly correct him.

"Yes, well, it's refreshingly honest."

I'm breathing heavily, fuming, my fire scorching over my affinity lines.

He doesn't say anything, just stands there watching me coolly.

"I wish I was a man," I spit out in defiance.

Vale gives a bitter laugh. "If you were, you might find yourself fasted to someone like Genna Thorne. You must admit, that would be a fair bit worse."

I shake my head. "I'm *sick* of not having any power. Not allowed to have a voice. Not allowed to make any important decisions or defend myself. Do you know how many times I've had to fight off attacks?" I pin him with my eyes and glare at him with white-hot ferocity. "If I'd been trained in the use of a wand…"

Vale's gaze turns deadly serious. "The Kelts would have strung you up for witchery."

I shoot him a steely glare, my lip curled in a defiant sneer. "They wouldn't have been able to catch me."

"I'll teach you," he tells me calmly, but I can feel his fire lashing in hot, furious strokes. Barely contained.

"You'll teach me *what*?" I snap at him.

"How to use a wand." He smirks again. "Without blowing yourself up."

My breath catches tight in my chest and I gape at him. "You would?"

"I'll even buy you a wand," he tells me evenly.

He's playing with me. He has to be. He can't honestly be offering me a wand. It's illegal to secure wands for Mages without Council approval, and for him to jest like this only stokes my anger higher.

"Go ahead, then," I taunt back. "Get me a wand. I might strike you down if you irritate me."

Vale coughs out a laugh. "You could try. I like to spar with the outrageously overconfident. I've a lot of practice with that."

"I don't need your help," I snipe at him. "I've used my grandfather's wand."

"And what type of wand was that?" Vale asks, his tone condescending.

My angry fire burns hotter. I lift my chin. "An Elstorth Oak wand."

Vale spits out a sharp sound of disdain. "The cheapest, most poorly made wands in all of Erthia. They work against power more than they work with it."

I remember the wand I used that terrible night. "Then get me a wand like that white wand," I counter.

Vale smirks. "I can't get you a Wand of Power. But I can get you a Maelorian wand."

I eye him closely. There's no slyness in his fire. It's coursing hot and steady.

"Sweet Ancient One, Vale, you can't actually be serious. Those are outrageously expensive wands. They cost as much as…as *Valgard*."

He narrows his eyes. "You do realize you have money now."

I stare at him blankly.

He gapes at me. "You really hadn't given that *any* thought?"

"I was too busy being…upset."

Vale gives an incredulous laugh, then shakes his head and grows thoughtful, his fire lashing out. His lips purse into a tight line of displeasure. "You're easily a Level Three Mage. Maybe even a Four, with the way you can layer power. If you were Noi, you wouldn't have to put up with any of this nonsense. They'd put you right into their Vu Trin guard, and they'd be the stronger for it. We waste half our fighting force. I find it deeply ironic that a woman is turning the tide for us."

I stare at him in dumbfounded surprise.

He notices my shock and shoots me a sardonic grin. "Not so bad having a fastmate with complete contempt for the rules, is it?"

"You'd really get me a wand," I marvel. "You're not joking."

His eyes glitter with fiery mischief. "Oh, Tessla, I'd get you a *very* nice wand."

Blinking at him, I sit rooted to the spot, my fire out of control, lashing out in angry fits and starts. I stare toward the Command Tent, and the flames briefly surge, coursing with hatred.

"Gods, Tessla," he says. "I can feel your fire even more clearly than my own. Would you like to get out of here?"

I turn toward him, incredulous, put off by his casual use of the blasphemous "gods." There's only one god—the Ancient One—and Vale's idle cursing is jarring.

"What about my brother?" I almost include *and my grandfather*, but I'm too hurt to even mention Grandfather, ready to lash out or burst into violent tears at the thought of his betrayal. "Wren needs me. I've no choice but to stay here."

His brow knits tight. "I'll not leave your family here. I have a home in Valgard. I'll arrange for a carriage to bring them there. Tonight. They'll be well cared for."

I stare at him, stunned. "You'd do that? You'd help them?"

His brow knits tighter. "Of course. Tessla, you've just made a very good match." His expression turns cynical. "At least in terms of money and connections."

"But if you're bringing my family to Valgard, then…where do you want to take me?"

"Somewhere quiet." He takes a deep breath and lets it out, staring at me like I'm a puzzle he can't quite figure out. "I have a second home by the Voltic Sea. It's just a small cottage, but it's isolated. Away from—" he motions toward the base as a whole "—all this."

Fear and suspicion suddenly flare to life inside me. What if the rumors about him and Fain are wrong? I'd be alone with him, and it would be all too easy for him to take advantage of that in order to consummate our sealing.

"I won't let you bed me," I tell him fiercely. There's an edge of pathetic desperation in my voice, and I loathe hearing it.

He stiffens with offense. "I have no desire to force you into my bed."

I waver, remembering what Fain said earlier. *We fit together, Vale and I. Like two pieces of a puzzle.* If Vale didn't want to wandfast at all, and he has no interest in pursuing our consummation…it must be because of Fain.

There's still one question left unanswered, though. "Why did you seal the fasting, then?" I challenge, raising my line-marked hand into the air.

There's a searing flash of irritation in Vale's eyes, as if his reasoning should be patently obvious. "I had them seal us to

bring you under my full protection, Tessla. Or would you prefer to stay under the partial guardianship of your grandfather?
That was going so *deliriously* well."

I let out a shaky breath, still furious at Grandfather. I realize that Vale was right to insist on our sealing. Right to strip
Grandfather of his power over me.

"Well, in any case, it's done," I observe flatly, turning my
hand side to side as more tears sting at my eyes. "It's over.
I'm…"

"Stuck with me, yes," he snaps. "But it's a fair bit better than
being stuck with Malkyn Bane. Of that, I can assure you." His
expression loses its sarcastic edge. He looks at me full on, serious and searching. "At some point," he says with a sigh, "we'll
make a trip to Noi lands and…try to undo this. I can't make
any guarantees. This magic is as strong as Elfin steel, but it
might be possible. All right?"

I look to him, his face drawn into hard lines, his fire raging.
But there's genuine concern at the edges of his gaze.

I nod in unspoken agreement. It's clear he doesn't want this,
either. Chastened gratitude pricks at me. "Why would you do
this?" I ask him.

He spits out a derisive breath, as if irritated by the question,
then locks his gaze on to mine, his eyes searing. "Because what
they were doing to you was monumentally unfair. Regardless
of what they think, you saved the lives of many of the Gardnerians in there. And, no offense, but your grandfather seems
like an idiot. And I hate idiocy."

I eye his wand with a glimmer of unease. "I suppose you're
my lord and master now. You're a Level Five Mage *and* we're
sealed."

"I would never force you to do anything."

"Except wandfast," I snipe at him. My words are hardly fair.
I know they're not. But I'm of no mind to be fair.

Vale's face twists into a sneer. "I know you don't want me. I know you don't want any of this."

"I'm sorry, Vale," I concede miserably. "You helped me. I know I should be thanking you."

"I don't want your gratitude," he says, fuming. "It was well worth it just to see the look on Malkyn Bane's face."

I stare at him, suddenly feeling lost and defeated as his fire lashes against me. My fire is as out of control as his. The pain of my grandfather's cruelty slices through me in jagged cuts and sends my affinity flames roaring higher.

"Are you ready to get out of here?" Vale asks.

I nod, hating them all. Hurt by them all. Everyone but my brother and Fain and Vale.

"I'm ready," I tell him, my voice breaking with despair. "If I stay here, I'll steal that wand straight from your belt and set them all on fire." I narrow my eyes at him. "And even your mother won't be able to stop me."

CHAPTER TWENTY-TWO:
Voltic Sea

My arms are tight around Vale as we ride, my body pressed up close against his back. We didn't pause to collect any belongings. Vale simply requisitioned a black stallion and pulled me up behind him, and we rode away, Vale's lineage and silver stripes giving him leave to go anywhere, do anything he dictated.

The wind picks up as we ride, pulling at my hair. Vale's cloak is wrapped around me to cut the chill, his heat fueling my own.

He feels good.

Too good.

His sparking fire radiates off his back, his affinity lines as out of control and fitful as mine, flaring violently at times.

Both of us passionately upset.

But there's also the matter of how exciting it is to touch him.

The muscles of his chest move under my hands, strong and sinewy, and my fire struggles to surge straight into him. Mortified, I pull my fire in hard, but it's like trying to control a raging storm.

I resist the urge to move my hands, to slide my fingers over the planes of his chest and trace fire all over it. I hold myself stiffly, but the movement of the horse is rhythmic and bumping and my fingers slide on their own. Every movement of my hands on him prompts a trail of explosive sparks.

We kissed, I think, my fire wanting to crash into him as we race through forests and farmland. *His mouth was hot on mine.* I realize, with a start, that I want him to kiss me again.

No, I rebuke myself, shocked by my own thoughts. *He won't ever kiss you again. He only did it to save your life, and you only want him because you fall into his affinity so.*

He belongs to Fain, not to you.

The rain begins to spit in fits and starts as the thunder grows closer and more insistent. I'm filled with a mounting frustration, and the chill wind doesn't do anything to dampen my hungry fire.

The desire to get even closer to him rocks through me. I want to get under the silk of his tunic. Feel his hot skin against mine. Forget everything in the whole world and drown in his fire.

My face is flushed hot. The heat he's kindling in me—it's all new. I've never had such brazen thoughts in my life. My fire sparks toward Vale in covetous flares and I struggle to rein it in.

Does Fain feel the same wild pull toward Vale? Toward his fire, his hard body? And does Vale want Fain that way, too?

A despairing frustration crashes through me that dwarfs the ocean scene opening up before us. Waves crash on the rocks below, the road abutting a sheer cliff dropping down to the Voltic Sea.

I'm fasted to a man who will never want me. Who wants Fain instead.

There's a flash of lightning and a crash of thunder as Vale's cottage comes into view. It's deeply isolated, set down near an arcing beach, with rocky cliffs rising to great heights all around it. The beach is dark, the clouds threateningly low, stormy as the churning water.

Of course it's isolated. Hidden away from everything. So Vale and Fain can hide what they are to each other. *And they can still have each other*, I bitterly consider. Fasting places control only over women. But still, I've complicated their already disastrously complicated lives. A sting of miserable regret stabs at me—regret over any hurt this might cause Fain.

The cottage is as stark as the landscape and blends in perfectly, traditional Gardnerian in style. It's constructed of Ironwood, carved to resemble a grove of giant trees, their limbs rising up to flow into the stone cliff. Part of the adjacent cliff is hewn into a side arch that's attached to the house. Trees are etched right into the stone, mirroring those carved into the Ironwood. There's an upper floor with a semicircle of long windows that open onto an sweeping porch. The porch looks out over the turbulent ocean.

It's beautiful.

This will never be your cottage, I harshly remind myself. *It's Vale's and Fain's. I'm an outsider in it. By virtue of their charity. A pitiful outsider, and nothing more.*

The heavens open up. Lightning cracks, and rain sheets down on us in glistening, spearing lines.

Vale rides down to the cottage and pulls the horse to a stop beneath a long stone arch. Rain spills off the arch's edge in thick streams, the thunder and lightning whipping up into a frenzy. There's a path to a cavernous and well-appointed stable cut right into the cliff, and I absently stare into it as my misery rises along with the storm's intensity.

Vale hastily gets off the horse, as if angered at me, and I feel the loss of his heat acutely. Like a blow.

He throws me a storming, tortured glance, and I glare right back at him, fighting off the urge to burst into tears. He looks away, his hand tight on the horse's bridle, waiting for me to dismount.

I hop off the stallion, made clumsy by my tear-blurred vision. Vale quickly leads the horse away, as if he can't wait to be rid of the sight of me.

It's too much.

I turn and walk away, straight into the storm, meet with the rain and surrender to my fury and anguish, letting my fire lash out in fractured spears. I walk clear away from the house, right up to a cliff's sharp drop.

There's a path that would take me right up to the edge of the Voltic Sea.

The rain's now pelting my face, chilling me to the bone, and I clench my fastlined fists and cry into it, staggeringly aware of what I've lost.

Yes, I can make a life for my family now. And I should be grateful. But Vale's enticing fire has, for the moment, singed all other thoughts to ash, save for one painful realization.

I splay out my hands in front of me, rain pelting the black, curling lines.

I'll never be loved. Never have a true fasting. I'll never have anyone.
Because of Grandfather.

It's all his fault, I seethe. *My arrogant, pious grandfather's fault.*
Anger rears up and slashes through me.

A wave of heat hits my back. "Tessla." Vale's hand touches my arm. Fire flashes through me with his firm touch, his hand so warm. It feels so wildly good, which shatters my heart anew.

I wrench my arm away from Vale and round on him, my breathing gone erratic and harsh, everything exploding out of me in a sudden rush.

"I took care of them for *years!*" I cry at Vale, teeth gritted, tears streaming.

Thunder crashes around us.

His hair and body are slick with rain, which only makes him more beautiful. His fiery green eyes sear into me. I'm pulling in staccato breaths, unable to control my despair. "I made *all* the money! Did *all* the hard work! The two of them sick, for *years* and *years*! And then he *forces* me! Gives me *no* say! Goes behind my back! It *hurts*! It *hurts* that he'd do that to me!" My chest is heaving so hard that my sobbing has grown painful. "I was powerless *there*, and I'm still powerless *here*. How *could* he? How could he do this to me?" I raise my cursed hands as my rage devolves into a wounded keening.

Vale's face is set tight. There's a whirlwind of conflict in his eyes. The rain has completely soaked him now, and I look him over with open longing.

His lips are drawn, and he briefly glances out over the steel-gray ocean. Then he turns back to me, his gaze fierce.

"If I'd only left a week earlier," I say with anguish. "I'd be there. I'd be in Verpacia *right now.*"

"Tessla," Vale says. "Come in out of the rain." There's an adamant insistence in his tone, but also something else. Genuine concern.

Lightning streaks and thunder crashes, and I'm suddenly aware of how cold I am. But I can't look to my fastmate to warm me.

No, he'll never warm me. He'll warm Fain.

The thought makes me cry even harder.

But he's trying to be kind. Trying to get me to come in to shelter.

I relent and follow him back under the stone arch. I slump up against the inside of the arch, weeping, not caring how pathetic I am.

Vale's eyes are on fire as he leans back against the opposite wall, facing me.

"Tessla, there's something you should know." He's biting off each word as if this is difficult to say.

"I know," I anguish, wiping at my tears. "I already know."

You love Fain.

"No, you *don't*," Vale says, his voice ragged. "Jules Kristian. He's one of my closest friends. Aside from Fain."

I raise my head and gape at him, instantly flooded with vast confusion. Not sure I've even heard him correctly.

"Jules? You're friends with *my* Jules?"

"Yes, *your* Jules." The words are tight and bitter, and shame washes over his expression. "I met him at the University. He's a brilliant historian. We've been close friends for almost three years." He pauses, as if momentarily at a loss. "When I saw him that night...when we came for all of you... I knew who you were immediately. Jules talked about you often." He hesitates, his words stilted, then shakes his head and spits out a short, wry laugh. "He's madly in love with you." He brings his hand to his forehead and massages his temple. "When he finds out..." He takes a deep breath and looks squarely at me. "I've betrayed him."

My heart speeds up. "Where is he?" I ask, breathless with hope.

He narrows his eyes. "I gave him a protective amulet against fire. He's...fine. He sent a runehawk. He's getting ready to cross into Verpacia. I have a small house there. I'm sending him funds."

I grasp at the wall behind me, going light-headed. "He's all right. Oh... Ancient One. He's alive." I can barely get the words out. Exhausted relief washes over me.

He's alive. All of us alive.

I glance up at Vale again. "His family?"

Vale's whole face pulls in tight. "They're dead."

The news is like a blow to my gut. "*All* of them?"

He nods, his eyes reddening, glazed with guilty tears. "My mother's fire." He almost chokes on the words.

Oh, Ancient One, no. "His sister, too?" Little Sarla. Ten years old and full of life.

"All of them, Tessla."

My throat goes sickeningly tight. "Oh, Vale."

I cry for a while into my hand, until I'm numbed from cold and grief.

"Did you send word to him?" I finally ask, my voice haggard. "Does he know they're all gone?"

Stricken, Vale nods. Then he looks down at his fastlined hands and grimaces, sagging against the wall. "He'll never forgive me for taking you away from him," Vale states with wretched certainty. "How could he?"

"Vale…" My voice is stuffy and strange from all the crying. "I was going to be fasted to Malkyn Bane. You saved me from being taken by a…"

"A monster?"

I nod.

"No," Vale says, his mouth tight with self-loathing. "All I did was destroy both Jules's happiness and yours." Anguish streaks across his face. "It's meaningless now, but… I'm sorry, Tessla."

"Vale," I say, shaking my head to refute him. "It's not how you think. I'm not in love with Jules. I *do* love him, a great deal. But…not in the way he was starting to feel. I…" I trail off, a stab of pain spiking through me. I look down at my hand, my fast-marked palm open and riddled with black lines. I know what this will do to Jules.

Vale's brow is tight with confusion. "But you were going to go *off* with him."

I give a long sigh. "I could have made a life with Jules. But… I don't know that I would have ever felt…anywhere near the way he did about me."

"So was there was someone else, then?" he asks, confused.

I give my head a tight shake, my lips trembling. I shrug. "No. I just… I had dreams of going to the University, apprenticing there as an apothecary. Learning how to use my magic." I pause for a moment, tears welling up again. "And I had this romantic idea. I'd meet a Gardnerian scholar there. Someone who loves books, like I do. Someone kind. I had this stupid story in my mind." There are tears dripping down onto my fastlines, and I absently smear them into the marks. "He'd bring me Iron-flowers. And he'd kiss me in a garden. And then he'd ask me to fast to him." I shrug again. "It was foolish."

Vale's gone very quiet and still.

"I'm sorry," I tell him, shaking my head. "I should be thanking you. Although…" I wipe my nose against my forearm and give a hard sniff. "I suppose we're helping each other. You saved me from a nightmare of a fastmate." I look at him straight on. "And I'm helping you hide your secret."

His brow rises. "My secret?"

I give him an incredulous look. "You and Fain. You…" I can feel myself flushing. "You fancy each other."

Vale lets out a short laugh. "No, we don't."

My face pinches with confusion. "What?"

He sighs. "Fain's like a brother to me."

"But he said…he *touched* you. That he knows your affinity like the back of his hand."

Irritation flashes across Vale's features. "Yes, well, he *has* touched me. My arm. My shoulder, perhaps. But not like *that*."

"But Vale," I counter, "he told me he cares for you."

Vale shakes his head. "Tessla, we're close friends." He swallows, a shadow passing over his expression and he looks at me askance. "If we weren't closely allied, do you know what would happen to Fain?"

I nod gravely. "He'd have to leave Gardneria."

Pain slashes across Vale's gaze. "Or he'd be imprisoned." There's a pleading edge to the way he's looking at me now. As if he's begging for my silence.

"Ancient One, Vale," I breathe. "I adore Fain. He's been—"

my voice breaks "—*so* kind. I'll *never* forget how good he was to me." I glance down at the soaked but exquisite clothes I'm wearing. The clothes Fain gave me.

Vale nods tightly, as if he's been carrying a heavy load.

"But..." I'm cast into confusion. "If not Fain...then is there another man?"

He shoots me a look full of amusement. "Tessla, I don't fancy men."

What? "Then...why don't you correct all the rumors?"

His face goes hard. "I don't care what people say about me. I'm too powerful to care, quite frankly. And it keeps away all the insincere attention from the women who want to fast to me for my connections. For my money."

I'm stunned. "So...you fancy women, then?"

He lets out a short laugh and looks at me sidelong, his eyes flaring. "Quite ardently."

I'm speechless for a long moment, gaping at him. "I thought..."

"Well, you thought wrong."

I blink at him. "So...you fasted to me...to protect me?"

He gives me a cagey, sideways look. "Partially." His face darkens with guilt. He looks down, his jaw tensing, then fixes his eyes on me. "I fasted to you to protect you, of course." He hesitates, his gaze heating. "And also...because you're the most beautiful woman I've ever seen."

Shock shoots straight down my spine.

"But..." I'm at a loss for words. "You called me low-class. And said that my looks were *rustic*."

Vale winces. "I didn't mean any of that. I felt such a strong pull toward you, and it unnerved me completely." The heat in his eyes flares. "Gods, Tessla, our affinities—your fire is *constantly* calling to mine. But..." His brow tenses. "I thought you belonged to Jules. I was trying to put as much distance between us as I possibly could." He pauses, his expression taut with remorse. "I'm sorry for what I said. The truth of the matter is... I've grown very fond of you."

His eyes meet mine with unwavering intensity. The fire in his gaze spreads down my neck like a fever.

"So," I say, still reeling. "You never wanted Fain."

He shakes his head.

"And you...like *me*?"

He nods. "And you don't love Jules."

"Not like that."

We stare at each other in rapt silence as the rain pours down around us.

Vale's eyes are momentarily blurred, like he's in a confused daze. "Would...would you like some tea?"

CHAPTER TWENTY-THREE:
Home

The kitchen is dark and chilled, but I can see carvings of sanded Ironwood trees rising up all around me, their stout branches supporting the walls and shelves and forming the rafters above.

Vale pulls his wand out and lights three wall lanterns, then points it at a fireplace set in between two tree trunks.

I jump back as a huge plume of fire bursts into life, the small kitchen suddenly glowing with orange light. A fierce wave of heat pushes through me, the fire's sparking tendrils almost setting my skirts alight.

I look to Vale, alarmed.

His eyes reflect the bucking firelight as he points his wand at the fireplace and murmurs spells under his breath. He pushes his palm forward, and the fire retreats back into the confines of the fireplace. Vale eyes it with a look of rattled frustration.

His careful control is shattered, and I can feel his affinity knifing in random patterns, straining toward me. Just like my affinity is flaring toward him, both of us trying futilely to rein it all in.

"Sorry," he says, glancing at me sidelong. The fire spits and hisses, but it's now confined to the fireplace, and the chill of the room quickly dissipates. But we're both soaked through, far too much for even an out-of-control fire to dry out.

I take in his kitchen in one sweeping glance.

It's part kitchen, part laboratory, with small stacks of books covering the wooden table in its center and more books piled on every available shelf. Beakers, retorts, vials and jars of metal powders are scattered about. Containers of small, gleaming stones are mixed in with canisters of tea and herbs and a haphazard assortment of pots and bowls.

It's chaotic, but utterly fascinating.

Some semblance of control regained, Vale sheathes his wand and shoots me a fierce glance, then distractedly pulls a mug and teapot from a cabinet. He spoons tea leaves from one of the many glass jars into the teapot, pumps water into it and points his wand at the teapot, murmuring a spell. Within a few seconds, steam is pumping into the air at a furious rate.

I stare at him, feeling as if I'm caught in a surreal scene. The son of the Black Witch, as wildly intimidating in appearance as his mother, with soaking wet tendrils of black hair spiked and flopping unevenly all over his head, using his overwhelming Level Five demon-slaying powers…to make me tea.

It's so…bizarrely domestic.

Vale pours the steaming tea and uneasily hands me the earthenware mug, warm to the edge of burning, and quickly steps back to lean against the counter. He eyes me, his wand held loosely in his hand, as if he doesn't quite know what to do with me.

Two black cats slink into the kitchen and twine around his legs, purring in a deep thrum. One is large and fluffy with pale green eyes. The other is short-haired with a yellow gaze and a questioning cock to its head.

"You've cats," I marvel.

"Yes, well," he says, distracted, as if he's carrying on a furious conversation with himself that's sapping all his focus, his hand gripping the counter behind him so hard his knuckles are white. "I'm partial to them."

"Do they have names?" I ask.

He nods, his lip quirking. "*Vorn'in* and *Strill'ian*."

High Elfin. I'm surprised and oddly delighted by this. It's so un-Gardnerian to use another language for things.

"Ah." I nod. "Midnight and…what's *Vorn'in*?"

"Coal," he says, his eyes hot on me.

I nod, then sigh deeply. "My clothes are soaked through, Vale."

He blinks at me for a moment, thrown into confusion. "Yes, of course." He looks around like he's absently searching for a solution. "We've no clothes for you…" He immediately stops himself, a spot of color appearing high on his cheeks. He looks away.

I suddenly realize that brash, suffer-no-fools Vale can be… shy.

He swallows and looks back at me. "Of course, I'll send for your things."

Sadness rocks through me. I think of our tiny cottage, and all our meager possessions. Momma's needlework. The small bear I sewed for Wren. A pretty camisole I embroidered with tiny pink roses. All of it rendered to ash.

And our cat.

My throat feels tight and raw as tears prick my eyes. I blink them back. "I have no things to send for, Vale. Everything was…destroyed."

His brow tenses as he searches my eyes, his fire flaring hot, angry on my behalf. "Well," he says tightly, the word clipped. "That will *change*." He says it with an assurance that's so rock solid, it momentarily cuts through my misery and softens the edges of my pain.

Vale looks around again, thinking. "Perhaps, just for a bit, you could…wear one of my tunics." He swallows, his eyes darting over me, and there's heat in his gaze. He quickly pulls back on it, drawing it firmly in.

My heart hammers against my ribs. I'm suddenly aware that I'm alone, in a completely isolated place, with a powerful young man. A man I'm fasted and sealed to.

A man who desires women and not men.

I take an almost imperceptible step back, my internal wall of fire rearing up.

His head gives a small jerk as he straightens, his gaze now edged with concern. He looks closely at me, then walks toward the spiraling Ironwood staircase at the edge of the kitchen, stops and turns back to me. "I'll show you to your room. You can take off those wet things." He swallows, his heat momentarily coursing outward, only to be quickly tamped back down.

I set my tea on the counter and tentatively follow him as he starts up the stairs.

He could force me to do anything he wants.

On some level, I know my alarm is unfounded, but it spikes just the same. With each step up the staircase, I become more and more nervous.

The upstairs is cast in shadow, but I can see his body straight and strong in front of me. The smell of him wafts back on the air—damp sweat and wool mixed in with the clean odor of wood smoke and something distinctly male. It sets my affinity fire flaring, and my irrational fear edging higher at the same time.

Vale reaches the top, turns around and looks surprised when he notices how much distance I've put between us.

He lights the sole lamp in the short hall with his wand and pushes the door before us open, stepping back with formal politeness as I reach the top floor. I hesitate, then peek inside the room, my unease mounting as I take in the sight of a canopied bed.

Large enough for two.

"This is my bedroom," he tells me, his brow knit in concern and confusion, his fire giving off a heat that's turned distractingly, overwhelmingly sensual. "It's your bedroom now," he tells me, his fire brushing against me in slow strokes. "I'll... um..." He glances back down the stairs. "There's a small room just off the kitchen. When weather's bad, Edwin stays in that room. I'll sleep there."

I round on him, stunned. "I can't take your room."

He blinks at me, as if I'm uttering nonsense. "I can't have my fastmate sleeping in such cramped quarters."

My fastmate. A disconcerting heat streaks through me at his use of the word—and relief at his reserved and thoughtful manner, so at odds with his aggressive fire.

"Vale, you shouldn't stay in cramped quarters either," I insist. "I can't possibly take your room."

His jaw tenses. "I'll be quite comfortable."

"But...all your things..."

"*Our* things," he insists. "They're *our* things now."

I'm thrown by this additional display of chivalry. Nervous amusement bubbles up within me. "Even your breeches?" My eyes go wide, and I flush hotly. "I meant...your clothing," I stumble. "I... I'm sorry..." I'm horrified, my flush deepening. "It struck me as funny."

He's gone still, watching me with narrowed eyes. "I doubt they'd fit you, Tessla. But you're welcome to them." His mouth turns up in a subtle smile.

I take a deep sigh, resigned to my scarlet face. "Thank you, Vale."

His mouth lifts in amusement. "You're welcome, Tessla." He

cocks his head. "I *will* have a wardrobe ordered for you. Until then…there's always my breeches."

A smile dances on my mouth, then widens. Vale's face lights into a grin that mirrors my own, our affinity fires suddenly loosened and curling around each other.

I realize I hadn't yet seen a smile on his face that didn't hold withering disdain or barely concealed malice. His green eyes are lit up with delight and affection.

He's handsome, I muse, flustered. *So distractingly handsome. And all that fire…*

"Let me just grab some dry clothing," Vale says, a bit falteringly. He shoots me another small, tentative smile, and I nod and step back. He's careful not to touch me as he passes, even though his fire brushes against me.

He lights a bedside lantern, strides over to the closet and quickly grabs a tunic and pants from a line of uniformly dark Gardnerian garb. Then he lights the room's woodstove with his wand, shoots me another small smile and stalks out, his fire trailing behind him.

I close the door behind him and turn the latch, then lean against the door, my palms pressed flat behind me. My heart is pounding, my breathing uneven.

His presence is overwhelming. I swear I can still feel the edges of his heat from a floor away.

I look around, feeling decadent in this new, private knowledge of him.

Mage Vale Gardner's bedroom.

It's as chaotic as the kitchen. His bed looks hastily made up, with deep green blankets over white sheets. Sturdy Ironwood posts support a plain, forest-green canopy. Ironwood trees, like the ones downstairs, flow out from the walls, their branches supporting the roof in an intricate tangle, more branches supporting shelves in their hollows.

Half the room pushes out into a semicircle that hangs over the lower story, and windows reach from floor to ceiling, continuing up to form a glass roof. A small side door opens onto an arcing balcony that looks out over the storming ocean.

Rain pounds the glass, the wind rattling the panes in violent fits and starts.

A table is set up against the wall of windows. It's covered with books, as well as a mariner's sextant, compass, scope and half-unrolled maps. A library of haphazardly arranged volumes is set into the surrounding walls.

He's quite the artist, Vale, and I find his drawings everywhere. Maps he's drawn, carefully detailed. Affinity patterns done up in multiple colors of ink. I can see he's tried to fit streams of elements together in elaborate, geometric designs. I pick up one of his patterns and study it, careful turning it this way and that, and immediately spot the errors in what he's working out, the equations worked in a firm, slashing hand along the edges. I can see the pent-up fire in his very handwriting—it's very similar to my own.

Weapons are scattered about, some even hanging from the walls. A number of swords, knives, three metal stars with runes engraved into them. I pick one of the stars up, the metal cold against my fingers. I gently touch the star's edge and draw in a sharp breath as it cleanly cuts through my skin, a small line of blood appearing, the sting following shortly afterward.

On Vale's bedside table sits a small tower of books. There's a slim white volume on top covered in complicated Alfsigr lettering.

I set the insanely sharp star down and go to his bed, sitting on its edge as I take the small volume in hand. I flip through it, making out scattered words in the flowing Alfsigr script.

Poetry.

And not just any poetry. Love poems.

I listen for Vale downstairs, awed by this secret discovery.

Vale's a romantic.

I momentarily forget how damp I am, set down the book and take in the riot of book titles on shelves all around me, my attention set alight to be in the presence of so many volumes. Grimoires. A number of Alfsigr books. Books on language. History. Science. Apothecary medicine. Mathematics. Military history. Shipbuilding. Metallurgy. And more grimoires.

I make my way over to his closet and peer inside at the row of tunics—all black silk or wool, well made without ornamentation. I finger one of them thoughtfully.

I hear his heavy steps downstairs and give a nervous jolt, releasing the fabric in my hands.

He's just below me. In Edwin's bedroom. Probably sliding out of his wet clothes.

My breathing quickens. I pull one of his tunics out, and a pair of pants, giving them an appraising look for size. I find some twine on his worktable and cut it to size with a jewel-handled knife.

Standing before the woodstove, glancing worriedly toward the door, I clumsily reach back to loosen my tunic's lacing. The wet laces have grown hard and tight, and loosening them takes some time. Finally, I peel off my soaked tunic, camisole and long skirt, hanging them over the backs of chairs to dry. I stand in front of the woodstove in just my pantalets, my shivers subsiding as the stove's warmth courses through me, quickly drying the skin of my chest. I'm suddenly aware of the uncurtained window, my naked chest, my nipples standing out in hard points, gooseflesh rising on my chilled skin. I hastily slide Vale's tunic on over me, the silk smooth over my breasts.

His tunic is loose and I have to roll up the sleeves, but it fits me like a short dress. The pants are disastrously ill-fitting, slightly tight in the hips, but huge in the waist. They pucker as I cinch them tight with twine, wrapping another piece of twine around my waist to secure his tunic. I hunt around and find a drawer of black woolen socks. I pull a pair on over my toes, the socks loose and bunching up, his feet so much larger than mine.

A hot thrill courses through me to be dressed in the same fabric he slides over his own muscular frame.

I sit down on his bed and run my hand over the covers.

He sleeps here. The man I'm now fasted to.

I try to imagine it. Serious, intense Vale, snuggled in under these very covers. His face blank and open in sleep. His black hair tousled on the pillow.

What does he look like when he sleeps?

I realize that I already know this. I remember him sleeping in Fain's tent. Staying there with me. All night. I remember how he looked.

Troubled and upset.

Glancing at the door, I listen closely for him. His steps thud across the downstairs floor, crossing directly below me.

I lean over and smell his pillow, briefly laying my body in the same spot I imagine he lays his. An exciting warmth courses over me. I can smell his scent on the wrinkled linen—fresh wood just catching flame on a chill autumn day, smoke on the crisp air. A hint of warm musk.

I like it, I realize. *I like the smell of him.*

Reluctantly, I set the pillow back, smooth the sheets to hide the evidence of my curiosity and go to join him downstairs.

He's in dry clothes as I haltingly make my way down to the kitchen, his too-large socks slippery on my feet against the pol-ished Ironwood stairs.

Vale watches me as I descend. He's leaning against the kitchen counter, his lips slightly parted, staring as if I'm a breathtakingly beautiful vision dressed in the finest silks and gems, coming down a stately flight of stairs to a lavish ball. Not an exhausted Lower River girl with damp hair wearing ill-fitting men's clothing and bunchy socks.

His eyes and his fire flicker over me.

He straightens, formal again, and blinks at me as if in a daze. "May I...may I show you the rest of the house?" One of his cats jumps onto the counter, and he idly pets it. "My library's through here," he says, pushing an adjacent door open to reveal a cozy room walled with bookcases, arching windows overlooking the ocean. There's a couch placed up against the windows with a stack of books on one side.

"It's good you have a library," I archly comment, glancing back toward the tome-laden kitchen table. "There's such a dearth of books around here."

He laughs and shoots me a sidelong glance of amusement. "No. No dearth of books. You've had a dearth of food, though," he says. "I'll show you the pantry. In case you're hungry for something."

I follow him through a door at the far corner of the kitchen that cuts into the stone of the surrounding rock, the temperature chilling as we walk down a short, cavernous path. Vale grabs a hanging lantern and quickly lights it with his wand, the guttering light flicking over the stone. Over us.

I'm struck again by a surreal sense that I'm in a dream—following a powerful Level Five Mage into his *pantry*.

Vale opens a wooden door that has a small door for the cats hewn into the bottom.

I immediately gape as I enter, transfixed on the sight before me.

The entire room is lined with deep shelves and large barrels of grain. Carrots and root vegetables are packed in sawdust on the floor. A row of shelves houses wheels of cheese and a large variety of preserved fruits and vegetables in glass jars. Dried meat, fish and sausages hang from the ceiling.

The cats flow in and wind around the room.

"They keep the vermin at bay," Vale idly comments, picking up and stroking the short-haired cat. The cat purrs loudly in response and pushes her head up against the sharp line of Vale's jaw, making it clear Vale's affection for these cats veers beyond the practical.

"It's not a lot," he apologizes, looking around. "Rather modest fare, but I hope you'll find it sufficient."

I stare at him, staggered.

It's more food put together in one place, in one home, than I have ever seen in my entire life. Like a whole market full of food.

I reach behind me for the edge of a shelf for support, slumping against it.

"Is Wren…is he going to eat like this?" I ask, my voice gone low, feeling suddenly light-headed.

"Oh, good gods, no," he says. "My house in Valgard is much larger. I have my own cook there. She'll let them draw up a menu. Their favorite foods, and so forth. With an eye for health, of course. For your brother." He gives me a significant look.

It's over. All over. Our struggle for food.

The crushing weight of our poverty is lifting so quickly that the world tilts beneath me, the very ground shifting. The struggle of years and years coming to an abrupt end.

"We never ate like this," I tell him, gaping at a hanging smoked ham. "I don't think you understand." I try to swallow, my throat gone dry. I stare at a row of berry preserves directly before me. "They stopped selling to us. So many of the Kelts. They wouldn't sell to Crows anymore. Jules would bring us things, but we didn't have money for much. Dried peas. Bar-

ley. Beans. Cheap food. I used to glean for the damaged vegetables that no one wanted. But…the farmers stopped allowing
it. And soon, Doveshire outlawed it. For our kind, anyway.
I… I've been through refuse bins, Vale. I've stolen food a few
times. There were times it got *that bad*."

My legs feel wobbly, and my hand slides down to find a
soft, solid surface. I look down to find the largest bag of grain
I've ever seen.

I own this. Wren has food. More food than he could ever eat…

"Tessla? Are you all right?"

"He's sick," I choke out, the floodgates suddenly flung wide
open, a storm of emotion coursing through me. "Wren's sick.
He's been sick a long time."

"I know," Vale says. He sets the cat down and looks at me
closely. "The Red Grippe. I left orders for my family's physician to tend to him. Fain will make sure he's given *Obsythian*
tonic this week."

All the blood drains from my face, and I stagger down until
I'm sitting on the floor.

He'll be cured of it. Just like that. He'll live.

"Tessla?"

I bring my hand to my eyes, overtaken by a staggering relief. "Oh, Ancient One. Vale. Thank you so much. Oh, Ancient One. Thank you."

"We're fasted, Tessla," he says, his voice low and gentle,
tinged with confusion. "Of course I'd do anything for you."

His noble sentiment and kindness send shockwaves through
me. I cry hot tears of overwhelming gratitude into my hand.

Vale is quiet for a long moment. Then I hear him come
closer, kneeling down before me.

"He'll be cured," he says, his voice near me now, his fire
coursing steady. "Completely cured. He'll have the best of everything."

"Where are they now?" I ask him, my face wet with tears.

"I suspect they're both in Valgard by now. Wanting for nothing. We'll visit them at week's end if you'd like."

"I can never thank you enough," I cry, breaking down again. "*Ever*. Thank you. Thank you, Vale. Thank you." I wipe at my tears with my tunic sleeve, realizing, too late, how messy I'm getting his clothing. "I know you've money, Vale, but still, *Obsythian* tonic—it's so wildly expensive."

He gives a short laugh. "Tessla, I'm *extremely* rich. And now you are, too."

I nod, trying to catch my breath. "Of course. Your mother's money."

He pulls his head up sharply. "No. *My* money. Tessla, I cleared the entire Salish Pass of kraken. There's a hefty bounty for that. Three years, on and off, at sea, killing the vile things. Plus, as a Wind Mage, dealing with storms and so forth—I've a fair bit of wind power, Tessla, just like you do. So I've more than enough of my own money. *None* of it from my mother."

"I—I'm sorry," I stammer, thrown. "I meant no offense."

Vale sits down against the shelf opposite me, the hard edges of his expression softening. "No offense taken." He takes a long breath and lets it out, studying me. "Tessla, you've been carrying a heavy load for far too long. Let me help you."

His large, green-eyed cat jumps up into my lap, purring. Weeping, I stroke the cat's silky fur, and it spins around to form itself into a contented, sleepy ball. A leaden exhaustion presses down on me. I shake my head from side to side. "I've been so lonely, Vale." The confession catches me off guard, but I'm starved for companionship. It seems to startle him, too. As if this moment of intimacy has pierced a constant feeling of isolation for the both of us.

"You're not alone anymore," he says, his fierce eyes hot on me. "You're safe here. And you never have to be alone again."

CHAPTER TWENTY-FOUR:
Blue Lightning

I'm exhausted but oddly restless when I return to Vale's bedroom. I pull off Vale's woolen breeches and climb into his bed, nestling in under the covers, dressed now only in his tunic, my pantalets and socks. Dark rain streams down the windows, but it's warm and cozy in here, with a roasting fire crackling in the woodstove.

Vale's short-haired cat, *Vor'nin*, jumps up on the bed to curl at my feet.

I turn, taking in the tower of books he has on his bedside table. The volumes are stacked unevenly in a way that seems quite precarious. I carefully pick up the Alfsigr poetry book and the language translation dictionary just under it, then puzzle through the volume for a good long while by the flickering lamplight. It's a good distraction, trying to translate the complicated Alfsigr language, and it slightly dampens the turbulent firestorm churning inside me.

I notice the book is heavily creased on one page in particular. I try opening the book several times to see where the pages open up to on their own, and always come back this poem.

"Sollil'lynir." Loneliness.

I spend a while piecing together the translation, the poem full of metaphors for painful solitude.

A winter moon. A frozen lake. A single candle in a midnight forest.

Vale's steps sound out below, and my heart quickens.

Is he as aware of me as I am of him, even separated by a whole floor?

Cheeks flushed, I go back to translating, but eventually, my eyes grow too heavy for the task, and I clumsily reach to set the book back on Vale's teetering tower of volumes.

Half the tower falls onto the bed, a heavy history of the Urisk clonking painfully against my shoulder.

My eyes watering from the painful blow, I inwardly curse at the ceiling, then turn back to the destroyed tower of books, now cut in half. Another slim volume rests on the small tower's top, its cover a tapestry of rioting colors, its spine embossed and hand-gilded. A Noi water god and goddess passionately embrace in the center of the riotous design, their hair made of the ocean's waves.

I immediately think of Fain's tent and his cacophony of Ishkart tapestries.

It seems so out of place among all the scholarly volumes, and my curiosity wins out over my crushing fatigue. I set it aside, restack Vale's volumes, then pick up the exotic book and flip through it.

My eyes widen as I take in the images that make up the volume. Each print depicts a divine couple, their water hair wild and flowing. They're dressed in intricately embroidered yet conservative clothing, but their tunics are unfastened, cast into disarray.

A surge of hot, titillating shock sizzles through me as I realize that the couples are copulating, their joinings depicted in shockingly graphic detail.

I close the book quickly, heart thudding, a bolt of sparking heat flashing through me, as if I'm committing a salacious crime and will be discovered at any moment. I look nervously to the door, furtive, hunching down. I bring up my knees to hide the book on my lap, ready to slip it under the covers at the slightest sound. Ears primed for any sign of Vale coming up the stairs.

But the house remains silent.

I sneak another peek at the book, a hot flush starting on my face, streaking down my neck. A warm, wildly disconcerting tension rises between my legs. I tense my thighs against it and keep looking.

I've never seen anything remotely like this.

Where did Vale come across such a book? I flip to the inside cover and find Fain's artistic script.

To Vale,
So you'll know where to put it.
As Always,
Fain

I flip through the book again and, like the poetry book, it opens easily to one heavily creased page. It's clear that this page has been returned to again and again, like a fly to a sticky sweet. It depicts a woman straddling a man, the man on his back. She's riding him like a horse.

I stare, mouth agape, both fascinated and shocked.

Is this what he likes?

I hear Vale's footsteps moving toward the stairs. I panic, fumbling with the book, dropping it on the floor, a giddy, nervous tension flashing through me. I scramble to reach it, then thrust the volume deep under the pillow behind me, my heart hammering, sure that he'll be knocking on the door at any moment.

But the knock never comes. Instead, I hear the downstairs door slam shut.

I go to the window and peek out to see Vale stalking into

the night, the storm moving off, the rain lessening. A full moon fitfully pokes through the fast-moving clouds, thunder still rumbling in the distance.

He's thrown off his tunic, the skin of his back glimmering a faint emerald in the dark. His wand tight in his fist, he follows the path down to the beach, then drops down on one knee in the sand and throws blue lightning out across the water. The bolt's crackling intensity casts blue light over the entire world, clear into the bedroom.

Vale stands and stalks up and down the beach, and I can just make out his expression, fierce and full of a tense frustration. He stops and hurls his arm out, lightning branching clear up to the clouds, piercing through them, sending more branches of lightning bolting sideways through adjacent clouds and then scything down to the ocean below.

The whole world pulses blue.

I watch him for a long time, my forehead pressed against the cold glass, in awe of his power. The ferocity of his magic. My breath sends foggy puffs to coat the glass's surface, rendering Vale's unsettled form misty. My eyelids grow heavy and I fall asleep for a few seconds at a time, jerking back awake at each new crack of his lightning.

Eventually, I rise, and take one last look at him as he furiously throws out bolt after bolt after bolt.

Then I slip under the warm covers of his bed, firelight and blue light pulsing over me. I turn and inhale Vale's enticing scent deeply, pull myself into a tight ball and surrender to sleep.

I'm running through the dark woods, twigs cutting at my face, my heart racing, my panicked breathing loud in my ears.

I'm prey. And they're after me—the huge ax-paladin and the Icaral demon.

The ax-paladin's hand clasps tight around my arm, jerking me back, blunt nails digging into my skin as the Icaral looks on, the creature's demonic fire coursing through me with churning ferocity.

I cry out as the ax-paladin throws me to the ground and falls on me, the demon close on his heels.

I struggle and scream as the ax-paladin pins my arms down and looks me over with manic eyes, excited by my fear and desperate struggle.

"Tessla!" Someone shouts my name from somewhere, far away.

I scream louder, wrench my wrist free and punch the ax-paladin in the face with all my strength.

My knuckles explode with pain, and the scene shatters around me. I'm thrust into immediate, wild confusion.

There's a half-naked man before me, cradling his face, one hand around my wrist as I buck and struggle and flail against him. He pulls sharply away, and I wrench my hand from his grip, scuttling toward the back of the bed, wildly disoriented.

"I'll kill you if you come near me!" I snarl at him, violence coursing through me like black fire, both hands clenched into fists. "I swear I will!" I turn, grab up a short sword from the head of the bed and pull it from its sheath with a metallic screech.

"Great gods, put down the sword, Tessla!" Vale's voice is muffled and he's doubled over, his hand tight over his nose, his palm out to halt me. "I'm not trying to attack you! You were dreaming!" He pulls his hand briefly away, blood all over his face, all over his palm, streaking down his chest.

I hesitate, heart hammering and sword held high.

He curses in Alfsigr, then puts his hand back over his nose, pivots and lies across the foot of the bed, arching his head backward.

"What are you doing?" I cry.

He glares at me. "Trying to stop the bleeding! Put down

the damn sword!" His voice is muffled, but stern, and it cuts through my senseless panic.

Everything falls together. *The dream. The terrible dream.* *I'm not in the woods. It was all just a dream.*

I take a deep, shuddering breath, my panic slowly receding. I lower the sword.

I punched him. I punched Vale.

It's a shock to see him sprawled out over his bed. Lean and muscular. The tops of his hipbones jutting up from his pants. His chest, streaked with blood. His head thrown backward, long neck arcing.

His half-naked state pushes my alarm higher.

"Why are you unclothed?" The question comes out as an unfortunate shriek.

"I heard you screaming," he grinds out, pinching his nose tightly. "I didn't throw on my tunic. I just grabbed my wand." He holds up his wand and flicks it idly in the air. "I quickly realized you were dreaming, and I was *trying* to wake you."

I huddle at the top of the bed, trembling and hating myself for it.

"Can I have a handkerchief?" he asks. "Top drawer, side table."

I fish out a handkerchief from the drawer and hand it to him with shaking hands. He takes it with a wary glance, keeping his head back.

I eye the blood on his chest. "That's a lot of blood," I say apologetically.

He throws me an incredulous look. "Well, you hit me *really* hard."

"I'm sorry," I say in a small voice.

He lets out a sigh that's muffled by the handkerchief and shakes his head, glowering at the ceiling. "It's not just because of you. I'm prone to this."

"Getting punched?"

He coughs out a laugh, then cringes. "No, nosebleeds. Whenever I pull air magic…if I pull too much, my nose bleeds. It's an incredible nuisance. Amuses Fain to no end."

There's a dark bruise blooming under his eye.

"Did I break your nose?" I ask, horrified.

He sighs. "I don't know."

"Do you have *arncian* tonic?" I ask, tentatively. "It's good for this sort of thing."

"No, I do not," he says drolly. "Being a *Level Five Mage*, I'm not often punched."

I hug my knees and wipe my residual tears away. The larger cat jumps up on the bed and then onto Vale's stomach. Vale's muscles tense in response. Then he shakes his head, as if resigned to mayhem, and strokes the cat.

After a few minutes, he sits up, still pinching his nose with the handkerchief. Slowly, he pulls it away, dabbing his nose, studying the soiled cloth.

"Am I still bleeding?" he asks me, both of his eyes anchored by dramatic bruising, though much worse on the left side.

"I don't think so," I say, shrinking down, chastened. "I'm so sorry, Vale."

Vale nods and looks around. There's a smattering of blood on the white sheets.

"Well," he says to me with a sigh and a weary glance. "Looks like we bloodied the sheets after all."

I gape at him, a bit put off.

Vale purses his lips, as if horrified with himself. "I'm sorry, Tessla. That was in poor taste."

I shake my head. "No. Don't apologize." I glance sidelong at his bruised eyes. "I suppose this isn't any man's dream of a sealing night."

"Punched and bleeding all over the bed? Not really," he readily agrees. "It does put a new spin on *Sanguin'en*, though."

I look to him sheepishly. "Both your eyes." I bring my finger up to trace under my own eyes. "They're blackened. It's really bad on one side. People will think I fought you off me."

He shoots me a level stare. "You did, in fact, fight me off you."

I sigh deeply and shoot him a rueful look.

"Well, this should be entertaining when we rejoin polite society." He arches his brow at me. "Don't you think?"

No consummation lines. Vale with two black eyes and a potentially broken nose.

"I'm sorry," I say again, the words sounding hollow.

Vale absently folds the handkerchief over in his lap, and I notice how graceful and long his fingers are.

"There's so many rumors about me already," he says with a resigned breath. "Why not add a few more?" He sends me a wry smile.

"I like you, Vale," I blurt out, shock spinning through me at my own admission.

He bursts out into a short laugh, then winces, reaching up to massage the bridge of his nose. "Thank you, Tessla. Thank you for clarifying."

His eyes light on something just behind me and flare wide open, his fire surging in sudden, chaotic streaks.

I turn and am horrified to see Fain's book peeking out from under my pillow.

The light in here is dim, but it's easy to see the deep flush now coloring Vale's cheeks. "It was a present," he tells me, looking mortified. "From Fain. In jest. He gave it to me a few years back."

I'm flushing, too. I can feel the heat of it on my cheeks, down my neck. I hug my knees, looking anywhere but at him. "I've never seen anything like…that. Ever."

He nods and swallows audibly. "Neither had I." He looks to the ceiling, as if wanting to be swallowed up by it.

I eye him, brow raised. "Those pictures. Is that…is that what you want?"

He takes a deep breath, then eyes me narrowly. "Tessla, I've had about as much experience with…these matters as you. I've no idea what's even logistically possible in that book. I seriously doubt some of it…" He trails off, his ruddy flush deepening.

I'm beyond embarrassed, but also painfully curious. "You like the one with the woman…riding the man…like he's a pony?"

He shrugs and looks sidelong at me. "It's…interesting." He lets out a deep sigh. "Not all people are as staid as ours. The Noi, they're more…open-minded." He motions toward the book. "You must be curious. I certainly was. You can look at it, if you'd like."

When I don't respond, he gives me a level look. "We're fasted, Tessla. No sense having secrets from each other. There it is." He points at the book. "My big secret. I own that book. I think, in the realm of secrets, it's quite minor."

"It's…it's wildly improper!" *And you looked at every single page*, I remind myself.

Vale spits out a laugh. "So is your having a wand, last I checked."

"This is entirely different."

He cocks his brow. "Is it?"

I glance sidelong at the book. "So," I say tentatively, "you haven't been with anyone?"

He spits out a laugh. "Women are terrified of me." His mouth gives a bitter twist. "Apparently I project a great deal of fire when I…kiss. It scares them."

"How many women have you kissed, then?" I trace a line of stitching on his quilt, feigning disinterest.

"Three."

I meet his eyes, waiting for more.

He lets out a long sigh. "There was a Salishen girl. I was sixteen and at sea for the first time. On board as their Wind Mage. The crew knew I'd never…" He gestures with one hand, a loose circular motion. "So they paid the girl and snuck her in with me. I'd been sleeping. She slithered under the covers, right on top of me. I thought I was dreaming. I…well, I kissed her. Sent fire through her." He looks down at the wand in his lap, rolling it in his fingers. "It's hard for me to control my fire when I'm that close to a woman." He looks at me, gaze intense, color burning high on his cheeks.

I flush. "What happened?"

He shrugs. "She ran away. Yelling that she'd been burned by a demon." His mouth gives a cynical twist, but I can sense his discomfort in how fitful his fire's grown. "I heard them outside, telling her that they'd already paid her. They threw her back into my room."

"What did you do?"

"Once she calmed down, we played cards most of the evening." He takes in my surprised look. "Well, I wasn't about to throw myself at her. And I didn't want them to abuse the poor girl. The crew just assumed…" He bobs his head and shoots me a pointed glance.

"Did you ever see her again?"

His face tenses uncomfortably. "A few years later, on the streets of Salish. She was strung out on nilantyr."

My brow furrows with a silent question.

"It's a powerful drug," he explains, then shakes his head, as if clearing away an unpleasant memory.

"And the second kiss?" I ask hesitantly.

"Ah, yes. That was a few years ago. At the University. A Keltic girl, friends with Jules and me. She was inexplicably fond of me. One night I kissed her, and it quickly cured her of both her attraction to me and all feelings of friendship. She avoided me from that point on. I overheard her telling another woman that kissing me was like kissing a bolt of lightning." The line of his jaw hardens. "Of course, once my mother took power, there were quite a few women who were willing to suffer through being with me. For power. For money."

I nod in understanding. "Like Genna Thorne."

Vale spits out a sound of disdain. "Genna Thorne would never have been able to handle my fire."

The room goes quiet. The only sound is the wind whipping outside.

"And the third?"

His eyes darken, and he looks probingly at me.

Astonishment washes over me. *Me. I'm the third.*

He takes a deep breath and looks down at the wand in his lap. "That night, you were coming untethered. You needed fire. And fast. Your affinity was disappearing. I tried to feed fire into you with my wand pressed up near your heart, the pulse at your neck. I tried several spells."

I remember his hands on me, and my cheeks grow warmer.

"It almost worked. But I couldn't get enough fire into you. And then I remembered." His mouth turns up in a crooked grin, his eyes two simmering coals. "Kissing me is like kissing a bolt of lightning." He pauses, growing quiet. "I'm glad it worked."

I loved it. I loved it. I loved it. The memory beats out with the rhythm of my heart.

"And you saved me."

"I saved you," he quietly affirms, but there's nothing quiet about the strength of his affinity fire billowing toward me.

"With a kiss."

His mouth turns up in a cynical grin, making light of it all, even though there's nothing light about the way his fire is raging. "So…was it like being kissed by a bolt of lightning?" He asks the question casually, as if my answer will be as insignificant as air. But I can feel how fraught with tension he is, and how easily I could shatter him.

"No," I tell him.

His eyes widen with surprise.

"It was like…" I flush, remembering, gripping at the sheets. "Like a torrent of flame. Broad and powerful and overwhelmingly hot. Flashing through me. It was…much more intense than a bolt of lightning."

"So…even worse." It's an attempt at dark humor, but I can practically feel the painful wound ripping open in him.

"No," I say, my voice almost a whisper. "Even better."

His fire sparks hard and hot. "You *liked* it?"

I loved it.

I give a tight nod.

His fire flares, running in a hot stream. When I look up at him, his eyes are pinned tight on me.

"I've scared someone with a kiss, too," I tell him, hugging my knees. "Like you scared those two girls. It was a few years back." I hesitate, my brow tensing. "A Kelt attacked me. One of the miller's sons. Dragged me into a barn. I screamed, but no one was there to hear."

"What happened?" he asks, and I can feel the change in his fire. An angry flare now. Fiercely protective. Wrapping itself around me.

"I kissed him," I tell him. "And I threw as much fire into him as I could summon."

His eyes narrow with approval. "Clever."

"He flew off me. Called me a demon whore. He told everyone I was a witch."

The memory saps my strength, and I suddenly feel the full weight of my crushing fatigue, my fire tamping down to a sullen simmer.

"It wasn't the first time," I tell him. "I was attacked twice in Doveshire." I'm trembling now, with pent-up anger. I've never told anyone this before, knowing that Grandfather wouldn't be willing to hear it. That he'd agitatedly wave me into silence and tell me not to speak of such things, to pray for renewed purity.

I look at Vale, straight in the eyes. "Prior to meeting you, I've never had a kiss that wasn't forced."

Vale winces at this and nods, staring at the floor. "Tessla," he says, his voice low and emphatic. "I will never, *ever* force myself on you. I hope you'll believe that, in time. I lack charm, but I won't abuse you."

I nod, his warmth coursing over me, my own fire bursting in chaotic fits and starts. Charm, at this moment, seems incredibly overrated.

"I'm a scholar, Tessla," Vale says, quiet and tentative. "Or was. At the University. And I love books. Just like you. I think that's patently obvious." The corner of his mouth turns up, and he gestures around at his scattered piles of books for emphasis. He shoots me a wry look, then grows serious. "All those things you've been wanting… I think you'll find you could have them with me. May I…may I court you?"

Ridiculous laughter bubbles up. I hold up my fast-marked and sealed hands, the design a perfect mirror of the marks on his skin. "Don't you think you're doing this *backward*?"

Vale laughs with me, his expression lightening. "I suppose I am." He looks to me, breathless with hope, and my heart skips a beat.

He's achingly handsome, especially in the firelight.

Everything is suddenly different. The whole world on its head.

Vale wants to court me. Wants to be touched by me.

And I want it, too.

"Will you," he says tentatively, "consider it?"

My head is spinning, and I can't suppress my smile. "Yes, Vale. You can court me. I'd like that."

His brow goes up in surprise, as if he'd never imagined I'd say yes. "Well then..." He trails off, looking around, as if he doesn't know where to start. All of his hard arrogance is suddenly gone. He blinks at me, speechless, and I'm struck by how young he looks in this moment.

"How old are you, Vale?" I ask him.

"Twenty. Just this past month."

I consider this. "I thought you were older."

He raises his brow. "How old?"

"I don't know. Twenty-six, maybe?"

He gives me a crooked smile. "It's those three years at sea. I'm weathered, apparently. And I look like her."

His features are so elegant and intimidating. I resist the urge to reach out and run my finger along the sharp lines of his cheekbone, along his defined jaw.

He swallows, transfixed, his fire meeting mine. "How old are you?"

The question catches me off guard. "I'm eighteen," I suddenly remember. "Or at least I will be, tomorrow."

His eyes widen. "Your birthday? It's tomorrow?"

I nod, as surprised as him.

"I'll take you to Valgard. To celebrate." His gaze is searching. "If you'd like. You can see your brother, and your grandfather." He pauses. "If you want to see your grandfather, that is."

"No, I do." In the wake of everything I've learned about Vale, my anger toward Grandfather has dissipated a great deal.

"I'll take you to hear the orchestra." His tone turns ardent. "We can dine on the finest food. Anything. Anything you want. You can buy anything you like."

"A horde of dragons?" I cheekily inquire, happiness unexpectedly blossoming inside me.

Vale laughs. "Of course." He beams at me, a defiant fire lighting his eyes. "And a wand to go with them."

CHAPTER TWENTY-FIVE:
Valgard

Vale is quiet on the carriage, peering out the window as if deep in thought, but his secret, grasping heat is palpable and makes me flush.

I realize I like how singularly his affinity fire is fixated on me.

I'm dressed in simple but elegant silken garb, Ironflowers embroidered in raised black designs along my tunic and skirt hem. A seamstress arrived this morning with a full wardrobe for me—compliments of Mage Fain Quillen.

I smile to myself, ever grateful for Fain's kindness toward me.

We ride over the crest of a hill, and Gardneria's capital city, Valgard, bursts into view.

It's a sight to behold, ringing the gleaming Malthorin Bay, sunlight spearing down through dramatic gray clouds hung low over the ocean.

We begin the descent toward the city. Jagged, jutting cliffs rise all around us, our carriage path slicing through gaps in the hillside. The road's sheer drop on my side is dizzying. Alarmed, I glance toward Vale to find him smiling at me, amused by my obvious discomfiture. I shoot him back a look of mock annoyance.

We ride into the heart of the city to find Valgard puls-

ing with the excitement of a nation reborn, jubilation ringing through the air. Our flag, outlawed in all the surrounding
lands, hangs defiantly everywhere I look—streaming from shop
windows and lodging houses, affixed to practically every carriage and horse's saddle. Knots of wide-eyed refugees in ill-
fitting black attire make their way through the city, many of
them accompanied by Gardnerians wearing white armbands
and acting as their protectors.

"It's so strange to me," I say to Vale, who's watching me
closely. "Our flag. Everywhere. Everyone dressed in our sacred clothing. It was dangerous to be Gardnerian for so long,
especially in Doveshire."

Vale's expression sharpens. "And soon it will be dangerous
to be anything else."

A few days ago, I would have bristled at this. Shot down his
pretentious views, deeming them anchored in his privileged
upbringing, always one step removed from any real suffering.
But after a forced wandfasting, I see things differently. I've
tasted the edges of something dark—something dangerous that
rides along the underbelly of our people's newfound power.

"Look at them," Vale says with an air of foreboding. "So
untroubled. So sure. So ready to rain the suffering done to us
down on everyone who isn't Gardnerian." Pain slashes across
his face, some private grief. I cast him a questioning look, but
he shakes his head and looks away. I study him tensely for a
long moment, then glance back out the window.

Gardnerians are out in force, packed tables spilling out into
the road at a multitude of restaurants and guest houses, people
eating, children waving small flags.

I draw back, surprised by the sight of pointy-eared, rose-
white Urisk women in light gray tunics and skirts dotting the
city—clearing tables, sweeping streets, their rose hair tied back
in tight braids.

"There are Urisk here," I blurt out, with no small amount of confusion and alarm.

Vale notes my shock with grave calm. "They're Uuril, Tessla. They're the lowest Urisk class, slaves to the other Urisk. Or they were. Years ago, a great many of them fled north." He lets out a deep breath and eyes me soberly. "The original Uuril refugees were welcomed here and treated reasonably well for a time. But that ended with the onset of the border hostilities." His expression darkens. "They were promptly roped into servitude—the men to help us build our own dragon army, the women forced into what amounts to slavery again."

Our carriage slows to a stop, and Vale watches as an elderly Uuril woman with a hunched back sweeps refuse off the street, sad sympathy in his gaze.

I look to the woman, her skirts edged with street dirt, her pale face deeply lined and filled with a palpable grief that's troubling to note. I was so recently a despised refugee myself, with nowhere to go. A conflicted compassion rises inside me for this outcast woman.

"I know how she feels," I tell Vale as I watch the woman labor.

"The Gardnerians seem to be in a contest with the Urisk," Vale says bitterly. "A contest to see who can treat the Uuril worse. It's hard to top the Urisk royalty for sheer cruelty, but I think we're currently winning." His frown deepens. "In any case, we'll be visiting that same cruelty on the Urisk upper classes soon enough."

"Good," I say flatly, remembering the terrifying blue-skinned Urisk soldiers, ready to set my family alight.

Vale shoots me a level look. "Really, Tessla? Should we kill them all? Their children, too?"

"Of course not," I answer, startled. "Not the children, but—"

"Where do you think this leads next?" he cuts in, gesturing toward the outside festivity. "Have you thought about it?"

There's an elderly Gardnerian woman with a white armband unfurling a Gardnerian flag from a window three stories up. The Gardnerian refugees on the street below applaud and cheer, ignoring the rose-haired Uuril woman as she sweeps.

"Our people are celebrating their freedom," I say, turning back toward Vale. "You should be happy about that."

"I am," he agrees, but his troubled expression doesn't waver.

The carriage lurches forward, the scene whisked from sight.

I let out a deep sigh as I take in the multitude of flags flapping in the sun. Vale's grown quiet, and I glance over at him as he abstractedly peers out the window, my eyes wandering over his long frame.

He cuts a fine figure, my fastmate—dauntingly severe in his dark garb, his blackened eyes only adding to his look of reckless danger.

"I'm glad we're not being killed anymore because of our prayer books," he finally says, frowning. "Or because of our clothing."

I consider this, my eyes drawn in by him, like a moth to flame.

"You know, it suits you." I gesture toward his clothes. "Our garb. I can't picture you in anything but black."

He eyes me sidelong and grins. "It mirrors my lack of mirth."

A short laugh erupts from me at this, and a tendril of his fire reaches out to pulse through me. Our eyes briefly meet, a small flush rising on both our cheeks.

Unsettled, I turn my attention to the docks we're passing, instantly fascinated by the variety of ships and skiffs.

"There," he says, pointing past the line of docks. "That's my home, there."

Far in the distance, there's a raised causeway leading toward a circle of land, a traditional Gardnerian manor situated in the middle, ringed by a small forest of trees.

"Killing kraken pays well, doesn't it?" I gasp.

"Quite well." He shoots me a significant look. "If you saw them, you'd understand."

Vale is a quiet presence as we disembark from the carriage, the salty wind whipping my hair as we enter his sizable home.

An elderly Uuril woman ushers us inside, her skin a pale pink, her ears sharply pointed, her large eyes a vivid coral. I struggle to tamp down my shock at finding an Uuril servant here, especially after Vale's words in the carriage.

She smiles broadly at Vale. "It's so good to have you back, Mage Gardner." Her accent is thick, but lyrical and lovely. She grows silent, her warm smile dampening as she takes in the sight of his bruised face.

"Please don't ask, Senal'lyn," he tells her with a resigned sigh, absently rubbing his nose.

Her eyes dance with amusement. "I won't." She turns to me, beaming, and gives a slight, gracious bow. "It is a true pleasure to meet you, Mage."

I can feel Vale's eyes on me, sense him almost holding his breath in anticipation of my reaction. The Uuril woman also seems to be breathlessly waiting, vulnerability showing in her eyes. I think of the hunched woman in the street, of my recent refugee status—all of us caught up in events far beyond our control.

"It's a pleasure to meet you, as well," I tell her, extending my hand, my heart pounding high in my chest. She takes my hand and relief brims in her eyes, a wavering smile coming to her lips. Vale's regarding me with open gratitude.

Senal'lyn brings us to a library that overlooks the ocean as she chats amiably with Vale about affairs of the estate.

My grandfather is sitting in a richly cushioned chair by a well-stoked fire, his head bent, spectacles low on his nose, a book in his lap.

A brief stab of hurt and anger spikes into me as I remember how he forced me into fasting. I can sense Vale behind me, his fire flaring and then banked rigidly back, his affinity lines almost vibrating with uneasy tension.

Grandfather looks up, and his face lights at the sight of me, his papery skin wrinkling into an expression of pure joy. "Oh, my sweet Tess," he cries and falteringly rises.

At once, my anger dissolves, and a staggering wave of relief washes over me.

He's safe. And fine. His silver glasses brand-new.

A gray-haired Gardnerian woman in a steel-colored apothecary apron springs forward to support Grandfather's elbow. She hands him his cane.

Grandfather teeters toward me, and all of my remaining anger falls away. I'm overcome by a wave of protective affection for him and embrace his thin form without any malice. I throw a quick look toward Vale, who seems unmoved by Grandfather's feeble state. He remains still, his eyes narrowed severely.

He won't soon shed his grudge, I realize. I take in Grandfather's clean, new clothing. The apothecary hovering nearby. His newly trimmed white beard. The healthy color in his cheeks.

Vale might not like him, but he's caring for him, and that's enough for now.

Grandfather bows repeatedly toward Vale, hardly daring to make eye contact. "Mage Gardner... I am honored." He's clearly overwhelmed to have a Level Five Mage in our family, and the son of the Black Witch, no less. I'm not sure if he even notices Vale's blackened eyes—if he does, he doesn't dare say anything.

Grandfather reaches over to cling to my arm with a trembling hand. "Tessla, your brother. He's doing so well." He kisses his other fist and shakily makes the sacred sign of blessing over his chest three times.

"Tessie!" Wren bursts from an adjacent room and runs toward me.

My heart lurches, and I fall down to my knees, throwing my arms around my brother's slender frame, tears coming to my eyes. We grasp each other tightly as I laugh and cry all at the same time.

I pull back to look at him, overwhelmed with relief and joy.

He's dressed in fine Gardnerian silks, his hair neatly cut and clean. The dark circles under his eyes are much less pronounced. And for the first time in I can't remember how long, there's color lighting his cheeks. Fragile, but there. And the spots around his mouth—I can scarcely believe what I'm seeing. Only one day on the expensive medicine, and they're already almost gone.

Wren tugs at my hand, his eyes lit up. "Come see, Tessie! Come see what I have!"

I let Wren drag me into his new bedroom, just off the library. Grandfather and Vale follow us in. Two gigantic glass doors are thrown open to let in the unusually warm early autumn air. A small white kitten sits in the center of Wren's mussed bed and looks quizzically at us.

"Fain was here," Wren tells me excitedly as he picks up the kitten. His usual wheeze is markedly lessened.

"*Wrenfir Harrow*," Grandfather weakly chastises my brother as he totters up to my side. "Mind how you speak of our great Mages."

Wren glances briefly at Grandfather, his smile momentarily dampening. "Mage Quillen," he corrects himself.

I turn and look questioningly at Vale. "Fain was here?"

Vale's eyes flick toward mine, but he remains silent, his severe look not budging, his protective fire flaring out over me.

"Mage Quillen brought us here, Tessie!" Wren tells me, filling me in. "And he gave me the kitten!" The small animal twists in Wren's hands and meows. My brother hugs the kitten to his chest, and it begins to purr. "She likes me!"

"Did you name her yet?" I ask, overwhelmed by Fain's kindness.

"Snowy!" he tells me, coughing. But it's not the bone-deep rattle I've gotten used to. It's higher up in his chest. Much higher.

I want to leap for joy and kiss everyone in the room.

My fire flows out toward Vale, and he stolidly meets it.

"Fain's nice!" Wren enthuses, then looks worriedly at Grandfather. "I mean, Mage Quillen. He gave me this, too, Tessie!"

Wren grabs up an intricate mariner's scope from the bed and hands the golden instrument to me.

My eyes widen as I take it. It's no child's toy, this scope, and probably cost a pretty guilder. I peer through it, out over the bay. The optics are exquisite. I can see clear over to the distant ship I'm looking at, the lines in the halyard rope as vivid as if I held the rope right in my hands.

A laugh escapes me. "This is a really nice gift, Wren."

"*And* he brought us chocolate and gave me a book!" Wren points to a colorful bestiary lying on his bed. "He's nice, Tessie. I like him."

"Mage Quillen is so very kind," Grandfather tells me, glancing uneasily toward Vale. "He's *everything* a Mage should be."

Vale's eyes are tight on my grandfather. I can feel his fire crackling like hot oil in a pan.

I consider Grandfather with a resigned sigh. *You only like Fain because you don't really know him.* I can't help it—the thought slips through like dark water.

"Vale," I say, gesturing toward my brother, increasingly worried that he'll frighten Wren half to death with his withering stare and intimidating silence. "I don't believe you've met my brother, Wren."

Wren loses his smile and looks sidelong at Vale, eyeing him with trepidation.

Vale strides forward, his serious expression not wavering. He gives Wren a slight bow. "I'm honored to meet you, Mage Harrow."

Wren looks down at his shoes.

New shoes. Brand-new, well-fitting shoes.

My brother dares to glance up at Vale, looks quickly down again, then seems to rally his courage and eyes him squarely. He cocks his head at Vale, as if confused. "What happened to your eyes? And your nose?"

Vale's lip quirks. "A minor altercation." He looks closely at Wren. "Are you finding the house to your liking, Mage Harrow?"

Wren nods, his intimidation seeming to lessen, but then his expression darkens. "Grandfather says you're powerful." His eyes dart to Vale's wand, his expression quickly becoming filled with an almost beseeching hope. "He says you can kill dragons. And demons. And their soldiers, too. That's what Grandfather told me." Wren looks back up at Vale with an expectant gravity far beyond his years.

"I can," Vale says with rock-solid assurance. "You're *safe* here."

Wren's lip quavers, and then his face falls, his whole body slumping.

Vale puts his hand on Wren's thin shoulder. I can feel him pushing his fire, a hot flare of it, into Wren, bolstering my brother with the warmth.

Wren's head hangs low as a tear streaks down his cheek. His

mouth turns down in a trembling grimace. "I'm worried that they'll come back," he says in a small, rasping voice, almost a whisper. He looks to Vale, his eyes gone wide with raw, undisguised terror.

Vale comes down on one knee, his hand still on Wren's shoulder. "I'm stronger than any of them," he says slowly, his voice laced with danger. "And you are now under *my* protection." Vale's fire blazes hot and he pushes it toward Wren.

Wren nods, looking relieved. He takes a deep breath, and my heart thrills at the sound of it.

It's the first clear breath I've heard my brother take in over two years.

CHAPTER TWENTY-SIX:
Kindred Lines

Vale stares out over the bay. A brilliant sunset breaks through the cloud cover and suffuses the gray clouds with a shimmering rose light that reflects off the water.

We're out on the outdoor balcony that wraps around the mansion's top floor, a beautiful view of Valgard and the sunset-colored bay splayed out in front of us. Lights are being lit all over the city, like a growing splash of stars.

"Your Uuril servants seem content," I observe. All five servants here greeted Vale's return with palpable relief. The haunted looks apparent in the Uuril we passed on the way here are markedly absent.

"I don't beat them or prey on them." His words are clipped, his fire flashing. He grows silent for a long moment, as if something dark and troubling is on his mind.

"Edwin and I were raised by a Uuril nursemaid," he finally says. "She was one of the refugees, fleeing north." He turns to me, his gaze probing in its intensity. "Edwin and I consider her to be our true mother." He sighs and looks back over the bay. "My Black Witch mother, once she started to come into her power...it *consumed* her. She had no time for child rearing. She hasn't the disposition for it, in any case."

"What of your sister, Vyvian?" I wonder, surprised by all this.

He shakes his head. "She had a different nursemaid, being a girl. Oralyrr. A different Uuril woman. She…wasn't kind." Vale spits out a bitter sound. "I had to threaten the woman several times when we were all children to keep her from taking the strap to Vyvian. Needless to say, my sister has no love for the Uuril. But Annel'lin—the woman who looked after Edwin and me—was very kind. Very loving. We were lucky."

We're both quiet for a time, looking out over the bay, watching a happy crowd gathered on one of the docked ships. They're sending paper lanterns up into the air.

"So, you see," Vale finally says, "hatred doesn't come so easily to Edwin and me. I'll rescue our refugees. Fight the Keltic and Urisk armies. Carve out a land where our people can be safe." He turns to me, eyes blazing. "But I won't slaughter our enemies' children. Burn their villages. Do to their families what they did to us. There are orders I *will not* follow, Tessla." His brow tenses. "I want our people to be safe. But I refuse to become as monstrous as the Kelts and the Urisk."

I let out a long breath. "They were pretty monstrous, Vale. It's better that we're in power. No matter the cost."

"If it means killing children?" he shoots back. "Really? Where does it end, Tessla? Where? We're simply dressing the nightmare up in different clothes. *Ours.*" Vale glances back over the bay. His fire is fitful, like a confined cat. "A few weeks ago we were at the southern border," he says in a low voice. "We arrived too late. The Kelts had already rounded up about ten of our families, and…" He breaks off, anguish streaking across his face.

"And what, Vale?" I ask him gently.

"I was sent to fetch Malkyn Bane later that day. And I found him." Vale's eyes grow tormented, and he looks at me. "He slaughtered every Kelt in the adjacent village. Everyone.

Speared some with ice. Froze most of them. There were babies, children. Old women. Caked in ice."

I remember how Malkyn killed Daisie and feel chilled to the bone.

"It was more than revenge," Vale continues hoarsely. "He… made *sport* of them." His eyes fill with outraged tears. "He hung them from hooks. Pierced them clean through before he froze them."

I look at him with horror. "What did you do?"

He shakes his head in obvious disgust. "There was nothing I *could* do, Tessla. *She* sent him there, knowing what he's capable of. She doesn't care. Not after what's been done to us. Before, when we were weak, Mother talked about killing them all. And it seemed like a rallying cry. Not real. Not truly the goal. But now, I'm wondering what I've aligned myself with." His face hardens. "I'm withdrawing from military service. The war will soon be dying down, in any case. Our neighbors falling at our feet like a house of cards. Surrendering everywhere." He looks back out over the ocean.

"Where is she?" I ask him. "The Uuril woman who raised you?"

He narrows his eyes at me. "Far away from here. Safe from what's coming."

A dark foreboding pricks at me. "What's coming, Vale?"

I know the answer to this before he says it. "Our *vengeance*."

I consider this, my fire now flaring and as troubled as Vale's. Images of being herded toward the barn invade my mind, the children crying and screaming. Soldiers leering at us. Cursing at us. Ready to kill us all.

Our enemies were so terrifyingly cruel.

But being grabbed at the altar. Forced to wandfast by a crowd ready to rip me apart if I had indeed been Jules's lover. A crowd of my own people, ready to treat me as viciously as the Kelts and Urisk had, if I had truly been *staen'en*.

It's changed everything.

I take a deep breath and push every last bit of my fire out toward Vale.

His eyes widen with surprise, then lock on to mine as our fires lash tightly around each other in kindred lines.

Vale and I walk into the city, my arm threaded through his. We're barely touching, but still, we're wrapped up in each other—wrapped up in our interlacing fire.

Twilight is descending, the sky now deep blue over the ocean, black over the city. A cool breeze blows in from the ocean as seagulls squawk and wheel above us.

I barely notice any of it. I'm too consumed by how closely we're knitting our fires together. Intentionally. Tendril by tendril, tighter with every step.

Wordlessly.

Vale leads me along a cobbled path lined with Ironwood trees, their branches dotted with blue Ironflowers. A row of merchants' shops are just past the trees to our left, a narrow canal past the trees to our right. The rippling black water reflects the Ironflowers' sapphire light in shimmering lines, and small boats filled with jubilant Gardnerians float past. My eyes light on a wandcrafter's shop, and a spark of longing rises inside me. There's a golden Mage Council *M* near the shop's door—a reminder that the Council strictly regulates the sale of wands.

Firmly keeping me out.

"Mage Vale Gardner."

A burly, bearded man is walking toward us, his gait heavy and suffused with muscular strength, his black tunic edged with mariner blue. He comes to a stop before Vale, goes military straight and hits his fist to his heart with a dull thump.

"How are you, Bron?" Vale asks with cool formality.

"Quite well, Mage," Bron replies in a husky voice, narrowed eyes darting toward me.

"Allow me to introduce you to my fastmate," Vale says, his fire snapped into a stiff wall. "Tessla, this is Bron Scullor. Captain of the *Raven*."

"Mage." Bron gives a short bow to me, his gaze going to our fast-marked hands, the lines heavy and intricate, indicating that we've been not only wandfasted but also sealed. I see his brow furrow as he realizes that the lines don't extend up our wrists.

Sealed, but not consummated.

Bron looks up at me, as if he's trying to puzzle us out, but then his face goes carefully neutral. He glances back at Vale.

A flush heats my cheeks. I imagine that, by not adhering to tradition, to the usual wedding night consummation, I'm causing Vale no small amount of humiliation.

And we're reinforcing the rumors that already circulate about him and Fain.

Vale's fire has consolidated. Cold along the side facing Bron, hot on the inside. I'm quickly realizing he's often like this in public. Coiled. Ready to fight. Ready to pull his wand and release his fire.

Bron taps under his eye as he studies Vale's two black eyes, his bruised nose. "In a brawl, were you?"

Vale's gaze remains cool. "A misunderstanding."

Bron eyes him quizzically, then shakes his head and huffs a sigh. "Ancient One, I'd love to have you with us again. Damned kraken spawned before you killed it. We've a Level Four Water Mage with us, but he's nothing compared to you. Blasts at them, but doesn't kill the godforsaken things. Took him what felt like a fortnight to clear the pass. Now, if we had your fire…"

Vale is unmoved. "Down the road, perhaps. If my fastmate wishes to travel."

Bron gives me and then our hands another quizzical look. He narrows his eyes at Vale, as if he can't quite figure out his game.

"It's taking us forever to even reach the Salish Pass," Bron laments, his tone brimming with a deep-seated frustration. "We need *real* Magewind. Level *Five* Magewind."

"Let Fain know," Vale offers. "He's done fighting. He usually feels the pull to be back at sea."

Bron's face tenses, and he shakes his head. "These are superstitious times, Vale. You know how crews are, what with their prayers and talismans. We've even had to get a priest on board now." He screws up his face with disgust. "Waste of resources, I say, but the men insist on it. They're taking *The Book of the Ancients* quite literally these days, especially that one passage about blessings on a boat." He leans in to speak to Vale more privately, ignoring me, as if I'm merely Vale's accessory. "Tell Mage Fain to find a lady friend like you did." He gestures toward me with his chin and shoots Vale a significant look. "It would squelch the rumors, and I could employ him again, eh?"

Vale's face shuts down, his fire rearing tight and hot with sudden anger. "I'll relay the message."

Bron gives a heavy sigh, and his expression loses all artifice. "I'm sorry, Vale. I have to skirt the waters of hypocrisy carefully, eh?"

Vale glares at him.

Bron looks at Vale with weary resignation, bids us a pleasant night and takes his leave, his broad back quickly swallowed up by the crowds and the dark shadows.

"They fear rumors more than they fear kraken," Vale says with cutting sarcasm. "That makes a whole world of sense." He turns to me, a blistering heat in his eyes. "Do you know how many Gardnerians Fain's saved?"

I throw him a questioning look.

"Well over a thousand," he says tersely.

"That's a lot."

"Yes. It is, isn't it?" His fire is whipping about in hot, troubled lines, riding along the edges of his anger and fear. Fear for Fain in this newly strident Gardneria.

Justified fear.

"Vale…" I slide my hand down his sleeved forearm without thinking and take his hand in mine.

The second my skin touches his, Vale's fire gives such a hard flare that I gasp from the startling heat of it. The flare builds as Vale threads his fingers decidedly through mine and grasps my hand with firm pressure. His rigid wall of fire surges out and suffuses my entire arm, coursing clear into my chest. My own fire, suddenly unbridled, flies toward him and twines tight.

"Gods, Tessla." His lips part in stunned surprise, his gaze gone blurred. "It feels *really good* to hold your hand."

"I know," I agree, as shocked as he is, my breathing gone deep and languid, my heart thudding warmly. I swallow, his fire coursing through me in pulsating ripples of heat, my own fire slowing to pulse to his same disconcerting rhythm.

He rubs his thumb slowly along the side of mine, sending out a delicious trail of sparks.

"Oh, Vale," I gasp. "That's nice."

His eyes are locked on me with molten heat. I run my thumb along his skin in a slow circle, and his breath hitches, the cords of his neck tensing, his fingers tightening around mine.

"What's that like?" I ask, my breathing becoming uneven.

"It like…a waterfall of flame. I can feel it rippling up my arm. It's so…" He takes a shuddering breath, his gaze gone liquid. "It feels very nice." He leans in toward me, and I can feel his warm breath against my ear. "Tessla, if it feels this good to just hold your hand…"

"And here they are," Fain's teasing voice rings out just be-hind us. "The happy couple!"

Both Vale and I stiffen and straighten at the same time. We quickly unclasp our hands, as if caught doing something illicit. I thread my arm lightly through Vale's arm, my heart pound-ing, trying to appear casual.

"I've got us a lovely table, just at the water's edge." Fain's smiling at us gleefully, his cloak thrown rakishly over one shoulder, his bearing and appearance dashing as ever, the silver Mage stripes that edge his uniform glinting gold and blue with reflected lamp and Ironflower light. His eyes dart toward our flushed faces, my arm threaded through Vale's, and I realize he can probably read how high our fires are running.

His expression takes on an edge of feline mischief. "Well, don't you two seem cozy?" He looks to me, lip quirking, eyes narrowed in amused appraisal as he leans in conspiratorially. "He's not inspiring the same terror in you that he does in most women, I see."

Vale's heat is straining to get at me, and mine is just as bad. "I'm not afraid of Vale," I tell Fain.

Fain laughs and shoots me a fey smile. "Of course you're not, love. I've read your affinity lines. You *are* Vale."

He looks to Vale, his brow knitting as he studies him even more closely in the darkness. "Sweet Ancient One, Vale. Were you in a battle?"

"Tessla hit me," Vale tells him evenly.

Fain blinks at us both, one eyebrow cocked in confusion.

"It's true," I tell Fain. "I hit him. As hard as I could."

I venture a glance at Vale at the same moment he looks at me. Amusement bubbles up, and we both grin like complete fools.

Fain takes it all in in one sweeping glance—how closely our arms are threaded, Vale's bruised face, our unconsummated fastlines. Our ridiculous grins.

"She almost ran a sword through me as well," Vale idly comments. He tries to pull his expression into its usual aloof severity when he says this, but it won't hold, and we're soon grinning stupidly again, basking in this exciting new warmth between us, our fires reaching for each other.

The two of us unexpectedly, deliriously happy.

Fain gives us both an arch look. "You two are a sheer abyss of contradiction. Do you know that?"

"I had a nightmare," I begin to lightly explain, smiling, as if merely recounting a tale. But my smile quickly fades, remembering the terrible dream. I feel Vale's fire coursing toward me protectively now, and when I look up at him, his gaze is full of concern.

Fain has grown somber, dark understanding lighting his eyes. "It doesn't matter, sweetling," he says with an affectionate smile, leaning in to pat my arm. He shoots Vale a look of mock disapproval. "I'm sure he had it coming to him about twenty times over. But enough of this." Fain smiles charmingly at me. "We've a birthday to celebrate! Let's join everyone, shall we? Edwin and Lucretia are waiting."

"Lucretia?" I question.

Fain grins, beaming. "One of my three sisters."

CHAPTER TWENTY-SEVEN:
Weapons

Vale's brother, Edwin, is disheveled and stocky compared to his elegant siblings, his black hair mussed, clothes wrinkled, wire spectacles slightly off-kilter and perched low on his nose. He has none of Vale and Vyvian's natural grace and aloof severity, nor anything of his powerful mother in his visage—save her deep green eyes.

Fain introduces everyone, deflecting questions about Vale's bruises with a vague, dismissive explanation.

Edwin takes my hand in his, blinking back and forth at Vale and me with an air of baffled confusion, as if he can't, for the life of him, believe that his stern brother has landed a now-willing fastmate.

"It's a great pleasure to meet you, Tessla," he says, shaking my hand warmly. I sense little magic in him, save the faintest tremor of earth. He's shy and unsure in his manner, yet I catch a quick intelligence in his eyes that mirrors Vale's.

I have a feeling that still waters run deep within Edwin Gardner, and I like him immediately.

"You're the musician," I say, remembering that night when I was still Magedrunk, when Edwin was playing a violin outside the tent by the fire.

"And you're the Mage who single-handedly fought off a

horde of Kelt and Urisk soldiers," he says with a trace of a smile. "Which explains why my brother hasn't scared you off yet."

I laugh at this and smile at Edwin, but it's hard to concentrate on anything but Vale—his fire is running so hot, straining relentlessly toward me, wanting to leap straight through the fabric that separates our arms.

Fain introduces the slim, bespectacled girl who stands beside Edwin, her black hair pin-straight and pulled neatly back, her posture straight and proud. At fourteen years of age, Lucretia Quillen greatly resembles her older brother, though her countenance is much more serious than Fain's.

"I'm pleased to meet you, Mage Gardner," she tells me with a self-possessed air that far exceeds her young age. I read her affinity lines as I shake her hand—she has a strong stream of water and wind magic. I look to Fain with mounting respect, remembering that he's essentially raised his sisters on his own.

"LuLu was just admitted to the University and has been pre-apprenticed with the Historians' Guild," Fain crows, throwing his arm around his sister and beaming. "She's brilliant, and I certainly can't keep up with her."

Lucretia gives her brother a wry smile. "Fain likes to brag," she tells us, obviously pleased.

Fain kisses the top of his sister's head and grins at us, clearly in his element here in Valgard, with his family, his people.

He's reserved a lovely table for us, right up at the canal's edge, and I take a seat next to Vale, Fain on the other side of me at the table's head. Ironwood trees and potted flowers surround us, the table covered by a rich green tablecloth and laden with gleaming, vine-patterned china. Fain's frolicking stream of anecdotes pulls even shy Edwin into conversation, some of his gossip so startling that my attention is pulled away from Vale for a brief moment.

"I don't suppose you've heard about the match of the season—two utter fiends, united in fasted bliss."

We all look to Fain, waiting, and he savors our heightened interest.

"Malkyn Bane has fasted to Genna Thorne." Fain gives us all a significant look, then goes about serving plump fillets of fish to each of us with silver tongs.

"Well, that has an awful symmetry to it," Vale says flatly as he holds his plate out so Fain can reach it. Vale and I exchange a swift, sober glance at the thought of Malkyn and Genna's union.

Fain piles my plate high with food, extolling the virtues of each dish as he does so. The food is bountiful and better than anything I've ever had in my entire life—fish poached with lemon and fresh herbs, followed by tender lamb with mint jelly, steaming rolls, a salad that's almost entirely made up of delicate, delicious flowers.

Vale reaches toward me under the table and slides his hand over mine.

I twine my fingers through his, my breathing going uneven, my heartbeat racing. The very air grows hotly charged as our fires feed into each other.

Vale leans toward me and whispers in my ear, "There's something I want to show you."

His deep voice sends a thrum of shuddering warmth through my body. I nod in decadent agreement, wanting to go. Wanting to be alone with him.

I glance up to find Fain watching us closely as his sister brightly regales Edwin with a story about her ill-fated attempts at cooking. Fain's eyes are darting back and forth between Vale and me.

Vale turns as Edwin briefly engages him in conversation, and Fain shoots me a wide, dazzling smile, rich in humor and genuine affection. He jerks his head toward the exit. "Go," he says, leaning in to whisper to me. "I can feel the affinity fire you two are throwing at each other from clear across the table." He pats my hand and gives me his feline grin. "Go take him home and change those lines, sweet Tessla. Before Vale simply explodes, right here, into a torrent of fire."

Vale leads me, my hand in his, down several alleys and meandering side streets toward the city's main public gardens, a lush park filled with succulent plants, bloodrose bushes and Ironwood tree groves. The gardens are edged by broad canals on all sides.

He guides me, his fire coursing hot through my arm, down the main path, cutting through the gardens toward a smaller path that leads down into a sheltered grove of Ironwood trees. We slow to a stop, and he turns to face me, the sharp contours of his face bathed in the Ironflowers' soft blue light. The two of us are suddenly all alone.

Vale releases my hand, reaches inside his cloak and hands me a long, thin package, his eyes bright with anticipation.

"For your birthday," he says.

Filled with a giddy curiosity, I set about opening it and gasp as the paper wrapping falls away.

A Maelorian wand. Black as midnight with a spiraling handle. Just as he promised.

Tears sting my eyes as I curl my fingers around it.

He's bucked some serious rules to secure this for me, likely having it crafted for himself. Only to break the law and gift it to me.

I'm overcome, my voice breaking. "Thank you, Vale."

The heat of his gaze is penetrating and searing, so singular in focus. "You are welcome, Tessla." A hint of a smile plays on his lips as he watches me. His expression turns ardent, almost pained. "Gods, you're beautiful."

Emboldened, I move closer to him, basking in the warmth of his affinity fire, breathing him in, while I consider the wand in my hand. I test the feel of it, my affinity lines snapping toward it with taut, satisfying force. I can sense the perfect craftsmanship of this wand, the layers of wood thinner than the thinnest parchment, perfectly laminated. And I can sense the quality of the wood as well—Star Maple, Frosted Hawthorne and Ironwood. Fine woods chosen to smoothly amplify magic.

"I saw the affinity patterns you were working out," I tell him. "Back at your cottage."

"*Our* cottage," he throatily amends, the deep thrum of his voice playing havoc with my heartbeat. "It's your house, too, Tessla."

I swallow, thrown by the nearness of him, disconcertedly heated up. "You're trying to work from the Waltherian Grimoire."

"Water spells," he concurs. "I've a trace of water affinity, like you. Not much, but still. I'm trying to utilize it. I just can't seem to access the water."

"Hook the roots," I tell him. "There's a natural attraction."

"Hook them?"

"Slow the stream down," I explain, pulling my hand down in a gradual arc. "So slow you can almost see it pulse." I mimic a slow rhythm with my fingers. "There's a hook in each crest. If you layer the streaming spell over the vine spell, you can latch right on to it and pull the water through."

He cocks his head to one side, and I can see him puzzling it out.

"I'll show you. Take your wand and roll up your sleeve," I tell him, heat rising in my cheeks.

He blinks at me, eyes searing, then complies. He pulls his

wand from its sheath and rolls his tunic sleeve up to expose his muscular arm. He raises his arm, ready to cast the spells, and looks to me.

Swallowing hard, I roll up my own sleeve, skim my hand down his arm and slide it over his fingers and around the wand. The entire length of my arm is pressed against his, skin to skin.

"Tessla," he breathes raggedly. "I don't know if I can focus."

"Try. Trail the water spell over the vine spell." I caress his hand. "Keep your fingers loose. Very light." His hand relaxes under mine, his fire flowing toward me. "That's good. All your fire's flowing away from the wand. Toward me."

He spits out a laugh. "Yes, it is."

"Do it. Send both spells through."

Vale murmurs each spell in sequence, a thin black vine jetting out from the tip of the wand to collide with and twine around the tree before us. I push my magic down against his, line to line, helping him guide the two spells together. The black vine is quickly limned by a small line of glistening water. The vine breaks from the tip of Vale's wand and falls just as the water collides with the tree and loses form. It streams down the trunk, seeping into the earth below.

Vale turns to me, eyes wide. "Brilliant." He looks back toward the tree in rapt amazement as I slide my arm off his. "Do you know how long I've been trying to figure that out?"

I smirk at him, challenge in my gaze, as his fire gives a hard surge. "Not bad for a Lower River—"

Vale pulls me firmly to him and brings his lips to mine, taking me completely by surprise. A shocked thrill flashes through me. His mouth is warm, his kiss startlingly intense, a wave of his fire flashing through me with breathtaking force. He reins it quickly in, his touch becoming more of a caress, his kiss turning slow and sultry. Then hesitant. He pulls back slightly to look at me, the Ironflower glow intensifying the brilliant green of his eyes, his breathing deepened.

I can feel his fire rising, sense him trying to bank it down.

My heart thudding, I lean in toward him, the side of his nose brushing against mine as we kiss again. He's careful now. Unsure. But the feel of him is so delicious, a restless hunger flares deep inside me.

His hands slide over my back, gradually pulling me closer, his mouth moving against mine as we drown in the surprising fire of this kiss. Small sparks ignite all over my lips, more sparks kindling wherever his hands touch my body. I caress the sharp line of his jaw and trace my fingers along his smooth skin. Vale's breath hitches.

He threads his long fingers through my hair as he pulls me against his hard body. I gasp into his mouth as a bolt of his fire flashes through me, lighting me up, stroking in long, sparking streaks down my affinity lines.

An overpowering craving to touch him takes hold. I press my palm against his chest and splay my fingers out against his taut muscles. I can feel his heartbeat, steady and strong. His delicious warmth courses straight through me from his mouth right down to my very core as he loses more and more control over his fire.

Both his hands are on my face now, his lips full on mine, kissing me deeply. His fire rushes through me, my affinity flame winding around his, blasting into him. I melt into his hot kiss and knot my fingers in his thick, luscious hair.

He's molten honey, his shuddering heat thick with forbidden pleasure.

The sound of jovial conversation breaks into my awareness as a group of young Gardnerians comes near our private grove.

Breathing hard, Vale breaks the kiss and looks toward them. They're just past the trees, chatting and laughing together.

"Let's go back to the cottage." His tone is thick with longing, the suggestion fraught with meaning, as if writ in flame and hanging in the air between us.

The cottage. Where we'll be alone. With all this fire.

I look to the ground, at the two wands flung down at our feet. Momentarily forgotten.

I step back from Vale, reach down and pick up our wands, handing him his. For a moment, I consider giving him mine to carry, as well.

No. I'll never be unarmed again.

I brazenly pull up the side of my skirt and slide the wand into the top of my stocking. Vale's fire flares in response.

I let my skirts drop back down and glance up at Vale. He looks like he's in a trance, his fire whipping out toward me in grasping, pulsating lines.

My heart pounds and my nerves flutter, but I know I want this. I want him.

"Yes. Let's go back," I say breathlessly.

He pulls me close and rests his forehead gently against mine. "Tessla," he says with passionate firmness, his gaze suddenly serious. "I… I've fallen in love with you."

I stare at him. Stunned. Thrilled. Disbelieving. I open my mouth to speak, my thoughts a tumult.

"Stay fasted to me." He takes hold of my hands, tracing the fastlines with his thumbs, sending a trail of sparks in their wake. "Even if we find a way to break this fasting." His eyes are hot on mine. "Let's not."

My heart takes flight, suddenly just as passionately decided as he is. "All right, Vale," I tell him, lacing my fingers through his. "Let's keep the lines."

CHAPTER TWENTY-EIGHT:
Alone

Vale reverts to stiff formality as we walk out of the gardens toward the main thoroughfare. He's quiet and subdued as he hires a carriage and tells the driver where to take us. The man immediately takes a submissive stance to this Level Five Mage before him, avoiding eye contact and nodding heartily in response to Vale's every request.

To the affinity-blinded masses, Vale's as cold and severe as he first seemed to me. But I can read the fire absolutely blasting through him. Barely contained.

I'm intimidated and giddily thrilled by it. Lit up.

Hungry for more of him.

Vale pulls himself into the carriage and shuts the door, both of us giving a small lurch forward as the driver sets off. He glances out the window, his pleasant, slightly dazed expression at full odds with the powerful fire that's violently lashing around inside him, lashing out toward me.

He turns and sets his eyes on me. Neither of us moves for a heartbeat, and the very air between us seems ready to catch fire.

In an instant, we are locked together. My hand clutches at his hair, pulling his mouth hard against mine. His arm grasps my waist, his lips hot and insistent.

He kisses me for a long time as the carriage drives away from the city, through farmland and forest, and I'm drowning in the taste of him, the heat growing, merging to flare even higher. His tongue caresses mine as we kiss deeply, our affinity barriers struck down, singed to oblivion.

His fists bunch in my clothing as he pulls me furiously closer, like he can't get enough of me, grasping at my skirts. Before long I'm straddling him, merged with the fire coursing through him, each lurch of the carriage pressing him deliriously harder against me. I can't get enough of him, enough of his heat. I want to strip the clothes clear off him to get at his skin, his fire…

The carriage stops, and we pull back, looking at each other in a flushed, chaotic daze. Our hair and clothing are hopelessly mussed, the windows fogged, my lips swollen and throbbing.

"We're here," Vale says, his voice throaty. He's panting and still clutching my hips, eyes blurred. "Gods, you're flushed," he says, looking at my face, the hollow of my neck. He shoots me a dark look, then smiles, teeth bared, as if he can't believe his luck.

Then he reluctantly pulls back, and I do the same, easing down skirts that have been pushed scandalously high. We're both breathing heavily, my fire whipping out toward him in desperate, hungry strokes. I try to subdue it, but the flames are running far too hot.

Vale sits back, neck arched, and stares at the carriage's ceiling, his breathing gradually slowing. He licks his lips and shoots me a scorching glance, then looks back at the ceiling and runs a hand through his mussed hair, trying to gather himself.

"Go on inside," he says, looking me over with lascivious heat once more, his fire sliding through and then under my clothing. He smirks at me. "I have to pay the driver."

We grin at each other and exchange a heated, knowing glance.

I lean over to slide my palm over his chest, to nuzzle his neck and kiss his hot cheek.

He laughs throatily. "You are not helping, Tessla."

I smile wickedly at him, then exit the carriage, the exciting thrill of him sizzling through me, my whole body lit up with desire.

As I step down from the carriage, the cold air coming off the Voltic Sea stings at my flushed skin. The waves lash turbulently at the rocks below, but an enticing lantern glow emanates from the inside of Vale's cottage. I glance sidelong at the driver, who keeps his face neutral, but there's a knowing glint of amusement in his eyes.

I wait in the kitchen, heart thudding, as Vale finally exits the carriage and pays the driver. The carriage drives off, and Vale strides toward the house like a powerful hawk, his cloak billowing like outspread wings. His eyes are dark with singular purpose.

He enters the kitchen and stops, his fire lashing out.

"We should go upstairs," I say, breathless, my fire slamming into his, our heat impossibly stoked.

"All right," he says, predatory eyes fixed on me. He swallows and looks me over.

My breathing uneven, I turn and go up the stairs, deliciously aware of his unsettling heat at my back.

I step into the bedroom and turn.

He's on me in a flash, pulling me close, his mouth hot on mine. I clutch his tunic in my fists, feverishly pulling him in. He's pressing me back against the bedpost with aggressive passion as I kiss him deeply, his fire rapidly flaring twice as high, his control fracturing.

Mine long broken.

He pulls back, breathing hard, his lip curled as he looks

me up and down. He's completely different from the reserved Vale I first met.

His hunger startles and excites me. I want to prod at the danger of it. To provoke him. To tease and tempt him into losing *all* control.

A wicked smile pulls at the corners of his mouth. "Tessla, I don't know how I'm going to hold back." His eyes fix on me hungrily. "If just your kiss sends me into this…frenzy. Just your mouth alone…" He stops and swallows, then glances at the bed. He turns back to me. "Gods, you're so beautiful." He threads his fingers through my hair and leans in to press his molten lips against the base of my neck.

A blaze of fire rocks through me, pulsing. I tense my thighs against it, knowing it's doing the same to him.

"You've taken over my mind," he tells me, his lips pressed to my throat. "All I want to do is touch you."

I caress the base of his neck. "Touch me, then."

He pulls slowly back, his eyes wide, then narrowing. He tilts his head in question, the words careful. "Do you *mean*…?"

I'm dizzy with desire for him and giddy with nerves. We're fasted and sealed. There's nothing wrong with giving myself to him. I nod, decided.

Vale presses his lips to mine again, hot and urgent, then draws back. "You're sure?" he asks.

"Yes," I say. My face and neck are so warm they're scorching. "You can share my bed tonight." I wince at my own presumption. It's his house. "I mean…*your* bed."

"*Our* bed," he insists, looking dazed.

"Our bed," I agree, equally dazed, my breath ragged. "From now on. If you'd like." I kiss his lips and send a rush of flame straight through his body. Vale groans and tightens his grip on me.

There's a hard knock at the door downstairs.

Both of us blink, startled. As if a magic spell has been broken.
Incredulous irritation flashes across Vale's sharp face. "If
ever there was an award for the worst timing in the world…"

Another knock. Louder. More insistent.

Vale takes a deep breath and rakes his hair back with his fingers, his eyes knife-sharp with desire. He looks me slowly up
and down. "There's no way I'll be able to talk coherently to
whoever is down there." He shakes his head. "If it's Edwin, I'm
going to melt him. Or Fain. I think I have sufficient grounds
to kill whoever it is."

I smirk at this, coloring, still not believing I've just invited
a man to share my bed. I feel scandalous. Deliciously, overwhelmingly brazen.

Vale walks to the door and hesitates, his hand on the door
frame. He leans into it and closes his eyes.

"What are you doing?" I ask.

His tone is clipped. "Trying to use what little water magic
I have to douse myself with ice water."

The knocking grows more insistent.

Vale looks at me and his eyes flash. "Perhaps I'll just ball up
some lightning and send it straight through the door," he says
tersely, then goes downstairs.

CHAPTER TWENTY-NINE:
The Selkie

I hover near the bedroom door frame and peek around its corner as Vale stalks down the stairs and through the kitchen to open the door.

Wind blows in from outside, sending the kitchen fire sputtering. Another storm seems to be quickly moving in, and I'm not surprised. Valgard is famously stormy in autumn, with choppy, dangerous seas.

Vale holds fast to the door as the violent wind threatens his grip. His eyes light with surprise. "Beck?"

"Hello, Vale." The answering voice is deep and grim.

Vale motions a young Gardnerian mariner inside, his black tunic, pants and woolen cloak all edged with a line of seafarer blue. He's as tall as Vale, but broad and muscular, a dark beard lining his square jaw.

His expression seems deeply worried.

"Were you…" Beck cocks his head in complete confusion as he takes in Vale's face. "How on Erthia was someone able to punch you?"

Vale shakes his head tersely. "It's no matter. Why are you here?"

Beck blinks at him in continued confusion, then grows somber once more. "I need your help, Vale." His hands grip the back of the kitchen chair before him.

Vale waits, brow raised in question.

Beck stares at Vale, his jaw tensing, as if he's fighting to hold Vale's level stare. As if he doesn't quite know how to phrase what he's about to say. "I've a Selkie lover, Vale," he finally blurts out. "She's in danger. I need someone to take her in, just for a little while. And...we have a child."

A Selkie?

I've heard tales of these seal-shifter women. Dangerous in their seal form—able to take down ships, kill sailors. But powerless without their silver skins.

Vale's eyes widen. "Did you say...a *Selkie*?"

Beck's jaw clenches tight as he holds Vale's piercing stare.

"Gods, Beck," Vale says, his voice low and tense. "You're *fasted*." This catches me off guard—that Vale lights on this as the most shocking detail.

"Yes, Vale," Beck says, his words clipped. "I *know* I'm fasted."

I stare at Beck's hands, at the heavy black lines that mark them and extend down his wrists. He's fasted and sealed. And the sealing has been consummated.

"I've never heard of a Selkie bearing a mixed-race child," Vale says, clearly astonished.

"Well, now you have."

Vale's face turns dark. "And what of Margryt?"

Beck's face hardens. "Margryt and I were fasted when we were *thirteen*. I had *no* say in the matter, and neither did she. Both of us *forced*..."

"That doesn't change the fact that you already have a child with her."

"Yes, I know I have a child with Margryt," Beck snaps. "And now I have another child, but *his* situation is far more complicated. And dangerous."

"Does Margryt know about any of this?"

Beck shoots him a wildly incredulous look. "Of course she doesn't!"

They're both quiet for a long, uncomfortable moment.

Vale finally speaks. "Where is she? The Selkie. And your child."

Beck motions outside with his chin. "By the ocean. Waiting."

Vale gapes at him. "Great gods, Beck, it's freezing out there. Bring them in."

Beck shakes his head. "The cold doesn't bother them. Not like you and me. And they actually like storms. Or any type of wet weather."

I turn, pad over to the bedroom window and look toward the small beach.

Lightning flashes, and sure enough, there's a woman sitting on the outcropping of black rock. She's staring out over the ocean and cradles a small bundle in her arms. Her hair glints silver with each flash of lightning. Astonished, I creep back toward the door.

"The men who captured her lost her skin," Beck wearily explains. "Tossed her overboard when they realized they didn't have it. They didn't want to risk her finding it and regaining her power. I came upon her, drifting in the ocean. She's not able to transform to her seal form without her skin, and she needs it to have enough strength to get home. I rescued her. Hid her in my cabin…"

"And then the baby." Vale's tone is hard, his hands on his hips, his entire demeanor judgmental.

"Yes," Beck snaps. "About a year and half later, the baby." He glares at Vale. "Not all of us are able to live like monks." Beck's eyes flick down, then widen in astonishment as they light on Vale's hands. "Great Ancient One, Vale! You're fasted!"

Vale takes a deep breath, his face gone tight with offense at Beck's great surprise. "Yes, I am."

Beck peers harder at the lines, clearly noticing the sealing marks. *Unconsummated* sealing marks. His brow knits in confusion. "When did you..."

"Yesterday," Vale puts in tersely. "And you should know that I'm not alone here."

"What? She's *here*?"

Vale glowers at him. "Of *course* she's here."

Beck's voice grows heated. "Great Ancient One, Vale, you should have told me! She might have overheard." He looks around, shakes his head, then massages his broad forehead. "I hope she can be trusted."

Vale shoots him an incredulous look. "Would I have bound myself to her if she couldn't be?"

Beck's mouth tenses into a tight line, and he gives Vale a narrow look. "I suppose not." He shakes his head again and looks around the kitchen blankly, as if searching for me. He turns back to Vale. "Who is she?"

Vale hesitates, his jaw tightening. "Mage Tessla Harrow. Well, Tessla Gardner now."

Beck's eyes light with shocked recognition. "Sweet Ancient One, Vale. *Jules's* Tessla?"

"The Tessla he talked about, yes," Vale staunchly replies, his level stare unwavering.

"Where is she?" Beck glances around again, clearly growing angered on Jules's behalf, his expression now severe.

My face heats, and I step out of the bedroom. "I'm right here." I make my way down the staircase, slightly unnerved by the tense silence and the feel of Beck's hard eyes on me. I look up in time to see his outraged gaze shift from me back to Vale.

Vale gives a long sigh and shakes his head. "Tessla, meet Beck Keeler. We were at University together." He turns to me with a humorless smile. "As you've probably gathered, Beck is also friends with Jules Kristian."

"A better friend to him than *you*, it would seem," Beck snipes, his eyes hot on Vale. "Yet you stand here and judge *me*." He looks at me again. "Does Jules know?"

Vale's gaze is coolly steady. "Not yet." The words are clipped.

"Let me guess," Beck snipes at Vale. "You bound her during one of those horrid mass fastings they're staging."

Vale sighs. "It was a slightly different situation."

"Really?" He turns to me, fire in his eyes. "Mage Harrow. Were you fasted to Vale of your own free will?"

I look to Vale, who shrugs at me, resigned. I turn back to Beck. "Well, I'm here at this cottage of my own free will."

"And the fasting?" he doggedly insists.

"Well, that was, in fact, forced, but…"

Beck rounds on Vale. "So you *forced* Jules's woman to fast to you?"

"I'm not Jules's woman," I emphatically put in, bristling.

Beck's head jerks back toward me and he grows silent, brow tensed, studying me with evident confusion.

I let out a heavy sigh. "It's a long story. Really. It's fine."

"It's…*fine*?"

"Yes," I insist. "I'm glad Vale and I are fasted. I've grown… quite fond of him." My cheeks grow heated. "*Very* fond."

Vale is eyeing me with surprise. Then his mouth quirks and breaks into a ridiculously wide smile, his gaze growing hot on me, his fire quickening.

Beck takes in Vale's besotted smile, my flushed face and our strangely unconsummated fastlines. He shakes his head with some disapproval. "I truly don't understand either of you."

"You don't have to," Vale says tightly. "Truly."

Beck's head draws back, his expression immediately chastened. He clears his throat and shifts awkwardly. Then, as if screwing up his resolve, he offers his hand to me. "Mage Harrow," he says with somber formality.

I take his hand, his handshake firm and warm. "It's Mage Gardner, actually. But I'm glad to meet you, Mage Keeler." I square my shoulders and hold his intent gaze. "We should invite your Selkie and your child inside."

A small measure of surprise lights his eyes, followed quickly by relief. He slumps down, as if profoundly tired.

"You're not able to keep your Selkie on the *Galliana*, then?" Vale asks. "I remember crews turning a blind eye to that sort of thing."

I stare at Vale in shock as I realize that Beck likely isn't the first mariner to take a Selkie as a lover.

Beck shoots Vale a sharp look of censure.

A bemused smile comes to Vale's lips. "Tessla's a refugee from Doveshire, Beck. She got caught up on the front lines. Do you honestly think you could say anything that would shock her?"

Beck looks at me with surprise, then gives me a respectful nod and turns back to Vale, sighing heavily. "Ray and I were always a bit suspect. It's one thing to have a Selkie on board… for sport." His eyes dart uneasily to me, and I huff out an impatient sigh, prompting him to continue. "But to fall in love with a Selkie…well, the word *staen'en* was bandied about. At first jokingly, but then as a true threat." Beck lowers his head. "They're putting priests on the ships now. There's no way to keep her with me anymore, especially with our baby. And she has nowhere else to go." He looks to Vale, imploring. "We're in a terrible situation."

"Her name is Ray?" I ask.

"I call her Ray, but that's not her true name," Beck tells me distractedly. "Her Selkie name is impossible to translate." Curiosity lights Vale's eyes. Beck takes a deep breath and makes an undulating motion with his fingers. "It means…'the shimmer when sunlight sparkles on the water on a hot, bright day. The way it looks from under the water, looking up. What the light does to the blue.' They have a lot of words like this."

Vale tenses his brow at Beck. "How do you know all this?"

"She uses Common Signage. I taught her."

Common Signage. I remember hearing about this—a language of hand gestures developed by mariners, so they could easily communicate with other mariners who spoke different tongues.

"And the child?" Vale asks, his tone slowly losing its judgmental edge.

Pain flashes across Beck's features. "His Gardnerian name is Gareth. His Selkie name is..." He makes a cage with his hands, turning his hands in toward each other, the fingers separated and curved into bars. He gives us both a weighty, sorrowful look. "It means 'trapped heart.'" Beck's face dissolves into sadness. "He's more Gardnerian than Selkie. He has a silver glint to his hair, but that's it. No gills."

"So he's trapped on the surface," Vale says sympathetically.

Beck nods. "I thought...perhaps they could live here. With you. Under your protection. You certainly wouldn't be the first wealthy man to keep a Selkie."

Vale's face goes tight, and I can tell he's trying not to take offense.

Misery clouds Beck's expression. "I'm sorry to be asking this of you. She's...they've nowhere else to go. Please, Vale." He turns to me, beseeching. "Tessla..."

My fire is running strong and decided. I know full well what it feels like to have nowhere to go. My eyes meet Vale's. "Let's go get them."

Vale nods in assent, his fire now flaring as decidedly as mine.

Vale and I follow Beck down the path to the arcing beach, a lantern swinging from Vale's hand. The rain is only spitting, but lightning still flashes, and muted thunder sounds over the ocean. Pin-like drops of rain are driven into my skin by the fitful wind, stinging and bitterly cold on my face.

Ray, the Selkie, recoils as we approach. Her thin form is lit by the guttering lantern light, and her gray eyes widen with fright. She looks cornered, hunted, and my compassion rises in response to her staggering fear of us.

She's hugging a baby in her arms, perhaps only a few weeks old. The child looks Gardnerian, with gray-green eyes that hint of a stormy ocean, shimmering skin and a shock of black hair. Touches of silver at the tips are the only hint of his true lineage. Ray is dressed in a Gardnerian man's tunic, pants and cloak, her silver hair whipped about by the wind, her white skin tinged with blue undertones. There's a row of gills on either side of her neck, ballooning in and out fitfully. She is stunningly strange, but very beautiful.

Vale and I slow to a stop at a careful distance as Beck goes to her, signing in a rapid stream. Her mouth trembles as she clutches wildly at her child, sure we'll steal him away at any moment.

I meet her eyes briefly, and an immediate sense of recognition lights inside me. My heart rushes out to her, fire blooming inside me in a protective flare as Beck tries to calm her, to no avail.

"Tell her I know how she feels," I call out to Beck over the howling wind.

Ray's head jerks toward me, her whole body flinching at the sound of my voice. Beck looks briefly to me, then places one hand on Ray's shoulder as he signs to her with the other.

Tears sting my eyes, my voice breaking. "Tell her I know what it's like to lose your family. To lose your home. To have nowhere to go." Vale is silent beside me, but I can feel his fire reaching out to me. "Tell her we'll help her."

Beck is furiously signing, clearly desperate to assuage her fears.

Her eyes are now locked on mine, and I can feel a kindred understanding taking root between us.

Her breathing is still erratic, the trembling of her mouth more pronounced, but the fear in her gaze has lessened, replaced by a profound misery. The sparse rain beads on her pale skin as we take stock of each other.

Then Vale's signing to her with formal grace, and I gawk at him before quickly reining in my surprise. Of course he knows Common Signage. He was on and off ships for three years.

Ray's body wilts, but she makes the same sign over and over to both Vale and me with emphatic force—her fist repeatedly hitting over her heart.

"What's she saying?" I ask Vale.

"She's thanking us," he says, looking to me with concern.

Ray sets her gaze full on me and lets loose a stream of conversation in a high-pitched, multitonal language, her gills flaring repeatedly, her hand shaking as she signs.

"I can't translate," Beck laments. "She's not signing clearly enough."

Ray's multiple tones coalesce into a deep, resonating wail as she looks to the ocean and points out toward the line of the horizon, her arm trembling, her palm turning up. Then she sets her ocean eyes back on me and starts another rapid stream of indecipherable multitoned words.

I don't need a translation. I'm clear on what she means.

Somewhere out there in the turbulent black water are her people. Her home.

CHAPTER THIRTY:
Runehawk

We bring Ray and the baby inside, just as the storm begins to gain force. I take Ray's wet cloak and guide her to a chair by the kitchen fire. Vale takes Beck's cloak and bag and sets them aside, the two men discussing Beck's danger-fraught journey here. Ray slumps down in her chair, seeming to fall into an exhausted trust of me, the gills on her neck now limp. She hands me her baby, her ocean eyes beyond weary, and then, to my great shock, pulls her tunic completely off.

A stinging flush rises up my neck, suffusing my cheeks. I quickly avert my eyes from her full breasts and large blue nipples. Ray reaches for baby Gareth, who squirms agitatedly in my arms and whimpers for her. Wildly uncomfortable, I hand Gareth over, and Ray pulls him close. Gareth immediately latches hungrily on to one of her nipples.

Face burning and not knowing where to look, I chance a quick glance at Vale.

"The Vu Trin are moving in to shut down the Eastern Pass," Vale is telling Beck, his mouth set in a hard line. "Nothing good will come of that, I can assure you." Vale grows darkly reflective for a moment as Beck sits and pulls at his boot laces. Then he looks toward Ray and gives a jolt of surprise at her state of undress, his eyes momentarily going wide. He shoots me a brief, stunned look while Beck tiredly pulls off one of his boots, throwing it down with a dull *thump*.

"I'll...fetch us some food," Vale announces to no one in particular, then flees to the pantry.

I strive to tamp down my embarrassment, realizing this must be her people's way of things. Shifting my focus to the comfort of our guests, I realize I don't know where anything is in this cottage. Bedding, cloths to use for diapers, something to turn into a makeshift cradle.

"I'll be right back," I say with an attempt at a congenial smile. Both Beck and Ray give me worn, distracted glances.

Vale's pulling a small wheel of cheese off a shelf as I enter the pantry. He places it in a woven reed basket on the small table before him.

"I'll put together the food," he tells me matter-of-factly, pulling down a jar of fig preserves, some sausage and salted fish with efficient industry. "They can stay in the downstairs bedroom. They'll need some bed things, of course—they're in the hall closet. Perhaps you could get the bedroom together for Beck and his half-naked companion."

His eyes flick briefly to mine with mischief, and I smile shyly, still somewhat mortified.

"It was a bit of a shock," I admit. "When she pulled her tunic off."

He gives me a look of wry agreement. "Yes, well." He pauses, then grows thoughtful, resting his hands on the table for a moment. "Perhaps they have the better way of it. Nursing comfortably. Out in the open." He shrugs. "Why should our women hide in the shadows with their babies?"

He goes back to picking items off the shelves, and I study him. He's incredibly open-minded, this fastmate of mine.

I eye him archly. "So I have your permission to go around the house half-dressed?"

Vale pauses, a wicked gleam in his gaze. "Oh, most enthusiastically granted, Tessla."

Our fires briefly flare, and I look away, both thrilled by his intense interest in me and slightly abashed. I remember that he's already seen me half-naked and knows what my breasts look like. I push the memory of that terrifying night away, but a cold unease lingers.

"But you don't need my permission to do what you want," Vale says, leaning toward me over the table, half-serious. "Do you, Tess?" There's affectionate understanding in his tone, and it bolsters me, his flare of heat softening to a caress that gently enfolds me.

And I like him calling me Tess.

As he turns back to the shelves, I have a sudden bold idea.

"I'm going to make the fires," I tell him decidedly. "In the downstairs and upstairs bedrooms. With my new wand."

"Tess," Vale says, a mildly cautionary note to his tone, "you were only just recently Magedrunk."

"I'll be fine," I firmly rejoin. I hike up my skirt and smoothly pull my wand from where I've sheathed it in the top of my shocking, well aware of the flash of thigh I'm giving him.

His heat gives a hard surge. Vale rakes his hand through his hair. "It drives me to distraction when you do that."

I give a throaty laugh. "Oh, I know it does."

I let my skirts drop, thrilled by the feel of my weapon in my fist. *My* wand. All mine. My magic hums toward it.

I slice the wand through the air and point it at him, my other arm arced theatrically over my head. I motion toward the food basket with my chin as I pose, regally straight.

"Go feed everyone, Vale Gardner," I say importantly. "*I'll* take care of the Magery in this house."

Vale laughs and narrows his eyes at me. "Look at you, so eager." He grins wolfishly, and I swing away from him, starting for the kitchen.

"We've quite a few guests," he calls after me, the words thick with amusement. "Try not to set the house on fire."

"Like you almost did our first night here?" I toss back over my shoulder.

He laughs. "You have an unsettling effect on me, my love."

I light up like dry brush at being called "my love." I pause, unsteady, then stop and turn to him, waves of delight washing over me. He tilts his head, studying me intently. I go back to him and pull him into a long, deep kiss, my hand knotted in his hair. His hands are light on my back, as if frozen with surprise. I pull away, reveling in how his eyes have grown dark and blurred as he smiles down at me.

"Go on," he prods, looking me over with sultry heat. "We'll pick this up later."

Flushed and disoriented, I head back to the kitchen, Vale's fire lapping playfully at my back.

As we enter the room together, he attempts to bank his heat, but the fire we've kicked up is still simmering.

I take in Vale's lithe grace as he moves, his long form bending to cut up cheese, bread, sausage. His shoulder tensing as he deftly sets out plates and drinks for Beck and Ray. His manner so formal and reserved.

I thrill in my private knowledge of him. What the heat of his mouth feels like. His wanton fire when he pushes his whole body relentlessly against mine.

Vale looks up at me as he sets out tea, as if feeling my attention. There's a flash of fire in his eyes that bolts out and shudders through me.

I look away, flustered. Ray is regarding us steadily as she

nurses with tired, languid eyes. Her mouth lifts in a knowing smirk, as if she can sense our thoughts. Her hair is even more spectacular in the lantern light and firelight, the silver shimmering like a waterfall and throwing off a cascade of reflections. Despite the warmth of the room, her white skin still looks faintly blue, as if she hides the essence of the ocean within herself. I find myself quickly adjusting to her half-nudity, my initial shock blunted to a mild embarrassment.

Wand in hand, I traipse up the stairs to the bedroom, throw open the woodstove door and send out a spell. A bolt of flame rips through the wand and almost knocks me off my feet, the spear of fire slamming into the woodstove with a rattling force that makes the floor vibrate. Heart thudding, I quickly step on several sparks to keep Vale's bedroom from catching fire.

"Keep a looser grip on the wand," Vale calls up from downstairs, and I frown down at him petulantly, as if he can see me. The fire I've cast has simmered down and burns with steady heat. I feel suddenly powerful and gloriously armed.

I just need some practice.

Gratified, I latch the woodstove's door shut and saunter down the stairs, wand in hand. I pause at the bottom of the staircase to stare smugly at Vale while I triumphantly twirl my wand.

"So, you gave your fastmate a wand?" Beck notes with unsurprised good humor.

Vale's sitting down, his long legs stretched out in front of him, watching me as he picks at the cheese. A small line of his fire caresses my waist, dances lightly on my cheek, brushes my lips.

"Of course I did," Vale affirms, his eyes tight on me. "She's close to a Level Four Mage."

Beck looks to me with surprise, then grins at Vale. "Well, I suppose she'd need to be. To handle you."

Vale laughs.

I have better luck lighting the fireplace in the downstairs bedroom, producing a tight, clean flame that catches almost instantly, sending off a minimum of sparks.

I rejoin everyone just as there's a hesitant knock at the door. Vale opens it to reveal Edwin, hunkered down against the driving rain. The wind rips the door out of Vale's hand and slams it against the outer wall. Thunder booms, rattling the window panes.

Edwin peers at us through rain-fogged glasses as he steps in, lugging a shoulder sack and his violin case. He blinks for a moment at the silver-haired, half-naked Selkie, briefly mesmerized, but recovers quickly, shyly averting his eyes. Sleepy Ray stirs and looks at Edwin with some alarm, then to Beck for reassurance. They sign back and forth, gesturing toward Edwin repeatedly.

"Hello, Tessla," Edwin says with a sheepish smile. His eyes flick toward the wand in my hand, but his neutral expression doesn't waver. He looks to Vale uncertainly. "Beck sent word to me. He told me to come."

"Oh, good," Vale says with tight sarcasm. He turns his sharp eyes to Beck. "Let's invite the entire population of Valgard here, shall we?" He gives a deep, resigned sigh, then takes his brother's things, helping him get settled. I go to the cook stove to boil more water for tea, using my wand to heat the water. I overreach and have to jerk back as the contents of the kettle burst into scorching steam, charring the bottom of the pot. I glower at the pot, as if the blackened bottom were its fault. I scour it out and rinse it, ready to make another attempt.

Vale quietly comes over and positions himself next to me.

"Would you like some assistance, Oh Great Mage?"

I shoot him a dismissive look as I pour more water into the kettle. "I'll figure it out myself, thank you." I loosen my hand, like he instructed me earlier, murmur a spell, pull all my concentration toward my line of fire that reaches for the wand and gently release a small stream of it.

The kettle chaotically sputters, then soothes to a smooth boil. I give Vale a wide, satisfied smile.

Vale's smirking at me. "Very good, Mage Gardner," he says, languid heat reaching out for me.

Mage Gardner. I've his name now, I marvel. It's still so foreign and new. I like the sound of it, and what it means to have his name. Like a wall of protection around my entire family.

I pour tea for everyone, including myself, then rejoin Vale at the counter, my gaze sliding down his long, handsome form. The mug of tea is warm in my hands, tendrils of steam wisping up in curlicues.

Vale shakes his head and examines the crowded kitchen. Beck's arm is draped loosely around Ray while the couple carries on their signed conversation. Edwin intermittently talks to Beck in hushed tones, and through him to Ray.

"We'll never get a chance to change these lines, will we?" Vale asks with a sigh, turning his palm over to stare at the thin, curling fastlines. "They'll stay exactly as they are," he jests with mock gravity. "Forever."

He's not looking at me, but his fire's kicked up again, reaching out to stroke my shoulder, the skin just under the collar of my tunic. It briefly skims the side of my breast, and I playfully bat it away. I eye the people sitting in front of us and raise my brow at him in light censure. Vale reins his fire in, shooting me a look that's both chastened and amused.

The Selkie looks over at us and signs to Vale. Vale cocks his head in question and signs back. Ray turns to Beck and signs emphatically to him, gesturing toward me with her chin, a broad smile forming on her lips.

When I look at Vale, there's a spot of color on his cheeks.

Beck's face takes on a look of surprise, then amusement. "Sorry, Vale." He gives Vale a knowing smirk, his eyes darting to me.

"What are they saying?" I ask Vale.

Vale takes a deep breath, the color on his cheeks deepening. "Apparently shifters can sense attraction."

I flush at this. "Oh."

Ray's grin broadens, and she signs to us emphatically, reaching around the baby to ball one of her hands into a fist. She brings her other hand around to clasp over her fist.

I mimic her movements to Vale, grasping my own fist. "What's this?"

Vale smirks and scratches his forehead, glancing sidelong at me. "It's joining. Of a couple. She thinks we'd best...go off together."

A flush heats my face as Beck laughs and hugs a grinning Ray. Edwin looks like he's trying to ignore us all as he averts his eyes and self-consciously focuses on his food.

Vale gives a short laugh and grins at me, his fire warm and steady. "We're such proper Gardnerians."

I nod and laugh, too. "I know."

We stay up late into the night, until both baby Gareth and Ray are asleep in the chair. Edwin and Vale are talking to Beck in low tones, the three of them studying a map, their expressions grave. I watch them intently, leaning back against the counter and sipping my tea.

"I received a runehawk from Collum late this afternoon," Beck tells Vale. "Just before we fled the ship. He's down in the southern lands, just off Vahrl'gul. Your mother's leveled all the villages there. They saw a piece of it from where they were anchored, not far from shore. The river of fire coming in. The dragons. *Our* dragons." He pauses, clears his throat uncomfortably. "The Urisk villagers made a run for it toward the water. Yelling for the ship, for help. The children were screaming. It was complete chaos."

Vale's face has grown dark, hands tight around his mug as he sits back, listening. Edwin stares at the floor in weighty silence.

Beck takes a deep breath. "The villagers swam toward the ship. Hundreds of them. And…our soldiers…they were ordered to shoot the survivors."

Vale winces, and Edwin remains frozen, a heavy tension thickening the air.

Beck's voice has grown hoarse. "A few soldiers tried to help some children who were near drowning. The children were promptly shot through with arrows, and the soldiers who tried to help them were tossed overboard. Collum said it was a massacre. And that charges of *staen'en* are being leveled at anyone who even shows sympathy toward the Urisk." Beck spits out a sound of deep disgust, his eyes fierce on Vale. "I never signed on for this. And now they're codifying the laws of the Ancient One. All those obscure religious edicts, now the law of the land." He shoots both Vale and Edwin a significant look, glancing toward Ray. "Those laws will be none too kind to the other races, of that we can be sure."

They all fall into a troubled, reflective silence as Beck taps out a disjointed, agitated rhythm on the wooden table.

Vale rises to replenish the food, and the conversation turns to less troubling topics. Ray wakes up and smiles sleepily at Beck. He starts signing everything we say so that she can loosely follow the conversation, our language too difficult for her ears to easily decipher.

Everything is hard for Ray without her skin, Beck tells us.

She's always weak and often slightly dizzy and off balance without water to orient her. She was training to be a diplomat, her lineage connected to the Selkie ruling family via her mother's marriage. I listen, rapt, as Beck talks about the host of shifters that exist deep in the ocean; whale-shifters, shark-shifters and others. Each group shares a shifting affinity and the characteristics of a certain animal.

"The Selkies are a peaceful people," he tells us. "They're trying to bring the various groups together. She's told me about where she lives. Beautiful caves on the ocean floor…"

Ray waves her hand, her face tightening with pain. Beck tenses his brow in concern and stops talking about her home, her family.

Vale gets up and offers her more food, salt cod he's steamed for her. She's already eaten a small bowl of fish and declines his offer of more with brusque signage, but gives him an appreciative smile.

Edwin pulls out his violin and busies himself rosining the bow and fiddling with the strings. He lifts the instrument to rest under his chin and sends out a gentle, mournful tune. The baby sleeps in Ray's arms as Ray drowsily listens to the music, her gray ocean eyes enraptured, her silver hair sparkling in the firelight. She seems wan and exhausted.

And I wonder what will become of her.

It's a strange scene. Four Gardnerians and a Selkie, being serenaded by one of the Black Witch's sons, the other son a Level Five Mage in a state of internal rebellion against his own people. And beside them, their Gardnerian friend, in love with a Selkie.

And then there's me, clutching my illegal wand, my affinity fire coursing out to wrap around Vale Gardner as his fire hungrily reaches out to meet mine.

It all feels like home. Like I'm finally, truly and completely home.

I turn to go up to bed, catching Vale's eye as I leave. He
throws out one long, questioning line of fire.

I hook on to it and pull.

CHAPTER THIRTY-ONE:
Fire

It's not long before Vale follows me upstairs.

There's a gentle knock at the door, tentative and polite, but there's nothing calm about the way his fire's running. I can feel it straight through the wood of the door, savagely hot and prowling around the door's edges.

A flush of excitement and trepidation rises up inside me. It's like preparing to welcome a tiger into the room.

"Come in, Vale."

I'm sitting on the edge of his bed as he enters and closes the door gently behind him. There's a soft click as it engages, and the sound seems so fraught with possibility that it raises a prickling line straight up my spine.

I nervously run my hand along the soft quilt beneath me, following an arc of raised thread.

Vale leans against the wall near the door, his eyes fixed on me, his face flushed, his fire licking deliciously out toward me. I can feel his hunger flaring hotter—the same hunger that's coursing through me.

I'm worried that if we touch each other, we'll explode like a lightning strike. It's all so new for us, and there are so many other people in the house.

"What will happen to Ray?" I ask Vale, gesturing toward

the downstairs bedroom where Beck and Ray are staying, trying to calm my nerves.

Vale takes a seat by me on the bed, the heat coming off him in shuddering flames. He takes a deep breath. "I don't know, Tess." He looks around, considering my question. "Probably nothing good."

"You know Beck's fastmate, then?"

"Margryt? She's a friend of mine." He shoots me a significant look fraught with conflict. "So, you can see I'm in a rather awkward situation."

"What will you do?"

He sighs gravely. "I think the question now is, what will *we* do? It's your house, too."

"We should shelter her," I tell him decidedly. "And the baby."

He nods in obvious agreement. "If they find her skin, and don't find her," he says, his expression darkening, "they'll burn it. And then she'll be as good as dead. Tessla, I'll do everything I can to help her, but the situation is a dangerous one."

Shock roils through me. "And the baby?"

Vale tilts his head, considering. "He could pass as Gardnerian. At some point, Beck will have to fess up to Margryt." Vale sighs. "And if Margryt is who I think she is, she'll raise the baby as her own."

We sit quietly for a long, somber moment.

I turn to him and take his hand in mine. His breathing hitches, his fire coursing straight up my arm.

Vale lets out a long, steadying breath, pulls a small glass bottle from his tunic pocket and hands it to me. "Fain got this. For us."

"What is it?" I ask, eyeing the brown root inside the bottle, trying to place it.

"Sanjire root."

My eyes widen at this. Sanjire root prevents pregnancy.

And it's illegal in Gardneria.

"He thought that we might not be ready for a child right now," Vale says. "And I...can't say I disagree. There's too much going on out there. Too much darkness."

I clutch the bottle, stunned to have a choice. Suddenly overwhelmingly grateful to have a choice. "How much of it do I take?" I ask him.

"Just one piece."

Emboldened, I unstopper the bottle, pull out a sliver of the root and chew on the soft, nutty root, then swallow it. I hand the bottle back to Vale, and he sets it on a side table. He shoots me a suggestive smile that sends a hard spark of heat straight through me, our fires flaring out even hotter now, my taking the Sanjire root a confirmation of what I want from him.

"How well can you read my affinity, Tessla?" he asks, taking my hand again, the heat flowing straight to my chest in rippling waves.

"With startling clarity." I give him a knowing smile as he caresses my hand. "How well can you read mine?"

His eyes grow dark and liquid. "Intimately." He smirks. "Your fire was playing with my neck earlier."

I flush. "Well, you've a nice neck." I reach over to trail my hand up along the warm skin of his neck, caressing it, slowly sliding my hand up and into his silken hair, trailing sparks. "Is this okay?" I ask, breathless.

"Gods, Tess." He leans in to slide his fingers into my hair and pulls me gently toward him. "Always."

His mouth covers mine, slow and sultry at first, holding back the torrent, but then I pull him toward me and kiss him deeply, sending my fire straight into him, striking down all our walls. Vale groans, his fire rearing, then shuddering straight through me in a searing, overpowering wave.

★ ★ ★

I remember everything of that night through a veil of flames.

Delicious heat courses down my spine as Vale fumbles with my tunic laces, trailing chaotic fire all over my skin as he pulls it off me. The two of us laugh as I artlessly tug at his tunic, almost tearing the sleeve. Vale stands, steps back and throws his tunic off, and my breath hitches at the ravishing sight of him, all lean muscle lit by the lantern's warm glow.

I rise, and he pulls me firmly into an embrace, his lips finding mine. My hands fan out over his muscular chest, riding over the hard planes of him. He kisses me deeply as my fingers trace swirling lines of flame all over his skin that make him gasp.

Vale pulls me back onto the bed, and I pull him on top of me, clutching at him as he presses his body against mine, our affinity lines pulsing hard, then merging to the same delicious rhythm. His tongue traces my collarbone as his fingers trail flame along my sides, my shoulders, my breasts. He pauses, his breathing erratic, and looks deeply into my eyes, as if he's making sure I'm all right. In answer, I slide my hands over his hips and send fire through him. Vale shudders, eyes momentarily widening. Then he kisses me with fervent passion and peels off the rest of my clothing, layer by layer.

I discover many things that Vale likes, his fire exploding when I touch him in certain ways, and he reads my affinity lines, as well, like a book splayed open. I quickly surmise that he likes to be touched, light and teasing, just behind his ear, the palm of his hand, the backs of his thighs. And he rapidly figures out that I like his tongue in my mouth and his fingers tracing heat down my spine.

His muscles tense rock-hard, and his affinity fire spikes with the strength of a fanned smith forge as I lightly trace the skin along the top of his pants and clumsily unfasten his belt. He pushes his remaining clothing off and kisses me deep and hard, his fire searing through me as we move against each other with a new feverish urgency.

We take each other once, then again deeper in the night in a wild torrent of flame.

By the time the pale light of dawn streaks through the window, the two of us are a mess of tangled limbs, our affinity lines finally dampened to a mellow glow.

I awaken encircled by Vale's warm embrace. Reluctant to wake him, I gently slide out from under his draping arm and sit up. I've a sheet wrapped discreetly around myself, but Vale is lying across the bed, stomach down, scandalously naked. I take in his long form, sprawled out like contented cat, his face calm in sleep.

He's beautiful, and I drink him in for a long moment.

As I rise, his hand snaps out to playfully grab at my sheet.

Shocked, I turn back to him, and he opens his eyes to peer at me with wicked mischief. His fire flares hot again and snakes out to slide along my body, a long line of heat flowing under my sheet.

I smack his hand away and he laughs, deep and throaty. "No," I tell him, adamant, but I can't help but grin. "I'm going to get food."

It's still new to me, this playful side to him, and I delight in it.

I tug away from him, but he won't release the sheet. His gaze turns serious and ardent. "This was a good fasting, Tess," he says.

"It was," I tell him softly.

"I love you." He says it with rock-solid assurance. As if he's saying *"There is a moon"* or *"There is a sky."*

"I love you, too," I tell him, my heart bursting open.

He reels me in and kisses me. "Go," he finally relents, caressing my face. He reluctantly releases the sheet, his eyes raking over me. "Before I take you again."

I laugh, and he smiles and looks down at his hand, briefly holding it up for my inspection. I look to my matching lines—dark swirling patterns that mirror his and run down our hands and around both our wrists now, the lines thicker and more numerous than they were before.

There's a smug, triumphant grin on Vale's face that I find amusing.

"Do you think anyone else is awake yet?" I ask as I grab up the clothing that's scattered all over the floor.

"I doubt it," he says, looking me over, his fire coursing up and down my form. "It's barely dawn."

I throw on my underthings and skirts as Vale brazenly watches me, then throw on one of his tunics instead of mine. They're easier to put on—no laces up the back.

Then I turn and make my way to the kitchen.

I reach the bottom of the stairs to find Beck cradling baby Gareth, sitting with Edwin and Fain at the kitchen table. Ray stands near the counter, eyeing me. They are all silent as stone, the Gardnerians abashed and averting their eyes.

Except for Fain. He grins at me with open glee, along with Ray.

I realize, mortified, how loud Vale and I might have been throughout the night. Vale groaning. The bed creaking.

"Hello, Fain," I say, my cheeks burning.

He looks me over with bold mischief. "Well, don't you look fetching in Vale's clothes." He gets up in one graceful swoop and comes to me, takes my hands in his and smiles. He glances down at my fastmarks and grows briefly serious. "Sweet Tessla," he says, eyes glassing over as he squeezes my hands. "I wish you so much happiness."

Tears sting my eyes, a tight knot in my throat. "Thank you, Fain. And thank you for helping my brother and my grandfather."

Fain releases my hands, throws his arms around me and kisses my head. "You've a lovely family. There's no need for thanks."

Footsteps sound on the staircase, and everyone looks up. Vale is there, blinking down over the assembled crowd. His hair is messier than I've ever seen it, an explosion of uneven spikes.

"Oh, good," Vale says. "The whole of Valgard is, in fact, here."

He comes down the stairs, strides over to me and slides his hand around my waist, a line of his fire coursing straight up my spine. "Would you like some tea?" he asks me, his fire whipping around me in caressing tendrils, hot and strong. Hungry. And not for food.

I gawk at him for a brief moment, stunned by his voracious appetite for this.

"Why yes, Vale," I say with exaggerated formality. "I would love some tea."

Ray breaks out into multitoned laughter, her gills fanning out. Gareth mimics her laugh and blows out a raspberry.

Vale hands me a mug and I sip at it, blushing furiously, but overcome with happiness.

Who would have ever guessed that I'd want this? With him?

Vale raises my hand to his lips and kisses the back of it, affection running hot in his gaze.

I've accidentally, unexpectedly, been given the perfect fasting. I can feel Vale's love for me flowing right through the fastlines.

EPILOGUE

"Mages," the Black Witch intones over the sea of Gardnerians, her eyes blazing with fierce pride. "We come together today to celebrate the wandfasting and sealing of my son, Vale Gardner, to Mage Tessla Harrow." She sweeps her arm toward Vale and me, and a protective wall of her great fire affinity swoops toward us in a powerful torrent.

The crowded Valgard Cathedral erupts into applause and cheers, everyone springing to their feet in a booming rush. Fain's up front with two fingers curled into his mouth, whistling loudly, an impish light in his eyes.

Vale's hand is tight around mine, our fires hot and merged, whipping around our arms in a unified coil. We stand on the cathedral's dais and face the crowd, then briefly meet each other's eyes with countless unspoken words and an edge of newfound worry.

Eight months have passed since Vale and I first met, and the Black Witch is back from the front lines.

Gardneria is now the greatest power in the Western Realm and ten times its original size, refugees of other races streaming away from our new borders. Mages have moved in to seize

the surrendered land and begin their new lives, and new Gardnerian military bases are rapidly being established.

It's a formality, this sealing ceremony, but one Vale's mother
insisted on, to the great delight of all Gardnerians. It's overwhelmed Vale and me, how rapidly this formal refasting and
sealing of the Black Witch's son has turned into a country-
wide celebration.

Wren beams at us from the front row where he stands next
to Grandfather. He claps with happy enthusiasm, his eyes momentarily locked on to Vale's with deep affection. He's taken
a wild shine to my fastmate, and Vale's become his teacher in
wandwork and sword fighting. My brother wandtested at Level
Three and his power is rising, the lessons in self-defense slowly
chipping away at his night terrors and residual trauma.

He's a different boy now, my brother. Completely healed and
filled out—and a good inch taller with access to so much rich
food. When he finally looks to me, his grin is wide and warm
as the sun. I bask in it, my affinity flaring out to embrace him.

I smile at Vale, tears stinging at my eyes as the applause
washes over us, and Vale's hand tightens around my own.

Grandfather is sobbing and praying, making the sign of blessing again and again over his chest as he leans heavily on his
cane. He throws a kiss toward me, and I throw one kiss back
to renewed applause.

I train my eyes on the front of the cathedral where Vale's
sister, Vyvian, stands next to Grandfather, grief etched hard on
her face. Compassion for Vale's harsh sister twists inside me.
I smile at her, but Vyvian frowns and turns her head sharply
away from me. It stings, her continued rejection of Lower
River me, but still, I never would have wanted such misery to
be visited upon her. She has a wide red armband around her
left arm, a symbol of mourning for her beloved fastmate, who
was cut down by Urisk soldiers only weeks ago, just before

our forces moved in and scorched the remaining Urisk lands. Fain is beside Vyvian, one arm tight around her shoulders, and she slumps into him, uncharacteristically worn and haggard.

I scan the room as the applause dies down. Everyone takes their seats, and the priest rises to intone a welcome prayer.

Beck Keeler sits with his family three rows back. Catching my eye, he briefly lifts his hand in greeting and attempts a wan smile, an ever-present sadness now in his eyes. Margryt, his fastmate, is by his side and cradling baby Gareth. The tips of the child's hair glint silver in the rays of sunlight that stream down into the cathedral through the stained glass windows.

Margryt is a plain, round-cheeked young woman, her expression stoic and gravely determined. Her three-year-old daughter stands on the bench beside her with a worried frown as she clutches at her mother's arm.

Ray, the Selkie, is gone. Her skin was found over a month ago by a cabin boy Beck had been kind to, freeing Ray to go back to the sea. She and Beck were devastated to part, but they knew what her discovery would mean for baby Gareth. In the end, it could no longer be denied that the safest course of action would be to raise Gareth as a Gardnerian.

Margryt was initially devastated, as well, shocked to hear of her fastmate's affair—and with a Selkie, no less. She spent many a tear-soaked night at our cottage, raging against her fasting to Beck at such a young age and his cruel infidelity. But in the end, Margryt's great kindness won out, and her compassion for this baby who was caught in the middle, just like her. Her growing affection for baby Gareth eventually overshadowed her grief and anger and rapidly morphed into a fiercely protective bond.

The cathedral quiets as Edwin Gardner walks up the side aisle, violin in hand, and joins us on the dais. He offers me a small, heartfelt smile, warmth in his deep green eyes.

"My congratulations to my brother, Vale." His voice wavers with nerves and emotion. "And to his beloved fastmate, Tessla."

He lifts violin and bow and launches into my favorite piece, "Winter's Dark." The sound of the massive crowd quiets to almost nothing, save the fidgeting of small children and the occasional cry of a baby. Edwin's melody gracefully winds around every column, and I remember the first time I heard him play this song. It feels like a hundred years ago.

I look over at Fain, who's listening to the music, his three sisters in a neat row on his left side. Lucretia gives me a brief, friendly smile.

Fain follows his sister's glance and catches my eye. He casts me his sly, catlike grin and throws out a tendril of cool water that I deftly meet, latch on to and warm up so hot that he has to quickly release it. His head bobs in a laugh, and I smile back at him with mischief.

Fain teases Vale and me to no end about our hunger for each other. Vale is so clearly making up for lost time, taking me away early from every event, pulling me into bedrooms, back rooms, closets, anywhere he can get his hands and his fire on me, the two of us burning through bottle after bottle of Sanjire root, which Fain generously continues to supply.

Fain enjoys making full sport of us, his jokes scandalously off-color. He recently bought three more erotic books for us and left them on our bed with a cheeky note.

To My Dear Vale,
Since you clearly know where to put it.
If you and your lovely fastmate ever come up for air, you can peruse these for more ways to…connect.
As Always,
Fain

I flush at the memory of this as my eyes wander away from Fain. My gaze lights on Rosebeth and Myles, who sit two rows back from Fain and his sisters. Myles's arm is wrapped protectively around my Lower River friend's shoulders. Their fasting has proven to be a good one so far—two good-natured people united in bliss.

Rosebeth cries joyfully into her handkerchief and sends me a small smile. I force a returning smile and fight back against an edge of bitterness that's still raw within me, and the unpleasant thoughts that rise with it.

She and Myles love me again, like so many do—now that I've been proven pure. Now that I'm sealed to the son of the most powerful Mage in Gardneria.

I've no dearth of admirers and friends now.

But things are forever altered for me. There are no clean lines anymore, no perfectly delineated sides.

Vale's standing stiffly, his expression frozen in place, and I follow his gaze to a cloaked figure standing past the crowds at the very back of the Cathedral.

"What's wrong?" I ask him in a hushed whisper.

His eyes glint with tears as he leans toward me. "Gods, Tess. It's Annel'lin."

I try to keep my face impassive, though my heart swells for him. Annel'lin, the Uuril woman who raised him. Coming here is a huge personal risk for her, as the women of all the Urisk castes are now indentured and forbidden from traveling freely.

But I can tell that her presence means the world to Vale. That she's here to see the child she loves refasted and sealed.

For the rest of the ceremony, Vale and I wear fake smiles and whisper to each other, putting on an affectionate show, as Vale quickly formulates a plan to bring Annel'lin with us to Verpacia. We'll sneak her back there under the guise of being our personal servant until we're safely across the border. It's a sound plan, and I can feel some of the turbulence in Vale's fire smoothing out.

"Please rise as we perform the sealing rites," the priest intones with a beatific smile, his arms stretched wide to embrace the crowd.

Vale and I take our places on either side of the small altar and clasp our hands tight over it, our eyes locked. Carnissa Gardner readies her wand. The priest opens *The Book of the Ancients* and reverently intones the long series of sealing prayers. He smiles as he finishes, and Vale's mother holds her wand over our hands.

It's unnecessary, the repetition of the spell. Purely for ceremony and show, but it suddenly strikes me that I'm here by my own free will this time.

I'm here with my whole heart. Full of a fierce love for the man who stands before me.

The spell won't do anything—we've already had the lines placed and set and well consummated. But I hold tight to Vale as his mother murmurs first the fasting and then the sealing spell. Her tendrils of power curl around our hands, our wrists. I'm suddenly overcome by my love for Vale. Love that's fully reflected in his ardent gaze as his fire blazes outward to merge with mine.

Carnissa Gardner's magic pulls into our hands and wrists, and I gasp as a series of impossibly intricate swirls bursts into life, adding to the lines that are already there. My love for Vale and his love for me wrap around and through the spell and out into the lines in a visible rush. The lines glow red for a long moment, and a collective murmur of overjoyed surprise goes up in the vast space. I look to Vale in wonder, and he smiles.

The Black Witch and the priests surrounding us all have tears glistening in their eyes as the crowd responds with thunderous applause.

"I love you, Tessla," Vale says with ragged feeling, his fire a warm caress all through me.

"I love you, too." I break into happy tears as he pulls me around the altar and brings his lips to mine. Cheers are shouted out over the applause.

We kiss, and I bask in the feel of his lips, his body pressed to mine, everything around us momentarily fading into background.

"*Sanguin'in!*" Fain rakishly yells out, and Vale and I laugh at the same time, breaking the kiss. We look to Fain, who's grinning at us, tears streaking down his face, his arm still tight around Vyvian.

"All will be well," I tell Vale with fierce assurance, patting the wand that's safely ensconced in my stocking. "We'll be in Verpacia soon." *Where Annel'lin will be safe.* My gaze wordlessly comforts him.

Some of the tight worry leaves his eyes. He nods and lets out a long breath. Then he smiles crookedly at me and leans in close. "It seems we'll get another chance at a proper Sealing Night."

A laugh escapes me, and I shoot him a suggestive smile.

Vale gives me a sardonic look. "Maybe don't punch me this time."

I caress his back, sending up a trail of sparks in my wake. "Don't worry," I whisper into his ear, my other hand tracing the now familiar planes of his chest. "That's not at all what I had in mind."

Vale laughs, pulls me firmly against him and brings his lips to mine, our fires lashing around each other like the lines that mark us. Sealed and tightly bound.

Forever.

★ ★ ★ ★ ★

LIGHT MAGE

To Walter—for everything.

Dear Reader,

There is a scene of sexual assault in *Light Mage* that is based on something that happened to me on a blind date when I was seventeen. The means I'm using to speak about my experience now may be within the pages of a fantasy novel, but the emotions here echo my own at that time, and so does the violence involved in the scene.

The assault occurs at the end of Chapter Three in Part Two of this story. If reading something like this would prove painful for you, please skip that section and simply know that an assault occurred. There is also a traumatic discussion of the assault at the beginning of the following chapter (Part Two, Chapter Four), where the main character is not believed or supported. The event is not referenced in any detail for the rest of the narrative and is only generally discussed, so if you need to skip over these two scenes, it is my belief that you can still understand and hopefully enjoy the narrative.

I had never discussed this incident of assault that happened in my own life until I sat down to plot out this story about two years ago. If you're wondering why I never talked about it, perhaps Sage's story will help you to understand how futile the idea of speaking out can feel to someone raised in a very strict environment where the culture does not support the empowerment of young women.

It is my wish that every last one of you has the power to speak out and be heard—and also, if needed, to walk away from oppression.

And, in time, fight back.

Laurie

Icelandic Mountains

North

Maeloria

Alfsigroth

Pyrran
Islands

Northern Lupine Territory

GARDNE

Malthorin Bay

Valgard

Voltic Sea

Rothir

W. F

Fae Islands

Southern
Lupine Territory

Keltania

WESTERN REALM

Northern Forest

Northern Caledonian Mountains

HALFIX

Northern Spine

AMAZ
TERRITORY

E. Pass

VERPAX

VERPACIA

LYNDON

Southern Spine

Southern Caledonian Mountains

Wastelands
(destroyed by war)

University

Vu Trin Military Base

Gardnerian Military Base

PROLOGUE

They're scared to let me see him. My demon child.

The elderly Vu Trin healer, Sang Loi, quickly wraps him in a dark blanket, hiding his wings from sight. She hugs him close to her chest, eyeing me with apprehension. Three black-garbed Vu Trin sorceresses flank her, watching me closely, their hands loose on curved swords.

Waiting to see what a Gardnerian will do to an Icaral child.

An Icaral demon. One of the Evil Ones.

And not just any Icaral—this child may be the Icaral of Prophecy. Destined to battle the next Gardnerian Black Witch. The Seers of every race are clear on one thing—somewhere out there, a new Black Witch is rising, and deep in the world's shadows, an Icaral is about to rise as well. A male Icaral, who will someday come into his power and fight against her.

His victory would be death to Gardneria. My country.

And this Icaral may very well be my son.

"Give him to me," I demand, my voice shaky. I'm propped up on my elbows, the sweat of a hard labor cloaking my back, my hair plastered to my head in wet tendrils, the pain of birth still reverberating through my body. "I want to hold him."

Sang and the row of Vu Trin sorceresses look to Chi Nam, their powerful rune-sorceress.

My gaze shifts to her as well. "He's just a baby," I rasp out to white-haired Chi Nam. "Not a weapon. And he's my child. Not yours."

Chi Nam leans heavily on her rune-marked staff and gives me a grave, considering look, then motions to Sang with a quick nod. The healer folds the blanket back and places the small, warm bundle into my arms.

My son's eyes glow like fire. Black wings, paper-thin, struggle to fan out from his back. His tiny hand wraps around my finger, the world circles around me at a dizzying speed, the enormity of it all pressing down, pushing the air from my lungs. Stripping away the last shred of everything I once believed.

I've become a pawn in a war that could be the unmaking of us all. And so has my child.

The White Wand sits on the table beside me, innocent as a branch, but I can feel it grasping for me. Drawing me near. A constellation of prismatic, shimmering light bursts into view and whorls around the Wand as the vision of a starlit tree pulses in the back of my mind.

The Wand has called to me ceaselessly for months now. Murmuring under my thoughts like a whispered song. Something that teases at my mind yet remains elusive.

I look into the eyes of my baby as realization crashes through me with the force of a gale storm. And I finally understand, with staggering clarity, what the Wand has been trying to tell me all this time.

PART ONE:

Six years ago...

CHAPTER ONE:
Wandfasting

I'm not supposed to touch Father's books. Especially not his Mage Council books.

But as I linger in the deserted sitting room, temptation swells inside me, my heart racing in my chest. Father's Mage Council tome is splayed out facedown on the arm of his favorite chair, practically begging me to take a peek at its pages.

Golden lumenstone lamplight flickers over the gilded Mage Council seal on the book's cover. The warm, glimmering color dances in my vision, and the light affinity lines deep inside me pull taut, my wand hand tingling with want.

Thunder rumbles somewhere outside in the storm-darkened night.

Don't be drawn in by the gold, I chastise myself. Gold is a Fae color. A bright lure of the Evil Ones.

I clench my wand hand and close my eyes in an effort to tamp down the pull of the forbidden color. The gold wash in my vision gradually clears, and I glance toward the sitting room's open Ironwood door, out into the shadowed hallway, making sure I'm still alone.

Emboldened by a desperate curiosity and acting hastily before I can lose my nerve, I take Father's book in hand and turn it over, breathlessly flipping through the pages until I find what I'm searching for.

Gardnerian Guard
Ledger of High-Level Elemental Forces (Levels Four and Five)
Fire Magery: 603 Mages
Air Magery: 78 Mages
Water Magery: 321 Mages
Earth Magery: 1,290 Mages
Light Magery: 1 Mage with rune-sorcery abilities

The last line stands out in bold relief in my mind.

Only one Light Mage.

I look down at my wand hand, the effects of the gold lingering in the metallic yellow hue that now suffuses my fingertips. Faint, violet veins of lightning flash through the gold, just beneath my skin, the lightning thin as fine thread.

I flex my fingers, anxious to clear the color from them.

My artistic hobbies used to be enough to contain my burgeoning light magery—painting, weaving and drawing in the permitted designs and colors. Black for our oppression; dark green for our subjugation of the Fae wilds; red for the blood of our ancestors; and blue, but only to depict the sacred Ironflowers. It says in our holy book that all other colors have been corrupted by the Evil Ones, and my family follows *The Book of the Ancients* to the letter.

But lately my light magery has been straining at the edges of me, like a prismatic waterfall threatening to burst as startling new abilities spring to life. I've recently discovered that I'm now able to magnify faraway images if I tighten the affinity lines around my eyes, and I can even see in the dark if I really concentrate, though everything seems to be lit by a reddish glow when I do.

An uneasy frustration flares inside me, a feeling that's been mounting for months now.

Why is it getting so hard to control my light affinity? And what could I do if I was a boy? If I was allowed a wand and access to light spells?

I know it's wrong to think these thoughts. I know it's not what the Ancient One has intended for me, or else He'd have made me a boy. *The Book* says that female Mages are supposed to pass on magic to our sons, not wield it ourselves. Only the prophetess Galliana and the Black Witch were granted the holy charge to wield magic and save Gardneria from the Evil Ones. Even so, I can't seem to stop myself from wondering what I could do with a wand.

Footsteps sound in the hall.

My head snaps up, fright rushing through me. I hastily set the thick volume facedown on the chair, the way I found it, then spring up, fleet as a deer, and make for the door. I peer into the hallway, my pulse thudding.

No one.

Slipping out of the sitting room, I freeze at the sound of shuffling in the library. Blending in with the shadows, I creep forward and glimpse movement through the slit in the library's door. Level Four Mage stripes gleam on the edges of Father's Mage Council uniform, the silver embroidery catching the flickering light from the fireplace with a lustrous metallic gleam. His wand is sheathed at his side.

A rush of longing catches inside me at the sight of the Blackthorn wand's smoothly carved handle. The rich colors of the room suddenly brighten, then fragment into an iridescent mosaic that encircles the wand like a spiraling flower of light.

I close my eyes and take a long, shuddering breath, flexing

my wand hand into a tight fist to shake off the wand's pull. Rattled, I open my eyes, the colors blessedly back where they should be, albeit heightened and pulsing with decadent vibrancy. I keep my eyes carefully averted from Father's wand and listen intently.

Mother Eliss, my stepmother, is gazing up at Father, her brow knit tighter than usual, her expression solemn. I frown and wonder if they're about to have the usual, troubled conversation about my increasingly uncontrollable light affinity.

"Sage needs to be wandfasted, and soon." Father's tone is stern, his voice low and implacable.

Wandfasted!

The word sears through me and my breath catches in my lungs as I'm thrown into disorienting confusion. *No. Not yet. I'm not even thirteen!*

A shamed flush pricks at my cheeks as I realize what's likely prompted this conversation. It's not my light magery—this is all because Mother Eliss found me alone with Rafe Gardner out in the woods yesterday.

There's no need for wandfasting, I inwardly rail, a raw, hot embarrassment twisting up inside me. *Rafe and I didn't do anything impure. We were just up on the property line talking—in full view of everyone!* Filled with secret guilt, I shy away from thoughts of Rafe's stunning emerald eyes. His warm smile. And my new, furtive curiosity about what it would be like to hold his hand or touch my lips to his, light as a feather.

My face burns with humiliation. When she found us together, it was as if Mother Eliss could look straight into my mind and read my deeply private feelings for Rafe. She practically dragged me away from him as I stumbled to keep up with her.

Thunder booms outside, and I flinch along with Mother Eliss. Rain begins to pound against the roof, sheeting down the library's arching windows as my thoughts storm in a tangle of emotion.

"She's so young for wandfasting." A shadow of bleak worry passes over Mother Eliss's face and she wrings her fastmarked hands.

"She has the figure of a *much* older girl," Father insists, as if I've committed some trespass. "It's time, Eliss."

I shrink back and look down self-consciously at the curves that are now so pronounced, even my modest clothing can't hide them.

"I've found a fastmate for her," Father announces with finality.

A fastmate? Panic trills inside me. I'm nowhere near ready to leave my home or my beloved sisters, Retta and Clover.

"Who is it?" Mother Eliss gives Father a questioning look.

"Tobias Vasillis," Father announces with slow precision, as if he's secured a prize. "Clover and Retta are to be bindingly promised to Tobias's young brothers as well, and fasted to them when they turn thirteen."

Mother Eliss gives a sharp intake of breath. "Oh, well done, Warren."

Well done? How can she say such a thing? Retta is only seven years old, and Clover just turned six. Why are our parents so eager to send us away?

Father deflects Mother Eliss's praise with a dismissive wave of his hand. "Sage was bound to attract a good match with her light affinity—she's sure to have high-level Mage sons. And she's a good girl, our Sage. She deserves to be well fasted."

I calm down a fraction, bolstered by Father's unexpected praise and Mother Eliss's unspoken agreement.

Our Sage. Not an outsider in the nest, but belonging just as much as my sisters. As much as my twin brothers. Even though Mother Eliss isn't my birth mother, or my older brother Shane's.

Momma died of the Red Grippe when I was just five years old, and Father fasted to Mother Eliss not long after.

I desperately want to please both of them. I'm afraid of being sent away like Shane, who was always arguing with Father and disobeying Mother Eliss.

I want to be their good girl.

Mother Eliss is quiet for a long moment, but then she sighs and nods, her tense expression softening.

"Eliss," Father says, his tone warmer, "I know how fond you are of Sage. She'll be fasted, and then we'll bring her home. But with her future secured."

It won't be so bad, I console myself. *Mother Eliss seems happy with Father's choice for me, and after the fasting, I get to come right back home again. With Retta and Clover.*

Thunder crashes again, and my head jerks back from the shock of the earsplitting sound. The frantic pitter-patter of small feet sounds around the curving hallway, and suddenly Retta and Clover are clinging to my skirts, a beseeching look on each of their faces.

Scared to be caught eavesdropping, I bring a finger to my lips and motion urgently toward the library to hush them. They remain carefully quiet, none of us wanting to invoke our parents' fury. I gently but hastily guide whimpering, wild-haired Clover and round-eyed, timid Retta back to their room and under their bedcovers. I snuggle in between them, hugging them close as the storm crashes and booms and pounds our estate. Retta's eyes are tightly closed, her hands pressed hard against her ears, and Clover clutches at me, chewing nervously on her ever-present quilted blanket.

"I don't want you to go away," Clover says, a stark plea in her tone, and I realize they were listening with ears pressed to the wall again.

"Don't get fasted," Retta chimes in, her whole body curled

into a ball and pressed up against my side. "Why do you have to get fasted?"

I hug them close and tamp down my lingering apprehension. "I'm not going anywhere, you silly ones. Not 'til I'm a lot older. And when I join my fast-family, you'll come, too."

Retta stares at me, wide-eyed. "We will?"

"Of course," I reassure her, still warmed from the glow of Father's and Mother Eliss's praise. "We'll always be together."

"Okay," Retta says in a small voice, seeming mollified. Clover's expression remains that of a soldier under siege. She grasps my arm even tighter, as if preparing to resist if someone tries to snatch me away. I playfully poke at her until she cracks a smile, and soon her grip on me loosens.

I sing them their favorite song, a counting song about baby animals, and stare up at the white bird mobile I've sewn for them, the design a reminder of the Ancient One's holy birds, who watch over us all and protect us from harm. The flock of cheery birds sways in the slight draft the storm has kicked up. My eyes slide down to a nearby shelf housing the cloth dolls I've made for my sisters. Smaller dolls fashioned from clothespins sit on the larger dolls' laps, all of them dressed in Gardnerian black. Beside that shelf is another, holding rows and rows of religious children's books.

Mother Eliss only allows religious books and religious songs and religious art in our house—and the art can only be in the permitted colors. She's always been strict with me and my sisters, and now she's often absent and wrapped up in the care of my twin half-brothers. But she often rewards us in little ways when we try to mind the rules—gifts of picture books left on our pillows, and a flower-press on the dining room table just last week with a note that read, "For My Good Girls." She doesn't like to play or sing songs, but I know she's been through terrible things, having lived through the Realm War.

Unbidden, a troubling memory surfaces from a few days ago, when I found Mother Eliss leaning against the wooden counter in the kitchen, sobbing, a small painting of her dead parents held loosely in her hand.

I'd frozen, my heart twisting with sympathy. "Can…can I help you, Mother Eliss?"

She'd given a brusque shake of her head, misery coating her in palpable waves.

Desperate to soothe her, I'd quietly poured her a cup of tea and fetched her favorite shawl, gently laying it around her thin, surprisingly fragile shoulders.

She'd reached out to gently squeeze my arm. "You're a comfort to me, girl." Her voice was stuffy, her eyes fixed hard on the counter. A single tear fell from her eye and splattered down onto the wood in a bulbous star.

"They're evil," she'd told me. "The Kelts. The Icarals. And those Urisk, too. Pure evil. Every last one of them. They killed my whole family. No one was spared, not even the children." She'd looked up and leveled her suddenly blazing eyes at me. "Never forget that, Sage. *Never.* Promise me."

Unease had spiked through me at her tone, but I'd nodded, hoping to please her. "I promise," I agreed, intimidated by the fierce grief swimming in her eyes.

"Another Black Witch is coming," she said, her grip on me tightening. "All the Seers have foretold it. The Reaping Times are coming, Sagellyn. And the Evil Ones will be rendered to ash and rent asunder."

I inwardly drew back from her, pulling my affinity lines protectively in. Scared of this talk of Evil Ones and the shadow times coming for us all.

Mother Eliss grew suddenly quiet, a jagged misery tightening her face as she released my arm, her hand coming to her eyes as she began to silently weep once more.

★ ★ ★

I hug my sisters tighter, chilled by the memory of Mother Eliss's implacable grief.

"It's looking for you, Sage." Clover's voice is tiny and worried as she clings to her blanket. Retta's huddled against my other side, fallen peacefully asleep while I've been lost in my own thoughts.

"What's looking for me?" I ask curiously. The wind rattles the windowpanes.

"The tree," she says in a small, sure voice. "I had a dream about it. It's calling your name. It sounds like the wind. *Sage. Sage. Saaage.*"

An uneasy chill pricks the back of my neck. "That's silly."

"It was a dream, but not a dream," she says in a singsong voice. "It likes you, Sage. Lemme show you."

Clover reaches over to the shelf that abuts the bed and picks up a framed painting I made for her—an illustration of our sacred Source Tree, wreathed in starlight and surrounded by a grove of dark brown Ironwood trees, each graced with deep green leaves and lush blue Ironflowers. Gardnerian children are dancing in a ring around the Source Tree, butterflies and birds flitting about, wildflowers strewn at their feet.

"This tree," she says, pointing to our Source Tree. "It wants to give you a branch. The White Wand."

Ah. She's being fanciful.

"It talked to you in your dream? The Tree did?" I'm half humoring her, half wondering if her musings about the Ancient One's Wand of Power would be considered sacrilegious by Mother Eliss.

"Not with its mouth," Clover insists, frowning. "Trees don't have mouths." She pats her chest. "In my heart. It's nice, Sage. It said you don't have to be afraid."

It's an odd thing for her to say and stops me up short, dampening my smile. I brush away a tinge of unease and arrange my face into a teasing expression. "Now why in the world would it want to give me the Wand?" I ask, playing along. Clover likes to spin tales.

"So the demons don't get it."

Surprise stabs through me. "The...*what*? Where would you get such ideas?" Lightning flashes.

"From my dream," she says, as if this should be obvious.

"Well, it was just a dream," I reassure her, fighting off a sudden chill.

"I'm scared of the demons." Clover pulls herself into a ball, her eyes darting furtively around as she tugs her blanket up over her nose. "They've got big shadow horns! And glowing eyes! And they're made of fire!"

"You don't need to be scared of anything," I stolidly insist. "It was just a bad dream."

Branches scrape across the window's glass, like claws. Like something trying to get in.

"No," Clover says urgently, eyes wide, her words slightly muffled by her blanket. "They're real. They're coming. They're coming for *you*. They *want* it."

"Clove, stop it."

"They want the White Wand," she presses, ignoring me. "They have the Shadow One already, but they want that one, too. You can't let them have it, Sage!"

"*Stop*. Really," I say, my heart picking up speed. I'm suddenly acutely aware of the cold darkness just beyond the walls. I focus on the window and pull the affinity lines around my eyes in tight so I can see outside. The darkness instantly brightens, as if illuminated by red torchlight, the trees outside the window gleaming in the varying shades of scarlet that my light magery allows me to see. I scan the red-lit scene anxiously.

Nothing. No demons. No monsters waiting. Just the wind-buffeted tree and the stormy night.

You're being ridiculous, I comfort myself, relaxing my affinity lines, the scarlet fading as my vision returns to normal. *There's nothing to fear. She simply had a nightmare.*

"Stop playing and go to sleep," I gently scold Clover, tucking the blankets tight around her skinny frame. "What do we do when we get scared?"

She answers me through a mouthful of blanket. "The Ancient One's Prayer of Protection."

"That's right."

Prompting her, we say the prayer together.

Oh, Blessed Ancient One. Purify our minds. Purify our hearts. Purify Erthia from the stain of the Evil Ones.

I make the Ancient One's star sign over her heart. "There," I emphatically state. "Protected."

Some of the fear in her eyes softens. Snuggling back in with her, I shake off my own edge of apprehension and stroke Clover's messy hair, drawing comfort from being close to my sisters. My own room is next door, but we often gravitate toward being with each other, especially on stormy nights like this.

And we'll always be together, I remind myself, a glimmer of relief passing through me as I remember Father's plans for all three of us. And maybe Tobias Vasillis will be as nice as Rafe and have his same lovely, emerald eyes. Perhaps he'll carve me a small bird, like Rafe once did, and tell me funny stories.

The storm rages and the darkness presses in around us, but I focus on these bolstering thoughts as the little white birds bob overhead, gently lulling me to sleep.

CHAPTER TWO:
Valgard

I'm breathless with equal parts anticipation and trepidation as I press my cheek to the sun-warmed glass of the carriage window. Mother Eliss and Father are seated across from me, wrapped up in low conversation.

Three weeks have passed since I was told I'm to be fasted, and I'm having a hard time keeping acceptably still. My legs fidget with nervous excitement beneath my heavy black skirt as our carriage draws ever closer to Valgard, Gardneria's glittering capital city.

For my wandfasting.

We crest a hill and Malthorin Bay comes into view, splayed out before us and shimmering with sunlight. I gasp as an impossible variety of blues cascade toward me in a glorious barrage—everything from cool, glacial tones to vibrant turquoise to midnight-blue.

Deliriously overcome, I reflexively breathe in deep and pull the color in. Swirls of blue that only I can see spiral toward me and straight into my affinity lines. I've a sense, in the back of my mind, of being suffused with a glorious rush of sapphire energy that sings through my lines of magic.

My wand hand starts to tingle, wrenching me from my

color daze. I glance down and see that my fingertips are glimmering blue. Not an acceptable Ironflower blue, but a bright, decadent turquoise.

Panic spears through me, and I force my gaze away from the bay, my heart now racing as I quickly pull my hand out of my parents' sight. I surreptitiously peek again, alarmed to see the iridescent blue has spread halfway down my fingers. I swallow hard, sweat breaking out on my forehead as I pull my hand further into my sleeve and anxiously glance at Father and Mother Eliss.

Father catches my eye and studies me with a questioning tilt of his head, then gives me a small, encouraging smile. "There's no need to be nervous today," he tells me. "You've earned this fasting. We're quite proud of you, Sagellyn."

Mother Eliss echoes Father's approval with a pleased nod. "You deserve this, Sage. To be fasted to a powerful, accomplished young Mage, and from such a good family. I'm so glad for you, child."

"Thank you, Mother Eliss. Thank you, Father," I say, clenching and unclenching my wand hand, desperate to loosen the forbidden color's grip and keep hold of their warm, always longed-for approval.

Father and Mother Eliss nod at me, then smile at each other, and my heart fills with gladness and belonging.

I secretly check my fingers, my hand curled to keep my fingertips from their view. My fingers have faded back to their normal, faintly verdant sheen. I breathe in a long sigh of relief and vow to do better. To be the best Mage—and daughter— I can possibly be.

The city's cacophony of colors and new sights are intoxicating, and I allow myself to fall into the overabundance of our holy colors. The design of every banner, every stained-glass window, every stone-patterned plaza is colored only in blessed blacks, deep greens, reds and blues—and the blessed hue of blue is only used to depict the sacred Ironflower.

Everything is so perfect and safe and beautiful.

Scarlet glass lanterns hang in rows in front of a furniture shop and flash their opulent ruby lights. Flowering emerald vines spill from rooftop gardens. A florist's stand sells bouquets of crimson roses. I tighten the affinity lines around my eyes and pull the image of one bloom so close, it's as if I could take the rose in my hand.

As the carriage pulls forward slightly, the scene shifts, and I'm suddenly face-to-face with a close-up view of a surprising image.

A young Snake Elf.

His ears come to swift points, and his silver eyes are set in a face covered with deep green, reptilian scales. The scales' interlocking pattern of small hexagons, intricately rendered in black ink, instantly captures my affinity and takes my breath away.

Beautiful…

"Warren," Mother Eliss says to Father, sounding rattled. "There's a Snake Elf loose in the city."

Her sharp voice shocks me back to my senses. I loosen my eye-lines and force the image of the Snake Elf away, his visage contracting as it flies backward to where it hangs, tacked onto the support beam of a tidy fruit stand.

A wanted posting for a fugitive Snake Elf named Ra'Ven Za'Nor.

Stupid, stupid. I mentally castigate myself. *You cannot be drawn in by the pattern of Snake Elf skin, of all things.*

Mother Eliss has taught us about these reptilian Elves—dangerous criminals that the Alfsigr Elves keep imprisoned underground.

Father regards Mother Eliss somberly. "He's an escaped prisoner of the Alfsigr. Part of the Snake Elves' mockery of a royal family." He gives her a look of reassuring gravity. "Don't worry, Eliss. His days are numbered. They've got the Mage Guard out looking for him."

We lurch ahead and the disconcerting poster is swept from sight, but my eyes dart around nervously now. I tighten the lines around my eyes and light up the shadows of dark alleys and alcoves in my vision, searching for the hidden Snake Elf. But there's nothing troubling to be seen anywhere.

We amble past a toy-crafter's shop, stocked with wooden canisters of play White Wands. Figurines of winged Icaral demons hang from the store's awning on strings. A little boy is trying to thwack a demon with one of the ivory wands.

Wands. Even though they're only toys, my light affinity insistently strains toward them.

Two young woman stride into view, laughing merrily, their arms linked. My eyes widen as my attention is wrenched from the wands. The first young woman's black garb is shockingly decorated with golden, looping embroidery, but the second young woman's garb is even more outrageous—her black tunic and long skirt are edged with glittering purple gems.

Purple!

My affinity hungrily lurches for the purple. Instantly overcome, I ignore every holy order and drink in the sight, the color washing over me, sweeping over the entire scene in a glorious violet filter.

How can she be wearing purple? I marvel, luxuriating in the exquisite hue. *She's Gardnerian.*

"Look at this display!" Mother Eliss spits out with piercing derision. Her words are a hammer, cracking down on my unholy rapture. "They've forgotten what our garb represents."

I reluctantly avert my eyes, a sullen frustration stinging along my lines as I fight the sudden, intense longing to own resplendent garb edged in glittering purple. Everything in me orients itself to this gravely forbidden Fae color. My affinity lines sometimes crackle a disconcerting purple just beneath my skin, even when the color isn't present around me. Mother Eliss has consulted our priest about this many times, deeply concerned for my Mage purity.

Father briefly eyes the women. "This is what comes of late fasting. Letting their daughters run rampant." He scowls and turns away with a disgusted breath. "One step up from an Issani whore."

I stiffen at the word as I tense my hidden wand hand. It's an important thing, I know, not to be a whore—a filthy, amorphous idea that I don't completely understand. But I do know I'm to be safe from it as soon as I'm fasted. Still, the idea of wearing a dress decorated with purple fills me with a yearning that's almost impossible to suppress.

Our carriage soon turns right and a huge plaza opens up before us, the mammoth Valgard Cathedral coming into view. I'm soon glued to the window again, mesmerized by the plaza's intricate mosaic floor of black and green stone. In its center rises a huge statue of our last Black Witch, Carnissa Gardner, chiseled in white granite, her wand pointed down at an Icaral demon lying dead beneath her feet.

I stare, transfixed. *Her face.* It's the absolute image of my neighbor, Elloren Gardner, the Black Witch's own granddaughter. Even though Elloren's only eleven, the severe lines of her face already match those of her powerful grandmother.

Our carriage comes to a smooth stop in front of the towering cathedral. Sweeping columns made of huge Ironwood tree trunks rise into the sky. The entwining branches hold a silver Erthia orb at their zenith, like a gargantuan forest leaning in to cup the world. A jittery apprehension rises within me as I gaze at the ornately carved doors.

Tobias Vasillis is somewhere inside. My soon-to-be fastmate.

I disembark from the carriage, filled with a quivering

sense of anticipation, and follow Father and Mother Eliss up the cathedral's stairs, careful to hide my purple-tinged hand.

There's a line of Gardnerian maidens seated in the pews at the front of the cathedral. A few of them turn around to look at us as Father, Mother Eliss and I make our way up the long central aisle. Large Ironwood trees are embedded throughout the walls and support the enormous ceiling, the trees' dark branches tangling overhead. It's like I'm inside a dark, majestic forest.

A gasp escapes me as I take in the sight of the stained-glass windows. Each one depicts a different scene from *The Book of the Ancients,* and I slow down, momentarily forgetting my nervousness, distracted by the stunning artistry. Though the images are rendered only in our sacred colors, rays of sunlight stream through the glass and criss-cross to create a kaleidoscope of other shades all over the cathedral, a blend of forbidden golds, oranges…and purples.

Purple. Oh, the purple.

The glowing, vivid beauty of it is almost too much to bear as my view of the entire cathedral interior is suffused with a violet hue.

Don't look, I caution myself, at war with my affinity. *It's the wilds trying to pollute this sacred space. Trying to pollute you.*

Mother Eliss gives me a gentle tug, cutting into the color's decadent spell. Heart hammering and the purple rapidly fading from my vision, I tense my wand hand and hasten my pace to escape the seductive Fae colors and keep up with my stepmother's fast clip.

There's a crowd of adults gathered to the right of the dais at the head of the cathedral, their conversations low and murmuring, their expressions solemn. Some of the adults turn as we approach, and several men break away from the crowd to greet Father, to shake his hand.

All of the Gardnerians here are plainly dressed like us—all black, with no ornamentation save the silver Erthia orb pendants round our necks and the silver Mage Level stripes on some of the men's tunics, as well as the occasional Mage Council seal pin. Every family here is part of the strict, Styvian sect of our faith, adhering with pure, unflinching submission to every rule in *The Book of the Ancients.*

The only true Gardnerians. The only true First Children, Mother Eliss likes to say.

We're met by a thin priest with a remote expression, the Ancient One's white bird embroidered on the front of his dark, priestly garments. He directs my parents to the pews on the right of the central aisle, where the other adults are taking their seats. Then he ushers me toward the young Gardnerian maidens sitting in neat rows to the aisle's left.

A heady excitement bubbles up inside me. I've never been around so many other girls my own age, and from my own sect—all of us strictly obedient and able to mingle without censure. I eagerly search the rows, wondering which girl is Gwynnifer Croft. Our fathers are both on the Mage Council, and I'm to stay with Gwynnifer's family for the duration of our visit while my parents lodge with my fastmate's family.

One of the girls turns to glance at me, then another. A surge of whispering rises for a moment before stilling into a tense silence, and the girls' looks of surprise change, almost in unison, to unfriendly glares.

A girl in the center of the group bursts out crying, and the young women around her lean in to comfort her. She's willowy and lovely, the crying girl, with vivid green eyes, a regal nose and full lips, her hair a cascade of lustrous black locks. Her eyes are red-rimmed, like she's been crying on and off for a while, and her almost palpable misery is the focus on this side of the room. But that's not what sets me flinching back.

She's staring at me with a hatred so daggered, I'm instantly thrust into a storm of confusion. Feeling unnerved, I awkwardly follow the priest's direction and take a seat at the far end of the front pew.

The button-nosed girl next to me jerks her whole body away as I sit down, then pulls her long skirt sharply aside so that not even her clothes will touch me. She has a haughty posture at odds with her pretty face, her black hair straight and pulled back into a simple, shining twist, her forehead large and curved like a smooth eggshell. She sniffs and briefly looks down her nose at me, then makes a point of whipping her head away as if the sight of me burns her eyes.

I hunch down in mortification, desperate to know why they all hate me so.

A white-haired priest is talking to our parents in a low, practiced drone about the importance of maidenly purity. The adults all nod solemnly in response, ignoring the commotion on this side of the aisle.

There's a startling jab against the side of my rear, and I turn to find the button-nosed girl sneering at me. Then she turns her head away again in an angry huff.

I glance down at the bench to find a small piece of paper pushed slightly under my skirt's edge. Heart thudding, I take the paper in hand, sparing a sidelong glance toward the adults to make sure they're still safely immersed in what the priest has to say, and discreetly unfold it.

It contains one word, hastily scrawled, and I inwardly recoil when I see it.

Slat'ern.

It's a word from the Ancient Tongue, but I know what it means. A girl with no morals. A girl who is filthy and coarse, who tempts men.

A whore.

CHAPTER THREE:
Tobias

I clutch the cruel note as tears sting at my eyes, sending up a fervent prayer that the malicious, crying girl isn't Gwynnifer Croft, desperate to not be staying with someone who inexplicably hates me.

The button-nosed girl eyes me sidelong with disdain, her face twisting into a frown. She leans toward me and hisses, "You've no right to fast to Tobias. He belongs to *Draven*."

My stomach drops and cinches tight as all the pieces of this terrible puzzle come together, the realization bearing down on me like a miller's stone. I slouch further down, lamenting my unfair treatment as I fight back tears. *None of this was my doing,* I silently rail against them. *Tobias was chosen for me by our parents and the priests and the Ancient One above.*

After a few miserable moments, the hairs on the back of my neck start to prickle, as if brushed by an invisible hand, and I'm overwhelmed by the sudden, uneasy sense that I'm being intently, silently watched.

I turn, and my eyes catch on a slight girl in the middle of the pew behind me. She has owlish, pale green eyes, and her black hair is a wild mess. Her small, pointed nose and face are all delicate sharpness, like a fox. Unlike most of the girls here, there's no malice in her stare, just a focused intensity that's unnerving.

The large Ironwood door to the left of the dais scrapes opens, and we collectively straighten to attention, craning our necks to see who's coming in. Only Draven remains hunched down, her weeping echoing off the arcing cathedral walls.

A young priest leads our fastmates in.

Instantly alert, we all watch in rapt silence as the young men awkwardly shuffle in, passing directly in front of us like horses on display, the silver lines on their tunics depicting their Mage levels. I search each face, my heartbeat fluttering in my chest.

Which one is Tobias?

They're all around thirteen or fourteen, like us, although one passes by who looks a fair bit younger, closer to eight or nine. *But he has to be at least thirteen to fast,* I reason, perplexed. He's skinny, with ears that stick out like the handles of an urn, his eyes darting nervously toward us. His whole body practically vibrates with pent-up energy.

Please don't let this be Tobias, I silently pray. I imagine my disappointment if this childlike youth is Tobias. I don't want to be fasted to a little boy.

But no, I soothe myself, *this can't be Tobias. Draven wouldn't sob over such a skinny little child.*

Some of the youths cast shy, unsure glances toward us as they pass. But there's one youth who doesn't seem unsure at all. My breath catches in my throat as he strides in. His gaze briefly rakes over us in one dazzling sweep, and a warm rush courses through me.

He's taller than the rest, already broad-shouldered, his stride confident, not awkward and shuffling like the others. He's even more handsome than Rafe Gardner, with a rakish smile on his lips and mischief in his eyes. And four silver Mage stripes grace his tunic.

A hungry hope lights in me. *Please, sweet Ancient One. Please, let this be Tobias.*

Chairs are set in a row to the right of the altar, and the young men are led to their seats one by one. The confident young man plops down and casts a self-satisfied grin at the stocky youth beside him. He seems to own the cathedral, and he eyes the priests with no deference whatsoever.

I'm instantly drawn in by him and swooning over his outrageously confident ways.

Oh, let this be him, I pray as a desire I never knew existed in me takes sudden hold; a desire to step outside the boundaries. There'd be such freedom with this youth, sweet freedom I can almost taste in my mouth. A sudden image lights my mind— myself, dressed in garb edged in glittering purple gems and dancing with him, the two of us smiling and laughing as we twirl around a ballroom.

The tall young priest walks up to the altar and gives us a perfunctory smile. He has a hawk's face, with sternly watchful eyes and an elegant, aquiline nose.

"Let us pray, Mages," he says, then leads us all in the familiar blessing. *Oh, Blessed Ancient One,* he intones, and we all join in—even Draven, with a tremulous, cracking voice full of tragedy.

Purify our minds. Purify our hearts. Purify Erthia from the stain of the Evil Ones.

The priest smiles again, his posture reed-straight as he surveys the room with satisfaction. "We are gathered here today," he says, his tone well-practiced, "to perform the most *sacred* of ceremonies. To bind for life those whom the Ancient One has brought together." He pauses, his satisfied smile fixed and unrelenting. He looks to us maidens and grows serious, almost disapproving, as if suddenly ready to chastise us. "Wandfasting is as binding as it is sacred. A blessed spell to keep you on the path of righteousness." He pauses again, frowning, his expression now one of great import as he looks to the assembled parents with a curt nod. "Let us commence."

He glances down at his notes. "I call upon Mage Stylla Gosslin and Mage Brin Paskal," he says, enunciating each word with clipped precision and scanning the room expectantly. "Please approach the altar, Mages."

The button-nosed girl beside me rises. The sudden motion startles me and sets my heart beating faster. Stylla stands frozen in place for a long moment, and I can sense her fierce reluctance in how rigidly she's holding herself. When the tall priest waves her forward impatiently, she forces herself into motion toward the altar, her eyes wide as a hunted thing. Her fastmate, a stout lad with a boyish face, reluctantly approaches as well, joining Stylla at the altar. He blinks out over the crowd as if he'd rather be anywhere but here while an older priest guides both his and Stylla's parents up to stand behind their children.

Stylla's lips are a trembling grimace, her gaze repeatedly darting toward her mother and father. She has a fierce, pleading look in her eyes that is met with firm shakes of her parents' heads, and I'm confused by how upset she seems.

The tall priest quietly talks to the young couple, but it does little to ease the tension. Stylla's and Brin's expressions are uncomfortable to the extreme as the priest quietly guides their hands together. Stylla's arms are stiff, her head drawn back, as if at any moment she might tear her hands away from Brin's and flee.

My creeping unease swells over their obvious distress as the priest pulls out a sepia wand and holds it over the young couple's stiffly clasped hands. He closes his eyes and drones out the fasting spell in the Ancient Tongue. The words to the spell are strange and lovely, no sharp edges or harsh sounds.

The couple flinches, and I gasp along with the other youths

as serpentine black lines flow out from the wand's tip. The lines spiral and twist, encircling the couple's hands like slender vines. Stylla and Brin suddenly appear to be trying to step back, their expressions now ones of fear, as if they're struggling to wrest their hands away from each other and can't. The lines abruptly pull in, and they both flinch again, the fasting patterns fusing to their hands. Stylla begins to softly cry.

I loose a breath I didn't know I was holding and look to Father and Mother Eliss, troubled by Stylla's unhappiness. Mother Eliss catches my eye and gives me a reassuring look, seemingly unaffected by Stylla's misery. The priest opens his eyes, lowers his wand and gives the couple before him a satisfied smile.

Stylla wrenches her hands protectively in and eyes her new fastmate with accusation. Her parents gather round, her mother kissing her head and embracing her as her father and the priest exchange an indulgent smile. Then the couple and their parents are guided toward seats together on the adults' side of the cathedral.

Pair after pair are called up, all of them quietly submitting to the ceremony. Some shy. Some overwhelmingly nervous. One couple blinks at each other as if momentarily disoriented, then break into wide, bashful grins, as if deciding on the spot that they're besotted with one another.

My anticipation reaches a feverish pitch.

I grip the pew seat, desperate to know who Tobias is. There are only four possibilities left: a rotund lad with disheveled hair and even more disheveled clothing who sits glowering hotly at no one in particular, his cheeks flaming red; a skinny, tall boy with thick spectacles who's blinking out over the crowd as if he's found himself in the wrong room; the fidgety little boy; and the powerful, confident young man. He's idly drumming his fingers on the wooden arm of his chair, the alluring grin on his face sparking an exciting warmth deep inside me.

"Mage Gwynnifer Croft and Mage Geoffrey Sykes," the priest calls out.

Gwynnifer Croft. The girl I'm to be staying with.

My attention piqued, I glance eagerly around the cathedral. The owlish, messy-haired girl rises and makes her way toward the altar. She doesn't walk so much as glide, holding her body oddly still, as if she's created a fragile refuge within it. Smatterings of derisive laughter crop up, but she keeps her chin high.

So this is Gwynnifer.

And then I notice it—the toy White Wand sheathed at Gwynnifer's side. My light affinity sparks to life, small prismatic stars pricking at the edge of my vision.

"Oh look, she's got her *toy*," one of the unfasted girls behind me mockingly whispers, setting off another fit of giggles. I shrink down, mortified by my desire to play with Gwynnifer's wand, and deeply put off by how mean some of the others are being to her.

The little boy, Geoffrey, bounds up to the altar like he's in a race and trips headfirst onto the dais. Most of the young women and quite a few of the boys, including the beautiful, self-assured young man, break into jeering laughter.

The small boy bounds back to his feet, fast as a hare. He briefly frowns at the mocking laughter, then turns and confidently strides up to the altar. He reaches out and decisively takes Gwynnifer's hands into his own as their parents join them. More mocking giggles sound from both the boys and the girls, and I notice that Geoffrey has a White Wand toy sheathed in his belt as well. Gwynnifer's face is serene as a still lake, even though they look a bit ridiculous together—not only do they have toy wands, but Gwynnifer towers more than a head taller over Geoffrey.

The priest eyes the laughing youths with obvious disapproval, and the smatterings of laughter quickly die down.

Geoffrey straightens in defiance of the jeering as the beautiful, confident youth turns to the stocky lad at his side and shoots him a sarcastic grin.

The priest raises his wand and intones the spell. The fasting lines form around the couple's hands and set quickly. Gwynnifer stares down at the marks, her serenity unbroken as Geoffrey gazes at her, his grin wide and brimming with happiness. Both sets of parents swoop in around the couple, fussing and congratulating before leading them off the dais. As Gwynnifer is ushered toward the other side of the aisle, she sets her owl eyes fully on me, and I inwardly shrink back from her penetrating gaze.

"Mage Draven Peltin and Mage Granthyn Emory."

I suck in air and turn as sobbing Draven is practically dragged up by the priests, her parents quickly falling in around her. They hush her in stern tones, and none of the maidens are giggling now. Draven bows down under the weight of her parents' obvious censure and looks to me, blistering hatred in her eyes. Then she glances at the gorgeous youth, and her hatred shifts to overwhelming grief. The beautiful young man appears completely disinterested in both her and the proceedings, his eyes casting around as if he's dreadfully bored. He whispers to the lad next to him, the two of them stifling laughter.

An uncomfortable concern pricks inside me, along with some measure of relief. If the handsome boy is Tobias, I'm heartened to find that he's clearly not interested in Draven the way she's interested in him. It would be horrible to have a fastmate who wants someone else. But still, he seems oddly callous in the face of Draven's misery.

The skinny, bespectacled lad reluctantly gets up to stand opposite a near-hysterical Draven, eyeing her with resignation as all the adults attempt to ignore her display. Draven's mother's hand is around her arm like a vise, holding her so tightly that her daughter is lifted up a bit on one side.

It's upsetting to watch her being forced like this, and I look to Father and Mother Eliss once again for reassurance. They're watching the troubling scene impassively, but they exchange a look, and I can detect the disapproval in their eyes over Draven's dramatic outburst. I realize that Draven must be overreacting, like Stylla did, and I resolve right then and there to behave in a way that Mother Eliss and Father will be proud of, even if Tobias isn't the handsome boy. Because whoever he is, he'll be the Ancient One's perfect choice for me.

"No. *Please*, no. Momma, I don't want to…" Draven frantically murmurs as her hands are forced forward onto the altar. Granthyn looks to his parents, unsure. His father sternly gestures toward Draven, and Granthyn relents, uneasily taking her hands in his. Her sobbing grows hysterical as the priest recites the spell.

Draven struggles frantically as the lines form, her whole body pulling backward, but both her mother and now her father hold her hands steady as the fastlines set.

And then it's over.

Draven wrenches her hands away and pushes violently past her mother, fleeing down the central aisle and out the doors of the cathedral. Her father takes off after her with heavy strides and slams the cathedral's door hard behind him.

Angry voices resonate just outside as we all wait. I look worriedly toward the doors when Draven's incoherent stream of protest devolves into a high-pitched shriek. I hear a deep male voice yelling and a thump that makes me flinch, followed by a broken cry.

And then silence.

The door pushes open, and Draven is dragged back up the aisle by her father, her head bowed as she quietly weeps, her right cheek a bright, angry red that shocks me. Her father roughly pulls her over to take a seat between himself and her mother on the adults' side of the aisle, and Draven slumps down onto the pew like some broken thing.

"Mage Sagellyn Gaffney and Mage Tobias Vasillis," the priest calls, and I'm almost jolted clear out of my seat.

Heart pounding and in a sudden, light-headed daze, I rise on shaking legs and come forward to take my place at the altar. I'm dauntingly aware of everyone's attention set solely on me and still acutely disquieted by Draven's anguish. My parents join me, and I'm comforted by Father's warm pat on my shoulder and Mother Eliss's encouraging smile. A stately couple also makes their way toward the altar, the man tall and impressively stern with Level Four Mage stripes, the woman gentle-looking and lovely as a lily.

The confident boy rises languidly from his seat, taking his time. My knees weaken as he looks me over with an enigmatic grin, and warmth flashes through me the moment his eyes meet mine, my apprehension rapidly diminishing.

Tobias's *eyes*. They're glorious. The whole, dazzling spectrum of green. Sun-drenched spring greens alternating with deep forest greens. Eyes I could stare into and get lost in forever.

I'm barely able to breathe, barely able to think as the priest directs us. And then Tobias reaches over the altar and takes my hands, his grip strong and warm.

I'm being touched by a boy. The outrageous thought sends another rush of heat through me as my hands tremble in Tobias's. I'm only half-aware of the priest sounding out the spell and its tight, instantaneous pull on my affinity lines as everything fades to the background. There's only Tobias's gorgeous eyes and the exciting feel of his hands around mine.

Sparking lines of energy brush against my skin, and I glance down to find the black lines of the spell wrapping around our clasped hands like dark, tendriling vines. I watch in fascination as the lines branch and loop and branch again into identical, elaborate patterns on our skin, stopping just short of our wrists.

Fastlines as beautiful as my new fastmate.

I glance up at Tobias in wonder. He smiles at me, and I feel like I'm suddenly floating on a cloud.

I never want this moment to end.

I'm in a giddy, flustered daze as our parents gently guide us away from each other and toward our new seats. My attention remains riveted on Tobias, who's now sandwiched between his parents at the other end of the long pew and has gone back to drumming a rhythm on his seat.

The priest reads his closing remarks and says the final prayer, and we all rise as delighted conversation swells. Father and Mother Eliss lead me over to Tobias and his family, briefly sharing congratulations with Tobias's powerful father and elegant mother, proud smiles on all the adults' faces. A warm flush of excitement stings my face as Tobias boldly stares at me, his mouth set in a crooked grin.

Then Tobias leaves with his parents, and I watch him go, wishing I could follow. Before he exits the cathedral, he turns and our eyes meet one last, thrilling time as he gives me an enticing smile.

He'll kiss me someday, I breathlessly muse. *And all the stars will light up in the sky.*

An insistent tug on my tunic sleeve breaks into my romantic haze. I turn to find Gwynnifer Croft standing close and staring at me with big, pale green eyes.

"Sagellyn Gaffney," she says with ominous gravity. "I have something to give you."

CHAPTER FOUR:
The White Wand

"The White Wand seeks you out," Gwynnifer says with great import, her focus singular, as if we're suddenly the only two people in the room.

I stare at the toy wand sheathed at her side as my affinity sparks to life with a buzzing prickle along my wand hand. "Pardon?"

"I had a dream about you, Sagellyn. The Wand wants to go to you."

I stare at Gwynnifer for a long moment, thrown by her bizarre statement, then cautiously look toward Mother Eliss. She's intently listening to what Father is saying to Gwynnifer's rose-cheeked, rotund mother and her gray-haired, bespectacled father, who has four Mage stripes marking his tunic. Gwynnifer's father is a skilled wandmaker for our military and in charge of the largest armory in Gardneria.

An armory stuffed to the brim with wands.

I turn back to Gwynnifer, a familiar longing rising inside me to have a wand of my own, along with anxiety that we'll get into trouble. "I'm not allowed to play wand games," I caution her. "Mother Eliss says it's sacrilege for girls to play with wands, even toy ones."

Gwynnifer's voice hushes to a near whisper, her expression full of drama. "This is no game, Sagellyn. Valgard has become dangerous. Shadow forces are rising. I've dreamt of glamoured demons on the streets. Two of them. Searching." She pats the toy wand at her side. "Searching for *this*. The Wand needs to escape. It wants to go with you. Back to Halfix."

Surprise bursts into being inside me as I'm reminded of the strange dream my sister Clover had a few weeks ago—a dream in which the sacred White Wand strove to get to me before demons could get hold of it. A tremor of unease rises, but I shake it off, realizing these oddly similar dreams must be a bizarre coincidence and nothing more. And Gwynnifer might be strangely theatrical, but she doesn't seem mean or mocking, unlike many of the girls here.

And she's offering me a wand.

I glance toward my parents, who are paying absolutely no attention to us whatsoever. My heart picks up its rhythm as I stare covetously at Gwynnifer's wand.

A chance to have a wand of my very own. Even if it is just a toy, the possibility is just too thrilling to resist.

"All right," I agree, barely able to tamp down my excitement and my sparking affinity lines. I can't fight the eager smile that lifts my mouth as I lower my voice to match her conspiring tone. "I'll save your wand."

"I only have one evening to teach you everything," Gwynnifer tells me with urgency as we climb several stories up her home's wrought-iron spiraling staircase, ascending all the way to the top.

I step off the stairs and gasp in wonder. Her bedroom is like something from a storybook—it sits on the pinnacle of their charmingly vertical house, one room stacked atop another, like a tower of blocks, as if the whole thing was built into the space between the armory and the estate next door as an afterthought.

I look around, mesmerized by Gwynnifer's circular, panoramic space and its breathtaking view of the city. Her bed sits to one side, festooned with a deep green velvet canopy. Arcing windows completely ring the tower, their forest-green drapes tied back with black-tasseled cords. The tops of some Ironwood trees are visible through the glass, the trees' Ironflowers glowing a soft sapphire that ripples through me in delightful waves. The tower's ceiling is a geometric glass skylight, stars twinkling above. Sanded Ironwood tree trunks are set between the windows, their tangling limbs rising up on all sides to frame the skylight.

Mobiles of white birds hang from the branches alongside silver Erthia orbs and glittering blessing stars attached to strings. I duck down to avoid one of the dangling birds. Paintings and drawings are affixed up and down the sanded tree trunks—depictions of wands, demons, the prophetess Galliana astride her giant raven, the white bird symbol of the Ancient One. Bookshelves are set into the walls beneath the windows, religious books and handwritten journals jammed haphazardly into them.

It's so excitingly different from our austere, tidy estate, and I feel a pang of jealousy. What would it be like to be so free? To hang drawings from the walls and own a ceiling of stars? Retta and Clover would be entranced, and I suddenly feel their absence acutely, wishing they were here with me to see this magical place.

Gwynnifer is hastily pulling thick texts out from under her bed and stacking each one onto a nearby table with a heavy *thump*. I'm filled with surprise when I see that the lettering on the books' spines is in a confusion of foreign languages. I'm also shocked to spot toy wands all over Gwynnifer's sprawling room, set on bookshelves and dresser tops, bunched in vases like bouquets. More toy wands are half carved on an art table that's surrounded by tools and discarded curlicues of wood.

All of the wands are identical to the wand sheathed at Gwynnifer's side.

My affinity lines buzz as I gape at them, stunned that her parents allow this. "Why are you making so many wands?"

Gwynnifer pauses for a moment. "Decoys. To throw the demons off. I'm going to scatter replicas all over the city."

Sweet Ancient One, she's fallen too far into this game of hers.

Uncomfortably spooked, I take in the sight of the smooth onyx stones that line the windowsill beside me. Golden runes are etched onto each stone in graceful, spiraling patterns. I pick one up and trace my finger along the design—a circle filled with what looks like a series of ocean waves. "What are these?"

"Ishkartan counter-runes. To weaken demonic tracking spells."

Apprehension strafes through me, and I quickly set the rune down, remembering Mother Eliss's teachings from our holy book. "First Children aren't supposed to play with heathen sorcery. Why do you have these?" I notice that the rune-etched stones are scattered all over her room.

"The Wand told me to etch the runes." Her voice is spookily certain. "And you're going to charge them with your light magery."

"Me?" I'm shocked by her outlandish idea. "How?" I know that Light Mages are the only Gardnerians who can perform rune-sorcery, since all runes are made of light, but I've no training in magic. As rare as my affinity is, Mother Eliss and Father always say that since I'm female, it's more important for me to follow *The Book* than to wield power. And following *The Book*'s teachings doesn't include wielding a wand.

Gwynnifer's gaze on me sharpens. "You won't need training

for this. The Wand will guide you and draw on your power. It told me so, in my dreams." Gwynnifer brings her palm down lightly on her tower of books and eyes me significantly. "I borrowed these grimoires from the armory. I've made copies of all of them for you to take home with you. They contain the designs for almost every runic system on Erthia."

I gape at her, incredulous. "There's no way I can take *any* of these home with me. Mother Eliss would never allow it."

But Gwynnifer is unmoved. "She doesn't have to know about them. Just keep them hidden." She sets a deep green volume on the top of the pile. There are circular runes made up of telescoping, geometric designs embossed all over the cover, glowing a shimmering emerald.

"I've never seen anything like this before," I say, suddenly entranced, touching my finger to the spine. The emerald glow washes over my hand as the beautiful runic designs spark my affinity, their shapes multiplying out at the edges of my vision.

"Snake Elf runes," Gwynnifer says, dark warning in her inflection.

I jerk my finger back, instantly chastened. *Snake Elves.* An image of the serpentine boy in the wanted postings fills my mind. I blink my eyes and struggle to clear the emerald rune echo from my vision. *What could be in a book like that? A Snake Elf grimoire…*

Gwynnifer is scrutinizing me, one thin eyebrow cocked, as if quietly taking my measure. "There's one more book. It's…a bit different." She pauses, seeming suddenly uneasy. "I tried to copy it, but the runes disappear almost as fast as I form them. So you'll have to take the original." She pulls out a weighty grimoire from the shadows under one of the bookshelves and slides it across the floor. It's all black, save for the stylized curling horns embossed on the front in shadowy gray, and there's a dark aura emanating from it.

"What's *that*?"

Her gaze doesn't waver, and her answer is disturbingly succinct. "Demon sorcery."

Serious trepidation strikes through me, and I nudge the grimoire back toward her with my foot. "No, Gwynnifer. *No.* You're playing with something evil here." I glance fearfully at the horned book, the very shadows seeming blacker around it.

Her eyes flash. "Don't you see? I'm not *playing*. Father says you've got some light magery, which means you'll be able to ward the Wand with protective runes. But you'll need to learn *all* the runes to be able to do it—even the shadow runes. And you *must* ward the Wand, Sagellyn. Or they'll come for you."

Something taps the window, and I almost jump clear out of my skin. My panicked eyes catch movement just beyond the glass.

Geoffrey's eager face comes into view, swaying in the branches, and my fright gives way to shocked alarm. "Your fastmate's going to kill himself!" I exclaim.

"He does it all the time," Gwynnifer calmly rejoins as she turns and winds the window open, the diamond-paned glass cranking out to let in the evening breeze and the fragrant smell of Ironflowers.

I let out a long, rattled breath and join them at the window. I glance down at the armory's carved roof and the evening military guard standing before its entrance—two Level Five Mages. I'm amazed Geoffrey was able to get past them.

Geoffrey rests his elbows on the windowsill and grins at us.

"Aren't you going to invite him in?" I ask Gwynnifer, stunned that she hasn't made a move to get him out of the tree, regardless of how improper it would be to have him in here.

"Oh, ho. *No*," Geoffrey protests with an emphatic shake of his head. "I can't come into her bedroom. I did that once, and her parents acted like the entire world had ended."

Gwynnifer nods solemnly. I stare at the identical fastlines on their hands.

"Did you two *want* to get fasted?" I blurt out, blinking at them in wonder.

They glance at each other and shrug, as if they've never really considered this, then nod in companionable agreement.

"They made us," Geoffrey readily informs me. "We snuck down to the bay one evening to gather stones for the counter-runes, and we got caught."

Out at night alone with a boy. I understand immediately why they were forced to fast.

"They just about lost their minds." Geoffrey gives a significant lift of his brow.

Gwynnifer huffs. "How am I supposed to be the Guardian of the White Wand if I can't come and go as I please?"

"And boy, were our parents mad when they found us." Geoffrey's eyes widen with mock alarm. "It was like the whole of Valgard exploded." He thrusts his arms out wide for emphasis, which causes him to wobble precariously before he grabs hold of a branch.

"They thought we went down there to kiss." Gwynnifer's tone is emphatic in its dismissal of the ludicrous idea. "But we were gathering *stones*. And looking for the demons."

"Kissing's gross," Geoffrey pronounces, and Gwynnifer nods in assent.

I blink at them, dumbfounded. I'm certainly interested in kissing Tobias, but I'd never admit that to anyone. Talking about such a thing would be highly improper.

"We're not romantic," Gwynnifer states matter-of-factly. "And who thinks of such things with demons on their trail, anyway?"

Geoffrey smiles at her, then looks back to me. "We're good friends, though. I'm glad we're fasted."

"I am as well." Gwynnifer looks at him approvingly. "He is a valiant companion." Then her expression lightens to one of wonderment. "And he always has candy!"

"My father's guildmarket is next to the biggest candy store in Valgard," Geoffrey crows. He pulls a crinkled parchment bag out of his pocket and hands it to Gwynnifer. She opens the bag and doles out handfuls of colorful, sugar-dusted blessing star candies to each of us.

I stare at the candy in my hand, hesitating. Mother Eliss doesn't allow candy in our house. Mages belonging to our sect aren't supposed to eat any food that isn't mentioned in *The Book of the Ancients*.

But I'm not supposed to have a toy wand, either, and I certainly plan on having one of those.

I grin at Geoffrey and Gwynnifer, feeling bold, and pop a bright red candy into my mouth. Sweet thistleberry flavor bursts over my tongue, thrilling me with its overwhelming deliciousness.

Geoffrey tosses almost a whole handful of star candies into his mouth, and I laugh. He looks like a contented moss squirrel in that tree, his cheeks stuffed to bursting. He motions toward Gwynnifer, his words muffled by the candy. "When we're both eighteen and sealed, I'm going to let her go down to the bay anytime she likes."

"I'll be able to do anything I want," Gwynnifer says with great dignity as she chews. "No more rules."

Geoffrey nods. "I don't like bossing people around."

These two are terribly odd. But as I sit here under the real stars and Gwynnifer's glittering fake ones, surrounded by wands and drawings and mobiles, my mouth stuffed with forbidden candy, my mind full of Gwynnifer's tales, I can't help but think that things didn't work out so badly for Gwynnifer and Geoffrey after all.

Because fasting partners are brought together by the Ancient One above, I happily muse, momentarily lost in the memory of my fastmate's beautiful eyes and dazzling smile.

I catch a shimmer out of the corner of my eye and glance toward the floor. The demon grimoire's horns catch the flickering lantern-light, and for a brief second, the air seems to vibrate as the shadows around the book deepen.

A thread of disquiet ripples through me, and for a moment, I get the ominous feeling that what we're playing at is much more than just a game.

CHAPTER FIVE:
Wand Lore

Heavy steps sound on the stairs, and Geoffrey's eyes go wide. He deftly throws two more bags of candy into the room, whispers, "G'nite, Gwynnie!" and disappears with a rustle of leaves. Gwynnifer expertly kicks the demon grimoire under her bookshelf, throws a cloak over the other grimoires and winds the window shut. She swings round and sits down demurely on a cushioned window seat, suddenly looking innocent as a lamb.

Gwynnifer's mother smiles jovially at us as she reaches the top of the stairs and enters the tower room. She's carrying a wooden tray that holds a plate of Icaral-wing cookies and a sloshing pitcher of milk, her face bright red from the exertion of climbing all the way up here. Two cats, one striped ginger and one fluffy black, enter the room behind her.

Gwynnifer's mother eyes the bags of candy on the floor. She briefly purses her lips and shakes her head, then casts me a warm smile. "Are you all settled in then, love?"

I nod with forced enthusiasm, scared we'll get in trouble for the candy—Mother Eliss would certainly never allow it. I search her face with trepidation, but she seems resigned to Gwynnifer's small rebellions.

She sets her tray down on the small table beside the bed.

"Well, don't stay up too late, you young Mages. It's been a big day for the both of you. You're fasted ladies now!" She gives Gwynnifer an indulgent look, her eyes glassing over for a moment, then good-naturedly insists on a hug and kiss from us both before descending back down the stairs, chatting animatedly with the ginger cat who follows her.

I climb up onto Gwynnifer's cushy bed as she solemnly pours me a glass of milk and hands me a small plate of cookies. I pick up a cookie and snap the Icaral wings in two, murmuring the usual protection blessing against the Evil Ones' winged power. Gwynnifer pulls out a thick journal as I take a bite, the cookie's warm, buttery goodness melting on my tongue.

"Everything I could find out about the Wand is in here," she says, offering me the hand-sewn volume. She's written *The White Wand* on the front in extravagantly looping letters. Doodles of blessing stars and wands and the prophetess Galliana astride a giant raven surround the title. I flip through the book and see that she's broken it up into chapters—histories of the White Wand from every race, even the Ishkart and Snake Elves.

My trepidation flares. Reading stories from other religions is flatly forbidden. Mother Eliss would surely want this book burned.

"You won't believe how outlandish some of these stories are," Gwynnifer breathlessly tells me. "The Noi think the Wand's a dragon goddess's *tooth*!"

"A *tooth*?" I exclaim.

Gwynnifer nods, her gaze wide-eyed. "And the Amaz believe their goddess grew the White Wand from a tree with a wave of her hand." She waves her own hand to illustrate.

I'm almost dizzy with conflict. It's a dangerous, forbidden thing, these fantastical stories, but I'm so curious.

"Go ahead and read it," she offers. "I'll stand guard." Gwynnifer hands me a small lumenstone lantern, then closes the drapes over all the windows and snuffs out the larger lanterns, casting most of the room in darkness. She stations herself by the window that overlooks the entrance to the armory, pulls its drape back a small fraction and cranks the window open a bit. She peers out, her hand protectively clasping the wand sheathed at her waist.

I glance at the wand covetously, my affinity colors sparking as I wonder when she'll let me take it in hand. I pull my knees up, ready to hide the forbidden book if Gwynnifer's mother comes upstairs again, then dare a peek inside, reading by the lumenstone's golden glow.

Gwynnifer starts her volume with the Wand's true story. She's drawn large, sweeping illustrations to go with the text, the drawings beautifully rendered in ink and watercolors. There's a series of drawings depicting the Ancient One pulling the sacred White Wand from our starlit Source Tree and gifting it to the First Children—the Gardnerian Mages. A two-page spread shows Galliana astride her giant raven, wielding the White Wand during the Demon Wars at the beginning of time.

I pet the fluffy black cat as it curls up beside me, only half-aware of the sound of carriages clopping by down below and the muffled, easy conversation of the Mages on guard in front of the armory. Moonlight washes its dim, silvery glow over the room through the geometric glass ceiling.

The Alfsigr Elf section of Gwynn's book tells of a prophet elf, Syll'en, who came upon the White Wand floating in a forest stream during primordial times. Syll'en wielded the Wand as a rune-stylus and battled a horde of the Shadow Wand's demonic monsters, thus saving the Light Elves from complete annihilation.

The Noi stories tell of the Vu Trin warrior, Chy Tan, who pulled the White Wand tooth out of their sacred dragon goddess's mouth. In the story, Chy Tan led her Vu Trin army, all of them astride wyvern shapeshifters, to defeat the Shadow Wand's demon army with the power of the tooth used as a rune-stylus. Chy Tan then returned the tooth to the sacred dragon, who hid it in a heavily warded underground lair.

I turn the page and find a picture from a Noi text, carefully cut out and taped into Gwynnifer's journal—a circle formed by a starlight dragon holding the White Wand and a dark gray dragon holding the Shadow Wand. My eyes freeze on the image, riveted. The two dragons flow together seamlessly, curling white against curling gray, White Wand against Shadow Wand. I'm pulled in by the image's beauty and the way the complicated symbol comes together, dragon on dragon.

Perfect.

I jerk back and give a quick shake of my head, as if forcing myself out of a spell. Unsettled by the image's hypnotic draw, I firmly close the book and set it aside.

I look to Gwynnifer, who remains standing watch by the window, still as a statue, her eyes pinned on the street below. I let out a long sigh, which triggers a wide yawn, then slouch back against the pillows behind me. The sleepy cat purrs as I pet him, lulling me into deeper relaxation, and I languorously splay my wand hand out in front of me, admiring the looping fasting lines.

So much has happened today.

A lovely, private warmth suffuses me as I think about Tobias's entrancing emerald eyes, his captivating smile. Soon the wagon traffic drops off, and the soldiers' conversation is low and soothing. My eyes flutter, heavy with fatigue, and eventually I give in and let them fall shut.

I dream of white wands. And white birds. And white dragons battling shadow dragons. And two horned demons searching, searching, searching for the White Wand…

★ ★ ★

"Wake up, Sagellyn."

Gwynnifer jostles my arm with urgency, and I spiral rapidly into consciousness. She's kneeling next to me, her eyes wide with fright. "They're here."

I blink sleepily as the lines of the shadowy room sharpen. "What...who's here?"

She gives a swift, terrified glance toward the window overlooking the entrance to the armory. I can just make out the echo of men's voices below, their conversation sounding oddly formal.

"The demons," she tells me, her words roughly stitched up with fear. "They've come for the Wand."

CHAPTER SIX:
Council Envoys

"That's them!" Gwynnifer whispers, moving over to the window. "The glamoured demons from my dream."

I kneel next to her and peer out the glass. The armory's two military guards face a pair of young men wearing Council envoy uniforms, all of them cast golden by the lantern-light. The Council envoys bear no Mage-level stripes, only the gold Mage Council *M* embroidered over their hearts.

My body slumps with relief. The Council envoys are square-jawed with refined features, one taller than the other, their expressions formal but pleasant. Decidedly undemonic.

Gwynnifer drops down, out of sight of the men. "I can't let them see me," she breathes, her brow knotted with urgency. "If our eyes meet, they'll know I have the Wand."

"They look perfectly normal—"

"They're *glamoured*. The Wand showed *everything* to me in my dream. It showed me what's coming—a shadowed, winged one. A river of fire. Demons. First these two, then a whole army of them. Bigger than the biggest army you can imagine."

I peek out the window and study the young men. The taller envoy is doing the talking, his voice deep and resonant as introductions are made. The other man looks on, serene and watchful, his posture relaxed, as if whatever they're here for requires no great urgency. The taller man's mouth tilts into a grin, and he says something in low tones that sets all the men laughing.

I breathe a sigh of relief. It's all quite placid, with no sense that demons are about to swoop down on our heads, or that the fate of the world rests on this encounter.

"They're in league with the Shadow Wand." Gwynn's voice is panicked, her hand clutching my arm. "You just can't see it."

"See what?" I glance back at the men, who are caught up in casual conversation and the idle showing of Council paperwork.

"They've glowing red eyes," she insists. "And spiraling shadow horns in their true form." She pulls the wand from its sheath on her belt, her fist tight around it. "If they find this, they will kill *everyone*. There will be absolutely *nothing* to stop the power of the Shadow Wand."

Gwynnifer looks down at the wand, a tortured look on her face. "I... I don't want to give it up." She lets out a long, shuddering breath and caresses the wand's spiraling handle with her fingers, shaking her head tightly as she gives me a grim look. Then she swallows, pulls the drape closed and thrusts the wand out toward me, as if with great effort. "Take it, Sagellyn. Take it, before I change my mind. You need to set the counter wards, *now*."

I draw back in alarm. "I don't know how—"

"You don't need to! You're a Light Mage. The Wand can access rune-sorcery through you. Just *take* it!"

The wand gleams bright, as if fashioned by moonlight. All my affinity lines snap tight and strain toward it, the sensation overriding all caution. Overcome, I reach out and clasp my hand around the wand.

Multicolored stars explode into my vision as every rune on every rune-stone surrounding us flashes with a bright glow. I gasp as a prickling line of energy shoots up from the floor, through my legs and my body, up into my wand-arm and out over the wand. The wand briefly flashes a blinding white that abruptly fades as the energy settles around my hand, and a warm sense of rightness floods over me, along with the fleeting image of a starlight tree with alabaster birds roosting in its branches.

I pull in a deep, shuddering breath and look to Gwynnifer, stunned. "Where did you get this wand?"

Gwynnifer ignores my question, her lips trembling. "Whatever you do, Sagellyn," she says, pointing her fingers in a V toward her own eyes, "*don't* look those men in the eye. Light affinity or no, if you look straight at them, they'll know you have the Wand."

Fear ripples through me as the opening of a door sounds out from street level.

"What brings you here?"

My attention is instantly riveted by the familiar, deep voice. I move back to the window with Gwynnifer as she pulls the drape open a sliver, my heart galloping.

Gwynnifer's father, Mage Croft, has come outside and is facing the two envoys, the armory's Level Five guards bracketing him.

Every muscle in my body is tensed as I ready myself to bolt out of view if the envoys' gazes lift even a fraction up toward our tower.

"Do you have a permit?" Mage Croft asks.

"We're looking for a wand," the taller envoy says. "A white wand."

The words rock through me, and Gwynnifer and I exchange a terrified glance. My hand tightens around the White Wand, which has started an almost imperceptible thrum, like it's gathering power. I hastily slide the Wand into my tunic pocket just as a soft rustling above me draws my eye. I catch a fleeting glimpse of white birds perched on the branch-rafters above, but they snap out of sight so quickly, I wonder if I imagined them. My gaze flits back down toward the men.

The tall envoy hands Mage Croft a scroll, which he carefully reviews before nodding and handing it back, as if satisfied.

"There's two wands here fashioned from pale wood," Mage Croft says, clearly well-versed in the armory's inventory. "One fashioned from Snow Oak." His tone takes on a rapturous edge. "Beautiful wand, that one. Magnifies affinity power *twenty*-fold. Thirty-two layers of wood. It was requisitioned by our navy, but proved to be unreliable in its ability to amplify magic. Caused one too many explosions. The other wand…" Mage Croft waves a hand dismissively. "That one is useless."

"These two wands," the tall envoy says casually, "are those the only white wands in the armory? Have any others been requisitioned? Or possibly…stolen?"

Mage Croft's posture grows rigid with offense. "No one has the keys, save for me and the Council." He gestures toward the armory guards at his sides. "And you can see we've Level Five Mage guards. This is the safest armory in Gardneria. Rune-warded, too."

"Does anyone else pass through here?" the envoy presses.

"No one. Only me."

The tall envoy's head starts to tilt up, and Gwynnifer and I pull down out of sight, our breathing uneven, my heart racing.

"And that building there," the envoy asks. "Is that your dwelling?"

"Yes," Mage Croft affirms. "I keep watch day and night over the armory, along with the guards. I'm a Level Four Mage myself. Only my young daughter and wife are here with me. They don't have access to the armory, of course."

"May we view the white wands?" the man asks as Gwynnifer and I peek back down again.

"Certainly." Mage Croft motions to one of the Level Five Mages, and the guard disappears through the armory's door.

My heart thumps in my chest, and I struggle to breathe normally. After a few moments, the Level Five guard returns with two white wands in hand, and I notice that one looks identical to the Wand in my pocket.

Mage Croft takes hold of the wands and offers them to the tall envoy. The young man accepts the wands, bouncing them slightly, one at a time, as if he's testing the feel of them.

They can't be demons, I adamantly tell myself, struggling to calm myself as panic mounts. Yes, it's odd that they're looking for a white wand, and odder still that the wand in my pocket seems to be magically firing up, but they don't look demonic in the slightest, and Gwynn's story of glamours seems far-fetched.

"What exactly are you looking for?" Mage Croft inquires.

The envoy worries the wands in his fingers. "A Wand of Power. Taken from the Urisk during the Realm War by Vale Gardner's fastmate."

Mage Croft nods and motions toward the wands. "That would be the longer one with the spiraling handle. I've tested that wand myself, several times over the years. The magic's all drawn out of it."

"We've our own wand tester at the Mage Council," the young man says.

"Well, I wish him luck," Mage Croft says starchily. "I certainly can't coax a thing out of it. What powers did it have?"

"Causes trouble. It's completely unpredictable. It's said to have freed a group of Urisk whores who promptly ran off to join the Amaz."

The envoy hands the spiraling wand and the shorter wand to his companion, who places both in a leather bag with a Mage Council *M* embossed on its front.

Both envoys bow their heads to Gwynnifer's father. "Thank you for your time, Mage Croft," the taller one says.

The envoys then salute the two armory guards, fists to hearts, and the two guards salute them in return. Then young envoys walk off into the night, chatting amiably as they go.

Normal men, normal night. Everything in order.

Gwynnifer's story partially deflates in the wake of their peaceful departure, although she looks wan and worn out, as if she's suffered a brush with death.

I deflate a bit, too, as the drama of the evening ramps down, some of the tension leaving my shoulders.

Did I imagine the glowing pulse from the wand? The flashing light of the runes?

I reach into my pocket and slide my hand over the wand, my fingers curling tight around its smooth, spiraling handle. I breathe in deep, and a subtle pulse of heat emanates from the wand like an answering caress. Disquieted, I reason that it's only the pull of my light affinity at work here, but it does feel so good and right to have this wand in my hand.

The image of the starlit tree filled with ivory birds takes hold once more, unfurling in the back of my mind.

CHAPTER SEVEN:
Escape

"You must take them if you're going to properly protect the Wand."

Gwynnifer is holding out a bag of the rune-marked stones. The night-blackened sky outside her tower bedroom has turned deep blue on one side, heralding the imminent arrival of dawn.

"You need to place them all around your home to keep the demons from tracking you," she insists, her tone imperative. "Bury them, so they won't be found."

I open the woolen pouch's green satin string and peer inside, shaking the bag of rune-marked onyx stones. Gwynnifer rifles through the grimoire copies she's sending along with me, like a military commander outfitting a soldier for battle.

My head is fair spinning from exhaustion. We've been up straight through the night, the excitement of our fastings swept aside by the Wand's dangerous, sweeping adventure.

What if her story is true? What if I really do need to save the White Wand?

"Remember what I told you," Gwynnifer says as she slides one more transcribed grimoire into a large bag.

"Don't look the demons in the eye," I answer somberly, braced for my getaway.

Gwynnifer nods. "You've got a real chance of getting out of Valgard, Sagellyn. If you can clear the city lines without them on your trail, the Wand will be safe. You will, in fact, be Galliana."

A slim line of fear pulls taut, even as excitement rises in me at being compared to the heroic Galliana. I slide my hand into my cloak's inner pocket and find the spiraling wood of the Wand's handle. The strange feel of a wand inside my pocket both thrills and unsettles me—power seems to imperceptibly thrum inside this Wand, and it sets off a barely detectable vibration against my thigh.

I close my fist around the Wand. "I'm ready," I tell her. "I'll get it safely to Halfix."

We finish breakfast before the sun is fully up, and my parents arrive soon after, fresh from their visit with Tobias's family.

As I get ready to board the transit carriage with my parents, Gwynnifer's mother gives me a warm hug and hands me some nut muffins wrapped in parchment. Gwynnifer stares at me grimly as Father and Mother Eliss exchange congratulations with her father.

"I'll write," Gwynnifer tells me, her tone adamant, as if willing my survival and receipt of future letters.

I'll miss her, I suddenly realize—a friend I'm actually allowed to be close to and share adventures with, unlike the Gardner children.

Tears sting at my eyes when I hug her goodbye, and I struggle to keep them at bay as the carriage door closes and my parents and I set off, the already bustling streets bathed in predawn blue. We amble past a sprawling guildmarket, and I spot Geoffrey dangling from a tree limb, grinning and waving goodbye to me. I smile at Gwynnifer's moss squirrel of a fastmate and wave back.

The streets are surprisingly busy with merchant traffic, farmers bringing in vegetables for the market, cider for the taverns, sacks of flour for the bakeries. Everything is now washed in a rose hue as the sun rises, turning a portion of the sky a stunningly bright red.

Red skies at night, sailor's delight. Red skies at morning, sailor take warning.

The ominous mariner's rhyme chimes in my mind as I press my face to the glass and watch a young man pick out a scarlet apple from an outdoor fruit stand. He drops some coins into the merchant's hand, smiles and takes a bite of apple. Then he turns his head toward me.

Our eyes meet, and an intense flash of recognition passes between us. Fright explodes through me and sets every hair on my body rigid.

The tall Council envoy. From last night.

And his eyes are glowing red.

I blanch and grip at the edge of the carriage bench. He loses his smile, drops the apple and starts for the carriage just as it lurches forward at a fast clip. I rapidly lose sight of him in the crowds, but a wave of nausea sweeps through me nonetheless, along with a rancid fear. *He knows I have the Wand. And now he's going to kill us all.*

"Sage, are you quite all right?"

I whip my head toward Mother Eliss.

"What's the matter, Sagellyn?" Father asks, a note of confusion in his tone.

We have to get out of this carriage. They're coming for us. I can feel it in my bones. I can feel it in the Wand that has begun a low, unsettling vibration against my thigh. *Don't look them in the eye.* Terror mounts as I remember Gwynnifer's warning too late.

"I… I'm going to be sick," I tell my parents with desperate urgency. "I have to get out! *Now!*"

I've never been this strident with my parents before, and it seems to momentarily stun them into taking me seriously. Father pulls the cord, and the transit carriage soon comes to a stop at the next carriage station.

I burst out of the carriage on shaking legs, my eyes darting from side to side like a hunted animal. The carriage station is a crowded bustle of activity, with knots of Gardnerian families and friends chatting amiably. Urisk women with bent backs and pale rose coloring sweep away the horse refuse, their eyes downcast.

Panicked, I grasp Mother Eliss's hand and drag her into the station. Bald terror races through me as I position myself at the edge of an arching, diamond-paned window, mostly hidden from sight.

I peer through the glass.

They're not there. Not on the road. Not in the crowd.

I clutch the wand through the fabric of my cloak's inside pocket, and my dizziness starts to abate. *It can't be real,* I desperately try to reason with myself. *I can't have the actual White Wand. I can't truly have demons after me....*

I watch as the carriage we were in fills with a new set of passengers. No demons in sight. No explosions of flame. *Nothing.*

I breathe a long, jagged sigh of relief.

Mother Eliss briefly walks away, then returns with a glass of water, her face tense. I slump down, chastened by her expression. Father is talking to the schedule master, fists on his hips as he arranges for another carriage.

"There now," Mother Eliss says, handing me the cool glass. I press it against my temple, my heartbeat throbbing against it and quickly morphing into a pounding headache.

"You've got yourself all worked up." She purses her lips. "You spent far too much time around Gwynnifer Croft—she's too fanciful, that girl." Mother Eliss crosses her arms in front of her chest and shakes her head, then strides over to join my father.

Feeling small and scared and foolish all at the same time, I turn back toward the carriage we were just in. My lungs constrict.

The two envoys have pulled up behind the carriage on horseback.

I recoil back from the window, my heartbeat slamming against my chest as I watch the envoys out of the corner of my eye, a mere sliver of my face pressed against the glass, my breath fogging one of the diamond panes.

The carriage pulls away from the station, and the envoys follow. It soon turns right at a fork in the road, and the envoys turn right along with it.

I stay glued to the window, a spiral of fear twisting inside me. I strain to keep the carriage in sight as long as I can, until both the carriage and the envoys who doggedly trail it are out of sight.

Then I turn and retch all over the floor.

Shocked murmurs go up as Mother Eliss rushes toward me. Father's face tightens with revulsion, but I don't care. All I can think about is the Wand hidden inside my cloak.

And the darkness that's closing in around it.

CHAPTER EIGHT:
The Wand

After our return to isolated Halfix, I read *all* of Gwynnifer's journals.

I commit every runic system to memory and carve protective wards into stones that I bury all over the property and place under floorboards, over arches. Anywhere I can get away with hiding them.

I carry *The Book of the Ancients* everywhere I go, reading it every day and resolving to follow its every stricture, repeating prayers over and over like talisman.

Mother Eliss takes note of my new, fervent devotion on the heels of my fasting.

"'Twas a blessing, that fasting spell," she tells Father one night. "It brought the Ancient One's light down on that child. She's filled with grace."

But it's not grace. It's fear.

Please, Ancient One, help me.

I pray and read from our holy book and wait for direction. I wait for a sign on the rays of the sun, in the shape of the clouds. In my dreams.

When Galliana had the Wand, I agonize, *how did she know what it wanted her to do?*

The years pass by, each day ordered and ordinary. The seasons turn. The crops grow, then are threshed, and then the fields are barren. I channel my light affinity into becoming an accomplished weaver, using only the allowed colors and designs, as my little sisters and baby brothers grow taller every year.

But the White Wand remains silent as stone.

There are no demons. No feelings of magic coursing through the Wand. No heroic or disturbing dreams. No signs. And my light affinity lines don't even faintly glimmer anymore when I hold the Wand tight in my hand.

Sometimes I feel like it's oddly quiet.

As if it's waiting for something.

By the time I turn sixteen, new thoughts creep in that Gwynnifer mirrors in her letters to me. We must have imagined all of it. We were so caught up in the bustle and excitement of Valgard, caught up in the thrill of being fasted. Caught up in Gwynnifer's imaginings.

I go over the details again and again in my mind. The vibrant red sunrise. Its reflection in the young man's eyes seeming demonic. The envoy appearing to spot me and take off in pursuit of our carriage. All of it, the work of our overactive imaginations, combined with lack of sleep after a momentous day. And it was pure coincidence that those envoys were riding out on the carriage's tail that morning.

Two more years pass, and the wand does nothing to refute these new thoughts. It doesn't whisper messages deep inside my mind. It's just dead wood.

Silent and empty as a child's toy.

PART TWO
Present Day

CHAPTER ONE:
University

I'm seated at a table for two, right up against the hip-level wrought-iron fence that encloses the Ironflower Inn's luxurious property. Birds warble in the Ironwood trees that surround me, the sky a sharp, dazzling blue that's almost too vivid to take in. The first shafts of early morning sunlight filter through the trees and softly illuminate the patio of black and green polished stones, cut to form a pattern of interlocking blessing stars.

"Sage?"

I turn at the sound of the feminine voice to find a young woman with large, owlish eyes approaching me, seamlessly weaving around the inn's outdoor dining tables. Her posture is so gracefully erect it's like she's floating toward me, a subtle smile on her delicate lips.

My heart leaps in my chest. "Gwynnie!" I eagerly get up and embrace the friend who's been my faithful correspondent for five whole years, though we haven't seen each other since our wandfasting.

Joy beats inside me like wings, and happy tears form in my eyes as Gwynn hugs me and laughs with disbelieving elation, our stiff silks sliding against each other. Both of us are dressed as sumptuously as our sect allows, our solid black tunics and skirts of the finest silk and perfectly pressed, glistening where the sunlight touches down on them.

Gwynn pulls back, beaming, and I marvel at how she's changed. A subtle shifting of her small, foxlike features has transformed her from a spookily waiflike girl into a delicate beauty, and she's grown almost a head taller. But her wavy, fly-away black hair forms the same chaotic cloud, and I'm oddly charmed by this. I haven't seen her in so long, but in some ways, it feels like we've never parted. We've been writing to each other almost every week for such a long time, Gwynn sending me not only letters, but volume upon volume of her fanciful stories.

"When did you get into Verpax?" She smiles serenely, arranging her skirts neatly and folding her small hands on the table as we both sit down, leaning forward with eager attention.

"Just last night," I say, brimming with excitement. "Oh, Gwynn. I'm so happy to be here."

It took my family and me a full week to get to Verpax University from remote Halfix, and my face was glued to the carriage window as we rode into the city late last night. Even as exhausted as I was, the sight of the pale Spine-stone buildings of the University city captivated me, with their clean lines, ivory-white turrets, huge domes and crisscrossing overhead walkways, so different from Gardnerian architecture.

It was fully dark when we finally reached the Ironflower Inn, an inn only for Gardnerians. I'd stepped down from the carriage, trailed by my sleepy sisters, practically quivering with travel fatigue and a jangling anticipation as Mother Eliss guided my twin brothers down the tree-lined path.

It had been a comfort to find an inn fashioned in the familiar Gardnerian style, built from dark wood with an overflowing roof garden and surrounded by a grove of Ironwood trees in full bloom. We had followed the amiable innkeeper, Mage

Edyth Gyll, down a path toward the inn's entrance as the sapphire glow of the Ironflower blossoms pulsed down my affinity lines and suffused me with an exhilarating euphoria.

Finally. Eighteen years old, and here in Verpacia. My life about to take wing.

"Some tea, Mages?"

Pulled from my recollection, I smile and nod up at Mage Gyll. I'm graced with a warm smile in return as she pours steaming tea from a lovely black porcelain teapot decorated with the inn's signature Ironflower motif.

It's a heady feeling to be having breakfast with Gwynn in such a beautiful place, like we're grown-up Mages. I've suddenly been granted more freedom than I've ever had before, a whole new world about to open up before me. In a matter of days, I'll be a newly minted University scholar, ready to start my apprenticeship with Gardneria's premier textile artisan and down the path to become a master weaver.

And I'll finally be sealed to Tobias, just as Gwynn will be sealed to Geoffrey, in only a few days' time.

I glance down at my fastmarked hands, both excited and incredibly nervous to become Sagellyn Vasillis forevermore. Just the thought sets heat pricking at my cheeks and neck. Our sealing has to be consummated that very night, and the consummation will cause our fastlines to magically flow down our wrists—proof of our union for all the world to see. But Tobias and I have never even talked. Or held hands. Or kissed. And I'll be expected to...

My cheeks sting hot, and I can't even finish the thought.

Mage Gyll sets a plate of currant scones on our table, along with a smaller plate of butter pats molded into Ironflowers. The scones' toasty scent wafts toward me on the cool morning air and lifts the edge off of my apprehension.

"Have you...seen Tobias yet?" Gwynn asks as I take a warm

scone and some butter. Her hesitant tone prompts me to look up, and I'm surprised to find her smile gone as she stares at me with the owl-eyed, unblinking look that I remember so well.

A nervous tremor ripples through me. "Tonight," I say. "We're having dinner with Tobias and his family. Here." I get that familiar stomach-tightening, anxious thrill I always have when I say Tobias's name. "I'm so nervous, Gwynn. I haven't seen him since the fasting." I trace the Ironflower pattern on my teacup's saucer with the tip of my finger. "I'm… I'm hoping he'll like me." It's not even half of what I truly mean, but I know, from the look in Gwynn's eyes, that she understands. I've thought about him every day since our fasting—beautiful, confident, powerful Tobias. I've dreamed about him, worked out elaborate romantic fantasies. I wonder if he's done the same while we've been apart, the two of us forbidden any contact in the strictest tradition of our sect. Mother Eliss, to my great chagrin, hasn't even permitted any letters.

Gwynn gently places her hand on my arm, her delicate face kind and earnest. "He's sure to be entranced by you."

My flush deepens. "Do you think so?"

She nods emphatically. "You're quite lovely. And it's meant to be." Gwynn gives me an encouraging smile.

I lean in toward her, whispering now. "Aren't you nervous?" I remember skinny, small Geoffrey, swinging from a tree. He was pleasant, to be sure, but she must be just as anxious about all this as I am.

Gwynn blushes, looking around to make sure no one can hear, and gives a small laugh. "A little."

A tall young man in a dark gray Gardnerian military apprentice uniform appears just beyond the iron fence, as if out of nowhere, and I give a start. He leans over the fence and playfully slaps his hands down onto the table near Gwynn. "Found you," he cheerfully announces, his smile wide and bright, his eyes latched onto Gwynn.

Gwynn's face lights up with delight. "Geoffrey!"

I gape at him. *Geoffrey?*

I study him, wide-eyed, as Gwynn springs up and they embrace over the fence. For a moment, it's as if I've disappeared into smoke, the two of them are so wrapped up in each other. I self-consciously grip my teacup as Geoffrey excitedly tells Gwynn about his trip here from Valgard and the family members who've arrived for their sealing. As they blissfully float in their happy bubble, I search for something of the Geoffrey I remember, and can make it out in his overabundance of energy, in the ears that stick out from his tousled black hair. He's a long beanpole of a young man, no longer the short, skinny boy he used to be. And…he's quite attractive.

And they're in love with each other, I realize, with equal parts surprise and amusement—and some envy.

They've had so much time together, whereas I've had exactly none with Tobias.

"We're ignoring Sage," Gwynn lightly chastises her fastmate.

Geoffrey looks over and blinks, as if noticing me for the first time. He grins at me, his smile as wide and welcoming as I remember it. "Hullo, Sage. It's been quite a while."

I let out a small, awkward laugh at this understatement, cupping the warm tea in my hands. All of us are so completely altered.

"It's nice to see you again, Geoffrey," I tell him, and he rewards me with another beaming smile.

At Gwynn's prodding, Geoffrey deftly leaps over the fence, pulls a chair over and joins us, straddling his chair backward.

"Remember that game you played with us?" Geoffrey teasingly asks Gwynn, bumping her shoulder with his. "With the toy wand? You had us convinced it was the White Wand and that there were demons about to eat us whole."

Gwynn brings her hand to her eyes, a slight smile of embarrassment on her lips. "Geoffie, stop…"

Geoffie?

Geoffrey laughs as he gently takes Gwynn's hand in his and plants an affectionate kiss on her palm. They share a heat-filled, private glance, then turn to me, both of them smiling widely, their besotted happiness on full display, and I marvel at how free they've been allowed to be with each other.

Warmth prickles along the back of my neck. *They know things*, I realize with daunting certainty. *They've probably kissed. Quite a bit. And possibly more than that.* Questions burn in me that I long to ask Gwynn. Questions about men and the sealing night.

"Do you still have the legendary White Wand?" Geoffrey asks me, his voice low with drama, his teasing as good-natured as it was when we were younger.

"I might," I tease him back, emboldened by his friendly nature. I eye him archly. "Do you still think kissing's gross?" I'm immediately aghast by my bold outburst, my face warming. Gwynn's eyes have gone even wider than usual.

Color lights Geoffrey's cheeks. "Um…no." He shoots Gwynn a bashful smile, then seems to laugh at his own embarrassment, his face brightening. "We rather like it now." Gwynn eyes him, like she can't believe for all the world he just said that. He laughs again then lifts her hand and plants a row of kisses along her knuckles as Gwynn loses her mortified expression and giggles, batting him away. Now they're looking at each other like they've both won the biggest prize in all of Erthia, and I'm both so happy for them and incredibly dismayed all at the same time.

How in the world will I possibly be this free and easy with Tobias?

Mage Gyll arrives with stacked platters of breakfast offerings, the heavenly scent of the hearty food prompting my stomach to rumble—a buttery gold mushroom frittata, crisped sausages, herbed red potatoes, and ham sliced paper-thin, edged with a brown sugar glaze.

"Mage Geoffrey Sykes." Mage Gyll beams, a delighted sparkle in her eyes. Geoffrey rises and gives her a formal embrace, kissing her on both cheeks. "Sit down with your lovely fast-mate," she tells him, gesturing toward the food. She shoots him a look of affectionate censure. "And sit with the chair the right way around, like a civilized human being."

Geoffrey grins and ceremoniously positions the chair facing the right way as Mage Gyll purses her lips at him, her eyes twinkling with amusement. He sits back down and she pours him some tea. I savor the rich, delicious food as Geoffrey regales us with his adventures as an apprentice cartwright with the Gardnerian military, and Mage Gyll asks about what seems like every single member of Geoffrey's apparently endless extended family, the two of them obviously well acquainted with each other.

My attention starts to wander toward the street and the constant stream of passing blonde Verpacians and black-clad Gardnerians, my gaze soon riveted on an unexpected sight.

Three Alfsigr Elves are striding silently in our direction, reed-straight and graceful as herons.

I'm instantly mesmerized, having never once seen Elves in my entire life. Their snow-white hair trails behind them like pennants of moonlight, their garments a spotless alabaster. They're heavily armed with intricately carved ivory bows, quivers full of arrows strapped to their backs. And their eyes. *Their eyes.* Glittering silver, like bright sun on snow.

My affinity lines pull taut, enraptured.

The Elves pass by, silent and ethereal, so close I could reach out and touch the intricate, spiraling white embroidery on the closest Elf's tunic.

My eyes are drawn across the street by a sudden flash of glowing gold. There's a man wearing a golden headband emblazoned with three runes that blaze a brighter gold, as if ignited by fire. He's black-bearded with deep brown skin, his long black hair tied back in looping, braided coils, and he wears bright yellow garb decorated with an entrancing purple star design. There's a strange glint along the edges of him, like he's standing before a late-day sun, the light raying out from him as he moves. My affinity sends up a burst of saffron stars that fizz at the edges of my vision in response to all the gold and his surprising aura.

The gold-limned man is standing just outside a smithery and securing its two large wooden doors open wide. Multiple Spine-stone domes top the smithery, and an Ishkartan Smiths' Guild flag flies atop the largest of the three domes, the design a black rune-marked hammer and anvil against a golden background.

The smithery's doors are covered with gleaming swords and axes, all hanging in neat rows.

A young woman emerges from the smithery's interior and joins the man, her pale skin the color of sand, her hair bright yellow, and she has the same golden aura as the man.

And her attire is absolutely mortifying.

She wears hide pants—*pants!*—and boots like a man, and her form-fitting, sleeveless yellow tunic is marked with runes that look like they were fashioned from molten gold. She's heavily armed as well, with rune-blades strapped to her arms and thighs and two rune-swords crisscrossed on her back. Glowing gold runes mark the skin of her face and arms.

The blonde woman pushes first one, then another large display table covered in jeweled rune-blades out in front of the smithery doors. Then she straightens and looks at the head-banded man, saying something to him that I can't hear, her hands brazenly on her hips, her stance fearless.

A woman. With so many weapons.

Everything about her is so bizarre and completely out of the range of what I've been taught is acceptable. I wonder if it would be possible for anyone in Verpacia to be more surprising in their appearance than she is.

Then a young Keltic man emerges from the shadows of the smithery.

He's tall, lean and muscular, his movements loping and powerful as he hoists several sheathed rune-swords to add to the outdoor display, and I've a sense of vast, contained strength in his body. There's a rugged elegance to him, his features long and sculpted, his expression watchful and restrained, as if he keeps close control of himself. He wears the leather, guild-marked apron of a smith's apprentice.

Every dire warning about the Kelts that Mother Eliss has pressed into me sounds in stark, blaring alarm, but he's so attractive, I can't seem to avert my gaze.

And his hair.

I've never seen anyone with red hair. And his hair is the most luxurious, heart-stopping dark red I've ever seen. Red like a blooded sunset, just before night closes in.

My affinity lines snap toward him with overwhelming force, and my wand hand starts to tingle as my vision is momentarily tinted a rich, deep scarlet. Alarmed, I blink hard and pull my hand under the table, catching a glimpse of the garnet hue forming on my fingertips.

Look away, I urgently warn myself. *Before the color spreads clear up your arm!*

But the red is so ravishing, I can't do anything but drink him in. And it's not just his hair—there's a subtle green shimmer coming off him that's only apparent when he moves. But it's not like our faint, Gardnerian emerald shimmer—it's as if he's edged in every hue of sparkling green.

Where is his green aura coming from? What could it mean?

He glances up and our eyes collide.

His gaze hits me like a bolt, his eyes taking on an emerald glow as if lit from within by green torchlight. Bright green sparks explode into my vision and strafe through my lines, and I draw back in surprise at the same moment he does, his gaze full of an astonishment that's almost angry in its intensity, his lips parted, his whole body frozen. There's a sudden, crackling tension between us that can be felt from clear across the street.

I tear my eyes from his as my heart pounds hot against my chest, deeply thrown by his obvious power and by our inexplicably intense reaction to each other. And by the strange aura surrounding him and everyone else working in the smithery.

Don't look at him again! I caution myself. *There's some type of sorcery at work here.*

I desperately force my gaze down to the table, to the swirling fastlines marking my hidden scarlet-and-emerald hand. Keeping my eyes set on anything but the startling red of his hair, the incandescent shimmer of his body or his relentless, verdant gaze.

I force myself to breathe deep, half-aware of the lively conversation between Geoffrey and Gwynn and Mage Gyll. When I finally dare to look back at the smithery, the red-haired apprentice is gone. I breathe out a hard sigh of relief.

"Who are the people in the smithery?" I nervously blurt out, breaking into their friendly morning banter.

Mage Gyll, Gwynn and Geoffrey all turn to me in unison, as if surprised that I've finally joined the conversation.

"The heathens?" Mage Gyll clarifies, with evident surprise.

I nod as I pull in a shaky breath. "There's something…odd about them." *They all shimmer colors,* I long to tell them.

And the young smith has emerald sorcery in his gaze. But I don't voice my thoughts, scared that this is my light affinity running amuck again after I've managed to keep it under pious control for so long.

Mage Gyll glances over at the smithery, her eyes narrowed, her lips pursed in deep displeasure. She gives me a cautionary look. "They're a sordid lot over there. And they should *never* have been allowed into Verpacia."

"Who's the man dressed in gold?" I ask, my heartbeat still tripping. *And the woman with the golden aura,* I think, but don't voice. *And the disturbingly stunning Kelt. With hair as red as Gardnerian roses and eyes that spark green lightning.*

Mage Gyll frowns begrudgingly at the smithery. "The one with the rune-marked headband? He's an Ishkart. From a highborn rune-sorcerer family." Her frown deepens. "All the Ishkart highborn wear gold. His name's Zeymir Nyvor."

I watch Zeymir Nyvor as he pulls a sword from the door to show to a Keltic customer.

Does his rune-sorcery have something to do with his sunlike aura? I wonder.

The heavily armed, golden-haired young woman is now sitting at a sharpening wheel. She's honing the blade of a sword, the wheel spinning as white sparks fly into the air. I can hear the grating, metallic screech of blade on stone from clear over here.

"He *was* a highborn Ishkart," Mage Gyll says with a cynical tightening of her lips as we scrutinize the smiths. "His own people cast him out."

"Why?" I ask.

"Because of the women. That's one of them there." She gestures toward the young woman at the sharpening wheel. "The Issani."

"I don't know much about the Issani," I say.

"It's what the Northern Ishkart people call themselves."

Mage Gyll leans close and lowers her voice to a discreet whisper. "He bought her. Like a sack of grain." Shock ripples through me as Geoffrey makes a sound of disgust and Gwynn glares in the direction of the smithery.

Mage Gyll eyes the young woman with dismay. "The other one's even worse."

As if on cue, a green-skinned woman with pointed ears emerges from the smithery's interior, and I draw back in surprise.

She has *scales*. Bright green scales that send off a luminous shimmer around her, like a verdant constellation that mingles with the glittering green aura encompassing her.

Her eyes are a dazzling silver, her hair a deeper green than her scales, her pointed ears rimmed with golden hoops. She's clothed like a man, in a deep green tunic and pants marked with glowing green Snake Elf runes. Her long, emerald hair is gathered in a large swath of yellow fabric marked with golden Ishkartan runes.

"A Snake Elf," I marvel. I turn to Mage Gyll, newly alarmed as I remember the chilling things that Father and Mother Eliss have told me about the criminal subland elves. "How can she be living here?"

"There's a few loose here," Geoffrey puts in, his hand protectively covering Gwynn's. He shrugs. "Verpacia allows it, as long as they have the right papers."

"She's why the Ishkart was kicked out of Ishkartaan," Mage Gyll says ominously. "That Snake Elf woman. His people could have countenanced the Issani whore, but he insisted on keeping the Snake Elf as well." She gives the smithery a dark look. "I've complained to the Verpacian Council about all this more than once. People with such low morals shouldn't be allowed into Verpacia."

A young child runs out of the smithery and up to the Snake

Elf woman. He tugs at her tunic and chatters excitedly in a foreign tongue. His ears are as pointed as hers and his skin is covered in green scales, but his eyes and his hair are black. He's in a yellow embroidered tunic much like the Ishkart man's, and like the rest of them, he has a spectacular aura—faint rays of gold and green light that radiate out, like he's his own tiny sun.

"There's the little viper they've spawned," Mage Gyll says with distaste, as if resigned to madness.

Her words are so unexpectedly harsh that they startle me. The child's appearance is surprising, to be sure, but his manner is distinctly childlike. He smiles up at the Snake Elf woman as she beams warmly back at him, caressing his cheek, and I'm thrust into confusion.

Her manner seems so kind. Not criminal at all...

And it's hard to keep from staring at both the woman and the child. Their snake scales are like glittering emeralds. And the strange, unique light auras they all possess...

Beautiful.

"He's so young," I say, thinking out loud. Maybe seven or eight years old.

"Yes, well, he's a child *now*," Mage Gyll cautions, "but he'll grow up to be a danger." She retrieves her teapot and tightens her mouth, grimacing at the smithery. "The next one they all spawn will have red hair and green scales. Mark my words."

I glance back toward the smithery as flames leap above the forge and illuminate the building's shadowed interior with a wavering, orange light. A heated surprise flashes through me.

He's there. The Kelt. Standing by the forge, the fire painting his dark, tousled hair with glints of crimson.

I'm instantly transfixed by him and overcome by the urge to see him more clearly. Staring at him sidelong, my head down to hide my fascination, I surreptitiously tighten the lines around my eyes and draw his image close.

His handsome form pulls into close view as he thrusts a broadsword into the flames and stares at it with a motionless focus that brings to mind the gaze of a predator. I watch him covertly as he studies the reddening metal gripped in his curiously ungloved hand, his stance as still as the surface of a summer lake. He lays the glowing sword atop an anvil, picks up an iron hammer and, with sudden violence, lashes down, hammer to sword, his aura trailing streaks of glimmering green. A shower of red sparks flies from the sword, and I can feel the force of his blows straight down my spine. Then he dips the glowing sword in a nearby barrel of water, sending up a great, hissing cloud of steam.

The fog of steam begins to dissipate and surprise rocks through me.

He's staring straight at me.

His gaze is unnervingly bold, and it jostles my affinity lines straight down to my core. But this time, I don't look away. For a suspended moment, the world drops away and I hold his stare, the color of his eyes like a strong, midday sun through vivid green leaves. I inhale sharply as the verdant color telescopes out toward me and sizzles down my affinity lines in a spangled green rush. Green runes burst to life in the back of my vision…

"Sage."

Gwynn's measured, disapproving tone jerks me from my decadent, shocking thrall. I immediately loosen my eye lines and wrench my gaze away from the young smith. The rune images lingering in my vision fracture, like glass shattering, the heart-stopping green abruptly clearing.

Gwynn, Geoffrey and Mage Gyll are all eyeing me with deep concern.

"I'm sorry," I stammer as I struggle to breathe normally and keep my color-washed wand hand carefully hidden. "He was staring at me."

What just happened? Why did I look at him and see runes?

Mage Gyll breathes out a sound of derision. "I'm sure he was." She casts a resentful glare toward the smithery that I don't dare look at again. "They try to ensnare our women." She turns back to us, grave resolve in her eyes. "You young Mages stay close to our kind here and you'll stay safe." She places her hand protectively on my back as I keep my eyes militantly plastered on the table, my heart pounding against my chest as my wand hand tingles with forbidden color.

CHAPTER TWO:
Rivyr'el Talonir

A few minutes after Mage Gyll's warning about staying close to our kind, my heart is still thudding. I risk a sidelong glance at the smithery to find the red-haired smith gone again, and I'm both intensely relieved and disconcertingly aware of the lack of him, as if a glimpse of his sorcery has lit a candle in me that refuses to go out.

Stop it, I chastise myself, dismayed by being so easily lured away from the Gardnerian fold. *Stop being so drawn in by them.*

Stop being drawn in by him.

Gwynn pauses in buttering her scone. We're alone at the table now, Geoffrey having left to meet his family, and Mage Gyll is a few tables away from us, pouring tea for two elegant Gardnerian women with gray hair and piously unadorned black garments.

"Sage, don't worry yourself." Gwynn glances at the smithery uneasily. "I did notice the Kelt looking at you rather strangely." Looking troubled, she turns back to me. "You'll be with Tobias soon. Don't forget that. And no one would *dare* bother you with a Level Four Mage by your side."

A prickle of nervous trepidation courses through me at the mention of Tobias's name, and I realize that this is my chance to ask Gwynn the questions that have been weighing so heavily on my mind—questions that I never dreamed she might have the answer to, until I saw the way she and Geoffrey are with each other.

"Gwynn," I haltingly begin, heat creeping onto my cheeks, "I'm nervous about…the sealing night."

I've read all the stories written for devout young women about the sealing night, searching for some clue as to what, exactly, will happen after the ceremony. We're to consummate our union that very night, but… I've never shown as much as an ankle in public.

The stories are full of chaste kisses, and even those are enough to set my imagination whirling and send warmth rushing through me, but…then what? Certainly we can't be expected to fully undress when we pair. Gardnerian maidens don't do such things.

Or do they?

Gwynn sets down her tea and eyes me soberly. I know she surmises immediately what I'm asking, without needing me to elaborate further.

Her cheeks redden. "You'll go off together…" She takes a breath, her brow tensing as she starts to speak, but falters. Then her eyes brighten, as if with remembered knowledge, and I lean forward, desperate for information. "And then," she lowers her voice, "the Ancient One will draw you together. *Seamlessly.*" She smiles beatifically, as if completely satisfied with herself for perfectly repeating something memorized.

I sigh inwardly. This is of absolutely no help whatsoever. "But…we don't know each other at all," I press, an anxious frustration rising. "He hasn't even been permitted to write to me. How can we be so close so *fast*?"

Gwynn shakes her head as if she's shaking away my worries.

"The Ancient One has drawn you together. That means that this is the perfect pairing for you both."

My unease refuses to be dislodged—it's stuck deep inside, like a large, dark burr. "But what about the couples at the fasting who seemed really unhappy about it?"

"That was years ago," she says, her tone lilting and good-humored as she dismisses this concern. "They were too young to think clearly. You need to trust the will of the Ancient One." She smiles at me, her gaze full of certainty. "You and Tobias were drawn together by the Ancient One's own hand. Your union is written in the stars."

I'm momentarily caught up in her flowery language, and it smooths the serrated edges of my fears, unspooling a sweet ribbon of hope inside me.

She's right. I need to trust in the Ancient One. Tobias and I will be perfect together, otherwise the priest wouldn't have fasted us.

But then, Gwynn loses her serene smile and turns sheepish as she rubs her fingertip distractedly along a seam in the inlaid wood table's tree design. "Sage," she asks haltingly, "you don't still have that wand Geoffrey mentioned, do you?"

I smile at her bashfulness about our childhood games, then reach just under my skirt's hem and slide the toy wand from where I've hidden it in the side of my boot. I often carry it there, my small, heartening secret—a remembrance of a time when I got to play at being a hero. At having power. And it feels so good to have a wand in my hand, even if it's just a toy.

I hold up the wand and flash a playful smile at Gwynn. "I thought you might enjoy seeing it again."

She sucks in air and freezes. "Please," she breathes, "put it away."

I'm instantly cast into confusion. "Why?"

Gwynn eyes the wand with extreme wariness. "It's…well,

it may not be the White Wand, like we were playing at…but it's a real wand."

My eyes widen. I quickly slide the wand back into my boot and yank my skirt's hem over it. "Great Ancient One, Gwynn!"

"Lower your voice, Sage," Gwynn pleads.

"I *cannot* have a real wand," I urgently whisper. "I don't have Council permission. Where did you get it?"

Gwynn eyes me guiltily. "Please don't be so put out. I stole it from the armory—"

"You *stole* it?"

"I replaced it with a carved replica," Gwynn says, blushing. "And then those Council envoys took the one I made. It's obvious no one gave it any mind, as no one ever mentioned it again." Her expression loses its defensive edge and melts into apology. "I don't know what possessed me to be so reckless. I was caught up in that whole fantasy." She gives me an imploring look. "Please, Sage. Just hide it away somewhere. Or destroy it. Truly, it was one of hundreds of wands that go through that armory. And this one was close to useless anyway. Father said it was as good as a toy even before I took it."

But it's not a toy.

It's a real wand. And I remember the terrifying tale she wove around it—glamoured demons hunting for it, ready to kill anyone in their path, the Wand wanting to escape Valgard to hide in Halfix.

Gwynn's expression tenses with real worry, but some of my alarm recedes as reason takes hold. If it's a useless wand, without power, no one is going to come searching for it after all this time. "I won't tell anyone about it," I relent, wishing she had told me the truth long ago.

Some of the tension drains from Gwynn's brow. "Thank you." She gives me a heartfelt look of gratitude.

The heavy clomping of horses' hooves draws our attention

toward the road. It's a busy place, Verpax City, and I find myself mentally calculating what proportion of its inhabitants are Gardnerian. I'm picking out the black-garbed Mages, about half of the people out today, and that's when I see them.

A devastatingly handsome young Gardnerian man is walking down the other side of the street with a Gardnerian girl on his arm, the two of them laughing and smiling like besotted lovers. The girl is beautiful, her black tunic form-fitting and scandalously trimmed in sparkling purple gems that set my affinity lines instantly flaring. The couple draws nearer, and my gaze locks onto the young man's dazzling green eyes.

All the breath tears from my lungs as a wild disbelief crashes into me.

Tobias.

The awful realization claws clear up my throat. My fastmate. With Draven. I recognize her with sickening certainty. Draven from the fasting, her willowy, doe-eyed beauty only brightened and enhanced with time. The same hateful girl who had a crush on Tobias. Who was distraught when he was fasted to me instead.

Tobias's eyes meet mine, and he throws me a contemptuous look before making a show of turning and smiling widely at Draven. Draven laughs and bats her eyelashes as she flirtatiously touches *my* fastmate's hand.

My eyes blur with devastated tears.

"Oh, Sage." Gwynn leans in to rest her hand gently on my arm. "I almost wrote to you about this." She eyes the happy, flirting couple, then looks back to me, steely-eyed. "You've already won, Sage. Don't forget that. Tobias is fasted to *you*."

Hurt knifes through me. "How long have you known?" I can barely get the words out. "How could you not tell me?"

"I didn't have the heart..." She bites her lip, then looks resentfully back toward Tobias and Draven. "It doesn't matter

how she behaves, don't you see? She can't have him. He's *yours*."
Her hand tightens around my arm, her large eyes going rigid
with determination. "You'll claim him. That's what you'll do.
You're far more beautiful than she is."

"No one is more beautiful than she is!"

Gwynn is undaunted. "You just need to get him alone…
and win him over."

Tobias and Draven pause to look at some trinkets on display in front of the jeweler's shop adjacent to the smithery. A
tear spills down my cheek, and I wipe it roughly away. Tobias
must know that my entire family is here, including my young
brothers and my sisters. For *our* sealing.

"I shouldn't have to win over my *own* fastmate," I counter,
my voice breaking as I watch them. I turn back to Gwynn
and search her eyes, desperately grasping for hope in a world
suddenly turned completely on its head. "And how could I
possibly win him over from *her*?"

"Sit next to him at supper," Gwynn tells me, her delicate jaw
set defiantly tight. She leans closer and speaks in a low whisper. "Touch his thigh."

Shock roils through me. "His *thigh*!"

"Trust me," Gwynn says, her cheeks lighting with a flush.
"Run your hand up his thigh. He'll forget all about Draven.
Then get him alone."

"But… Gardnerians aren't supposed to…" My voice trails
off to a constricted whisper. "We're not supposed to do things
like that…"

"Well, you will," Gwynn states firmly. "If you want to make
him forget Draven ever existed."

My face and neck have grown sickeningly hot from misery
and embarrassment. I take in Gwynn's decisive expression. She's
so sure, so full of secret, guarded knowledge about men. I re-

member the heated glances that passed between her and Geoffrey. How besotted he seemed.

"How high?" I ask in a choked whisper, as beautiful Draven chimes out a laugh from across the street. Desperation cuts through me. "How high up his thigh?" *Surely not that high...*

Gwynn sets determined eyes on me. "As high as it takes to win him back."

I struggle not to sob right there in the open. I shouldn't have to win Tobias back! I shouldn't have to do this...outrageous thing. He's my *fastmate*. He's supposed to love *me*.

Draven shoots me a devious grin that hollows me out. Then she turns and walks off with my Tobias the way they came, the two of them quickly swallowed up by the street traffic as my world threatens to completely fall apart.

"Why so glum?"

I give a start at the male voice.

An Elfin youth around our age is leaning rakishly over the iron fence. I blink at him, disoriented by his sudden presence. He's slender and as coolly beautiful as a glacier, like all the Alfsigr. But he's also screamingly different. A glittery cloud of rainbow metallic dust highlights the shimmer of his Elfin eyes, and he has a relaxed posture that's decidedly *un*-Elflike. There's a constellation of ruby gems fastened to his braids and multicolored hoops rimming his long ears, and his blindingly white Elfin tunic is edged with looping red, purple and gold stitchery.

And he has a prismatic, silver aura about him that takes my breath away.

"I could cheer you up," he offers, his Alfsigr accent fluid and lilting, his silver eyes dancing.

Before Gwynn or I have time to react, he tilts his head and grins at me, and suddenly all the color of the world contracts toward his gaze. I'm instantly bolted to it, my mouth hanging dumbly open as the riot of reflected color in his eyes practically ransacks my light affinity and takes it hostage. It's like falling into a sunlit lake filled with broken glass. For a moment, the pain of Tobias's rejection fades to nothing, and I float suspended in a world of prismatic beauty, veins of violet lightning pulsing through it.

His eyes flash with recognition. "Great gods, you're a Light Mage. How incredible."

The prismatic colors all around me intensify, intricate silver runes forming inside each shard, coming to life and rotating like intricate gears. It's mesmerizing. So beautiful...

I'm barely aware of a hard voice calling for me from the direction of the inn.

"Oh, they've left you vulnerable, haven't they?" The Elf's words are a sultry caress. "Probably never even put a wand in your hands." He sighs, and I can feel it ripple through me. "Focus on me, *ti'a'lin*. I'll set up a protective ward."

A faint tingle of warning whispers in the back of my mind, but I ignore it. I'm enticingly lulled, swimming in silver as he brings his eyes closer. *His eyes.* His lovely eyes. Full of spiraling silver runes that whirl toward me and light up my vision. I can feel the runes sizzling down my affinity lines in rolling, concentric patterns as I float in his gaze, only vaguely aware of something pressing against the palm of my wand hand.

"You have rune-sorcery, did you know that, *ti'a?*" His voice comes from everywhere in the prismatic lake. "All Light Mages do. But they never taught you how to use it, did they? Or else you'd have warded yourself."

New runes start to form in the center of my sight, drawn suspended in the air and glowing like silver fire.

A door slams, and I'm wrenched from the prismatic lake, reality crashing down as the real world floods into my vision. I recoil back against my chair, my head spinning from vertigo, fright slashing through me. The Elf is pointing what must be a rune-stylus at me.

Shock overtakes me. *An Elfin rune-sorcerer.*

"Get away from her! *Now!*"

Edyth Gyll's Level Four husband, Mage Korin Gyll, is stalking toward us, two young Level Three Mages just behind him. Gwynn and Edyth trail the Mages, their expressions full of outrage, and I realize Gwynn must have gone to summon their help.

How long was I under the Elf's thrall?

The three Mages pull their wands on the glittery Elf, and I notice that every other breakfasting Gardnerian has retreated behind the line of Mages or fled. I blink at them all in confusion, struggling to steady myself, my head spinning as I grasp at the edge of my seat to keep from falling clear over.

The Elf smiles at me and slowly straightens. His silver eyes flick toward all the pointed wands as if he finds them incredibly amusing as he idly twirls the stylus in his hand.

"What did you do to me?" I rasp out, outrage warring with fear.

The Elf gives a short laugh and bares his perfect teeth at me. "You're a Light Mage. I'm a rune-sorcerer. The combination can kick up a thrall that could be dangerous to you, drawing all of your power away from you and into me. You needed to be properly warded to keep that from happening, so—"

"I said, get away from her!" Korrin Gyll booms.

The Elf coughs out a laugh and gives Korrin and the other Mages a narrow look of appraisal. "Such a jolly lot, you Gardnerians." He takes in the lodging house with a sweeping glance. "*That* is why I love this place. The welcoming air." He grins at them, plucks up a small scone from my table and takes a cheeky bite from it. His eyes briefly widen as he nods with somber appreciation. "Mmm. *Wonderful* food. I adore currants." He looks to Edyth Gyll, who's glowering at him furiously. "Did you cook this?" The words are slightly muffled with scone. "It's quite good—"

"This place is for *Gardnerians*," Korrin Gyll snarls. "Not heathen *filth*."

Another laugh bursts from the Elf as he looks Korrin over with contempt. "Don't you ever get tired of all that black? Shining One's piss, I get tired of all this white." His eyes suddenly go wide, and he twirls his scone in the air, his lip lifting. "We should have a special holiday! The Alfsigr could dress all in black, and your lot could wear silver and white. So glorious and confusing." He turns and rakes his gaze over me. "*You* would look stunning in silver brocade."

I'm afraid to look directly at him, so I glare at him sideways, still horribly dizzy. "Don't use your sorcery on me again."

"I couldn't if I tried," he flippantly answers. "I warded you."

"What does that mean?" I demand, scared of him.

"I *told* you what it means," he throws back condescendingly. Something further down the walkway catches his eye, and his mouth tightens into a grimace. He rolls his silver eyes and breathes out what sounds like a low oath in Alfsigr.

Five Alfsigr Elves are storming down the walkway, coming in like a blizzard of white. They're armed with swords, with bows and quivers strapped to their backs, and they wear silver-plated armor. One of them is taller than the others and has the same chiseled features as my tormentor.

The glittery Elf flashes a too-wide smile at the tall Elf. "Ah, Yllyndor. My humorless brother." His eyes flick to the Elf standing rigidly beside Yllyndor. "And Kryl'lin. His equally humorless second." He shoots me a look of deep forbearance, the silvered pull of his gaze much fainter now. Barely there. And the silver aura around him is gone as he smiles at me.

"This morning keeps getting brighter and brighter, my sweet Crow. Don't you think?"

Before I can even formulate a response to the slur, Yllyndor has launched into a livid stream of High Alfsigr and is gesturing sharply toward all of us Gardnerians while the glittery Elf tries to get in a word edgewise, scratching the back of his head in frustration when he's unable to. Kryl'lin is grasping his sword hilt tightly, as if ready to murder the glittery Elf at the slightest provocation.

"We are taking you into custody," Yllyndor sternly announces in the Common Tongue, as if to notify everyone listening of his intentions.

"Ha!" the glittery Elf coughs out in disbelief, one hand on his slender hip. "To be dragged back to Alfsigr lands and thrown into prison? I think not."

Prison?!

The tall Elf lets loose another stream of unforgiving Alfsigr.

"I can't steal my own inheritance," the glittery Elf shoots back sarcastically. "And you have no jurisdiction here, Yllyndor. I have an open-ended residency permit and good luck getting *that* rescinded. You may be powerful, but you're no match for the bureaucratic nightmare that is Verpacia."

Yllyndor stares coldly at his brother.

"I'm getting the distinct impression I'm not wanted here," the glittery Elf rues to me as he polishes off his small scone and expeditiously slaps his hands free of crumbs. He straightens and addresses the entire crowd, his voice clear as a bell. "I must take my leave, although I know it will grieve you all to hear it. Good day, you incredibly festive people."

Then he turns on his heels and walks into the momentarily emptied road, whistling to himself as he goes.

Without warning, Yllyndor whips out an ivory stone imprinted with a silver rune. He extends his arm and points the stone toward his brother, his thumb sliding over its center.

A stream of silver light bursts from the stone, and I recoil back as the light spears toward the sparkly Elf's back. It slams into him with an explosion of white light, the Elf's garb lighting up with glowing silver runes. I gasp as the white light explodes a second time into silver sparks, causing passersby to shriek and rush away as nearby horses spook, one rearing as its Keltic driver yells and pulls hard on the reins.

The sparkly Elf turns slowly to face down the other Elves.

His air of cheeky sarcasm is gone. Hard defiance lights his steel-cold eyes now, a mirthless smile on his ivory lips.

"I am well-warded, you close-minded, tedious, intolerant *fools*." He launches into a vicious stream of Alfsigr, then stops, turns and looks directly at me, pointing a finger emphatically. "You are *wasted* where you are." His nostrils flare as he shoots his brother another look of pure fury before turning back to me, a hard flash of rebellion in his eyes. "You should try a dress in violet, *Light Mage*." A note of bitterness darkens his tone. "Truly, *ti'a'lin*, black is *not* your color."

He throws one last look of hatred at his brother, then turns and strides toward the smithery. I can feel his fury practically vibrating on the air.

Gwynn breaks down crying and rushes to me. Edyth Gyll follows close on her heels, both of them fussing and trying to comfort me as my equilibrium slowly returns. The Elves are apologizing to Korrin Gyll, the tall Elf assuring him that he'll inform the Alfsigr royal council. I can barely follow their tense conversation, I'm so thrown by the young Elf's confusing words and distressing level of power. Eventually, the Elves finish speaking with Korrin, send joint hard glances toward the smithery, then take their leave.

"Why can't they arrest him?" Gwynn implores. "Who is he?"

Mage Gyll shakes his head. "He's the most powerful Alf-sigr rune-sorcerer to come along in ages. His name is Rivyr'el Talonir. He's the son of Alfsigr royalty and the disgrace of his family." He glares at the smithery. "I've never known an Elf to act like he does. He came into his inheritance, left Alfsigr lands and promptly went insane."

"He said he warded me," I tell Mage Gyll, my voice shaky.

Mage Gyll gives me a dismissive look. "There's no need to ward you, child. You can't possibly have enough magic in you for a ward to catch hold."

I shrink down, not understanding any of this.

That Elf did something *to me, though,* I worriedly think to myself. And after he did it, his aura was gone, and so was the wild pull of his silver eyes.

Edyth Gyll casts a hateful look toward the smithery and gives my shoulder a squeeze. "Come, luv. You're safe now. That's all that matters."

Safe from these frightening, unpredictable foreigners and their dangerous sorcery. Safe with my own people.

Tobias's betrayal slices into my thoughts, but I force the horrible remembrance down as Edyth and Gwynn guide me up on shaky legs and lead me towards the inn.

Once Tobias and I are sealed, all will be set right, I tell myself, feeling bereft. *And he'll forget Draven and protect me from all the threats of the world.*

"*Crow Princess,*" Rivyr'el's insolent voice rings out from across the street.

I flinch, my pulse tripping higher, and turn even as Edyth and Gwynn both urge me not to look at him.

Rivyr'el Talonir smiles rakishly from where he stands just inside the smithery's doorway, his silvered gaze dark with rebellion. He brings an elegant hand to his ivory lips and blows me a kiss.

CHAPTER THREE:
Fastmate

"He'll be here momentarily," Tobias's father states, his voice hard, as if this is an unassailable fact that had best not be questioned. Tobias's empty chair and untouched dinner are like a slap, his pristine bowl of soup sending steam up into the outdoor restaurant's evening air.

I draw myself tightly in, unable to eat the rich leek soup, my cheeks and neck burning with a miserable knowing. And an even more miserable wondering if Mage Vasillis knows why his son is not here with us for dinner—and whether that accounts for his hard tone.

Tobias's mother keeps her head carefully lowered, taking measured sips of her soup as Father falls into conversation with Mage Vasillis about the "heathen problem" in Verpacia and how Gwynn and I were accosted by an Elf. Normally, Mother Eliss would take a keen interest in this topic, but tonight she's distracted, her brow drawn tight, her eyes darting around the outdoor dining area, up and down the increasingly lamplit street—searching, no doubt, for Tobias.

She doesn't have to search long.

Tobias suddenly descends like a storm, stalking around tables, his dark cloak streaming behind him. He's beautiful and severe and full of furious glory, and he doesn't even so much as glance at me.

My insides constrict at the way he ignores me. *He's Draven's. All hers,* my erratic heartbeat drums out. *He doesn't want you.*

"Ah, Tobias. You've finally graced us with your presence." Tobias's father observes this mildly, neatly wiping his lips with his black cloth napkin, but there's steel just under his casual tone.

Tobias pulls back the chair next to me with as much force as he can muster, and I flinch at the harsh scraping sound. He falls heavily into the seat and throws a contemptuous glance at me.

My ears are burning, my head filled with a sick desperation. The despair spikes to an overwhelming distress when my eyes meet Mother Eliss's harsh stare, her gaze boring into mine. Her eyes flit pointedly toward Tobias and back to me. Her meaning is clear—*Remedy this, and quickly. Or it will be your disgrace and ours.*

I can barely hear all the niceties being spoken as Mage Vasillis and Father pointedly ignore the undercurrent of gut-churning tension while Tobias seethes beside me. His mother continues to mechanically sip her soup across the table.

I have to win him over, I breathlessly realize. *I just have to. And I will. I'll win him over, and everything will fall into place as it should. He'll be the devoted fastmate I've always wanted.*

Tobias throws me a withering sidelong glance, and the harsh reality of the situation slashes away my brief attempt at hopefulness.

The Ancient One will right this terrible thing. He has to.

My gut clenches tighter as our fathers idly talk about the University. Mother Eliss gives me a look of extreme censure, as if I somehow caused this.

Did I? Should I be seeking him out aggressively like beautiful Draven? But, that's not what they taught me to do. Tobias is supposed to like me shy and demure. But I'm quickly learning that nothing in this world is as it's supposed to be.

I can practically feel the ire coming off Tobias. He's like a panther I'm scared to spook, wound up as tightly as he is.

Run your hand up his thigh…if you want to make him forget Draven ever existed.

Gwynn's shocking advice pulses in my mind.

I look at Tobias, desperate, but he stubbornly refuses to acknowledge me.

I wait until our parents are engaged in heated conversation, Mother Eliss forgetting about her displeasure with me for a few moments to rail against "Snake Elves and deviant Alfsigr Elves allowed to run free, accosting our daughters." I glance sidelong at Tobias, heart thudding, knowing it's now or never.

Trembling, I place a hand on his knee.

Tobias's head gives a subtle, surprised jerk, his whole body stiffening.

My heart beats wildly, but I keep my hand lightly in place, scared to be so brazen. His knee is warm under my hand, and I can feel his muscles clench. It's exciting and frightening and embarrassing all at once, to do this forbidden thing.

My hand quivering, I slide my hand slightly up his thigh, and Tobias inhales sharply.

Where do I stop? I have to stop. Where would Draven stop?

His thigh tenses again, rock hard, a ruddy flush now filling his cheeks as he stares straight forward, his breathing deepened. He turns his eyes fully on me, and I realize with a start… it *worked*.

All the anger is gone from his gaze. Only a blurred, surprise remains, as if he's truly noticing me for the first time.

A fragile hope rises in my chest. I lean in, my throat dry, my heart fluttering as I whisper to him unsteadily, overcome with jagged nerves. "Would you…would you like to take a walk with me after dinner? And…perhaps we could talk a bit?"

He swallows, his whole attention fixed on me. Only me. His fastmate.

I did that. With just my hand on his thigh.

He nods, mesmerized.

I pull my hand off him carefully, desperate not to break this spell, and give him a trembling smile. "I haven't seen the University yet," I tell him.

His mouth tilts into a grin, an enticing glint now in his beautiful eyes. "Well, I'll just have to give you a tour, won't I?"

I break into a wider smile, encouraged. "I'd like that. Very much."

We'll talk and get to know each other, I comfort myself. *And he'll forget all about Draven.*

I glance at Mother Eliss and can tell by her approving look that she's noticed our friendly exchange.

Tobias and I eat in silence as our parents somberly discuss Mage Council affairs, but there's a new, palpable tension present between us, our focus on each other now vibrating heatedly on the air.

Dessert finally comes, and I'm savoring a spoonful of spiced whipped cream when Tobias's hand slides over my thigh.

I freeze, my spoon suspended in the air. His hand is quite high up on my leg and sparks an exciting warmth deep inside me, mingled with a sharp spike of unease. His hand tightens—too tight. Hard enough that it pinches. But still, I look at him and force a shy smile, wanting to stay in his good graces. Wanting to stay in everyone's good graces.

He glances at me sidelong and sends me a flirtatious smile in return, his hand loosening and sliding off my thigh.

"Father," Tobias announces, and all the adults turn, wide-eyed and blinking at his sudden participation in the conversation. Tobias shoots his father a brilliant smile. "I'd like to show Sagellyn around the University."

His mother looks up, but remains as silent as she has throughout the meal. Tobias's father studies him, brows raised, then turns to glance at my father, who indulgently nods permission. Mother Eliss shoots me a look of hard caution, her eyes flicking to Tobias. Her meaning is clear. *Preserve this new civility between you.*

"Very well," Tobias's father says, giving Tobias a quick, dismissive look before turning his attention back to his food. "Stay on the main thoroughfare. And be back before the twenty-first hour."

Tobias rises and gives me a dazzling smile that tangles my thoughts and sends me reeling over my sudden, blessed change of fortune. He holds his warm hand out to help me up, then dashingly offers me his arm.

I'm in a heated, disoriented daze as I take his arm and he leads me silently away.

As soon as we're away from our parents and the restaurant, Tobias's aggressively polite bearing changes. He now seems like he's in a distracted haze, silent and radiating an intense energy that sets me alight with nerves.

My mind whirs with a pained uncertainty. *Should I say something? Touch him in some way? What would Draven do?*

I work to keep up with his long, powerful stride through the University's iron gates and down its cobbled Spine-stone walkways. The sky is darkening and lanterns are being lit by Urisk workers, the alabaster Spine-stone buildings washed deep blue in the dying light.

Tobias guides me into the stately Gardnerian Atheneum, the Ironwood building darkened to black in the twilight, the structure's rich wood a sharp contrast to the pale Spine-stone buildings that surround it.

"Oh, it's so lovely!" I enthuse as we step inside. I'm instantly lit up by the beautiful, sanded trees set into the walls and acting as supporting columns, dark branches tangling over the roof of the Atheneum. It's like a mysterious forest of knowledge, with bookshelves everywhere. Crimson glass lanterns are hung on the walls and set on broad Ironwood tables, and in the center of the vast space, a wrought-iron spiraling staircase rises up several stories, drawing ever closer to the stained-glass image of a white bird on the domed, glass apex of the grand building.

I look to Tobias, excited to be in such a wonderful new place. He flashes me an enigmatic smile as we walk, and the heat in his beautiful green eyes sets an enticing warmth kindling through my affinity lines.

Will he kiss me here? In between the shelves? My heart takes flight with nervous anticipation. I can feel the warmth of his arm through the fabric of his tunic as I cling to him and follow his lead.

"I've never seen so many books in one place before," I tell him brightly. "And...it's so beautiful here."

Tobias doesn't reply as we cut through the maze of shelves, but his eyes flit to me, intense with heat, a cryptic smile on his lips, as if he's both intensely interested in me but not even registering my words. Trepidation creeps into the edges of my mind, but I push it firmly away. *He's my fastmate. I can trust him completely. Or the Ancient One wouldn't have picked him for me.*

"Where are we going?" I ask hopefully.

He smirks and looks fully at me, a flash of disdain in his eyes. "As far away from all of *them* as possible."

It's clear from the hard rebellion in his tone whom he's referring to: Our parents.

I'm drawn in by his boldness, suddenly wanting to be bold, too. "It'll be good to get away," I tell him.

I'm rewarded with a captivating smile, and elation leaps

in my chest over our sudden camaraderie. Tobias guides me through a side door and down a wooden staircase to a long, bookshelf-lined tunnel cut into the underground Spine-stone. The air is much cooler down here, almost chilly, and I tamp down a flicker of unease over how flagrantly we're disobeying his father's command to stay on the main street.

Does it really matter that we're off alone? We'll be sealed at week's end. And maybe we'll finally have a chance to talk to each other.

"Where does this lead?" I ask, my voice echoing slightly off the stone walls.

"All around," he answers evasively as we descend another staircase into an empty, circular room lit by a single golden lumenstone lantern. Tobias guides me toward the far wall and I glance around, searching for a door or hallway leading to somewhere else. But...there's nothing.

I turn and smile nervously at him. "What's this?"

Without warning, his mouth comes down hard on mine, and I fall back against the cold stone wall, bumping my head with a painful thud, his harsh kiss muffling my cry of surprise.

I'm so stunned that for a moment, I don't feel anything but shock as his mouth grinds against mine, his teeth pressing so relentlessly into my lip that it stings.

Outraged confusion roars through me. *What's happening? Why is he doing this? This isn't how it's supposed to be!*

I jerk my head roughly to the side. His wet mouth slides away from my lips and he pulls back a fraction, his breathing hard, his face flushed.

"Tobias...wait..."

His mouth slams down on mine again, and I cry out against his lips. He grabs hold of my breast, his fingers digging into my flesh with small spikes of pain.

Shock flashes through me, with shame tight on its heels. *This can't be happening. There's been some mistake.* Even as it's happening, I can't believe it's happening.

I push hard against him, force my mouth away from his and try desperately to pull his hand away from my breast. "Stop... *wait!*" I plead with him, distraught. "I don't *like* this."

He laughs as I push against him, his mouth curled into a sneer, his eyes hard and bright. He grabs my wrist and forces my arm against the wall, his other hand tightening on my breast as he forces himself relentlessly against me, my other arm pinned under his elbow.

Everything in me spirals into bewildered, outraged chaos. I wrench my hand away from his grip and shove him away from me as hard as I possibly can.

Tobias falls back and almost stumbles. He catches his balance and looks me over with angry surprise, eyes narrowed, breathing heavily. His expression darkens, and his lips curl back in an enraged snarl.

His arm rears back and he smacks my face so hard, I almost lose my balance.

My hand flies up to my stinging cheek, horror coursing over me. Tobias lunges forward and grasps my arms in a viselike grip as he forces me back against the wall, my whole world crashing down around me.

"You're mine now," he snarls. "You don't get to say *'stop.'*" He utters the word in a high-pitched mockery of my voice. "I can do whatever I like with you. We're *fasted.*" He looks me over lasciviously. "I could strip you right here if I liked."

He moves to put his hands on my body again, and something inside of me snaps.

"No!" I cry, spittle flying out at him. I devolve into fists and nails and flailing limbs, scratching and hitting and fighting him with everything in me as he struggles to hold onto me, my nails slashing a bloody line down the side of his face.

"Help!" I cry out, but I know that no one can hear me, down here in the bowels of the University.

I wrench myself free of him, his fingers bruising my arm as I pull it loose, and make a run for the stairs, almost stumbling as I flee. I grab hold of the bannister just as black, roping Mage-lines cinch painfully tight all over my body, driving the air from my lungs and pulling my arms hard against my sides. I skid backward toward Tobias, his magic biting into my skin. The white wand buzzes frantically against my calf.

I cry out in horrified rage, straining against the magical vines. *I can't escape him. He's a Level Four Mage, and I don't know how to use a wand.*

When I reach him, his hand clamps around my arm and the black vines dissolve. Seeing an opportunity, I spin around and smack the wand out of his hand so hard that it flies across the room.

And then I run.

CHAPTER FOUR:
Abyss

"I can't be fasted to him anymore." My voice is muffled by tears as the eyes of my parents and Tobias's parents bear down on me with heated force.

I feel small, terribly alone and crushingly humiliated as I sit in the Ironflower Inn's small, private library, my hands tightly clasped as I wring them together, my head hung low. Tears plop down onto my hands and my lap in wet, dark splotches.

"Fasting is *forever*," Mother Eliss reminds me, seeming stunned by this turn of events.

I shake my head. "It doesn't matter. I can't be fasted to him."

"You claim my son attacked you." Mage Vasillis's coldly commanding voice is low and threatening.

I nod, sniffling, humiliation roiling inside me. *This can't be real. It's not supposed to be like this.*

"Yet your fastlines have not changed," comes his icy reply.

I open my mouth to protest and raise my eyes, withering under his cold stare. I can't speak. How can I possibly tell them exactly what Tobias did? How he grabbed at my chest and forced his lips against mine? How can I speak of these forbidden things?

But don't they see the bruise on my cheek? I can feel it, red and raw.

Tobias's father lets out a disgusted sigh. "So, your fastlines are unchanged. No lines of consummation spread down your wrists. Yet you claim your fastmate, who you will be sealed to in a matter of days…*attacked* you?"

My throat is dry as chaff as I sit, frozen.

Mage Vasillis's mouth curls into a contemptuous sneer. "My son informed me that you were acting inappropriately during dinner. That you—" he shoots my parents an accusatory glance before pinning his eyes back on me "—had your hands on him under the table."

Mother Eliss lets out a startled gasp, then drops her head and shakes it from side to side in disavowal of me. Father's face has paled and he's looking at me like he doesn't know who I am.

Shame rocks through me with hollowing force. I grip at the edge of my chair to steady myself.

"And then," Tobias's father continues tightly, "even after I told you both to stay on the main route, you enticed him to go off with you, away from everyone. Prior to being sealed. Without *any* chaperone."

I open my mouth to protest, my lips trembling, but I can't form the words. Mage Vasillis turns to my parents, his gaze blistering. "Is *this* how you taught your daughter to behave?"

"No. *No*," Father insists, shaking his head, his brow tight with humiliation. He can't even look at me.

I want to die right there. To be swallowed up by Erthia whole.

"Is this how your other daughters are likely to behave?" Mage Vasillis challenges Mother Eliss.

"I can assure you, *my* children would never behave in such a disgraceful manner." Mother Eliss spits out the words, her face twisted into an unforgiving grimace.

The full meaning of her words slices through me—I'm nothing but a stepchild. Easily discarded, our bond thin as parchment.

"So," Mage Vasillis continues, pinning his flinty eyes on me, his tone full of barely concealed loathing, "my son follows you out after you...*handle* him. Like a heathen whore. And now his face is bloodied with your *claw marks*. He actually had to *defend* himself from his own fastmate. And yet you have the gall to claim he attacked you?" His eyes narrow with fury. "How dare you bring such shame down upon my family's name."

I can't hear his words clearly anymore as blood pounds in my ears with a deafening roar, drowning everything, submerging it, the whole world suddenly unstable and staggeringly cruel. A hot rush of shame streaks down my neck. The world has been rent asunder, the safe, loving and secure life I thought I had suddenly ripped clear away.

Whore. Heathen whore.

The terrible words spear through my fog of shame as I start to cry, my fastmarked hands limp in my lap and slick with tears and snot. The sight of my fastlines triggers a swelling nausea.

And then Tobias's parents are gone, and I'm left sobbing, alone in a room with Mother Eliss. Dirty and despised and all wrong.

Mother Eliss gets up to stand before me, fists hard on her hips.

"*This* is how you act?" she demands, her voice trembling with outrage. "Like a Keltic *slut*? I took you in." Her voice cracks with emotion. "I raised you. Like one of my own."

I can barely hear her as I continue to cry. Why did I touch him in such a shameful way? How could I have done that?

Whore. Heathen whore.

The words beat down on me until I'm drowning in them.

"You are going to apologize to your fastmate," Mother Eliss

snarls through gritted teeth. "Tomorrow morn. Do you understand?"

I nod dumbly as I whimper.

Mother Eliss lets loose with a staccato stream of demands. "You will not only apologize to your fastmate, you will apologize to his father and to his mother and after that…"

The words fade to a hurtful buzz, lining the edge of the black fog that's rushing in to fill my mind.

Mother Eliss grabs my arm so hard it hurts, pressing on the bruises from Tobias's horrible grip. "Do you understand me?"

"Yes." I force the word out through my tears, head hung low, not even knowing what I'm agreeing to.

Whore. Slut.

Why did I do those things?

"…and from here on out, you will behave *appropriately* with your fastmate."

I nod, crying.

Mother Eliss is quiet for a moment, and I raise my eyes pleadingly to hers, but she's glaring at me as if she can no longer stand the sight of me. "You are a disgrace," she spits out, her eyes glassing over with tears. "Get out. Get away from me. Go to your room and stay there."

Everything around me is blurred through my tears as I get up, hunched over, wanting to disappear. I push open the heavy wooden door and leave the library.

I do not go to my room.

I walk down the long hallway, tears still streaming down my cooled cheeks. I don't bother to wipe them away.

In a numbed fog, I stumble out of the lodging house. The night air is warm and dewy as I walk down the Ironwood tree-lined path to the gate, the gentle beauty of the glowing Iron-flowers only heightening the pain inside me.

I will destroy my life if I walk away.

But I can't go back to *him*.

This final thought is the only sure, solid thing left in my world. So I open the iron gate and walk through, latching it behind me with a terrible, decisive click of iron on iron.

Feeling oddly disconnected from my body, I put one foot in front of the other as I make my way through the streets of Verpax City. The streets are empty at this late hour, the street lanterns casting long shadows over my new world. The world that no longer holds a place for me, because I know my parents too well.

I have only two options—go back to my fastmate, or leave.

If I stay, they will absolutely make me go back to him. And I can't do that. Not ever.

I drag my feet listlessly, attracting a few scattered, curious stares. There are heathens all around me, now that I've walked aimlessly away from the center of the city.

I slowly walk past shops and Keltic taverns with boisterous music inside. Past the occasional parked or slowly plodding carriage. Past Verpacian merchants shuttering stores. I'm like a ghost, with no destination but one.

Away.

A woman's low moan sounds from a darkened alley. I turn and spot a young Alfsigr Elf pressing a blonde Verpacian maiden against the Spine-stone wall. Feverishly kissing her.

Rivyr'el Talonir.

I know it's him by the colorful patterns edging his Elfin tunic and the gems sparkling in his ivory hair. He's kissing the young woman ravenously, his hand buried under her skirt, and around the back of her rear, her thigh and garter scandalously flashing. She laughs throatily against his mouth and pulls him harder against her body, her eyes closed, her head thrown back in rapture as he trails his lips down her neck.

A warm sting of shock flushes through me that quickly curdles into despair as I rush past them.

I aimlessly turn down a broad street and soon pass by a raucous gathering. Partygoers are packed into a large inn, the crowd spilling out onto a second-story balcony and also flowing from the first floor out onto the road, everything lit by crimson lanterns. Young Verpacians and Kelts are laughing aggressively loud, most of them young males.

Two blond Verpacian men are hanging over the balcony railing, drinking from amber bottles and watching the passersby. One of the men's eyes meet mine and light with sudden focus, sparking red in the lantern-light, and I've a vague remembrance of the envoy in Valgard whose eyes seemed to flash red.

The young Verpacian straightens and smacks the man next to him with the back of his hand to get his attention, never taking his glinting red eyes off me. Fearful to be drawing his attention, I hurry my pace as a group of three young men passes close by and blocks my view of the balcony. When the balcony appears again, the red-eyed Verpacian and his companion are gone.

"Hey, Crow girl!"

The words lash into me and I flinch, startled. I lower my gaze to find a Kelt with a red face and beady eyes leaning against the outside tavern wall, leering at me. "You're a pretty little Roach, ain't'cha?"

I stiffen in fright and speed up, veering away from the tavern.

"Leave her alone, Mordin," another Kelt chastises. "Are you mad? You want trouble with the Mages?"

I worriedly glance over my shoulder to find Mordin's eyes set on me with both anger and heat, his words slurred. "Hey, I'm talking to you, Crow!" He stalks toward me.

His unchecked pursuit sends a bolt of panic through me. All I can think about is Tobias, pushing me against the wall, forcing himself on me.

I break into a sprint down an alley, fast as a hare as fear scythes through me. I turn sharply onto a side street, zigzagging first left, then right, frantically checking over my shoulder, my breathing painfully hard and fast.

Eventually, I slow to a stop, heart thudding and anguish rising as I stand in a deserted alley, my hand pressed against the cold stone wall.

What am I going to do?

My world has split into two impossible halves—Gardnerian and non-Gardnerian—and I'm the despised outsider in both.

My sisters' faces flash into the back of my mind, and grief rips at my throat. I picture Retta and Clover tucked into their beds, whispering to each other, and a fierce longing to be with them whips up inside me as I start to cry once more.

No, I realize, the grief suffocating me. *I don't have a family anymore. They've been torn away from me, along with everything else, because I will not go back to my fastmate.*

I'm all alone now.

I walk on, quietly sobbing as the side streets grow increasingly deserted. Choosing any road that seems to lead closer to nothing. Eventually, I'm enveloped by dark woods, the staccato sound of crickets filling the dark forest.

I hear water up ahead and sense some vast space. As the trees thin out, the sound of water grows stronger. Then the woods open up, and I'm walking toward a long, stone bridge that arcs over a gorge. I pause at the bridge's edge, one sweeping glance registering the devastating height. Moonlight glints off the turbulent current and the jutting black rocks far, far below.

The bridge is lit by a single blue glass lantern, and its cobblestones are gray and worn. The stone railings are deeply weathered, many of them crumbling apart.

Dangerous.

That word would have mattered this morning. Before my world was stripped from me.

I walk onto the bridge, half-aware of a slight sense of vertigo. I'm so high, and the gorge is so incredibly deep. I keep walking, straight up to the highest point in the center of the bridge.

I stop, dull and deadened, then turn, lean over the railing and peer down at the water rushing by beneath me.

The gorge is impossibly deep. The black current races along, choppy and foaming. Dark earth rises to form vertical cliffs on both sides of the gorge, roots twisting out of the soil. Some trees are bent down as if contemplating whether to hurl themselves into the obliterating chasm.

The rail is cool beneath my hands as I bend forward, listening to the swoosh and slosh of water, driving relentlessly in one direction.

Away.

It's cold and clean, the water. The only clean, pure thing left in the whole world. I lean in and inhale the water's scent, the smell fresh and cold and sweet. The mist is cool against the muggy warmth of the night.

And I wonder—what it would feel like to join with the black water? To dissolve?

I tilt closer, mesmerized by the water's cold beauty. It would be a sharp, painful embrace, but it would strip me clean, dissolve me. Erase me. Carry me into it and with it.

Forever away.

I brush a pebble off the rail by accident and watch it fly down, down, down. I don't even hear it as it's caught up in the black current.

I tilt out further, my stomach on the railing as I push myself slightly over, wanting to get closer to better hear the water. To imagine it closing up around me.

A faint thought glimmers in the back of my mind.

My sisters. Sisters that will be fasted.

To his brothers.

I teeter toward the water and almost fall as a sharp jab of fear slices through me.

My sisters. They need me.

And then another thought, drowning out all the others.

I have to save them.

My feet slide on the slick stone, and I slip treacherously forward. I gasp, heart pounding, as my hands scramble to find purchase on the slippery railing. I cry out as panic rips through me and I start to topple over.

Boot heels sound on stone.

"Stop!" a deep voice commands as firm hands take hold of my arms, tugging me sharply back. I lose my balance and fall onto the hard cobblestones of the bridge, my elbow slamming down on the cold ground.

A spike of pain bursts through my elbow from the impact, and every terrible thing washes over me in one great, overpowering wave. Grief crashes through me, and I break down into savage tears, crying as if everything inside me is broken and rushing out at once.

When I finally get ahold of myself, I open my eyes to find brilliant emerald eyes set on me.

A young, strapping Kelt is crouched down beside me, wearing an expression of deep concern. He radiates an unnerving intensity, almost as unnerving as the vivid green of his eyes.

The red-haired Kelt from the smithery.

CHAPTER FIVE:
Search Spell

There's a tight line of tension between the Kelt's brows, and for a moment I hold his fervent stare. He's crouched down on the bridge with me and grasping my upper arm, his unnaturally brilliant green eyes boring into mine. "Don't do it," he says, his voice pitched low with implacable vehemence. "Whatever's led you here…still, don't do it. I was right where you are once. Ready to hurl myself off that very same bridge. *Don't* do it."

My lips are trembling with overpowering anguish, and his powerful presence is wavy through my tears. In some small recess of my mind, I realize I should draw away from this Kelt. That I should be alarmed by his large, strong hand keeping firm hold of my arm, and the remembrance of his mysterious sorcery. But my anger and hurt and grief have laid waste to all caution.

"Are you glad you didn't?" I challenge him, almost angrily, my voice coarse with a despair that's so strong, it's hard to breathe.

The intensity of his gaze doesn't waver. "Yes," he says emphatically.

I hold his unyielding stare in silent, fierce challenge to his affirmation. He silently, relentlessly holds onto my stare as well, his hand remaining doggedly firm around my arm.

There's a sudden pull on my affinity lines as a flash of emerald sparks in his eyes, and I'm abruptly swept up in the dizzying sensation of us both falling toward each other, even though we're completely still. He seems to feel it, too, his lips parting and his gaze tensing with evident astonishment.

Running steps thud to my right, along with what sounds like cursing in another language.

"Holy hells, Ciaran! Get your hands off of her!"

The Kelt—Ciaran—loosens his grip on my arm, the spell-like force pulling us toward each other abruptly broken. Shaken, I turn to find a young, blonde-haired woman sprinting toward us.

The Issani. From the smithery. In her outrageous rune-marked clothing, swords criss-crossed on her back and rune-blades strapped to her arms and thigh. Two large, golden hoops hang from each of her ears and *clink* against each other as she moves.

I abruptly realize that the colorful auras that used to radiate from each of them are gone.

Ciaran rises to his feet, his lean, strong frame now towering above us both, his jaw tightening as he faces her down.

"Ciaran," she spits out as she comes to a halt before him, her eyes blazing, her heavily-accented words lashing out. "What in the name of the gods are you doing?"

"*Wyla*," he answers with hard emphasis. "She tried to throw herself into the gorge."

"Well, you should have let her!" The metallic hilts of her weapons glint in the sapphire lantern-light, and her pale blue eyes are full of fire. Golden Ishkartan runes mark her cheeks, casting her face in a warm glow. She points unforgivingly at me, keeping her fierce eyes on Ciaran. "Leave her be, Ciaran! She's one of the Styvian Crows. The strictest Crows of them all! You will bring the wrath of the Mages down on your head if you are seen with this girl!"

Crows. I inwardly recoil from the vicious slur. Despair washes over me with renewed force. *I'm all alone. I have absolutely nowhere I can go. Nowhere I'll be accepted.*

I grip at the cold stone railing beside me, my face tensed with overwhelming anguish. Ciaran remains rooted to the spot he's standing in, his eyes fixed on Wyla, blazing with defiance.

"Ciaran, *no.*" Wyla swipes her arm toward me again. "She needs to go back to her own people!"

My anguish explodes. "*I. Have. No. People!*" I snarl at them with withering force.

Wyla's eyes fly to meet mine, as if she's surprised enough by my outburst to finally look at me. Her gaze grows more focused and then narrows in tightly on me. Like a wall shattering, all the anger drops from her expression as she takes in the sight of my bruised face and my fastmarked hands in one sweeping glance, shocked outrage now flashing in her eyes.

I startle as she rushes over and drops down to one knee in front of me. She grabs up my hand, and I instinctively draw back from her touch as she glances down at my fastlines. "When did they bind you?" she demands, but there's an unmistakable solidarity in her ferocious tone.

"I was thirteen," I choke out, a vortex of furious emotion storming through me.

Wyla studies my hand for another moment, then raises her eyes and looks deeply into mine, a pained understanding edging her fiery gaze. She reaches up and lightly touches my bruised cheek, and I flinch back from the unexpected contact. Her face tightens with concern as she immediately pulls her hand away.

Fury sparks in her eyes. "He did this to you?" Wyla grinds out accusingly, her teeth bared as she gestures toward my face. "The one you are bound to?"

I nod jerkily.

She abruptly stands, one of her hands fisting around the hilt of the rune-blade she has sheathed at her waist. Then she looks at Ciaran as if unflinchingly decided. "We hide this girl."

Surprise jolts through me, and I see my emotions mirrored on Ciaran's face as well.

"What is your name?" Wyla asks me harshly, but there's an undercurrent of fierce kindness to her commanding tone.

"Sage," I force out, wiping at my tears with the back of my hand, their figures momentarily blurred. "Sagellyn Gaffney."

Ciaran lets loose with what sounds like a low oath in a foreign tongue. He turns to me with forced calm. "Your father," he asks me, his tone carefully measured. "Is he Mage Warren Gaffney of the Mage Council?"

When I nod in affirmation, Wyla pulls in a harsh breath, closes her eyes and shakes her head, murmuring to herself under her breath.

"They'll get their Mage Council involved," Ciaran says to her, looking as if a thousand thoughts are churning in his mind. "They'll send out search spells."

Wyla drops down in front of me again, a heightened urgency in her gaze. "When are they likely to know you are missing?"

Mother Eliss, I think. *There's no way she'll be able to resist one last lecture.*

"They already know," I tell her, hopelessness thick in my tone.

Wyla grimaces and grinds out what sounds like more cursing. She looks to Ciaran. "We'll hide her. In your room."

His room?!

Ciaran lets out a harsh breath and eyes her with disbelief, shaking his head. "It's clear she was just attacked, Wyla. She doesn't know me—"

"I'll stay as well," she snaps, tearing away this concern, the blaze in her eyes making it clear how vicious the catastrophe that's coming for me is likely to be. "Your bedroom is heavily warded," she insists, eyeing him significantly. "It's her *only* hope of escape."

Warded? Somewhere in the back of my misery-choked mind, I wonder why on Erthia this Kelt would have a heavily warded bedroom.

Ciaran looks to Wyla, their gazes welded tightly together, as if immersed in silent, fraught communication. She gestures toward my Gardnerian dress. "She needs different clothing. And I'll need to ward her with a *shyrnol*."

"What's that?" I ask, fear spiking.

Ciaran turns to me, and our eyes fuse with that odd intensity again, as if we're staring each other down and drawing each other in all at the same time. I'm swept up in the magical current of it, every color of him intensifying, his green aura momentarily reappearing. Ciaran swallows hard, looking momentarily thrown and swept up in the current as well.

"A detection rune," he explains, forcing the words through our sudden thrall. "If you're not warded with one, the tracking spells will be invisible to you. You need to be able to see them to avoid touching them."

"Roll up your sleeve, Sagellyn," Wyla orders as she pulls a glowing rune-stylus from a sheath on the side of her belt.

I'm wary of their rune-sorcery, but I'm desperate to avoid going back to Tobias, so I hastily comply. Wyla grasps my wrist and brings the tip of her rune-stylus to my bare forearm. A crackling energy sparks along my skin as she draws a golden design with nimble, practiced strokes. Once finished, she draws back and I stare, mesmerized, at the glowing mark. I immediately recognize the Ishkartan runes from the grimoires that Gwynn gave me so many years ago—*detection* encircling *search*. The designs curl around each other and start a slow rotation on my arm that trails a mild sting along my skin.

"Get her out of sight," Wyla directs Ciaran. She nods toward the woods on the other side of the bridge. "I'll go get some clothes for her." Without another word, she sets off at a fast sprint across the bridge and back toward the city.

Ciaran holds his hand out to me, an imperative force to his gaze, but there's also kindness in his eyes, and that draws me in as powerfully as his magic. "We need to get off this bridge," he says gently.

I beat back the fear that's clamoring to keep me trapped as I reach up and take his proffered hand, his grip strong and sure. He pulls me to my feet, and the two of us pause for a split second, our hands firmly clasped, a daring look passing between us as my magic gives a hard pull toward him.

Then we rush across the bridge and make for the woods.

Ciaran guides me down a small embankment, my smooth bootheels sliding on the soil and slick leaves. I grip his arm as I start to skid, scrambling for purchase. Ciaran immediately catches hold of me, his arm sliding around my waist as he deftly guides me to the base of the embankment. My heart thunders against my chest from a mix of fear and the strangely welcome sensation of his hand closing protectively around mine as we crouch down behind some low brush.

I can just make out the deserted bridge and its blue lantern through the leaves and twigs. A cool, gauzy mist is rising up from the gorge, tinted a soft cerulean by the light.

Ciaran's grip tightens and he brings a finger to his lips, cautioning me to be quiet, his eyes full of warning. We hide down in the embankment for a while, my every sense primed, the smell of loamy, wet earth and fresh greenery heavy on the air.

What if they find me? I agonize. *I can't go back to him. I won't.*

I look to Ciaran, fear racing through me, desperate for reassurance. He holds my gaze and my hand with a firmness that steadies me, his long, chiseled features deeply shadowed as I cling to him. The green of his eyes abruptly flares in the darkness, and suddenly I'm falling into that verdant color again, like a tide drawn to the moon, my affinity lines lighting up and pulling toward him in a mesmerizing rush. He seems to feel it, too, this recurrent thrall between us, his gaze gone unblinkingly fervent, as if I've become hypnotic to him.

"Sagellyn," he says, sounding overwhelmed, "are you a Light Mage?"

Dull footsteps sound on the dirt road leading to the bridge, breaking both our thrall and Ciaran's line of thought. We both jerk slightly back from each other with a look of mutual surprise, his hand falling away from mine as we turn toward the sound.

A figure pops into view, running across the bridge, clasping a bundle, and relief washes over me as I realize it's Wyla. She quickly locates us and slides down our embankment, thrusting the bundle out to me. "Quick," she says. "Put these on. We've got to get rid of your Crow clothes."

I accept the balled-up clothing and unfurl an Ishkartan tunic and pants in a variety of woven colors. It's hard to make out the exact hues in the dim, blue light, so I take a deep breath and pull on the light affinity lines around my eyes, the colors momentarily brightening as if illuminated from within— a lush, interlocking star design of forbidden golds and purples. The bright purple sparks into the edges of my vision as everything I've been taught about these colors fills my mind and a sting of reluctance sweeps through me. *Fae colors. Hated by the Ancient One.*

To put on this garb is to bring down the disfavor of the Ancient One. To possibly be cast out forever.

Panicked defiance rises within me. *I won't go back. Which means I have to shed my Gardnerian blacks.*

But pants! a shrill part of me rages. *How can I wear such forbidden garb?*

The Ancient One already hates me, I bitterly counter, at full-blown war with myself and everything I've ever been told. *I'm already cast out, since I'm running from a sacred fasting. What does it matter now?*

I glance sidelong at Ciaran, wondering how I'm supposed to change with him here. As if sensing my thoughts, Ciaran turns and addresses Wyla. "I'll stand watch." He gives me a significant look. "With my back to you."

I nod stiffly, and he moves in a crouch nearer to the bridge. I'm trembling as Wyla helps me undress and quickly pull on the pants and the brightly colored tunic. Then Wyla wraps a large golden scarf around my head and lower face. She grabs up my Gardnerian clothing, rushes through the brush and onto the bridge, and hurls them over the railing.

I watch the shadowy bundle drop into the gorge and feel momentarily light-headed as my old life is irrevocably swept away, along with my sacred black garb.

But the wand. I reach down to find it still pushed into the side of my boot. *I still have the wand. And it's not a toy.*

Wyla returns and stoops down before me. She fishes a dark stick out of her pocket and tells me to hold still, then lines my eyes thickly with kohl, like hers. She hastily pulls my dainty Ironflower enamel earrings from my earlobes, pushes them into the dirt with her thumb and replaces them with heavy gold hoops. Last, Wyla unsheathes her rune-stylus and draws runic symbols on my cheeks.

She sits back and studies me closely, her pale eyes narrowed. "Good," Wyla says, nodding in satisfaction. She rises and palms the hilt of one of her blades. "Now, you follow us. Stay close."

I rise to my feet and we climb back up the embankment, making for the bridge, Wyla and Ciaran in the lead. Just as we reach the top, multiple thin streaks of deep green light arc through the sky from the direction of the city and stream toward us.

Both Wyla and Ciaran skid to a halt and turn, alarm in their eyes as they launch themselves at me.

"Get down!" Ciaran cries as they pull me roughly to the ground. Ciaran throws his long body on top of mine while Wyla drapes herself over my exposed shoulder and arm as the streaks of light curve down and explode into bursts of light when they make impact with the ground. One lands only a few handspans to my left, the light-bursts spearing out multiple rays of light.

For a split second, I'm thrust into a wild panic. Ciaran's breath is hot and heavy against my ear, his heartbeat insistent against mine, his body heavy. Wyla's sharp chin juts into my shoulder, and I feel so trapped I almost launch into a crazed resistance.

Ciaran grips my arm, his forehead pressed to my temple. "Sagellyn, stay *down*. We're trying to protect you."

I draw in a frightened breath as another line of deep green light pulses over us, arcing to the earth and bursting into multiple lines that fan out over the expansive gorge and the woods surrounding it.

"They're tracking you," Wyla hisses. She looks to Ciaran, savage urgency in her gaze. He pivots his forehead on mine to glance at her.

"What happens if the light touches me?" I ask in a haunted whisper.

Wyla's jaw tightens. "They will know where you are." Rebellion lights her pale eyes. "So we will not let that happen."

Roots dig into the back of my head, my shoulder. The side of Ciaran's nose is brushed up against mine, his chest rising and falling with steady, strong breaths. Another spear of light courses just above us, and my lungs constrict as Ciaran's hair is momentarily illuminated in a deep green halo.

We wait for what feels like a long time as the lines stop streaking through the sky, our breathing dangerously loud to my ears. Slowly and carefully, both Ciaran and Wyla venture up and off of me, then rise to a crouch as I hesitantly sit up, my gut clenched tight with fear.

Ciaran's eyes narrow as he looks toward the city, but he motions us up with a wave of his hand and cautiously stands. "Let's go." He offers me his hand, then pulls me swiftly to my feet, glancing at Wyla and pointing across the bridge to the distant woods. "We'll follow the edge of the gorge and bring her through the back."

I hold tight to Ciaran's hand and look fearfully to the sky as we rush across the bridge and into the woods that abut the curving gorge. We weave around trees, moving through the forest at a fast clip, and I almost stumble on the thick roots underfoot.

After what seems like forever, we near Verpax's outskirts, the backs of the moonlit city buildings now visible through the trees on my right, the rushing waters and dark wildness of the gorge to my left. The late-night echoes of voices and horses can be heard just past the line of Spine-stone buildings, and the sounds send a trill of panic through me.

We're running back toward everything I'm trying to escape.

My heart beats high and fast as I cling to Ciaran, and he briefly meets my gaze. He tightens his grip on me, as if he's reading my fear and wants to soothe my mounting panic.

We slow down as the forest constricts to a slim line of trees edging the narrowing gorge, the three of us weaving around unhitched carts, barrels and other detritus that lie along the rear of the homes and shops. I keep my head carefully down, in a surreal state as we move in the direction of the Ironflower Inn.

Before long, we come to the back of a multidomed Spine-stone structure topped with an Ishkartan Smiths' Guild flag that I immediately recognize as their smithery. Wyla breaks free of the shelter of the trees first. She rushes into the deserted clearing behind the smithery, looks in both directions, then waves for us to follow.

Ciaran and I run toward the smithery's back door as Wyla opens it, all of us swiftly slipping into its dark interior.

There's a metallic, ashy tang on the air, and the space holds an otherworldly, runic glow. Lines of black rune-marked discs cover a broad table, the runes etched on them glowing Snake Elf green and Ishkartan gold, casting the smithery interior in their eerie light.

Ciaran closes the back door and bolts it. He picks up a rune-stylus from the table with the rune-stones, then pauses, shooting me a sidelong, unreadable glance. He looks to Wyla and gestures sharply with his chin toward a curtained door, the black fabric glowing with rows upon rows of emerald Snake Elf runes that are slowly rotating at different speeds and in different directions, the effect somewhat dizzying. I recognize some of the runes from Gwynn's grimoires—*barrier, invisible, strengthen.*

Wyla is looking at the rotating runes with an unnerving gravity, as if she's reading something alarming in them.

"Bring her in there," Ciaran directs, hard urgency in his gaze.

Wyla grabs hold of my arm and guides me toward the curtain. She pulls it aside, and I gasp as a narrow, closetlike room comes into view. It's like I've fallen off of Erthia and into the stars.

There are runes everywhere. Snake Elf runes that glow emerald and a few scattered Ishkartan runes that shimmer gold. The runes are worked into the deep green tapestries that line the ceiling, walls and floor, and countless green and gold circular runes float, suspended in the air, their internal designs slowly rotating in complicated patterns.

Two narrow cots are pressed up against the tapestried walls with barely enough space to walk between them. Dark blankets woven with a golden star pattern cover both cots, and rune-weapons are scattered throughout the room, some hanging from the walls. Strewn all over one of the cots are several splayed-open journals with intricate drawings of runes on their pages, as well as what look like multiple runic grimoires and a history of the Eastern Realm.

The shuttered window adjacent to that cot is heavily warded with runes etched into its frame, as well as a mass of small suspended runes that float all around it.

The Ironflower Inn is right across the street, I realize, stunned by the thought. *I could probably see it through that window.*

My whole world.

My sisters.

A sharp pang of heartache stabs through me. Then there's a flash of deep green light around the shutters, and I instinctively flinch back. All the runes in the room briefly flash white, and an additional line of tiny emerald runes bursts to life around the window.

Bootheels scuff on stone floor just beyond the curtain, and Ciaran enters the small room. His gaze immediately flies to the window, then to Wyla, and the two of them exchange a tense look of relief.

"Well, those held well," Wyla says tightly, giving an impressed nod to the window.

The deep green glow suddenly pulses around the shutters once again, and I stiffen in response. Wyla and Ciaran pull me down into the space between the two cots as all the runes pulse an echoing shade of darkened green. Tendrils of shadow suddenly undulate from the runes like curling smoke, and the runes start to whir so fast that they look like solid wheels of deep green light.

Ciaran curses and looks to Wyla. "What dark magic are these Crows mixed up in?"

"What do you mean, 'dark magic'?" I ask, my voice gone unsteady with a clamoring panic.

"There's shadow magery woven in with the tracking spell," Ciaran tells me. He points at the runes surrounding the window, which are spitting out silvered black smoke. "That dark smoke. Shadow sorcery is the only thing that does that to wards."

I remember the stories Gwynn used to tell of demons with horns made of spiraling shadow, and a hard chill snakes up my spine.

Wyla stares at Ciaran for a long moment, green light pulsing over both their faces. When her voice comes, it's riddled with an anxious dread. "Will the wards hold?"

"They will hold," Ciaran grinds out. There's a faint edge of an accent to his voice that wasn't there before. A deepening of the sounds. And he says *vill* instead of *will*, and drops the *h* in *hold*.

The runes pulse deep green again, and a cold sweat breaks out over my body. I cling to the star blanket hanging off the bed behind me as we wait. And wait. Tensed in coiled silence.

Until the green pulse of light dies down and all of the runes grow still.

Hours later, no new search magic has pulsed in, and the defensive runes around the window have dampened to a sullen deep green glow and slowed their rotation. The other runes have returned to their original emerald green, and the suspended runes hang motionless in the air.

"Stay low, Sagellyn," Ciaran cautions. He rises, peers through a slit between the shutter and the window, then straightens up, seeming satisfied. I marvel at his unfaltering calm and am struck by how imposing his physical presence is in this small space.

Ciaran lights a small stained-glass lantern patterned with multicolored stars, and a rainbow of light illuminates the room, the color flashing through my affinity lines. I breathe in deep and reflexively pull on the color, the soft hues tamping down my fear. I glance down at my tingling wand hand and see my fingertips each glowing a different hue. I move to tense my hand, to press the color down, but stop myself.

Why subdue it? I bitterly consider. *What does it matter now?*

I glance up to find both Ciaran and Wyla looking at my wand hand. Wyla's brow is raised high, but Ciaran doesn't seem surprised at all. I meet his gaze with unspoken recognition.

"You're a Light Mage," Wyla breathes out, stunned, her mouth agape. She turns to Ciaran and falls into a rapid-fire conversation with him in another language. Ishkart, I assume. Wyla is waving her hands around and gesturing to me as Ciaran calmly fields her obvious concerns with a staunch gravity that I'm coming to realize is his way.

Feeling hollowed out, I let my eyes dart around the room. I can pick out aspects of some of the Ishkartan and Snake Elf runes. *Destroy. Evade. Barrier. Invisible. Strengthen. Protect. Dismantle.* A thread of tense confusion flares. These aren't just runes—they're high-grade, defensive wardwork. Protected military wardwork.

Something's hunting him. Something powerful.

"Wyla," a woman lightly calls out just past the curtain, the name followed by a stream of words in another language.

I freeze, my heart picking up speed.

Wyla and Ciaran exchange a quick, intense glance, as if silently coming up with a plan of action.

"I will go and lead her away," Wyla whispers to Ciaran,

barely audible. She turns to me, her voice still low. "You will stay here, Sagellyn." She gives me a look of firm encouragement. "Dawn will dismantle the Gardnerian search spells, as they only work in the dark."

"Wait, no." I reach up to take hold of her arm, desperation rising.

Wyla's gaze intensifies, as if willing me to listen. Her eyes flick to Ciaran's, then back to me. "He will not harm you. And I will be back as soon as I can." Wyla gives me one last fierce, troubled glance before pulling back the curtain a fraction and slipping out of the room.

I remain crouched down in the narrow space between the cots as I struggle to grapple with the mounting sense of vulnerability that's taken hold of me.

Ciaran sits down on a cot behind me, silent and vigilant as he listens to the voices of Wyla and the other woman conversing amiably in another language just past the curtain. Their footsteps begin to move away as they talk. A door opens and closes, the sound of their voices now muted and rapidly fading.

Then silence.

Ciaran lets out a deep breath and leans forward, his hands on his knees. Our eyes meet and my affinity lines snap toward him. I'm suddenly acutely aware of that seductive, emerald thrall hidden deep in his gaze. The masculine line of his jaw. The hard elegance of him. He radiates physical power, his frame the broad-shouldered physique of a practiced smith. But his mouth—its sensual lines bring up a panicked remembrance of Tobias's cruel lust, of Rivyr'el Talonir's hand slid up under that Kelt girl's skirts.

I've a sense Ciaran won't hurt me, but that's meaningless. I never dreamed Tobias would attack me until he did. A jagged apprehension whips up inside of me that quickly overtakes my gratitude for his help.

"Thank you for...for hiding me," I tell him haltingly as I pull myself up onto the cot facing him, wanting to put a little more distance between us. "But...you leave me alone tonight." I point at his cot, my finger trembling. "You stay on *that* bed, and don't come near me."

Ciaran's green eyes narrow, as if he's reading something in me that's complex and troubling. "I wouldn't," he says.

"I've been told what Keltic men do," I challenge, jittery with my mounting fear of him. His strength. His obvious hidden sorcery.

Ciaran holds my glare, his voice calm and reasoned when it comes, but with an unmistakable edge. "It seems like that's what *your* people do."

I don't know what to do with his logic. I'm instantly tangled up in it, because he's right. I fight back the sudden swell of rage-filled tears as I grip at the blanket beneath my hands.

They were supposed to protect me, my people. They warned me and warned me about heathen men and their cruel, unbridled passions. But when the attack came, it came from the person they told me I could trust the most.

They *lied* to me. *Lies* upon *lies* upon *lies*.

"Sagellyn," Ciaran says, his green eyes now full of concern. "I would not do this thing you fear. You have my *word*." That accent again, touching the edges of his voice.

"They *lied* to me," I tell him, teeth gritted, a raw anger overtaking my fear of him.

Ciaran considers this, studying me for a long moment. "Yes, Sagellyn. They did."

This new realization strafes through me as I'm assaulted by the memory of vicious Tobias. Of my family's rejection of me. Thoughts of the gorge suddenly fill my mind, and the powerful black water rushing through its abyss.

"When you didn't jump," I say to Ciaran, my voice thick with profound hurt, "what stopped you?"

Ciaran looks probingly at me, the intense set of his eyes more pronounced in the rune-light. "Zeymir," he says with succinct gravity. "The owner of this smithery."

Zeymir. The Ishkart smith with the golden rune-marked headband.

"Why did you consider jumping?" I haltingly ask.

Ciaran winces, his mouth tightening into a hard line. He turns away and looks at the rune-marked wall, as if wrestling with his thoughts. After a long moment, he finally speaks, his voice a jagged whisper. "I lost everyone."

The tears stinging in my eyes roll down my face and slide over my lips, salty and warm. "I'm sorry," I tell him, barely able to get the words out.

After a few moments, Ciaran releases a deep, shuddering breath. "Sagellyn," he says, his odd accent there again. "You should try to sleep. I remember..." He pauses, and his gaze goes momentarily unfocused, as if he's looking at a memory instead of at me. Then his face tightens, as if the memory has become too difficult to look at.

"I remember when Zeymir took me in." He pauses again. "I didn't sleep for two days. But finally... I passed out." The hard edge of his expression softens as he looks to me. "Try to sleep, Sagellyn."

I nod, and as Ciaran moves to clear the piles of books off the cot that I'm sitting on, I notice that he's extraordinarily careful to avoid brushing up against me. I listlessly slide under the dark, star-patterned blanket and ball up under it, feeling lost and grief-stricken.

Ciaran lies down on his cot, on top of the blanket, not bothering to take off his boots either. He stares fixedly at the ceiling for a long moment, his face tight with unease as he reaches up to run the fingers of one hand through his dark crimson hair, as if he's deeply unsettled. Then he turns and our eyes collide, the heavy edge of sadness in his gaze a twin to the knot of misery in my chest.

"I want my sisters," I tell him, choking on the words. "I want to go home and be with them."

Ciaran's eyes widen with a profound understanding that rushes toward me in a fierce, bracing wave. "I'm sorry, Sagellyn. I know what—" His voice breaks off, and when he speaks again, it's ragged with emotion. "I know how terrible this thing is."

"My sisters," I say hoarsely. "I'll never see them again." My breath catches tight in my throat. "I'll be cast out. Banished if I don't go back. But I can't go back. I can't *ever* go back." Raw anger rushes in and overtakes the grief, my voice turning harsh with it. "I *won't* go back to him. I will *never* go back to him."

For a moment, I stew in the rage, letting it build, the dark storm churning inside me. But then a vivid image of Retta and Clover fills my mind, and I imagine their devastation upon finding me gone. The storm breaks apart into a heartbroken grief as tears fill my eyes and I choke on them.

"Sagellyn," Ciaran says, his own eyes now sheened with tears. He extends his hand to me and turns it palm up.

"I want to go home," I cry, unguarded and cracked open, letting him see my full misery.

"I know," he tells me, heartbroken understanding in his eyes, his hand still extended.

I look to his hand. Every last thing about where I am in this moment is forbidden and supposedly a dire threat. Asking for an attack. Taking his hand, especially here in his bedroom, is flatly forbidden and inviting unspeakable danger.

I momentarily war with myself. *Forbidden by who? Your people? Who would have you fasted to a monster? Who fed you nothing but lies?*

Rebellion rising up within me, I reach out and take hold of Ciaran's hand.

Our fingers clasp around each other, his hand warm and steadying, his grip bracingly firm.

"Don't leave me," I say, almost a demand as I tighten my grip on him.

"I won't," he promises with the force of a vow.

I hold on tight to him as the storm inside me lashes and churns, his steadfast presence keeping my head above water.

Ciaran never moves from where he's lying. Never touches me, save his hand in mine. He holds my eyes with his kindred gaze deep into the night, when finally, sleep takes hold and pulls me under.

CHAPTER SIX:
Za'ya

I wake up the next morning disoriented and confused by the green tapestries with embroidered runes all over the ceiling and walls, and the strange smells of warm, unfamiliar spice on the air. A hard rain pelts the roof and a dim morning light prowls around the shutters, a rumble of thunder sounding in the distance.

Shock jolts through me as it all comes flooding back— Tobias. The attack. The terrifying tracking spell.

I sit bolt upright, my heart pounding, momentarily unable to catch my breath as panic swamps me. I look down to find my sweaty, rumpled self covered in a tunic and pants, the fabric an interlocking star pattern of purple and gold. Small multicolored stars are embroidered along the tunic's edges in a spectacular rainbow of hues, a riot of forbidden color that lights up my affinity lines like a Yule tree.

Nothing is right. Not the foreign tapestries and runic designs. Not my clothing. *Nothing.*

And this room is warded like it's ready for a military siege.

A small table sits beside me with a golden pot of tea on a black lacquered tray inlaid with golden stars. The elegant pot is slim and curving and etched with filigreed designs, steam curling up from its slender spout. A teacup made of delicate glass is nestled in a gilded holder. There's a plate holding flat green biscuits coated with unfamiliar black seeds along with an odd brown paste. And next to that lies a small bouquet of Ironflowers, a slight glow to them in the dim light of the lamplit room.

I pick up the bouquet, suddenly overcome, tears stinging at my eyes.

Ciaran. He must have left them for me.

He must have stolen the blossoms from across the street. From the Inn's trees.

It's such a lovely gesture that my heart struggles to hold onto it, and it momentarily softens my great, blanketing grief. Ironflowers are our sacred flower. A flower representing escape from oppression. And freedom.

Does he know all this?

His gift helps to soften the strangeness of my surroundings, and keeps me from feeling so completely alien and lost and unwanted.

I drink in the delicate flowers, sparks of their vivid blue suffusing my vision. Ironflower blue ripples over my fingertips, but I don't tense the color away. I vow to never tense the color away again. What does it matter if my wand hand is blue or gold or purple? I've crossed clear over to the other, forsaken side of this world.

I lift the bouquet to my nose and breathe in deep. The flowers' sweet, almost beeswax smell is a comfortingly familiar thing in this strange new world I've landed in.

Clutching the bouquet, I peek through the slit between the window shutter and the window frame, the morning rendered gloomily dark by the storm.

Thunder sounds and lightning flashes, briefly illuminating the sight of the Ironflower Inn across the street, its form wavy through the rain-streaked window. Ironwood trees bend slightly in the stiff wind, and my heart gives a hard twist.

Retta and Clover are likely there. Just a few steps away over the rain-slicked, cobbled street. But they might as well be in another land, past a treacherous sea. The divide would be just as wide.

Tears well in my eyes and burn at my throat as a staggering desolation washes over me. I press my forehead against the hard wooden shutter and stare out the window, passersby and horse-drawn carriages with drivers hunkered down against the driving rain periodically blocking my tear-soaked view of the inn.

Is my family still here looking for me? To force me back to Tobias? What did Father and Mother Eliss tell my sisters? Did they tell them I'm their sister no more?

I'll never see Retta and Clover again.

The terrible thought rips my heart apart, and I slump back onto the bed, clutching the small bouquet to my chest. I turn my back on the food and tea, curl myself into a heartsick ball, close my eyes and weep.

"Did you at least find out who she is?"

A sonorous, accented man's voice sounds from just past the curtain. It jostles my attention from where I still lay in my grief-stricken state. A thread of fear pulls taut in my gut.

"Sagellyn Gaffney." It's Ciaran's voice, low and soothing. Everything in me wants to reach out and grasp firmly onto the refuge of that voice.

There's a tension-fraught silence, and then, "Ciaran. Her father is on their Mage Council." The words are slow and heavy with import.

"I know."

"You cannot provoke the Mages." The man's tone is filled with dire warning.

"I don't intend to provoke them, Zeymir," Ciaran returns. His deep voice kicks up a disquieting tangle of feelings deep in the center of me, and an echo of the feel of his hand tight around mine. *All night long. Staying with me. Keeping me safe.*

"You have one of their fasted maidens in your bedroom," Zeymir says. "The daughter of a Mage Council member. He's a *Level Four Mage*, Ciaran. Do you know what they will do to you if they find her with you? They enforce their racial purity laws across borders. That girl's fasting is a *battle zone*."

"They fasted her at thirteen!" Wyla's strident voice blares out. "Her fastmate beat her! And gods knows what else! If we don't give her shelter, they will throw her right back to him!"

Another woman's accented voice sounds out, her melodious tone grim. "And if we do shelter her, Wyla, they will come for us. And they will spare no one. They have shadow magic at work to find this girl. Demon magery! Her plight is terrible, I am sure, but we cannot endanger all of us—"

"So," Wyla's disgusted voice cuts her off, "you can endanger all of us for *your* people only?"

"This girl is not your people either!" the woman cries. "She is a *Mage!*"

"No," Wyla spits out, her voice breaking with ferocity. "She *is* my people. You forget, Za'ya. I understand this thing…this thing that has been done to her."

Everyone grows quiet for a moment as the memory of what Tobias did slices through me, along with the horrible realization that Wyla has endured something like this, too.

"Ciaran," Zeymir finally says, his tone low and adamant, "you *cannot* be found out. This girl will draw first the Gardnerians and then the Alfsigr straight to you."

My confusion mounts. *Why would the Gardnerians and Alfsigr be looking for Ciaran?*

"I have made it this far," Ciaran says coolly. "And I will be in Noi lands soon enough."

"You've made it this far," Zeymir counters, "because the Mage Council is not setting its best trackers after you—which they *will* do to find this girl."

"Zeymir," Ciaran says, his tone hard, "she stays."

"She is a danger!"

"Well, so am I!" Ciaran snarls, low and dangerous.

I draw back, surprised by his sudden capacity for venom.

"They will *kill* you if they find you," Zeymir grimly insists. "They will not kill her."

"She'd be as good as dead!" Wyla growls. They all devolve into an argument in what sounds like more than one language.

I clutch at the blanket draped over me, islanded in a sea of confusion and desperate questions. *Where will I possibly go if they cast me out? And why is Ciaran being hunted?*

Abruptly the curtain pulls back and I flinch, my heart thudding against my chest.

The green-scaled Snake Elf woman sets her bright silver eyes on me. Her emerald splendor is so beautiful, it's almost confrontational. Her long, green hair is tied back in a golden, jeweled Ishkartan scarf, and her tunic and pants are a rich green with looping black runic embroidery along the edging. Ciaran, Wyla and Zeymir stand behind her, the rune-marked golden band of an Ishkart highborn wrapped around Zeymir's head.

A child clings to Zeymir's golden tunic—the black-haired, pointy-eared, green-scaled child I saw from the inn yesterday. He's dressed in golden Ishkartan clothing like his father and peering in at me with a look of stunned concern.

The small viper. Heathen spawn. Edyth Gyll's harsh description of this child sweeps through my mind.

The Snake Elf woman's determined expression freezes, then morphs to one of shock as she takes in my bruised face.

Zeymir looks just as stunned. He turns away, his face tightening, and shakes his head. My hand involuntarily comes up to self-consciously cup my bruised cheek, and for a moment I want Erthia to swallow me whole.

My eyes meet Ciaran's, and my affinity lines brighten and pull taut toward his emerald gaze. I straighten a bit, and the blanket that's half covering me slides down a fraction. Surprise lights Ciaran's gaze as his eyes are drawn down. I follow his gaze to find my wand hand still clutching the Ironflower bouquet and washed with a glowing sapphire all the way to my wrist.

"She's a Light Mage," Zeymir breathes, staring at my blue hand. He looks to the ceiling and closes his eyes for a moment, shaking his head slightly, as if clearing a groundswell of alarm. Then he gives Ciaran a loaded glance, his look conveying that we've all just jumped into the abyss below the abyss.

Za'ya, the Snake Elf, studies me closely.

Snake Elves. Dangerous Elves. Evil, venomous serpents. They need to be locked up underground and kept there. Everything I've been told about this woman's people sounds warning bells inside me and whips up a wild confusion.

And then Za'ya's fierce look shifts, and the same heartbroken understanding I felt in Ciaran's gaze last night breaks through. It's so unexpected, an ache gathers in my throat and pulls tight.

"I want to go *home,*" I tell her, hopelessness pulling me under. "I just want to go home and… I'll never be able to go home again." I close my eyes tight and begin to cry once more.

Everyone is silent for a long moment, and then I hear the sound of footsteps just before the cot dips under Za'ya's weight. Her hand comes to rest gently on my arm, and I peer up into her silver gaze, her brow knitting hard.

"Everyone here," she tells me, her lilting voice raw with emotion. "Everyone you see, child. We all wish we could go home."

I glance toward the Ishkart smith, Keltic Ciaran and Issani Wyla. The emerald-scaled child. And this Snake Elf woman, trying to comfort me. And for the first time, I realize just how mixed their group is.

"Sometimes," she tells me, her voice breaking, "you cannot go home." A tear streaks down her cheek, and she squeezes my arm, her eyes holding onto mine. "Sometimes, you have to make a new home." She smiles to herself and laughs through her tears, closing her eyes for a moment. Then she opens them, glances at the people waiting in the doorway and smiles warmly at me. "And...it can be good, hm? You must hold onto the faith of this."

A new home. But I don't want a new home! My despair rises higher.

"My sisters," I rasp out through a strangled sob. My voice is muffled as I choke on tears and talk in a tangled mess. "When they turn thirteen. They're going to fast them to the brothers of...of *him*. They're *promised*. To a family of *monsters*..."

I break down, unable to say more.

Za'ya takes my blue hand in hers and lightly traces my fasting lines, grimacing. "Ah, yes. Well. That is a serious matter. And one that cannot be resolved at the moment." She sighs deeply, as if resigned. "Perhaps we think on this in a few days, hmm?"

She strokes my hair. Overwhelmed, I nod, falling into an exhausted acceptance of her kindness. It's almost too much for me to look at her, her glittering scales bursting with brilliant color and reflected stars of lamplight, the stars multiplying at the edges of my vision in a disorienting rush.

Za'ya bends her head closer to me. "So now, Sagellyn...you eat. And wash, hm?"

The little boy slips into the room, quiet as a small deer, his emerald scales glittering like his mother's. He clings to Za'ya's arm and looks me over for a moment, his brow knotting in confusion as he turns back to his mother. "What happened to her, *Ma'mya*?"

Za'ya takes a deep breath and strokes his hair. "She has lost her home, Na'bee."

Na'bee's brow tenses tighter. "Like the Elfhollen, *Ma'mya*? And like us?"

She considers this for a moment. "Yes, *Al'mya*."

Na'bee's lips tug this way and that, as if he doesn't know which words to form. Finally, he steps closer to me and puts his small hand on my hair, stroking it lightly.

"Don't cry," Na'bee says. I notice he has no accent, unlike both his parents. His serpentine appearance is so strange to me, but his dark eyes are innocent and wide and kind. He looks to his mother again in confusion when I cry harder over his kindness.

"Would you like me to draw a beautiful rune for you?" Na'bee asks hopefully, smiling at me. His smile creates deep dimples in his scaled face, his cheeks puffing out. I don't understand what he's offering, but an overwhelming, disorienting thought hits me. He and Retta have such similar smiles— round-cheeked and heartbreakingly gentle.

I realize in that moment, in a great, blinding flash, as I stare into this child's infinitely kind eyes, that everything I've been taught about these people is completely, unbelievably and horribly wrong.

I nod at the child, my words stuffy. "Thank you. I'd like that."

Na'bee's hand moves to my shoulder and he looks at me with serious intent. "I'm going to draw you a *Sornith'yl* rune." As if this mysterious rune is the medicine that will cure every last thing in my life. But his intention is so heartfelt that it inspires a laugh and a small, quavering smile from me.

"Come," his mother says, rising and holding her hand out to me.

Feeling stiff and storm-battered, I let Za'ya pull me up. I'm sweat-soaked and I know I smell sour, but if Za'ya notices any of this, she doesn't comment. Numbed, I let her lead me out into the smithery and toward another door. Zeymir, Ciaran and Wyla remain behind, murmuring gravely to each other in Ishkart, locking doors, closing shutters.

Ciaran turns and our eyes meet, the unsettling pull of him once again suffusing my affinity lines in a sudden, disorienting rush. He glances down at the Ironflowers still bunched in my hand, then raises his eyes back to mine, his fervent gaze full of the intimacy that's sprung up between us after a night of clasping each other's hands and sharing an unspoken, profound understanding.

As Zeymir pulls out a golden, glowing rune-stylus and marks new runes on the wall facing the street, a morbid chill passes through me.

They're golden Ishkartan battle runes. Search-destroying runes.

Created to protect me.

CHAPTER SEVEN:
Smaragdalfar

Za'ya brings me through the door leading out of the smithery and into a small, circular library, a tunneling Spine-stone staircase in its center. I follow her down the stairs, my steps heavy with exhaustion and grief.

At the staircase's base, there's a small, sparse foyer cut into the white stone and a chalky corridor before us. I follow her through the hallway, breathing in the spicy smell of incense on the air. There's a kaleidoscope of color up ahead, woven into tapestries on the floor, walls and ceiling. A whole, forbidden garden of color.

Emerald, gold...purple...

I pause at the threshold of a domed common room and blink at what lies before me.

For a moment, I'm overcome by the sheer abundance of color, my affinity lines lighting up in chaotic bursts along the edges of my vision. The cavernous room is lit by flickering golden runes suspended inside multicolored glass orbs that hang from wrought-iron stands. My vision momentarily sparks with an echo of the orbs' amethyst, saffron and crimson hues. Emerald tapestries adorn the stone walls and stretch across the ceiling, woven into intricate runic designs. Purple rugs patterned with golden stars overlap beneath my feet.

It should be cold and claustrophobic here in this stone cavern beneath the ground, but a rune-stove suffuses the color-rich haven with a caress of warmth that loosens a sliver of the bowstring-tight tension in my body.

A sizable circular wooden table stands near one of the arcing walls, its ebony surface marked with an inlaid wooden star. It sits low to the floor, green velvet cushions positioned around it where chairs should be, and there's a ladder affixed to one wall that leads up to a loft bedroom cut into the stone.

I look over toward the other side of the room, and a hard sizzle of shock passes through me. A small goddess statue is set on an altar, flower and food offerings placed before it, as well as a gleaming censer with incense smoke tendriling into the air from it.

Idols. Despised by the Ancient One and railed against in our holy book. Sure to bring a curse down on the heads of all these kind people. My breath momentarily hitches with both fear and dismay as I consider all the dire warnings and strictures I've been taught about idolatry.

But I'm here now. With them. Dressed in Fae-colored garb and running from my sacred fasting.

And I won't go back.

I'm cursed, too, I realize, with a sensation of gut-wrenching, spiraling descent.

In a disoriented haze, I follow Za'ya out of the room and through another tunneling passageway that leads to an austerely appointed washroom cut into the alabaster stone.

Za'ya hums a soothing tune and tenderly helps me get undressed. I listlessly let her pull my tunic up over my head, and she abruptly stops humming when I lower my arms and she takes in the sight of them. I glance down, and my gut heaves as I confront the series of bruises on my arms where Tobias's cruel hands and vicious magery restrained me. I quickly look away, my breath shuddering through my lungs as tears sting at my eyes. When I turn my gaze back to Za'ya, her expression is one of grave sympathy.

Za'ya gets fresh clothing for me—deep-green tunic and pants edged in black embroidery, much like what she's wearing. She steps out of the washroom while I finish undressing, wash myself and put on the fresh clothing.

I look down at my unfamiliar garb, everything so outrageously surreal that I feel vaguely disconnected from it. I reach down and pull up the hem of my pant-leg, then slide my white wand back into the side of my boot.

Za'ya brings me into a bedroom that's covered with tapestries and rugs similar to the ones in their common room. She's exquisitely gentle with me as she combs out my hair and elaborately braids it, humming to herself. It's unsettlingly strange to be in pants, the fabric sliding over my thighs as I move, scandalous in how they show so much of the shape of me. The cut is much closer than the loose Ishkartan pants Wyla gave me before, and I feel strangely weightless and almost half-naked without my heavy skirts.

Sounds of the smithery have fired up above us, and I can hear the dulled thump of hammers clanking against anvils straight through the domed ceiling. I look to Za'ya with blatant fear, picturing the wide smithery doors flung open, exposed to everyone. Exposed to Gardnerians.

"Sagellyn," Za'ya says, pausing, her slender hands on my shoulders as her reflection peers back at me from the jewel-framed mirror before us. "Don't be afraid. They must continue on. Or it would draw attention to you." I nod miserably, my insides clenched up with sadness and sheer exhaustion.

Za'ya studies me, her brow knotting as she takes in how obviously worn down I am. She motions toward her bed. "Rest, child. I'll come back for you in a bit." She squeezes my shoulders and gives me a bolstering smile before she takes her leave, and I spend most of the day curled up on Za'ya's bed, swept up in a turbulent sea of agonizing questions.

I can't ever go back, but after this, where can I possibly go? What will I do?

I have nowhere else and no one else to run to. No money. No belongings. No knowledge of how to use my magic.

Nothing.

That evening, Za'ya leads me back toward the common area, the scent of unfamiliar foods wafting on the air. The smithery is closed for the day, and everyone is gathering for dinner.

As Za'ya draws back the curtain at the threshold of their communal space, I slump down self-consciously in the shadows of the narrow hallway, feeling wildly underdressed in my slim pants and close-fitting tunic, and wondering what Ciaran will make of my outfit.

Men should never be provoked. Mother Eliss's oft-repeated warning to be modest and to always wear modest clothing sounds in the back of my mind, but a jagged anger rises along with the thought.

Why should I listen to anything you told me, Mother Eliss? After you fed me lies and fasted me to someone so cruel.

I look to Za'ya, and she smiles encouragingly at me as she holds the curtain back.

She's in pants, too, I remember. *And so is Wyla. This is normal for them, not scandalous.*

I step toward the common room and my affinity lines give a hard, bright flare when I see Ciaran. He's sitting at the star-patterned table next to Na'bee, one knee up, his muscular arm resting on it.

And he's dressed in purple. Vivid purple. The color washes over me in a tingling rush, sparks coursing over my wand hand at the decadent sight of handsome Ciaran dressed in such a shocking, tantalizing color.

Ciaran turns and our eyes meet, his green eyes widening with obvious surprise as his gaze flicks up and down my body, riveted by my emerald clothing. He averts his eyes and swallows, as if momentarily overcome, and my face heats from the intensity of his interest and how my lines of magic are pulling so relentlessly toward him and his purple garb.

Wyla is grinning as she looks me over with dumbfounded glee from where she sits, perched like a bird at the edge of the bedroom loft. "A Gardnerian in Smaragdalfar clothing." She shakes her head and huffs out a sound of incredulity. "Now I have seen absolutely everything."

Za'ya casts a sharp glance at Wyla, then murmurs gently to me in her language and invitingly prods me toward the circular star table before she goes over to talk to Zeymir, who is stirring a large iron pot on the stove, with thick, fragrant steam rising from it.

"Come sit by us, Sagellyn!" little Na'bee says brightly, bouncing a bit on his cushion.

Heatedly aware of purple-clad Ciaran, I take a seat across from Na'bee and next to Ciaran. Ciaran glances over at me and smiles, his gaze darting down just beneath the table's edge and catching on my wand hand with another flash of surprise. I look down to find my tingling hand suffused in purple, and my cheeks sting hotter, abashed to have my forbidden color fixation so glaringly on display.

"I'm… I'm very drawn to purple," I stammer out to him in an awkward whisper. "Your tunic…"

"You don't have to hide it," he says.

"You don't understand. It's the most forbidden of the colors in our religion," I explain, voicing what I've never spoken so honestly about in my life, emboldened by our kindred connection. "But…my Mage lines love purple. I've fought against its pull my whole life…"

"You could stop fighting it." His words are a gentle invitation, lightly said, but explosive in their potential ramifications.

I hold his gaze as I consider the subversive possibility. *Why hold back? I'm already cursed and cast out. Why resist any longer?*

Emboldened by the rebellious idea and our inexplicable magical bond, I let my eyes slide over the purple of Ciaran's tunic and breathe in deep as the color flows over and then floods straight through me in a euphoric rush, tinting my vision with its decadent splendor, a shiver of delight racing along my lines. I look back up at a now purple-tinted Ciaran, my vision completely steeped in the intoxicating color.

A sudden tremor of apprehension takes hold, and I abruptly feel like I've just jumped clear off of a cliff with no way to scramble back to safety. My breath tightens in my throat as I pull the sleeve of my wand hand slightly up, shock stinging through me when I find my entire wand hand and forearm colored a deep, rich violet.

"I've never let go like this…" I say, invigorated and lit-up and absolutely terrified all at once, no solid ground beneath me.

Ciaran's hand slides over mine, and he gives my purple hand a bolstering squeeze that sends warmth skidding through my affinity lines.

"If I was a Light Mage," he says quietly as I let myself fall into his captivating gaze, "I imagine my wand hand would be green right now." He glances at my emerald garb, seeming as swept up by me as I am by him. "The color suits you," he says, kind and emphatic. "And so does the violet."

There's a gravity to his statement that speaks of some undercurrent of unguarded emotion, and I've that unsettling sensation again of falling into him as he falls into me, my light magery orienting toward him and his mysterious, powerful draw.

Ciaran gives me a quick, abashed smile, seeming a bit flustered as he pulls his hand and gaze away from mine, breaking the magical connection. The purple tint of my vision rapidly dissipates as I avert my eyes as well.

Ciaran leans away to quietly talk to Na'bee in another language, gesturing in the air with his finger, as if prodding the child. Na'bee smiles at him, bumps his forehead into Ciaran's arm and giggles, as if the two of them are involved in some delightful conspiracy. The child pulls out a golden stylus and draws two runes in the air, one Ishkartan gold, one Smaragdalfar green, as Ciaran shoots me a quick half smile. Fantastically, the runes hover just above the tabletop and then merge as Na'bee prods them together with his stylus, deftly linking the two patterns with dotting swirls of his stylus's tip. My eyes widen as I take in the shimmering colors.

"Here, Sagellyn," Na'bee says brightly. He pokes the intertwined runes gently, and they float toward me. Entranced by the rotating pattern, I hold up my purple hand and catch it. The runes burst into small green and golden sparks that send a burst of warmth through my hand and clear up my arm, their color twinkling in my vision.

"You can link runes," I marvel, surprised by Na'bee's obviously adept rune-sorcery at such a young age—and not of just one runic system, but two.

Na'bee's smile broadens, pride lighting his eyes. "I'm Ishkart *and* Smaragdalfar, Sagellyn. I can combine both powers."

It's significant, this statement. Each runic system has its strengths and weaknesses. The Smaragdalfar runes are most powerful underground, and oriented toward battle runes and lighting. In sharp contrast to them, the Ishkartan runes are charged to their full power by sunlight and geared more toward shielding, agriculture and healing.

What new magic could be wrought from combining the two?

Zeymir leans over our table and sets a tea service tray in its center. "Amber spice tea," he announces with some formality, his voice a deep thrum. He goes about pouring steaming tea into all the cups on the tray.

I look down at the table, suddenly uneasy as I anxiously wonder what Zeymir's thinking, a sudden wash of vulnerability overtaking me. I remember his reluctance to have me here and worry that he might wish I was gone instead of still being here, endangering his family.

"It's very good. Try it, Sagellyn."

I look up to find Zeymir handing a cup out to me, smiling warmly, as if there's no longer any question in his mind regarding my welcome place with them.

His unexpected, casual kindness makes my chest ache, and I wordlessly take the teacup, afraid that if I speak, I might burst into sudden tears. I take a quavering breath and cradle the steaming tea. It's delicately fragrant and crystalline orange in color. I sip at it and am surprised by the richness of the spice, which is similar to vanilla. Delicious and warming on my tongue.

"It's very good," I tell Zeymir, my voice cracking with emotion. I glance up to find him staring at me, and the grave compassion in his dark eyes makes the sea of conflict inside me roil higher.

Za'ya clicks her tongue and murmurs to me kindly in her language as she and Zeymir exchange a knowing look. Zeymir then starts ladling out bowls of food that Za'ya hands out to each of us. She presses a warm, full bowl into my hands and pushes a bizarre, V-shaped utensil into it. Everyone around me lapses into a variety of languages and settles down around the circular table to eat—everyone except Wyla, who remains happily perched in her loft, wolfing down her food.

Ciaran is quietly watching me, and when our eyes connect, he gives me a smile that's so full of acceptance and his alluring magic, it not only bolsters me, but sends a flush straight through my lines, emerald sparks shimmering at the edges of my vision.

I stare down at the food and my warm feelings are quickly erased, replaced by a stomach-churning revulsion. Za'ya has handed me what appears to be a bowl full of black worms. They're curled up at the bottom of the broth, a variety of unknown vegetables floating above them. I've heard tales of this—how the reptilian Snake Elves eat insects.

"Eat," Za'ya prods me cheerfully as she sits down, picks up her bowl and begins slurping up the wormlike food by pinching hold of it with the strange utensil.

I poke at the food with the V-shaped sticks that I'm supposed to use to grab it up, tears stinging at my eyes. "I'm sorry, Za'ya," I finally tell her, desperate to not lose her good favor. "These can't be…these aren't worms, are they?"

Ciaran's head snaps up, and everyone freezes as a flash of offense fires in Za'ya's eyes.

I realize, immediately, that I've inadvertently said something terrible.

"Those are not worms, Sagellyn," Za'ya tells me gently, but dismay still tightens her gaze. "They are *nu'duls*. Made from rice and cave squid ink. And I am not a reptile, *ti'a'lin*."

A chastened flush sears my cheeks. "I'm sorry," I say, barely able to get the words out.

Za'ya rises, comes over and takes a seat beside me. I can barely look at her, my face burning with shame. She gently places her hand on my arm and pulls up her sleeve. "Look at my arm, Sagellyn. What do you see?"

"Green scales," I haltingly tell her.

"Look again," she says with great patience. "Touch my arm. See if what you say is true."

I look closely at her arm. It's stunning, the scales like small, interlocking gems, reflecting the lantern light and throwing off both a green and a gold that brightens my affinity lines. I glance up at Za'ya to make sure it's truly all right, and then I touch her arm. I'm immediately filled with surprise. Her skin is smooth. Completely smooth. Just...patterned.

"Just as you are not a crow or a roach," she tells me, "we are not snakes, *ti'a'lin*. We are Smaragdalfar. The Emerald Elves. We do not shift to snakes or sleep in dirt burrows. We do not eat bowls of insects. Or sting people with hidden tails."

"You're beautiful," I blurt out, mesmerized by the flashing greens of her skin and what the color does to my affinity. I draw back, immediately embarrassed by my sudden outburst.

Za'ya grins. "This is true, *ti'a'lin*." She puts her arm around me. "As are you." She gestures toward my food with a wry smirk. "Now eat all your worms like a good child."

Her irreverent teasing cuts through my misery, and I give her a shaky smile, wiping away my tears with the back of my hand. "I'm sorry," I tell her again, my smile falling away as my voice breaks around the words. I think about how much I hate it when I'm called a "crow" or a "roach," and I'm ashamed to have ignorantly done the same type of hurtful thing to her.

"Eat," she tells me, momentarily serious as she pulls away, but there's forgiveness in her eyes, and I'm grateful for it.

I glance up to find Ciaran's gaze set on me, his brow knotted with evident concern.

"I didn't mean to say something so awful," I tell him. "I didn't know..." I look away, unable to finish the thought.

His hand briefly slides over mine, and I tentatively meet

his gaze. "We understand," he says as he and Za'ya exchange a quick, somber glance.

"Truly, Sagellyn," Za'ya says, her expression lightening as she gestures toward my food, "you need to eat."

At Za'ya's insistent prodding, I finally dare to take a bite of the *nu'duls* and am immediately stunned by how rich their flavor is. The *nu'duls* are slippery, but delicious and coated in the savory broth, their texture like nothing I've ever had before.

"Do you like them?" Ciaran asks, his lips quirking into a small, wry smile.

I nod enthusiastically, suddenly aware of how starving I am, and how long it's been since I've eaten anything. I take another bite of the *nu'duls*, wrestling a bit with the odd utensil, then smile self-consciously at Ciaran, my mouth full of the wonderful food.

Ciaran smiles warmly back at me, but then his expression shifts, his eyes seeking mine and full of questions as the invisible pull flares between us. Our silence deepens and grows charged, as if crackling with latent power. Ciaran's eyes flash emerald light, and I'm suddenly overcome by the urge to hold his hand in mine again. I begin to wonder if he's having the same thought as we both color and look away, the action taking obvious effort, both of us seeming reluctant to break the connection.

After dinner, Za'ya insists I settle back on some cushions with a cup of tea, and Na'bee leaves for his room. Everyone else clears away the plates, chatting animatedly and affectionately, and I try to parse out the Ishkart language from the Smaragdalfar. The languages are very distinct, and I'm soon able to at least identify which is which.

Ciaran is scrubbing down a pot, his back to me, the muscles of his shoulders flexing, and I wonder at them all doing such work themselves without Urisk servants. I've never cleared a table in my life. I watch the warm way they help each other, fascinated. Za'ya shoots Zeymir flirtatious smiles as she works, and he smiles lovingly in return. She repeatedly touches him on the arm or the shoulder as they pass each other, and once, he gently pulls her into an embrace and kisses her.

It sends a warm confusion through me—all this physical affection, given so freely and openly. Mother Eliss and Father never touched each other in our presence, and Gardnerian men *never* help with the cleaning or cooking. I look around at the forbidden colors and designs surrounding me, and try to understand why all of this is so utterly despised by the Ancient One.

I struggle to force down the blasphemy that's threatening to overwhelm me. It's all so different. Wildly different. But it seems...*good*.

Abruptly, steps sound upstairs, and I'm instantly seized up with fear.

Almost in unison, Za'ya, Zeymir, Ciaran and Wyla pull rune-blades, and it stuns me how stealthily armed they all are and how lethally smooth their combined motion is, nothing fearful or clumsy about it.

They all look to the ceiling and calmly follow the footsteps as they make their way toward the staircase and then down it. I hold my breath, feeling every step resonating straight through my spine.

The steps sound out in the hallway, drawing closer, and my heart lodges in my throat as Rivyr'el Talonir, the rebellious, criminal, glittering rune-sorcerer Elf, sweeps into the room.

CHAPTER EIGHT:
Zalyn'or

Rivyr'el stands before us, smirking, his ivory cloak thrown rakishly over his shoulder, a gleaming flask in his hand. The prismatic glitter around his eyes sparkles in the lantern light, like outrageous constellations.

He opens his mouth to say something to the assembled crowd, then stops cold as his gaze lights on me. His eyes widen, then narrow as his mouth lifts in a sardonic smile.

"I remember you," he purrs with a tilt of his head, his expression animated with mischief. "The Crow Princess." He enunciates the words, a lilting Alfsigr roll to his *r*'s. He glances pointedly at me and looks brightly at everyone else in the room, his eyes flicking over all the rune-blades. "*So*. I expect the Gardnerians will be by at any moment to murder us all." He takes a long swig from his flask and shoots me a droll smile as everyone mutters at him in Ishkart, sounding exasperated, and sheaths their weapons. The Elf throws the stopper of the flask back into place, shakes his bow and quiver off his shoulder and leans them against the nearest wall. Then he glides over to sit next to me in one fluid movement.

Alarmed by his closeness, I edge away toward Ciaran, remembering what it was like to fall under the thrall of the Elf's prismatic, rune-magicked gaze.

He sighs as he takes in my obvious trepidation. "I *warded* you," he says impatiently. "I *told* you that."

"I still don't understand what that means," I counter, frustrated, part of me stunned that I'm even here, talking to this outrageous Elf.

He blinks at me, as if surprised by my level of ignorance. "I warded you," he says again, somewhat condescendingly, "to help you resist the magical pull that rune-sorcerers have on each other. Because you, little Light Mage, are a rune-sorcerer. So now, your light magery won't just fly straight into me, which would essentially turn you into my willing minion." He smirks, his eyes flicking over me lasciviously. "Of course, if you *want* to be my willing minion..."

"Let her be, Rivyr." Wyla's voice is sharp with irritation. She looks as if she'll leap from the loft and throttle him if he steps out of line.

"How did you ward me?" I press, thrown by all this new magical information.

Rivyr's silver gaze narrows, his mouth tilting up slightly. "I pressed my rune-stylus into your palm and sent an Alfsigr barrier rune into your lines. I could remove it right now, if you'd like, but I wouldn't advise it."

I look at him with astonishment as a broader realization takes hold. I remember the strange aura shimmering around Rivyr and everyone else here when I first saw them—all of it gone after Rivyr warded me. And the intense pull of Ciaran's gaze when we first laid eyes on each other—a magical pull that's still overpowering, but now allows for some coherent thought around it.

"Before you warded me," I say to Rivyr, the pieces starting to fall together, "you all had this aura of light about you..."

Rivyr's sly smile inches wider. "That's because we're all rune-sorcerers, *ti'a*."

Incredible. The ability to practice rune-sorcery is rare in every land, yet somehow, I'm sitting here in a room full of rune-sorcerers. Confusion rises in me, and I look to Ciaran, his expression having taken on a guarded cast. *How is a Kelt a rune-sorcerer? Kelts generally don't have magic...*

"And now," Rivyr says, grinning and leaning in, "you get to be part of our happy lot of outcasts." I notice that he smells strange, like something bitterly medicinal. He flicks the stopper off his flask again with his finger, takes another swig and grins. "Come now," the Elf chides, his gaze liquid and jaded. "The dark side isn't so bad. You'll get to have weapons." He looks me over. "And you already have *much* better clothing." Rivyr holds his flask out to me with a rakish smile. "Here, *ti'a*. You'll like this."

Ciaran coughs out an incredulous laugh utterly devoid of any mirth. "Rivyr, *truly*? I'm sure you can guess what she's running from. What exactly are you doing?"

Rivyr's smile is hard and brittle. "Welcoming her into the fold."

"Well, find another way to do it." Ciaran bites out each word, his tone weighted. He looks to me. "Those are strong spirits, Sagellyn." He cuts Rivyr another glare. "You might want to pass on that."

"And she's probably never had them," Wyla chimes in sharply. "Being *Gardnerian*."

Rivyr ignores Wyla and peers suspiciously at Ciaran, as if there's some realization dawning. Then his silver gaze narrows back in on me, one ivory brow arching. He glances down, taking in the sight of my wand hand, my fingertips still suffused with purple. I ball my hand self-consciously against my side.

"Ciaran's a bit protective of you, isn't he, *ti'a*?" Rivyr purrs.

I flush at his implication. Can they all sense the strong magical pull that's sprung up between Ciaran and me? "He's been very kind," I tell Rivyr, put off by his probing gaze.

"Oh, I imagine he has been," he says laughingly. "A beautiful Crow maiden. Living here." His head swivels back toward Ciaran, his eyes going wide with delight. "Is she staying in your room?"

"Yes, Rivyr," Ciaran says, his tone long-suffering. "Because it's *warded*."

Rivyr snorts a laugh and glances back down at my purple hand. "Oh, is that why? This is getting more interesting by the minute." His eyes flit to Ciaran and then to me with undisguised mischief. "Did he tell you he's wrapped up in the Resistance? You've fallen into a nest of revolutionaries, sweet Sage."

I blink at him, stunned to hear him make such a dangerous statement so blithely.

He gives a low laugh. "Oh, Ciaran didn't mention any of that, did he? Why do you think he needs all those high-grade wards? My guess is he's tried to blow up one or two Gardnerian military outposts. But you didn't hear that from me."

I stare at Rivyr, thrown by his behavior and his reckless accusations. He's absolutely bizarre—Elves are graceful, ethereal beings. Always subdued and calm. And I've never even heard of an Alfsigr Elf drinking spirits. Or wearing a hue other than ivory or silver. Or making inappropriate or inflammatory comments.

I remember what Edyth Gyll said about Rivyr having been banished from Alfsigr lands, and reckless curiosity overrides my intimidation. "You're quite a bit different from the other Elves."

He laughs heartily and gives me a thin, condescending smile. "Oh, you've noticed that, have you?" His lip curls. "You've never met an actual Elf. You've met a *mirage*. Except for me." He tries to hold onto his obnoxious grin, but it fades, rapidly replaced by a look of scorn. He sighs and sets his flask down, then fishes in his tunic pocket and withdraws a pendant that hangs from a slim, sliver chain. Elaborate silver knot-work encircles the gleaming pendant, the oval disc marked with multiple Alfsigr runes.

"I don't wear this," the Elf tells me snidely. He holds it out for me to take, but I hesitate. "Go on," he chides, with an exasperated roll of his silver eyes. "It won't bite." His gaze turns salacious. "Although *I* might."

Ciaran says something terse to Rivyr in Ishkart, and the Elf holds up a hand. "Kidding. I'm *kidding*, Oh Humorless One." He holds the necklace back out to me, a jag of what seems like long-standing bitterness shadowing his expression. "Take it, *ti'a*. Take a look at the reason I was banished from Alfsigr lands."

I look to Ciaran.

"Just don't put it on," he cautions with a conciliatory tilt of his head.

I take the necklace from Rivyr. The silver disc is cool in my palm, the chain draping over my thumb. "What is it?" I ask.

"It's a *Zalyn'or*." Rivyr'el spits out the word mockingly as I study the gleaming pendant. "Given to every good little Alfsigr boy and girl when they reach their twelfth year."

I look back at him, uncomprehending.

He eyes me with half-lidded disdain. "Haven't you ever wondered why the Alfsigr Elves are so gloriously uniform and ethereal? Swanning about like lofty creatures made of moonlight?" He leans in conspiratorially and whispers. "The *Zalyn'or* tamps down desire. Renders the wearer placid and serene and free of *all* rebellious thoughts. Part of the *Great White Herd*." He grins wickedly and bares his teeth. "But I rather like rebellious thoughts, so I decided not to wear it." He raises his pale brow at me significantly. "*That* caused a bit of a stir."

He straightens and gives a hard sniff, as if the whole Alfsigr race is now beneath him. "I was promptly banished. You can't live in Alfsigr lands and not wear the stifling thing."

"So you darken our door," Zeymir puts in, a slight smile on his lips as he starts another pot of water for tea.

"So, I *grace* you with my *scintillating* presence," Rivyr starchily corrects, mock-frowning at Zeymir. He holds out his hand for the pendant. I give it back to him, and he slides it into his pocket. "I'm supposed to be thrown in prison for not wearing it," he tosses out, like some insignificant detail. He snorts a derisive laugh. "But I'm on Verpacian soil, so good luck with that."

I gape at him. "Was that why your brother was coming after you? For not wearing a necklace?"

"Seems a bit excessive, doesn't it? Rather humorless lot, my people." He smirks. "Much like Za'ya."

Za'ya counters with something sarcastic in Ishkart as she sets out a plate of triangular, nut-dusted cakes, her mouth tilting into a grin, and Rivyr laughs. He leans in toward me with a theatrical whisper. "The prison is underground. With *Snake Elves.*" He shivers like this is terribly frightening and eyes Za'ya, who is now doggedly ignoring him, her mouth set in a tight line. "But it's still probably a jollier place than being here with Snake Elf Za'ya."

"Why do you come here then?" I challenge him harshly, suddenly protective of kind Za'ya. It's clear that she doesn't like being called "Snake Elf" any more than I like being called "Crow." Ciaran's eyes land on me, and I can feel his surprise at my sudden spark.

Rivyr smirks at me sidelong. "I adore children. They haven't been…*ruined*. Not yet, anyway. And Za'ya and Zeymir happen to have one of the most wonderful children on all of Erthia." He glances at the cakes and flashes a smile at me. "And Za'ya's a *phenomenal* cook."

Za'ya eyes him shrewdly, pausing in her assembly of a fresh

tea tray, a smirk on her lips. "You come because you feel the pull of *Oo'na*. Like an itch that cannot be scratched." She looks at me, but I get the sense she's still talking to Rivyr. "The Great Mother, *Oo'na*, wants him to leave his selfish life behind and choose the path of the hero."

Rivyr gives a mocking laugh and turns to me. "You'll find that Za'ya's a religious fanatic. She thinks the purpose of life is to be dour and fight unwinnable battles."

"They are winnable." A serene smile forms on Za'ya's lips.

Rivyr's eyes widen mockingly. "Against the full might of the Alfsigr Elves and their Gardnerian Allies? Oh, wait—you have your little goddess statue! Well, we're all saved then. No matter that there's talk about how the Gardnerians have their next Black Witch. Oh, and I almost forgot about how the Gardnerians have *the biggest dragon army on all of Erthia*." He shakes his head and grins obnoxiously. "But you've got some rune-marked weapons and your tiny goddess statue, so *thank you*, Za'ya, for enlightening me. Of course you'll win. I'm so sorry for thinking you're completely and utterly deluded."

"We wait," Za'ya insists, unfazed as she spoons leaves into the teapot. "And we prepare. For the day when Ra'Ven will lead us to claim our homeland in the East."

"Who's Ra'Ven?" I put in, looking to Ciaran in question, the name seeming strangely familiar.

Everyone has gone silent, like they've collectively paused in their breathing. They cast dark, furtive glances around. Everyone except for Rivyr, who rolls his eyes.

"Their Blessed Savior," the Elf sneers.

"He is the last surviving member of my people's royal line," Za'ya tells me, her chin held high, her words bright with passion. "And he is a great rune-sorcerer. The greatest *ever*, and blessed by *Oo'na*. He will lead my people to freedom and reclaim our ancestral sublands." She shoots Rivyr a poignant look. "And he is going to provide refuge not just to the Sma-ragdalfar, but to the unwanted *everywhere*."

An image of the wanted posting I saw in Valgard the day of my wandfasting comes to mind. *That's* where I've heard the name—a Snake Elf named Ra'Ven. The postings are even present here in Verpacia now, and likely still in Valgard, although the picture of the Snake Elf on the posting has changed from an angry, slender boy to an intimidating young man.

"Nothing can stop the weapons he makes," Za'ya crows.

Rivyr rolls his eyes again and leans in toward me. "Don't spend too much time with this lot. They'll draw you into one hopeless cause after another."

"You should join with us, Rivyr'el Talonir," Za'ya states with unassailable certainty. "To be heroic is your true purpose, yet you fight it so mightily."

Rivyr's voice turns velvet, his arm coming around me. "Sweet Za'ya," he purrs, "the purpose of my life is to pick all the flowers I come upon."

"Rivyr," Ciaran says warningly.

I remember seeing Rivyr in the alley, pressed up so wantonly against that woman. Steel rises up within me and I cut my eyes towards him. "Get your arm off of me."

Rivyr's smile wavers. There's a flash of bitterness in his eyes that quickly morphs to a chastised hurt. He nods and stiffly complies, pulling his arm from my shoulder and putting a respectful distance between us. He shoots me a sidelong apologetic look, and for a moment, I get an unguarded glimpse into eyes filled with glittering pain. Pain I recognize, which makes me regret speaking so harshly to him.

He's an outcast, like me.

Just then, Na'bee runs in, shrieking with delight in Ishkart. I only understand the name "Rivyr'el!" in the flurry of foreign words.

Rivyr's face lights up like the sun. His sharp edges fall away as he rises, his arms opening wide as Na'bee practically hurls himself at the Elf, almost pushing him over, the two of them laughing and hugging.

"I have something for you, young prince," Rivyr happily reveals.

Na'bee's eyes light up brightly with anticipation as he bounces up and down and lets loose a string of breathless Ishkart. Rivyr pulls a carved wooden, jointed toy from his cloak pocket—a beautifully wrought white stallion with an Alfsigr Elf in alabaster military garb on his back. Na'bee takes the toy into his hands and hugs it to his chest, exclaiming his happiness in a tangle of both Ishkart and the Common Tongue and hugging Rivyr once more.

"No, Rivyr'el," Za'ya says, shaking her head, her expression tense and pained. "I know you are trying to be kind, but he cannot have this thing."

I look to Za'ya, surprised by her rejection of a toy. Rivyr's eyes narrow with irritation. "Well, it's too late, Za'ya, since it's a gift, and I've already given it to him."

Za'ya's eyes flash. "Thank you, Rivyr, but I said *no*."

Tension descends upon the room, thick and volatile, as Rivyr and Za'ya launch into an argument in what sounds like Alfsigr as Na'bee looks on worriedly, clutching the toy to his chest. Finally, Za'ya gets up and stalks toward them, holding out her hand to Na'bee for the toy.

Na'bee frowns, lip quivering, and hands the toy to his mother, who promptly goes to the rune-stove, opens the door to the fire and casts the toy in, her eyes like lightning on Rivyr.

Rivyr looks to the fire for a moment, his jaw ticking, as if struggling to contain his anger. He gets hold of himself and forces a smile at Na'bee. "It's no matter," Rivyr says, beaming, though his expression seems hollow. "I got you two things, and that wasn't even the best of it. I'll bring the other by for you tomorrow. What do you think of that?"

Na'bee rallies somewhat as Za'ya beckons to him. Unsure, Na'bee goes over to his parents, and Zeymir kneels down to his level and has a low conversation with him in Ishkart, patting him warmly on the shoulder. Na'bee nods and slowly loses his troubled expression.

"Say good-night to everyone," Zeymir prods him kindly as he rises, his hand coming to Za'ya's back.

Na'bee runs to Rivyr and the Elf embraces him warmly, his eyes closing momentarily.

A finger of cold remembrance traces down my spine. *Nightfall. The search spell.* I turn to Ciaran. "Won't it be dark soon?"

"There's about three more hours of daylight," Ciaran tells me, the protective look in his emerald eyes and his ever-present steadiness reassuring me. "I'm watching, don't worry."

I turn, and suddenly Na'bee is before me, holding his arms out for a hug. I reach out and we embrace warmly.

"Good night, Sagellyn," he says, hugging me close.

"Good night, Na'bee." A sorrowful pang cuts through me. *My sisters. What are they doing right now? What were they told about me?*

Na'bee leaves, and Rivyr's smile leaves with him. He faces down Za'ya, his eyes flashing. "Have you completely lost your mind?"

Za'ya's outrage instantly rekindles. "You bring my child an Alfsigr Elf soldier as a toy? They *enslave* us, Rivyr'el."

"It's a toy, Za'ya," Rivyr scoffs. "I'd bring him a Smaragdalfar toy to play with, but *they don't make toys like that.*"

Her eyes catch fire. "And why is that? Why *exactly* is that, Rivyr'el?"

They launch into a fierce argument in Ishkart, occasionally

lapsing into the Common Tongue. I sense this is just one part of a larger, ongoing clash of wills.

"Shall we wage war on the toy shop?" Rivyr'el cries, throwing up his hands. "Good use of your time, that is!" Frustrated, he pulls out his flask again.

"Oh, you think you are such the rebel." Quick as a flash, Za'ya grabs his flask, unstoppers it, opens the woodstove and casts the spirits into the flames, the fire exploding outward. "This is not rebelling," Za'ya seethes, letting the flask clatter the floor.

Rivyr's silver eyes simmer with indignation. "Those were ten-year-old Keltic spirits."

Za'ya ignores him and gestures at his tunic, her silver eyes hot with challenge. "You think putting on this colorful clothing is rebelling? You are no true rebel, Rivyr'el Talonir."

Rivyr's expression grows haughty, his tone now coldly dismissive. "You're so bitter. All because my rune-sorcery can best yours. I could strike you down with three short moves, Za'ya Nyvor. And you know it."

Za'ya gets right up in his face, unmoved and unintimidated by his height. "So, you'd strike me down? Rather than hear the *truth*? The truth about yourself?"

His sneer returns. "The truth? All right. Here is the truth, Za'ya. I do enjoy your cooking. And your bonfires. And your simple Snake Elf ways."

Za'ya grows silent, sparks flying in her eyes. "I am going to forever pretend you did not just say that, Rivyr'el Talonir." She stalks back to Zeymir, gesturing toward Rivyr and lapsing into passionate Smaragdalfar.

"Of course," Rivyr grouses to me. "I'm winning our latest debate, so she switches to Low Alfsigr so I can't understand what she's saying."

There's a collective intake of breath. Za'ya slowly turns, combat fire lighting her eyes.

"*LOW* Alfsigr?" Her voice is a wave of fury. "It is not *LOW* Alfsigr. It's *Smaragdalfar.* An older language than yours by far, you sun-bleached fool!"

Rivyr stares at her, eyes wide with a shock that soon fades as he coughs out a derisive laugh. "*Sun-bleached fool?*"

"Get out," Za'ya hisses at Rivyr. "Get out of my sight before I run a rune-blade through you."

Rivyr's face tightens into an incredulous grimace. "So you're kicking me out now?" Misery slashes across his coldly handsome face.

I'm stunned. Arrogant Rivyr is suddenly the picture of vulnerability.

Za'ya takes a deep, shaky breath, glaring at him. "I am kicking you out for *tonight,* Rivyr'el. Not permanently, because you are my *friend.* And because I believe a noble thing exists within you that you do not yet see. But right now, I am *furious* with you, Rivyr'el Talonir. You *must* go."

The Elf nods stiffly at Za'ya. He looks to me, all levity gone, hard bitterness back in his expression. "We have more in common than you think, Gardnerian." His voice breaks with emotion. "Even if you despise me, our lot is the same."

For a brief moment, his anguish is laid bare. And I recognize the fierce loneliness in his eyes.

"I don't despise you," I tell him, and am surprised to find I mean it, upset as I am over his treatment of Za'ya.

He blinks at me, seemingly caught off guard, then shoots a hurt look at Za'ya, grabs up his bow and quiver and takes his leave, slamming the upstairs door behind him.

The tension in the room leaves with him.

"Why do you put up with him if he bothers you so?" Zeymir asks Za'ya as he pours the tea.

Za'ya closes her eyes and takes a long, shaky breath, as if to calm herself. She opens her eyes and looks to Zeymir. "He is only nineteen. And he is more than what he thinks he is."

Zeymir shakes his head. "He's a child of privilege. He'll never change."

She shoots him a poignant look. "Like you never changed?"

They launch into a low conversation that's a combination of Ishkart and Smaragdalfar. It's dizzying, how they can all switch and combine and meld languages.

Suddenly, I'm feeling very isolated here. An outsider, removed from their history with each other.

I turn to Ciaran. He has one leg propped up, his arm resting on his knee as he watches me intently. His protective focus on me is comforting, and it quickly diffuses some of the tension built up inside me from witnessing Rivyr'el and Za'ya spar so intensely. I suddenly realize how much I like and appreciate Ciaran's quiet manner.

"Are you friends with Rivyr'el?" I ask him.

He looks down at the table, his focus momentarily drawing inward. "I am. As much as he'll let anyone be friends with him." He looks back over at me. "He's had a rough time of it. Don't let his bravado fool you."

I think of the pained vulnerability in Rivyr'el's silver eyes that momentarily broke through and nod in understanding. Then I hold Ciaran's emerald stare for a moment, his magic drawing me in. "Can I stay in your room again tonight?"

He nods and gives me a searching look. "It's the safest place for now."

With all those runic wards. More protective wards than anywhere else in this dwelling. "Is it true that you're a rune-sorcerer?" I ask him.

His open expression becomes inscrutable. "Yes."

I wonder at this. I've never heard of a Kelt with rune-sorcery, but perhaps he has mixed ancestry. Except he doesn't look Noi or Alfsigr or Ishkart or Smaragdalfar, and only the Fae can glamour. So...how is it that he has so much rune-sorcery inside him? And why am I so drawn in by it?

"My light magery is drawn to your power," I admit, flushing a bit as I relax into his magical pull. It feels like a caress along my affinity lines, drawing me in toward him and heightening my color sensitivity, the hues of everything in the room brightening.

"I know," he says, his voice throaty, as if he's momentarily giving in to the pull as well. "I feel it, too. It's *strong*."

My flush deepens. It *is* strong—so strong that I have to resist the urge to move closer to him. "Is your rune-sorcery warded? Inside yourself? Like Rivyr warded mine?"

He nods, the green light in his eyes intensifying.

I study him closely. "I wonder...what it would be like to be around you if Rivyr hadn't warded me."

Ciaran's mouth quirks into the suggestion of a grin. "Dangerous. It's good he warded you."

My eyes widen a bit at this. So it's true. He's as powerful as I suspect.

I suddenly remember what else Rivyr said about Ciaran. "Are you truly a revolutionary?" I've heard Father describe revolutionaries as dangerous criminals and killers, and he's talked about their Resistance in cautionary tones, always followed by Father reassuring Mother Eliss that the Resistance is always easily crushed every time it rears its head against the Gardnerians and the Alfsigr.

Ciaran's eyes fill with unshakable conviction. "Yes, Sagellyn. I am."

Sweet Ancient One, he is. He's part of the Resistance.

Ciaran remains quiet for a protracted moment, but when

his words come, they're low and certain. "You're a revolutionary, too."

I tense my brow at him in confusion.

"You walked away from oppression," he says. "Turned your back on everything you've ever known, and at great personal risk. That was a revolutionary act."

I turn this over in my mind, stunned by the idea. "What are you fighting for?" I ask him. I've been told that revolutionaries are a pack of thieves, out to destroy the Magedom and steal our land—all of them criminals bent on smuggling spirits, pit dragons, illegal elixirs, weapons and dangerous refugees across our borders.

He's silent for a bit, his gaze steady on me. "Nothing is as you probably think it is. The Smaragdalfar aren't criminals or depraved beasts. They're like Za'ya, and they're being imprisoned underground by the Alfsigr Elves as laborers in the mines. Even children as young as Na'bee are given lumenstone quotas, and if they don't meet them, they're beaten and sometimes killed. That's what I'm fighting for. For freedom."

His words throw everything I've ever been told by my parents completely off-kilter. But now that I've met all of them—especially now that I've met Za'ya—I'm inclined to believe the shocking things he's telling me.

"You're right," I tell him, disturbed by it all, "that's not what I've been told."

"Of course you haven't. The Mage Guard is helping to enslave the Smaragdalfar." There's a jaded look in his emerald eyes as this new information rocks my world. "The Gardnerians are aligned with the Alfsigr militarily because the Gardnerian Guilds benefit from access to the mines."

I think of how Za'ya cast the Alfsigr toy into the fire, the pain on her face as she argued with Rivyr'el, and I begin to understand.

"The Resistance isn't made up of debauched criminals," he says, seeming to read the spark of troubled awareness in my expression. "We're fighting for a new world, where everyone can be free. No matter what culture. Or race. Or religion." There's a sudden, seditious fire in his eyes. "At least, that's what I'm fighting for."

Freedom. I look down at my fasting lines. What would it be like to live in a place where everyone is free?

"When you talk about everyone," I ask him haltingly, "do you mean Gardnerians, too?"

The hard resolve in his eyes doesn't waver. "Yes. Even Gardnerians. If they could accept every group as equal."

Could that even be possible? Everyone together instead of so rigidly separate? Together—like Za'ya, Zeymir, Wyla, Ciaran and Na'bee are here? It's possible for them, which means it might be possible for more people.

I lean in toward him, feeling suddenly lit-up by the explosive thought. "Tell me about your ideas."

We spend the next few hours talking, right up to the edge of nightfall, about the politics of the Realm and the strengthening Smaragdalfar Resistance. We talk about how the Mage Guard is massing on the Keltanian and Lupine borders, threatening an invasion if they don't turn over large swaths of borderland to the Magedom and the Alfsigr. He tells me about the increasing flow of desperate Urisk, Elfhollen, Smaragdalfar and Fae refugees out of the Western Realm.

And we talk about the Resistance—and their goals to build something better.

A fierce light shining in his eyes, Ciaran tells me of his desire to help the Smaragdalfar Elves build a new land in the Eastern sublands with a new type of rule, and with the ability to defend themselves against the Gardnerians and the Alfsigr and their allies.

I feel like someone is walking into my darkened world and firing up a million lanterns all at once. No one has ever talked to me like this, as if the workings of power are something I have the right to dissect. And it's a heady idea, that change could be possible. But…what if there *could* be a place where everyone could be free and together? A place for Za'ya and Na'bee and Zeymir and Wyla?

And a place with no wandfasting. Maybe even a place for a Gardnerian running from her family and her fasting.

The odds are insurmountable, but still, just the idea of it is like a beautiful, fragile, winged thing.

"I want a different world, too," I tell him, glancing at my fastmarked hands. When I look back up at him, the sudden empathy in his emerald eyes is a palpable thing.

And it strikes me—he's so completely different from the young man my parents bound me to. I look down again at my hands as frustration claws at me.

Why did they have to bind me to Tobias?

I'm suddenly distraught and desperately wishing that I could strip the fastlines from my skin.

But I'm trapped—I could run to the other side of Erthia and jump clear into the Resistance, like Ciaran, but I'll never really be free.

And I'll never get to choose who I want to love.

"Sagellyn?" The obvious concern in Ciaran's gaze only feeds into my frustration, and I have to turn away, tears stinging at my eyes as I wring my cursedly marked hands, finding it momentarily too painful to look at him as the immensity of what's been done to me presses down.

"I have to set the wards," he says after a long moment, his words edged with lingering concern.

I nod and draw away from him and his lulling pull and his hope for a different world.

I'll never have anyone and I'll never be free. They've ruined that for me. Forever.

Heavy with grief-filled exhaustion, I slump back against the cushions behind me as Ciaran leaves, and soon I drift off into a dark sleep.

I waken to the sound of Zeymir playing a mournful tune on a triangular stringed instrument, his low baritone warm as he sings in Ishkart. Ciaran is not in the room, and I immediately feel the lack of him.

Za'ya is sitting cross-legged and still as a statue in front of her small altar, straight-backed and peaceful. A series of tiny oil lamps are lit in a semicircle in front of Za'ya's goddess statue and send up a soft glow.

I think of how my people would view this. Idolatry is one of the worst crimes possible in Gardneria—a crime my people are hoping to avenge with death someday. But…she's so tranquil, her arms gracefully lifted, her palms up as she quietly chants in her language, as if she's waiting for a gift.

I settle deeper into the cushion and allow myself be lulled by Zeymir's rich voice, by Za'ya's gentle chanting, and I realize that they all did find a home here. Maybe not a home where they wanted it to be, but a warm, colorful new home.

My eyes are drawn back to Za'ya's goddess statue and the ring of purple flowers at its base. Her skin is patterned with emeralds like Za'ya's, her arms open wide, her face serene. On her shoulder is perched a small, white bird.

Za'ya grows silent and turns to look at me. I flush and look to the floor, embarrassed to be caught staring at her.

Za'ya's soft footfalls pad in my direction, and she sits down beside me. "I didn't mean to be staring at you," I tell her, abashed.

Za'ya rubs the back of my hand. "What's troubling you, Sagellyn?"

"Watching you pray…" I trail off. "It's just… I used to pray, too. All the time. And now… I'm cursed." I'm suddenly overcome with the hopeless certainty of this, and a tear courses down my cheek. "I'm running from a sacred fasting, and now the Ancient One will cast me off."

"No," she says gently, reaching up to stroke my hair. "Your people's *stories* about the Ancient One have cast you off. Not the Ancient One. Not *Oo'na*."

Za'ya must see the confusion on my face, because she pulls her necklace off and hands it to me. There's a beautiful white bird pendant hanging from it. "That's your bird, is it not?" she asks me.

I shake my head, not understanding. "No, it's your bird."

"It is. And yours, too. Take it, *ti'a'lin*. A gift."

Unsure, I take it and examine the dangling pendant. *The Ancient One's white bird*, I think. *And her Goddess's bird, too.* Here. In this place. It's such an outrageous thought, it sends a ripple of rebellious amusement through me that feels unexpectedly and deeply comforting. I slip the necklace over my head and tuck the small bird inside my tunic. Za'ya pulls me in and hugs me close, and I smile shakily at her. Then she rises, humming, and sits down before a weaving loom near her altar.

I fall asleep again to Zeymir's mournful tunes coaxed from perfectly tuned strings, to the soft clacking of Za'ya's loom, my thoughts on ivory tree branches and beautiful white birds.

"Sagellyn."

Ciaran's warm, deep voice wakes me, his hand gentle on my shoulder.

"It's time," Za'ya says to me from beside him, her tone low and cautionary.

I nod, bleary-eyed, and grasp Ciaran's hand as he helps me

up, but am soon fully awakened by a rush of fear that speeds my heart.

Nightfall.

Ciaran keeps his hand firmly around mine and I make no move to pull away from him—instead, my grip on him tightens. I turn to find Zeymir and Za'ya taking in our clasped hands with a trace of unease, but they remain silent, a resigned, shadowed look passing between them.

I'm awakened a few hours later by the deep green searchlights pulsing through Ciaran's room, sparking off the wards, feeling wildly disoriented as I struggle to wake.

Retta? Clover?

My chest tightens as I frantically search for my sisters before remembering where I am. Fear surges through me as I gasp for air and sit up, panic swiftly overtaking me.

"Sagellyn."

Ciaran kneels down by the edge of my cot, his hand coming to my arm as he looks at me with the same pained understanding that was there last night. I struggle for breath and it all comes rushing back—how I'm permanently cut off from my family, my people. From my sisters.

His hand comes to my shoulder as he murmurs to me in another tongue, his thumb gently brushing along my neck, and I hear the word *ti'a'lin.*

My breath shudders and I reach out to grab onto his arm, holding tight to him, my hand trembling. Ciaran pulls me into a comforting embrace, and I cling to him as the search spell pulses and fear whips through me.

"*Ti'a,*" he murmurs, caressing my hair. "You're safe." He holds me tight until my ragged breathing steadies and I get hold of myself again.

"I can't go back," I say into the crook of his neck, my whisper rough with rebellion. "I won't go back."

Ciaran's lips brush against my hair. "You won't have to, *ti'a*." He strokes my back, holding me close, and it feels so right—so completely right and safe to be held by him.

I take another deep shuddering breath, my lips brushing against his long neck as I do so, my Mage lines pulling toward him. "What does *'ti'a'* mean?" I ask him, suddenly even more aware of his comforting warmth, his solidly masculine presence, his hand splayed out on my back, his breath against my hair.

I draw back slightly and hold his gaze, fractals of green light sparking in my vision in response to his rune-sorcery, my affinity lines tingling warm and bright as I let myself fall into his magic and he lets himself fall into mine.

"It means 'beloved,'" he says, an impassioned longing in his eyes.

I don't know who initiates the kiss, but his mouth is suddenly on mine, soft and seeking, as I draw him close. I don't know who initiates our second kiss or our third or our fourth. I only know that kissing him is everything I've ever longed for. Everything I've ever wanted. Like coming home to a place I was always meant to find.

We cling to each other and kiss deep into the night, soft and gentle, lingering and careful. And then not so careful, as the search spell pulses around us and all through the surrounding darkness.

CHAPTER NINE:
Rune-Blade

When I stir from sleep, Ciaran is already gone, the blankets around me mussed in a fitful tangle that mirrors my emotions at finding him absent. I touch my lower lip, my face warming as I remember the feel of his mouth on mine, the two of us wrapped around each other for most of the night—a new thrall cast over me that has nothing to do with his rune-sorcery.

This sudden strong attraction to him is what I was supposed to feel for my fastmate on the day of my sealing.

A thought jolts through me with staggering force.

It's today.

Today is the day I was supposed to be sealed to Tobias. I glance down at my spidery fastlines, my heartbeat kicking up. Nausea sweeps through me and I grip at the edge of the bed, feeling like I'm about to retch.

"We'll need to move you soon," Za'ya tells me gently over breakfast.

Zeymir and Za'ya are sitting inside with me while everyone else is off working. Na'bee has been sent to do lessons in his room. The low table holds a teapot full of amber tea and a platter of fried breakfast cakes made from leftover *nu'duls*, colorful cave mushrooms, eggs and spices.

"We have a safe house in Eastern Verpacia," Zeymir tells me, setting down his tea. "Ciaran is there now, warding it against search spells."

"I can't leave for good without my sisters," I remind him.

"There is nothing you can do for them now without endangering yourself, Sagellyn," Zeymir says. "Your family has reported you missing to the Verpacian Guard and to the Vu Trin forces, as well as to your Mage Council. The Verpacian Guard is going to allow Fifth Division Gardnerian trackers into Verpacia to find you. Postings with your face on them are being hung everywhere."

Za'ya's hand comes to mine. "Do you understand now why you need to be moved, *ti'a*? And quickly?"

I struggle to blink back the tears that well up at the thought of leaving Retta and Clover behind…and the thought of leaving everyone here. But I also don't want to place them at risk, especially when they've done so much to protect me.

And I want a chance at a new life. A life that I can truly call my own.

Za'ya's emerald hand tightens on mine. "Sagellyn," she says softly. "We are not abandoning you. We know what it is like to be alone in a strange place. With nowhere to go, and no way of ever going back. We are all headed toward the Noi lands eventually, and there may be a way to get you there as well, since—like all of us—you possess something that is very rare. And potentially very useful to the Noi military."

I wipe my tears away with the palm of my hand. "I might have quite a lot of light magery," I tell them. "My parents wouldn't tell me my Mage level, but I've overheard things… I know they were concerned about the Mage Council finding out about my level of power." My tone takes a bitter turn. "They felt that following *The Book of the Ancients* was more important than my being a Council Light Mage. Because *The Book* says that females aren't supposed to have wands."

Za'ya considers me thoughtfully. "Rivyr'el was able to ward you. Which means you must have significant power."

I shake my head. "I don't understand."

"Barrier wards, like the one he warded you with, can only be drawn in by a strong magical pull. Magic is like a magnet to those wards," she explains. "So you must be a powerful Light Mage and rune-sorcerer."

I blink at her as her affirmation of what I've always suspected sinks fully in.

"But unlike us," Za'ya continues, "you will be able to work the runes of any system and link them together into new powers, because Light Mages can fabricate any rune. The Noi will have a strong interest in this, and for this reason would most probably accept you, even though you are Gardnerian."

"They would likely enroll you in the Wyvernguard," Zeymir says.

"What's that?" I ask curiously.

"The Noi military academy," Zeymir tells me. "Where they train the Vu Trin soldiers."

Shock roils through me at the idea, followed closely by a clutch of sudden distress. "I have to save my sisters," I insist, desperation rising. "I can't leave for the Eastern Realm without them. I just can't."

Za'ya takes a deep breath and tilts her head slightly in acknowledgment and agreement. "You will save them—someday. But first you have to save yourself."

At midday Rivyr'el shows up, his flamboyance dampened to a chastened wariness, as if he's trying to regain Za'ya's favor—and perhaps win mine. He gives me a dazzling glass prism that dances with rainbows as it catches the light, the beauty of it stealing my breath away.

"So you can remember," Rivyr tells me with a wry grin, "that there's more than black in this world." He winks at me, his eyes flashing with glitter.

I look down at the sparkling prism, the diamond-cut crystal sending a prickle of delight through my affinity lines and prompting an entrancing rainbow of sparks to appear in my vision. I glance up at Rivyr, who momentarily appears covered in rainbows, and smile. "Thank you," I tell him, touched by his kind gesture.

Rivyr dips his head with graceful formality, his eyes gleaming with amusement. "You are welcome, my sweet rune-mage."

Za'ya watches Rivyr with her arms crossed tight as he strides over to Na'bee, pulls a wrapped package from under his cloak and hands it to him. Na'bee excitedly pulls open the parchment wrapping and exclaims something happily in Ishkart as he holds up a black stallion toy and a whimsical stuffed bear wearing Keltic clothing to sit astride it. Na'bee launches himself at Rivyr, hugging both the young Elf and his new toys tightly. Rivyr looks sidelong at Za'ya, an impish grin on his face, and Za'ya snorts. She motions for him to sit, then roughly sets a bowl of *nu'duls* down in front of the Elf with a clatter.

Later, after Rivyr has taken his leave, a rumpled, ash-sullied, leather-aproned Wyla briefly stops in to grab food and talk to Za'ya in Ishkart. Their eyes dart toward me occasionally, and my ears pick out my name a few times. Finally, Wyla strides over to me, a fiery look in her eyes as she pulls one of her daggers from the holster on her thigh and hands it to me, handle out.

It's a gorgeously wrought Ishkartan rune-blade, with deep violet leather wrapped around its hilt and glowing golden Ishkartan runes set along the length of the blade.

"For you," she says. "You will learn to use your wand and you will learn to use this blade."

"I can't..." I protest.

"Yes, you can," Wyla insists, pushing the blade forward. "Take it. You have cried much over this terrible thing that happened to you. But it is time to stop crying, Sagellyn." The burn in her eyes becomes a blaze. "Soon it will be time to fight them instead."

I take hold of the knife, the Ishkartan runes glowing brighter as I take it in hand. The circular aspects of the rune design widen and fill in with more intricate runic markings, the blade and hilt suddenly pulsing with every color imaginable. The blade is lighter than I would have expected, with a wickedly sharp edge, and I can make out some aspects of the golden runes that are coming to life on its hilt and blade, remembering them from Gwynn's grimoires.

Accuracy, conflagration, decimate.

I don't see Ciaran again until just after nightfall. It turns out to be a quiet night—no search spells. The runes in his bedroom are peaceful and still as I sit on the cot by the window, immersed in one of his books about the history of the Eastern Realm.

Ciaran's eyes immediately find me when he enters the bedroom, and his face lights with a quiet elation. My heart starts a slow, pounding rhythm in response to his nearness and the intensity of his attention, my affinity lines drinking in his deep red hair, the vivid green of his eyes, the handsome lines of his face.

I have a million questions to ask him, but all my thoughts tangle in on themselves as I remember our wonderful, heated kisses.

Ciaran sits down next to me and opens a palm on his knee

in invitation. I set aside the book and slide my hand into his, shivering with delight when his fingers close around mine. I smile at him as warmth slides through my lines.

"I missed you," I tell him shyly as he trails his thumb over mine, my heartbeat tripping over itself in response to his caress.

"I missed you, too," he says, the green light in his eyes sparking, his magical pull wrapping around me. "We've only known each other for a few days, but… I want to be with you all the time now."

"I feel the same way," I breathlessly tell him, loving his calm, reflective manner and how he listens to me in such fully absorbed silence. "When I'm with you, I don't feel so alone anymore. I feel…understood."

He gives me the trace of a smile. "Maybe we should always stay together, then."

My mouth twitches into a besotted grin. "I like that idea."

Ciaran's smile widens, mirroring my own, and I feel like we've just made a quiet, unshakable declaration, the two of us aligned now, from here on in.

Ciaran's gaze lights on the rune-blade that's now sitting on the small table at the head of my cot. He looks to me questioningly. "You've a rune-blade now?"

"Wyla gave it to me. She wants me to learn how to fight with it. Along with the wand." I gesture toward the belt-sheath that sits on the table beside the blade. "She gave me a sheath for the blade as well."

Ciaran's lip lifts at this. "Wyla likes her weapons."

"How did she come to live with all of you?" I ask curiously. "I heard a rumor that Zeymir's married to both Za'ya and Wyla. That's not true, is it?" I've noticed that Zeymir has a paternal manner around Za'ya, and he looks old enough to be her father.

A shadow passes over Ciaran's face. "Zeymir *is* married to Wyla. On paper, at least. It was the only way he and Za'ya could rescue Wyla from a brothel she'd been sold to. She was fourteen."

Shock blasts through me, and I draw in a tight breath, horrified.

"He married her as a formality," Ciaran explains. "It was the only way to get her out of Issani territory. Zeymir and Za'ya had traveled there because it was the only place that would allow them to marry. While they were there, they happened upon Wyla, who begged them for help. So Zeymir married Wyla as well, which broke the brothel's legal hold on her, and then Zeymir and Za'ya took her in. She's like a daughter to them."

I understand this thing that was done to her. Wyla's impassioned words flash into my mind, and an even fiercer gratitude for her help swells inside me—and a bone-deep sorrow for what Wyla's probably endured.

"Why wasn't she able to free herself with her magic?" I ask him.

"Her rune-sorcery didn't surface until a few years after her rescue."

I consider this. "What would have happened if Zeymir hadn't rescued her?"

Ciaran inclines his head in thought. "Probably an arranged marriage to a warlord, once her rune-sorcery became apparent."

"After being forced into a brothel," I say flatly, frustrated over how little control both Wyla and I would have been given over our lives if we hadn't escaped.

Ciaran nods grimly, and I can see my own outrage mirrored in his green eyes.

"Did Zeymir rescue Za'ya, too?"

He shakes his head. "No, Za'ya rescued herself from the Alfsigr-controlled sublands. She was an escapee from the mines, and she went to work forging runes for an Ishkartan smithery that Zeymir's family owns. He caught her fabricating weapons to smuggle back west and into the sublands, but he never turned her in. Za'ya convinced him to join her cause instead."

I let out a short laugh at this, affection for Za'ya lighting in me. "I can believe that. Za'ya's persuasive."

Ciaran smiles at this. "They began working for the Resistance together, and Zeymir soon fell in love with her."

"That's easy to believe, too," I say, growing serious, emotion abruptly overtaking me. "Za'ya's very kind."

Ciaran is silent for a moment, and his voice breaks when he next speaks. "Zeymir and Za'ya are…some of the best people I have *ever* met."

"How did you come to live with them?" I ask hesitantly.

"My family died," he says simply, a stark grief suddenly in his eyes. He doesn't elaborate further, and he's in such obvious pain that I don't press him.

I lean into him as we hold hands, resting my head against his broad shoulder. I glance up at the ceiling tapestry, filled with the sudden longing to kiss him, like we did last night. I follow the swirl of a circular rune with my eyes as a flush blooms on my cheeks and neck, the unsettling heat his presence sparks refusing to be confined or willed away.

I turn to find Ciaran staring at me, his cheeks ruddy, his eyes full of this longing for each other that seems to have overtaken us both.

"Sage," he says, his voice filled with emotion.

At first, I almost smile to hear him use the same name my family and friends do. But as I gaze back at him, I'm rocked by a sudden, overwhelming, viciously futile desire to be fasted to Ciaran instead of Tobias.

I hold out my free hand to him, palm up, my skin riddled with fastlines. He looks at them unflinchingly. "I can never be with anyone else," I tell him, my voice breaking as tears glaze my eyes. "I can never be with anyone but…"

Bile rises in my throat. I can't do it. I can't say my fastmate's name without retching. A nauseous heat burns at the back of my neck.

"You don't know that," Ciaran says, his tone defiant. "Spells can be broken."

"Not this one."

"*No.* Any spell can be broken." His grip around my hand tightens.

"Even if it could…" I extend my arm, the emerald glimmer of my skin catching the rune-light. "I'll always be Gardnerian."

"I don't care," he says, his defiance unwavering.

Ciaran lifts my hand and presses his lips to the back of it in a slow, gentle kiss right on the fastlines, his eyes closing, his expression overcome with feeling. His breath shudders against my hand, and I inhale sharply. Then he kisses the bend of each finger with deliberate slowness, one at a time, his warm mouth gentle, his rebellious eyes lifting to mine as his lips brush over my knuckles in a featherlight line.

He's nothing like Tobias—he's what my dreams of my future fastmate were. My heart thuds hard against my chest as Ciaran reaches up to lightly caress my cheek before threading his fingers through my hair and bringing his lips to mine.

I fall into his ardent kiss, his loving, gentle touch filling my heart even as the awareness of my fastlines breaks it.

I'm awakened late in the night by Ciaran tossing and turning on the other cot and frantically calling out in fluent Smaragdalfar.

"*Ma'mya! Ma'mya! Ohn! Ohn!*" I've picked up enough Smaragdalfar in these past few days to understand these simple words. *Mama! Mama! No! No!*

"Ciaran!" I sit up as he moans, his face distraught, the blankets wrapped chaotically around his long limbs. I tap the rune-lantern beside me and it sparks to life, casting the room in its soft, multicolored glow, hoping the light will wake him from his nightmare.

"*Ma'mya! Fav'ya! Ohn'a'yir!*" *Mother. Father.* And something else I don't understand.

Why is he dreaming in fluent Smaragdalfar? And what happened to his parents?

"Ciaran." I go over to him and take hold of his shoulder. He cries out, tears streaming from his eyes, struggling as if the blankets are restraining him, kicking at them like he's trying to escape. I grip his shoulder more firmly and shake him, my heart going out to him. "Ciaran. You're dreaming."

He inhales sharply and flinches, his eyes flying open, glassy and reddened. He blinks around, wildly disoriented, his mouth opening and closing, wet with tears. He's breathing hard as his gaze locks onto mine, and for a brief moment, I see it all. How he lost everyone.

His hand clamps down on my hand, his eyes tight on mine. Holding onto me as I've held onto him.

"Stay with me," he rasps out, seeming still half in the nightmare. "Don't leave."

"I won't," I promise.

I stay there for a long time, holding onto him, his hand grasping mine as his hard breathing shudders and then slows to a more normal rhythm. Eventually I lie down beside him and soon drift off, my arm draped over his chest, his hands clinging to me all night long.

CHAPTER TEN:
Secrets

I'm awakened by a high-pitched scream, followed by my sister Clover's voice.

"*Sage! Sage!*"

I jolt up, my heart lurching, and scramble to peer through the slit between the shutter and the window.

Mother Eliss is dragging Clover over to a waiting carriage as she angrily hisses something at my sister. Clover's feet drag against the cobbled street, trying to gain purchase as she's dragged forward.

"No!" Clover cries out. "I want *Sage!*"

Gentle Retta emerges from the inn, red-eyed and looking traumatized. Father's hand is tight on her arm, firmly guiding her to the carriage as well. Still childish at twelve, she's hugging one of the cloth dolls I made for her.

Clover yanks free of Mother Eliss, fists balled, and glares hard at her as Father all but pushes Retta into the carriage, my gentle sister quickly cast in shadows. Retta's terrified, distraught eyes soon appear at the carriage window, blinking out, miserably searching.

Searching for *me*, I sickeningly realize.

"I won't go!" Clover yells at both Mother Eliss and Father. "I won't go without Sage!"

Father lunges forward and grabs Clover, but she continues to scream. He rears back and slaps her face so hard that she falls to the ground, weeping and calling my name. I jolt back from the blow, as if struck myself, covering my mouth in horror.

Mother Eliss's face is twisted in fury as she glares down at rebellious, eleven-year-old Clover. She turns her back on my youngest sister and gets into the carriage as Father jerks a now limp, sobbing Clover up and forces her into the carriage, slamming the door shut. He stalks back toward the inn, where a knot of Mages and Verpacian soldiers are gathered. Gwynnifer is there with them, talking with earnest concern, pointing down the road, toward the smithery, toward the University.

Gwynn. Pain twists inside me as Ciaran's hand comes to rest comfortingly on my back. I want to run to my friend. To open my heart to her and tell her how everything went so horribly wrong. How everything we've been told is full of lies. But I know her all too well—she's so strictly Gardnerian, she'd never believe me. Anguish slashes through me as I realize beyond any doubt that Gwynn would fully reject me if she knew where I was right now. If she knew how I held Ciaran through much of the night. How I ran away from my fasting.

The carriage lurches to a start and drives away.

I want to throw myself straight through the wall. Run after them and save my sisters. Pull out my wand and force back anyone who dares stand in my way.

"Sage..."

"They're going to lock them up," I rage, knowing this to be true with crushing certainty. "That's what Father did to my brother Shane when he rebelled. Clover will rebel, too, and they'll beat her into submission. Then they'll fast them both, as soon as possible. And they'll be trapped in that family of monsters." A vision of gentle Retta, of skinny little Clover being controlled by Tobias's family slices through me. The possibility of my beloved sisters being attacked and then blamed for it, and belittled like I was, is too terrible to bear.

I turn to Ciaran, reckless outrage overtaking me. He's watching me with deep concern in his eyes, his hair a wild mess from sleep.

"I've got to get them out of there," I say vehemently, sliding around him to get up from the cot. I buckle the belt-sheath around my waist and shove my rune-blade into it, my wand already stowed in the side of my boot.

Ciaran rises, his hand coming to my arm. "Sage, you *will* save them. But not yet. You have no spells. No training. But there's time. You told me your sister's fasting is still a year away…"

I rake my hand through my hair as furious tears well in my eyes. "It *kills* me to see them treated like this. And they won't know what became of me."

"No, they won't." Ciaran reaches up to caress my shoulder. "I'm sorry. Resistance is a long game. A *long* one. You'll go to a safer place, and you'll get hold of a grimoire. You'll learn light spells and rune-sorcery. And *then* you will save them."

I struggle to breathe normally, swallowing back the tears. Ciaran pulls me gently into his arms for a long moment, and my body slowly melts into his, comforted by the contact of his long form against mine. I slide my arms around him as he caresses my back, a shudder passing through my affinity lines.

My eyes are briefly drawn to his long neck, the collar of his tunic askew, giving me a shadowed glimpse of his muscular chest. There are tattoos of multiple chains holding small, emerald runes running all over the skin under his clothing.

I reach up and brush the edge of his collar with my thumb. "Ciaran, what are those tattoos on your chest?"

Ciaran stiffens and pulls slightly away, his previously open expression abruptly closed.

THUD THUD THUD

Both our heads jerk up as someone slams against the front entrance door to the smithery.

"Open up!" a rough voice demands. A voice I know. The blood drains from my face.

"Father," I whisper, meeting Ciaran's eyes in horror.

Outside the room, a door slams open. Bootheels thud through the smithery and then down the spiraling stairs. Za'ya's shriek comes from below us. Then a crash.

Ciaran bolts toward his bedroom's curtained entrance, peering out. He turns and motions for me to be quiet, then reaches out to grab my arm, pulling me toward the curtain, toward him.

"Get down!" Father growls from the downstairs living space. The demand is echoed by several other men. There's another crash, followed by Za'ya's screech.

Na'bee cries out, "*Ma'mya!*"

"We're searching the premises for my daughter, Mage Sagellyn Gaffney," Father's voice booms up from below. "You have a Kelt here. Where is he?"

"Please, Mages," Zeymir's deep voice tries to reason, "this girl is not here…"

A sharp thud. Za'ya and Na'bee crying out in Ishkart.

Outrage blasts through me, and I move to push through the curtain, to do *something*, but Ciaran holds me firmly back.

"Mages, please," Zeymir tries again, his words slightly muffled this time.

"Shut up, heathen," Tobias's cruel voice snarls.

Shock explodes through me as it all floods back. Tobias holding me down, restraining me with magic, forcing me…

I can barely rasp the words out. "That's *him*."

Ciaran's eyes widen, then narrow with lethal calm. "Do you trust me?" he whispers.

I lock onto his emerald glare and nod, terror crackling through me.

He pulls me out of the bedroom, through the smithery and out its rear exit as Father yells at Zeymir and Za'ya and Na'bee. There's another crash as Ciaran pulls me out the back door, the gloomy gray sky above spitting a chilled rain.

There's a huge, gray-skinned Elfhollen man standing at the head of a heavily loaded wagon and holding the reins of two black workhorses, seeming ready to flee. Surprise flashes in the Elfhollen's silver eyes as he catches sight of me. He glances in the direction of the angry voices and gives Ciaran a look heavy with warning. "Ciaran. *No.*"

"We've got to get her out of here," Ciaran snarls in a whisper. "There's no other way, Kol." He finishes his thought in a rapid stream of Ishkart.

I can make out the edge of a slatted crate just underneath the canvas that's tied down over the wagon's back with heavy twine. *Weapons,* I frantically realize, the glint of blades visible through the crate's slats. I've spotted one of these crates ensconced in Ciaran's room under his cot, filled with rune-blades..

They're smuggling weapons out. Today.

Oh, Ancient One.

Ciaran doesn't wait for Kol's response. He pulls me toward the back of the wagon and lifts the edge of the cloth. "Get in," he whispers, eyes adamant, his dark red hair deepened to russet in the gloom. "They *can't* find you here in the smithery."

Na'bee cries out from below ground. I can hear Za'ya pleading, and I realize how much danger they'll all be in if my family does find me here.

I scramble, half-pushed, half-lifted by Ciaran into the darkness under the cloth. He pulls the edge of the canvas higher for a moment, and in a brief flash of illumination, I realize the crates aren't the main cargo of this wagon. They only line the very edges of the sheltered space.

The wagon is filled with people, most of them children, lying tightly pressed against each other on their sides. Smaragdalfar like Za'ya, their skin patterned with gleaming emeralds, eyes like stars, ears coming to swift points. All of them are silent and still as death, their eyes wide and brimming with suppressed terror. I slide down between the close-packed bodies and Ciaran replaces the canvas. The stench of wet wool and fear swamps me as the glowing emerald shimmer of my skin becomes apparent in the darkened light.

I pull on my affinity lines, brightening my surroundings. There's an old woman in front of me, her hair white as snow. She's got her arms around a little girl who looks to be about six years old. The child is completely still, clutching a worn cloth doll with skin of emerald fabric, pointed ears and green yarn for hair, the doll's eyes glinting with silver thread. Despite the toy in her hands, there's a gravity in the little girl's fear-stricken eyes that belies her young age.

I glance over my shoulder. There's a young Smaragdalfar woman behind me. She's around my age and glaring at me with blistering hatred. All around us, the silver eyes of children blink at me, like small animals in the woods around a forest campfire.

I can't stop trembling, and I struggle to get hold of my fear with the steadiness these small children are managing. I realize, in a searing flash, exactly what Ciaran, Zeymir and Za'ya are involved in. They're not smuggling spirits or pit dragons or young women or illegal elixers, like my people accuse them of doing. They *are* smuggling rune-weapons for the Resistance.

And they're smuggling refugees.

The carriage gives a sharp lurch and sets off bumpily, the young woman's elbow shoving painfully into my back, our bodies jostling against each other. Father yells an unintelligible command from far off, and I flinch at the sound.

"Search out back!" Tobias's hard voice calls out.

A wave of terror hollows me out as the wagon bumps along, my cheekbone jarred against the hard wood beneath me. I'm trembling as the men's voices grow fainter, but I know they could catch up with us in an instant—we're a heavily loaded wagon, and they're Mages who can travel swiftly on horseback.

If they find us, they'll take me back. I'll be forced into captivity by Tobias's family and beaten until I break. I'll never learn to use my magery, and I'll never save my sisters.

And who knows what terrible things they'd do to all these refugees.

The yelling fades, the rain increasing, heavy drops now pelting the canvas. I'm so scared, I'm shivering violently, and I feel like I can't breathe. Then a gentle hand comes to rest on my arm, and I look into the old woman's starry eyes. She murmurs something to me in Smaragdalfar, her voice coarse, but her tone warm and kind.

The young woman behind me hisses something in their language, but the old woman ignores it, her silver eyes locked on mine. She pushes a stray strand of my hair back behind my ear as she murmurs to me softly, and I'm touched by her kindness. My trembling lessens as I hold her compassionate, rock-steady gaze. The child reaches out and puts her small hand on my arm, light as a butterfly, and tears sting at my eyes.

The other woman won't let up her ceaseless protest, her elbow periodically jabbing painfully into my back and the old woman's voice briefly rises into a stream of strong censure. The young woman doesn't stop hissing her stream of hate into my back, but she does stop hurting me.

The old woman and the child hold onto me as we ride for what seems like a million years, the smell of sweat and grime a sharpening tang on the damp, rancid air. Eventually, the child nods off, her small hand sliding down to fall onto mine, and I tenderly grasp it, steadied now and flooded with thoughts of my sisters and wanting to protect this little girl.

Why is this child here? In a wagon? Is she running from the Alfsigr?

Father and Mother Eliss have talked about Snake Elves escaping from underground, like demons slithering up from the bowels of the earth. Dangerous Evil Ones, ready to align themselves with the powers of the Shadow Wand to wage war on the Blessed Mages.

But they never told me the Evil Ones would be a small, terrified child, clutching a worn rag doll.

CHAPTER ELEVEN:
Forest Lair

As we ride, the sounds of the city fade. Soon there's just the pat-
ter of the rain and the occasional clomping and creaking of another wagon passing by or the thudding gallop of a lone horse.

Finally, Kol's deep voice sounds out to the horses in another
language, his tone calm and unflappable, and the wagon slows
to a stop.

The little girl is awake now, but remains as still as she was in
sleep. Heavy steps thud nearby, to my left, moving around the
wagon, and my exhaustion is wrenched away by a new rush of
fear, my heart racing.

Gray light floods into the wagon as the canvas is wrenched
back, and we all blink at the sudden brightness, the little girl
rubbing her eyes and pushing herself up. Kol's face looks down
on us as my eyes adjust to the gloomy light.

Standing behind Kol is a heavily armed Wyla, her face grim
and determined, and relief floods through me at the sight of her.

"You're okay," Wyla tells me as she helps me out, my legs
shaky. The rain has stopped, and a muggy fog hangs in the air.
I glance around and get my bearings, my feet sinking into the
wet ground.

A small, gentle hand slips into mine, and I look down to find the small Smaragdalfar girl with the doll staring up at me with wide, starry eyes. I tighten my hand around hers, smile through my trembling and give her hand an encouraging squeeze. I can see her doll more clearly in this light, lovingly embroidered, dressed in a small version of the green traditional clothing of her people. I glance around at the refugees milling about, murmuring softly to each other in Smaragdalfar, blinking at our surroundings, the children seeming lost. It's almost all children, about twelve of them, along with four women. The refugees' clothing is uniformly bedraggled—worn green garments, soiled to the edge of dark gray. One of the children has what looks like a lash scar that cuts diagonally across her face, and my heart gives a painful twist at the sight of it.

They're too thin. Too quiet. They all have a haunted look, and when they glance at me, most of them seem terrified.

My sisters' faces fill my mind. *What if they were on the run like this?* The thought of children—*any* children—in danger like this is almost too awful to bear.

The shock of their obvious fear of me and of being faced with the awful reality of their situation sets thick in my chest, so thick that for a moment, I can barely breathe.

Devastated, I glance down at the little girl holding my hand and give a small jerk of surprise. There's a white bird perched on her shoulder, translucent and serene. Startled, I glance around to see the gauzy shapes of white birds perched on the shoulder of every child, but the children seem oblivious to the ghost birds.

As one, all the birds turn and set their eyes on me.

"Oh," I gasp, blinking, but then the birds are gone. I blink several more times, hard, thrown by the vision.

Get ahold of yourself, Sage, I caution myself, heart racing. *You're seeing things that aren't there.*

"Sagellyn?" Wyla asks from beside me. "Are you all right?"

I rub my bleary eyes and nod at her, then take a haggard breath, glancing around as I try to calm myself and take stock.

"Where are we?" I ask.

"Still in Verpacia," she tells me. "A few hours east of Verpax City."

We're surrounded by dense forest, the narrow, muddied road we came in on marked with carriage wheels and dirt turned up by the horses' hooves. Up a low, short hill before us is the large, flat stone face of a sizable hillock. To the far right are some ramshackle horse stables, visible through a thin grove of pine trees. An iron firepit lies directly in front of us, and long logs are arranged around the firepit as makeshift benches.

The little girl takes a seat on the nearest log and talks quietly in Smaragdalfar to her cloth doll as Wyla touches her rune-blade to the logs in the firepit. The wood is quickly enveloped in flames, and I'm surprised by her casual use of rune-sorcery.

Huge Kol is gently coaxing a frightened, balled-up child out of the wagon's back as the dull, heavy thud of horses' hooves sound down the path. Along with everyone else, my head jerks toward the forest-bracketed road, a cold blade of fear cutting through me.

Air floods back into my lungs as Za'ya rides in, rune-weapons strapped all over her body. Ciaran rides in behind her and his searching eyes immediately light on me. Our gazes lock tight, warmth exploding through me. Na'bee sits on the saddle in front of Ciaran, and my heart lurches as I take in the sight of his bruised, reddened cheek and the brave smile he attempts when he spots me. Zeymir brings up the rear, two rune-swords strapped to his back, the side of his face bloodied, his runic headband gone, his long black hair untethered and loose down his back.

Shame on behalf of my people floods through me. They hit Na'bee and Zeymir, and they must have ripped the runeband from Zeymir's head—I just know it. A sickening disgust twists in my gut at the thought of my supposedly upstanding, perfect people being so devastatingly vile.

Ciaran helps Na'bee down as Wyla catches the child. Wyla briefly goes down on one knee to talk to him. Na'bee nods and gives me another wavering smile that I attempt to return before his mother swoops him up into an embrace.

"Sage." Ciaran is off his horse in one, lithe movement. He strides over to me, his expression blazing, his emotions completely on display. I throw every last bit of caution into the abyss along with my Gardnerian blacks, my old life cast clear away as I make for Ciaran.

Ciaran throws his powerful arms around me and hugs me fiercely, murmuring to me in Smaragdalfar. I hug him back just as tightly, tears coming to my eyes, devastated by what's happened, but overjoyed to be encircled by the solid, sure strength of him.

Ciaran pulls back to look at me, his warm hands caressing the sides of my face. He presses his forehead to mine, his breathing heavy and uneven. "Oh, Sage."

I never want to let him go. I hold my forehead against his until our breathing slows and Ciaran withdraws slightly, his impassioned gaze conveying the depth of his feelings.

We pull away from each other as Zeymir approaches. I take in his bruised, bloodied face and am suddenly so overcome with shame, I can barely meet his eyes.

"I'm so sorry," I tell Zeymir, my voice coarse with regret. It's all my fault. All of this.

Zeymir's hand comes to my shoulder. "We knew the risk we were taking. Do you understand that, Sagellyn?"

I nod and fight back the tears, wanting to keep hold of myself for the little girl who is quietly watching us.

"Are you all right?" Zeymir asks me.

"Yes," I tell him, devastatingly aware that my situation is far better than what all these children have been faced with. "I'm fine."

Zeymir squeezes my shoulder and gives the little girl an encouraging smile. Then he says something in Ishkart to Ciaran and gestures toward the stable.

"I'm going to help them with the horses," Ciaran tells me, his hand briefly coming to my arm, and I nod my agreement. He strides off with Wyla and Kol, little Na'bee breaking away from Za'ya to trail after Zeymir.

Za'ya climbs up the hill and up to the stone face of the hillock. She pulls out a stylus and begins to draw a large, glowing green Smaragdalfar rune on its surface.

I watch, transfixed, having never seen Za'ya perform rune-sorcery before.

Circular emerald runes burst to life all over the stone wall, then dissolve like mist to reveal a large double door. Za'ya pulls the doors open to reveal a rough shelter inside a cave, furnished with rune-lanterns glowing a warm gold, chairs, tables, crates of supplies and even a rune-stove. Za'ya's clear voice rings out as she takes charge and ushers the refugees into the cave and out of the cold, spitting rain.

The old woman who comforted me is standing by the stables, talking to Ciaran in fluent Smaragdalfar. I blink at Ciaran, wondering, not for the first time, about his grasp of the language. The old woman reaches up and pulls his head down, touching her forehead to his, both of their eyes briefly closing in what I realize must be a Smaragdalfar greeting. Then she and Ciaran both walk back toward me and the little girl. The little girl gets up and moves to cling to the old woman's bedraggled skirts, looking up at all of us with wide-eyed curiosity.

The old woman studies me for a long moment with a shrewd, narrowed gaze, then takes my hand in her calloused one. She says something to me in serious tones, and though I can't translate the words, I understand her inflection. It's an attempt at comfort, and I'm deeply moved by it, tears coming to my eyes. She squeezes my hand, then walks to the cave with the little girl, who turns back once to look at me over her small shoulder.

Ciaran is watching them go, his expression grim but calm. *He's used to this*, I realize. *He's seen all this before, again and again. How many refugees have they smuggled through here? How many children?*

"What happened back in the city?" I ask him.

Ciaran frowns. "They roughed up Za'ya, Na'bee and Zeymir. Searched their home. Made a show of magery and left." He tells me all this with disturbing matter-of-factness, and I realize my people's cruelty is normal to them. "They're looking for me," he says. "Apparently one of your friends saw me looking at you that day you arrived. And she's right—I was looking at you."

Gwynn. You don't understand, I want to rail at her. *You don't understand anything.*

The Smaragdalfar refugees are moving around inside the cave. Za'ya's handing them what looks like flat pieces of dense bread that she's pulling out from a storage crate, a hurried air to the proceedings.

"So many children," I observe.

"Escapees," Ciaran says, eyeing the crowded cave. "From the mines. They set them to working in the narrow lumenstone mines when they're five, because they can fit through the smaller tunnels. Many die. *Many.* If not from the mines caving in, then from sickness." His face tightens with disgust. "The Alfsigr don't care. Smaragdalfar children are expendable to them."

Shame pulls at me. I think of the expensive golden lumenstone lighting our estate and the Ironflower Inn back in Verpax City.

"Where are you taking them?" I ask.

"East. To Noi lands. It's a difficult journey. Across the desert." His brow furrows. "We can't move too many at a time. We've only so many guides who can protect them." He frowns, his tone bitter. "Quite the trade has sprung up in people pretending to take refugees to safety. Then they sell them into slavery or prostitution."

"But…they're children!" I protest, shocked by all of it.

Ciaran shoots me a level stare, as if he's surprised by my naivete. "Yes, Sage. They are."

Outrage whips through me as I catch a glimpse through the cave doors of the little girl with the doll now climbing into the old woman's lap as she's handed food and water by Za'ya. The sound of multiple people speaking Smaragdalfar emanates from the cave.

"Do you think that old woman with the little girl is her grandmother?" I ask Ciaran. "She was…very kind to me on the way here."

Ciaran gives me a look of wry amusement. "I'm glad she was so gentle. That's To'yir. She does constant runs to rescue children. She has about ten rune-blades under those rags she wears."

I look to him with surprise. "Another rune-sorcerer?"

He nods, a smile touching the edge of his lips, a sardonic look in his eyes, as if I've said something inadvertently amusing. "Oh, yes. She is."

"They're scared of me," I tell him, looking toward the cave. "Most of them. Except for To'yir and the little girl."

He gives a short laugh. "Yes, not much scares To'yir."

I shiver from the damp air and hug myself to fight off the gathering chill. Ciaran reaches up to caress my cheek. "Go sit by the fire for a moment. Warm yourself."

Another wagon sounds and Ciaran straightens, his hand falling away.

A bespectacled Keltic man and a Smaragdalfar man ride in on a large wagon, two stout workhorses pulling it. The Kelt holding the reins is about Zeymir's age, with messy brown hair and an intelligent expression. The Smaragdalfar man is young with erect posture, his features long and elegant, his ears pointed. He wears immaculate, deep green Smaragdalfar attire covered in rune markings and edged with black embroidery.

"Who are they?" I ask Ciaran, concerned.

"You're safe, Sage," Ciaran tells me, his tone assured. "They're University professors active in the Resistance—Jules Kristian and Fyon Hawkyyn. They're helping us bring the refugees east."

Ciaran holds up a hand up in greeting and strides over to meet them. "Jules! Fyon!"

Jules and Fyon get down from the wagon and greet Ciaran. The Smaragdalfar Elf narrows his star eyes at me, looking me up and down in apparent confusion as he takes in my Smaragdalfar attire. Jules motions in my direction, and I can make out a cautious "Gardnerian" in their mostly too-low-to-hear conversation, and I imagine Ciaran is explaining my situation.

Jules briefly looks to me with savvy eyes, then nods in silent greeting. He resumes his conversation with Ciaran and Fyon in low tones and gestures toward the wagon, then down the road. The three men open up the back of the wagon and Jules removes two boards across the bottom of the wagon's rear, revealing a secret compartment set back slightly under the wagon's floor, big enough to hide people in.

Thunder sounds overhead, and I glance up at the dim sky. Ciaran returns to my side as Jules and Fyon get back into the wagon. "I'll be back shortly," Ciaran assures me. "We're picking up some grain to load onto the back."

As a ruse, I realize. The real cargo hidden below.

I glance up at the sky worriedly. "It's getting late."

Ciaran spares a quick glance at the afternoon sky and nods. "You'll be safe as long as you stay here. I've strengthened all the wards around this clearing. Even halfway down the road." He gestures toward the cave with a tilt of his head. "And I have a more heavily warded room in there."

This sets my mind whirring.

Another heavily warded bedroom. There may be a search on for me, but it's clear Ciaran is being even more heavily sought after. But why? Why, out of all of them, does Ciaran have the only heavily warded room everywhere he goes, when they're all rune-sorcerers?

What's hunting him?

"Ciaran," Jules calls from where he sits on the wagon's front seat. "We don't have much time."

Ciaran shoots me a brief, conflicted glance, pulls the hood of his cloak over his dark red hair and joins Fyon and Jules, jumping into the back of the wagon and leaving with them.

I watch the carriage disappear into the forest and glance once more at the darkening sky.

CHAPTER TWELVE:
Alfsigr

I linger, warming myself by the outdoor fire as I wait for Ciaran to return, hesitant to go into the cave and spook the children. I watch the sky slowly slide into a deeper gray with trepidation, the fire spitting off sparks, the thunder growing more insistent to the west.

Horse hooves echo in the distance and I rise, my heart picking up speed as I look toward the curve in the dirt road, realizing the sound isn't that of a wagon, but a single rider moving at a fast clip.

Rivyr'el rounds the corner on a breathtaking white mare, his bow and quiver on his back. He rides up the forest-bracketed road like a blizzard roaring in, like a warrior riding into battle, straight up to me.

Rivyr throws himself off the mare in one lithe movement. "What happened?" His tone is hard as a blade.

"My father," I tell him, nauseating shame clenching at my stomach again as I relay the story. "He tracked me to the smithery and came after everyone there. He brought…" My stomach clenches at the thought of Tobias. "He brought my fastmate and some other Mages and I think my people might have torn apart their home, looking for me…"

"They did," Rivyr affirms, danger in his silver eyes.

And now they can't go home. Because of me. Guilt rips at my insides.

"Where is Na'bee?" There's a cold command not just in his tone, but also in his eyes.

"He's inside," I tell him.

"Is he all right?" Rivyr demands.

I nod, barely able to speak. Barely able to picture Na'bee's bruised face without being overcome with outrage. "They're all here," I stammer. "They all got away."

"It's lucky for your father that I wasn't there," Rivyr says icily.

He gives the cave a narrow look, the doors now partially closed to fight off the encroaching chill, but lamplight and movement are visible through the slender opening. He turns back to me. "They're smuggling refugees, aren't they?"

Rivyr looks back at the cave, not waiting for my answer. His figure is blindingly white in the gloom, the glitter over his lids and the multicolored hoops hanging from his pointed ears catching the bonfire's light. He looks around the area, one hand on his hip as if surveying his conquered domain, his usual arrogance seeping back into his expression. "So this is their little hideaway."

I eye him with confusion. "You've never been here?"

He shoots me a derisive look. "Of course not. They enjoy being very stealthy and secretive. I'm too Alfsigr to be a full member of their club, apparently." He cocks one white brow. "But they've brought a Gardnerian here so..." He sniffs, pulling off his bow and quiver and setting them aside, then slides an ivory satchel off his shoulder.

Rivyr throws the edge of his cloak over one shoulder with an elegant flourish and takes a seat beside me, setting his satchel down. "I have a present for you, Lady Mage." He pulls a long, slim package tied with silk string and a small, leather-bound tome out of the satchel. He hands the package to me first.

I unknot the smooth, silk string and the package falls open.

"Oh, Ancient One," I breathe, my affinity snapping toward the mahogany wand as soon as my hand makes contact with it, multicolored whorls of light tendriling around its spiral handle.

Two wands. I have two wands.

Rivyr hands me the small book, smirking. *Elemental Spells* is embossed on the black leather cover in elaborate silver calligraphy.

I inhale sharply. "Oh, Rivyr…"

He smiles crookedly. "Go on then, Light Mage. Have a look."

I flip through the grimoire, looking for light magery spells. I find six toward the end of the book—spells for Camouflage, Color Glamour, Color Bending, Rune-Shaping, Blinding Flash and a violent-sounding spell called Light Strike.

A heady rush of shock ripples through me. "How…how did you possibly get hold of these?" I know the Mage Council keeps tight control over wands and grimoires.

Rivyr makes a sound of disdain. "I'm wealthy, Sagellyn. I can find anything." He tilts his head close, like we're sharing a decadent secret, and points at the light-strike spell with his pale finger. "You can explode things with this one." His finger slides to the Camouflage spell. "And this one…apparently it's known as the 'Chameleon' spell."

"Chameleon?"

He grins. "Color blending. According to your heart's desire, little Light Mage." He flicks his finger toward the grimoire again. "There's variations on it. Practice hard, and you could blend in with your surroundings. Render yourself invisible." Mischief glints in his eyes. "*That* could come in useful."

My hand comes up to cover my mouth. *Real spells. And he bought me a wand.*

"Oh, Rivyr. Thank you."

He dips his head, a glimmer of satisfaction in his sly gaze. "You are most welcome, lovely Sagellyn." He looks back toward the cave, his brow tightening. "Are there children in there?"

I give him a sober look. "About twelve of them."

He takes a deep breath, then shakes his head, as if clearing the darkness away. He pulls a small jute sack out of his cloak pocket. "I've confections. I brought them for Na'bee, but all the little ones can share." He stands in one, graceful movement and moves toward the cave.

My hand rushes up to grab onto his cloak. "Rivyr, I don't know if that's such a good idea. You might scare them."

Rivyr looks at my hand, then at me, his face tightening with offense. "I'll do no such thing."

I stand, letting go of him and gripping the grimoire and the wand to my chest. "Rivyr, don't go in there. Truly. Don't."

He rolls his eyes. "Sweet gods, they're rubbing off on you. Everything so dire all the time." He indicates his handsome self with a sweeping gesture. "Do I look frightening to you?"

"You're Alfsigr," I stress. "They're escapees from the mines. Those children have probably only ever been exposed to Alfsigr soldiers."

Rivyr glares rebelliously at me, his eyes sparking with temper, and starts for the cave.

"Rivyr, *wait!*" I trail after his long stride, running to keep up with him as he makes his way to the cave.

Rivyr reaches the doors, pushes them open and explodes into the room. "Greetings! Would—"

Chaos erupts the second the refugees catch sight of Rivyr. The women and children bolt up, chairs knocked over, food and drink crashing to the floor as the children clumsily flee backward, away from Rivyr. The adults deftly pull rune-blades, and green rune-targets burst to glowing life all over Rivyr's chest. There's a green flash of light that makes me jump as the room charges up with magic, the energy prickling all along my skin.

To'yir, the elderly mage, stands with her hands raised, two elaborate, rotating emerald runes suspended just before her rune-marked palms. Not taking her eyes off Rivyr, she lashes out a phrase in Smaragdalfar and six glowing blades appear, sticking out from each rune circlet.

Za'ya throws herself between Rivyr and all the rune-blades, her arms out, the rune-targets now on her chest. She lets loose with an impassioned stream of Smaragdalfar, sounding like she's urgently making a case for Rivyr's life. To'yir listens as she keeps her eyes pinned on Rivyr with lethal calm.

The children have grown deathly silent, silver eyes bugging out with abject terror as they clutch at the adults. One of the smallest children, the small boy Kol had to coax out of the wagon, starts to sob in big, heaving gasps. The little girl with the doll begins to weep quietly but convulsively, as if she's struggling for breath.

Rivyr is frozen in place. It's like he's in a daze and can't move, his mouth open, his eyes riveted on the little girl with the lash mark across her face.

"*Get out,*" Za'ya orders him over her shoulder.

He doesn't move.

"*Rivyr!*" she grinds out through gritted teeth. "Leave. *Now.*"

Rivyr turns to her, his expression one of pure shock, as the women look to Za'ya in harsh question, keeping their weapons carefully aimed.

Za'ya holds Rivyr's gaze for a split second. When she speaks again, her voice is firm. "Rivyr'el. You *must* go."

Rivyr takes one last look at the little girl with the scarred face, then abruptly turns and flees past me, leaving a trail of devastation on the air.

For a moment I'm bolted in place, stunned by the force of their reaction to him. I realize, even more clearly, how nightmarishly monstrous the Alfsigr military must be toward the people of the sublands.

Za'ya is everywhere at once, speaking in a stream of Smaragdalfar as the women lower their weapons and To'yir vanishes the suspended rune-blades with a flick of her hands. Za'ya's voice is firm and measured as she motions repeatedly toward where Rivyr went as children cry and women debate with her. Za'ya continues to make a case, probably in support of Rivyr's life, to To'yir. To'yir listens, then eventually inclines her head and nods at Za'ya, as if guardedly convinced.

The woman who jabbed me in the wagon casts a dark look in my direction, points the tip of her rune-blade toward me and lets loose to Za'ya with a torrent of angry Smaragdalfar. I realize I need to go, too.

I leave the cave and rush down the hill, my stomach tightly knotted. My eyes search for Rivyr'el everywhere, but he's disappeared. I make my way past the fire as the sounds of weeping, traumatized children and women locked in fierce debate recede into the distance.

"Rivyr?" I search the cloud-darkened woods all around for a sign of Rivyr, circling around the area. Finally, I catch sight of a flash of ivory through the woods, just past the horse stables.

I slip into the small clearing and find Wyla and Kol, the huge Elfhollen, watching Rivyr gravely, a lantern in Kol's broad hand.

Rivyr has his back to us. He's facing the dense woods, his head down. Wyla eyes me with concern as I approach, and pats the air to caution me. I slow to a stop.

"Za'ya was right," Rivyr says without turning around, his

voice low and deadened. "About *everything*." He murmurs something in Alfsigr, his tone vicious. Then he reaches down, pulls a rune-knife from his belt and begins slashing his long, elaborately braided and gem-decorated hair off with silent fury.

"What are you doing?" I ask, shocked.

"I'm going to offer myself up to them as a guard. Then I'm going to escort those Smaragdalfar children across the desert." Rivyr's tone is low and dangerous as he jaggedly slices off another lock. He turns to me, silver eyes blazing, fist tight around his rune-marked knife. "And I'm going to cut down anyone who tries to harm them."

We watch as he violently chops the rest of his hair off, lock after lock, his face a mask of grim resolve, until there is nothing left but short, uneven spikes of white.

We silently watch as Rivyr pulls his white tunic off, his eyes flashing, and throws it to the ground. The white of his skin is startling—so pale, like new-fallen snow. I avert my eyes for a moment, flushing at the sight of his bare chest, his nipples exposed, silver rings outrageously pierced through them. Men are never unclothed like this in Gardneria, especially not in front of young women.

I watch Rivyr sidelong as he pulls off his earrings one by one. His pendants, bracelets, every ring, throwing a small fortune to the ground. When he's finished, he bends down to retrieve them and holds them out to Wyla.

"Take all this," he tells her, his voice hard. "Sell it all and give the money to Zeymir to help the children get out."

"You can't go with them," I gently reason. "You'll draw the Alfsigr Elves right to them!"

His gaze bores into me. "No. I won't. You're going to glamour my color."

Wyla's and Kol's heads whip toward me. "Is that a grimoire in your hand?" Wyla asks, her voice rough with shock.

Rivyr moves toward me as I try to adjust to his partial nudity. "Glamour me, Sagellyn Gaffney," he says, silver eyes blazing. "Change my color."

I gape at Rivyr. "Change your actual color?" I sputter, disbelieving. "I've never even used a wand—"

"Then *start now*." He bites off each word, his gaze relentless. "Are you going to go on being powerless?" He steps closer to me. "Or are you going to be a *Light Mage*?"

I hold his stare, feeling as if I'm on the cusp of something dangerous and unpredictable.

Rivyr picks up his discarded tunic in his fist and holds it out to me, like a dare. "Start *now*, Light Mage. Test the Color Glamour spell on this."

I hold his glare for a long moment, then glance at the dark wand and grimoire in my hands, my heart thudding against my chest. I open the grimoire and flip through it until I locate the Color Glamour spell. There's an incantation, along with instructions to pull a color through my lines as I recite it.

"I don't know how to pronounce this spell," I tell Rivyr.

"Then practice," he tells me.

I swallow, biting my lip, and come down to one knee. Rivyr drops his tunic in front of me and I place the grimoire on the ground, holding it open as Kol sets his lantern down beside me.

I take a deep breath and pull the color that's easiest for me through my affinity lines.

Purple.

Then I place the tip of my wand on Rivyr's pale tunic and stumble through the unfamiliar words of the spell, crafted from the Ancient Tongue.

Nothing.

I try every variation of inflections and pronunciations I can think of, methodically going through each possibility.

"Forget everything around you," Rivyr says. "Focus on a color."

I take a deep breath, then another as I close my eyes and concentrate with all my might, but still...nothing.

Disheartened, I let out a frustrated breath just as a warm buzz kicks up against my ankle. I straighten in surprise—it's been years since I felt something from the wand Gwynn stole from her father's armory.

I reach under my skirts and pull the white wand out of my boot, a subtle vibration emanating from it. Barely perceptible. Newly alert, I press the mahogany wand into my rune-blade's belt-sheath, sit back and rearrange Rivyr's chalk-white tunic over my lap.

Wyla is eyeing the white wand in my hand dubiously. "I thought you said that wand was useless."

"That's what I was told," I say, gripping the wand's spiraling handle. "But it's worth a try." I take a deep breath and set the tip of the white wand on Rivyr's tunic, then close my eyes and concentrate.

Luxurious purple fills the back of my mind, loosening my muscles, as I sound out the words of the spell.

Nothing.

Pushing back a jagged disappointment, I try several more pronunciations of the three words to no effect, then attempt different tones, as if I'm singing the spell.

Nothing.

Stubbornly determined, I think back to the fasting spell, the lulling, shushing sounds of the Ancient Tongue. I soften the consonants of the glamour spell to a nub and try again. And again. And again.

Then I try emphasizing the first syllable of each word of the spell and drop all of the consonants, mimicking my memory of the cadence of the fasting spells.

The wand's handle tingles against my palm, and like the effortless flow of warm water, the violet slides right through me, down my arm and toward the wand.

Wyla gasps, and I open my eyes to find color bleeding out of the wand's tip and into the tunic. My heart pounds hot in my chest. "Holy Ancient One," I marvel with a spark of light-headed excitement. "Sweet lord, Rivyr. I'm doing actual light magery."

Rivyr's eyes glitter with determination. "That's it, Light Mage. Push *all* your magic into it."

I force a few shuddering breaths and close my eyes. I fill my lines with violet and can feel the wand practically yanking the glorious, forbidden color straight through me.

When I open my eyes again, Rivyr's entire tunic is deep purple.

"Holy hells," Wyla spits out, eyes wide. "Holy *all the hells.*"

I look up, stunned, and Rivyr grins. "There's a reversal spell, too," he tells me, flicking his finger toward the grimoire. "See if it works."

I glance down the page to find the reversal spell. After a number of false starts, I hit on the right pronunciation and can feel the wand pulling the color back into itself and through me in a warm, satisfying rush as the tunic returns to its original ivory. Reflexively, I breathe in deep, filling myself with the pulsating violet, everything around me momentarily tinted purple.

Everyone's eyes have gone wide.

"Oh, Sagellyn," Wyla breathes out, and I'm pulled out of my sensual color haze by the dire way they're all looking at me. Worried, I glance down to find my normal Gardnerian emerald glimmer is gone…replaced by a glowing, bright purple sheen.

"Holy Ancient One…am I purple?" I ask, stunned, an edge of fear riding along the question.

"Quite a bit purple," Wyla says, with no small measure of concern.

With shaking hands, I pull my hair forward and feel myself blanch. It's purple, too. "Oh, no." I turn to Wyla. "My eyes?"

Wyla swallows nervously. "Purple."

I pull my rune-blade from its sheath, look into its gleaming, reflective surface, and give a hard start.

I'm completely purple. Vivid purple skin, violet eyes and hair that's every shade of purple.

I frantically try the reversal spell on myself, but the color refuses to budge, which only ramps up my apprehension.

Mouth open, I gape at Rivyr, who seems oblivious to my screaming purpleness. Kol has launched into a low conversation with him in Ishkart, and the light of an idea seems to ignite in Rivyr's eyes, his jaw tightening with what looks like renewed determination. He turns and holds his forearm out to me.

"Sagellyn," he says calmly. "Glamour me gray. Like Kol. Like an Elfhollen."

I look at him, overwhelmed. "Are you sure, Rivyr? A tunic is one thing, but I might permanently turn you gray. Look what I just did to myself!"

"Don't you see?" Rivyr insists. "I can protect the children if you glamour me, without drawing the Alfsigr right to us."

I look at Kol, stunned. The huge Elfhollen man is leaning against a tree, his muscular arms crossed in front of himself, his silver eyes narrowed appraisingly at Rivyr'el. He and Rivyr'el converse briefly in Ishkart again, Wyla joining in, her brow tense. Wyla glances at me, then looks back to Kol and nods her head in carefully considered agreement.

They all turn to me as Kol pulls up his sleeve and shows me his rugged forearm. "Match this color, Light Mage," he says, his voice weighty and deep.

"Are you sure this is a good idea?" I ask Kol. He nods, his

expression betraying no doubt. I turn to Rivyr, heart thumping. "What if I can't change you back?"

"I don't care," he says with icy defiance.

Rattled, I practice a few more times on the tunic, turning it several different shades of gray, then pulling the color out, half expecting my skin to start shimmering silvery-gray, but the violet on me stays alarmingly stuck.

Rivyr holds his taut forearm out to me. I eye him, unsure, my heart pounding as I tense myself against the slight tremble running through my body.

I place the tip of the wand on Rivyr's skin and then take a deep breath, filling my mind with slate gray and sounding out the spell before I can reconsider.

A warm vibration kicks up along the wand's handle as a foggy gray comes to life inside me, like gathering mist, rising and rising. The ashen color seeps out of the wand and curls over Rivyr's forearm like smoke, tendriling up his arm, over his chest, face, ears, hair—evening out and solidifying until the whole of Rivyr'el Talonir is glamoured storm gray.

I blink at him like he's a mirage, stunned that I've actually managed to work this spell.

Rivyr holds up his hand and turns his forearm over, inspecting it, his jaw tight. He looks like he's stopped breathing. He turns to me, his eyes now pale gray, his skin the color of dark storm clouds. He slams his fist onto his chest, dips his head and murmurs what sounds like a formal show of gratitude in High Alfsigr.

I'm overcome by his fierce gratitude. And by my budding power.

"Sagellyn," Wyla says excitedly, a sudden spark in her eyes, as if she's lit up by a bold idea and can barely contain it.

I glance at her questioningly, and she gives me a significant look. "You could glamour the children."

My eyes widen. "What? You mean…glamour them gray?"

She nods as Rivyr and Kol exchange a weighted look, both silently deliberating the ramifications of this.

"You could glamour them to look Elfhollen," Wyla says, her tone ignited with the bold idea. "Then they'd escape the notice of the Alfsigr Elves as well."

"Would the children definitely have a better chance of survival if they looked Elfhollen?" I ask them. "The adults, too?"

Wyla holds my astonished gaze. "Yes," she says, almost breathless with the possibility. "Yes, Sagellyn, they would have a *much* better chance of survival."

"Holy Ancient One," I breathe out.

Wyla turns to Kol. "Get Za'ya."

CHAPTER THIRTEEN:
Light Mage

Za'ya and To'yir stride into the forest clearing, Kol trailing behind.

Rivyr straightens up at the sight of them, his expression determined as he strides forward to meet Za'ya and comes to a stop before her. He stares at her for one long moment, tension mounting on the air between them. I flinch in surprise as Rivyr drops to one knee in front of her, slams his fist over his heart, and lowers his forehead in a posture of formal supplication, then lets loose with a stream of low, beseeching Alfsigr.

Za'ya goes very still and listens as Rivyr continues on in a formal cadence without any sign of stopping. There's a fierce, relentless quality to it, like he's doing penance for a crime.

"Rivyr'el," Za'ya finally says, cutting in. "It is enough."

Rivyr doesn't budge as he renews his stream of contrition. Then his voice breaks and he starts to sob, low and choking.

Za'ya lowers herself to his level, her hand coming to his shoulder. "Rivyr'el," she says, "I forgive you."

Rivyr grows silent, breathing hard as he lifts glassy eyes to hers. "I pledge myself to you, Za'yalor Shi'mar Nyvor. I pledge my life to you. To you and to the defense of your people." He lapses back into Alfsigr, his head dropping down once more.

"Rivyr'el," Za'ya insists, hands on both his shoulders now.

"I was wrong," he tells her, his voice rough with emotion. "I was wrong."

Za'ya rises and looks down at him for a long moment, hands on her hips, as if taking his measure. Finally, Rivyr lowers his arm and glances up at her, his cheeks slick with tears.

Za'ya holds her hand out to him, her arm rigidly straight. "I forgive you and accept your pledge of fealty. You will now rise, Rivyr'el Talonir, as my second."

Rivyr takes her hand and rises to his feet just as the clomping of horses' hooves sound. I catch sight of Ciaran's crimson hair through the trees as he rides in on the wagon, Jules and Fyon now absent. A heady anticipation floods through me at the sight of him.

Za'ya's hands are on Rivyr's shoulders as she peers deeply into his eyes. "You have finally found a life worthy of you, hm?" She looks him over. "So, you are glamoured to appear Elfhollen." She turns to me. "Your doing?" She looks me up and down. "Well, clearly so, as you are now violet."

Heart fluttering, I nod, clutching the white wand and the grimoire in my sweaty palms.

Za'ya's eyes flick toward the wand and the grimoire. She shakes her head and makes what seems like a sign of blessing over her heart. She kisses her fist, looks briefly at the sky, then back at me. "*Oo'na* works in mysterious ways, *ti'a'lin'el*."

Ciaran strides into the clearing and our eyes fly to each other, my heart picking up speed. His mouth falls open as he takes in my altered hue. He glances at gray Rivyr, then back to me. "You can do this?"

I nod, overcome. "And…perhaps more."

"I'm going East with them," Rivyr tells Ciaran, gesturing toward the cave with his chin, a storm of emotion in his voice. "As an armed escort. Across the desert."

Ciaran makes a rough sound of surprise, his gaze welded to Rivyr for a moment. Then he takes hold of the Elf's shoulder with a firm grip, leans in and touches his forehead to Rivyr's, murmuring emotionally in Smaragdalfar. When Ciaran pulls away, tears are streaming down Rivyr's fierce, gray face.

Wyla's voice bursts forth. "The children would have an easier time escaping if they looked Elfhollen, too." Everyone goes silent and turns toward her.

Za'ya gives her a sharp look, rife with conflict, and I immediately feel chastened and unsure about Wyla's plan. I know Za'ya wants a world where the Smaragdalfar can exist as they are—not glamoured, not in hiding, but able to celebrate who they are and establish a new homeland. And part of me doesn't want to be involved in altering any of the Smaragdalfar one bit.

Za'ya sets her sharp gaze on me. "Can this glamour be reversed?" she asks.

I hold up the grimoire like a weak offering. "Yes. It can."

"Show her," Rivyr puts in, stepping forward, holding out his arm.

I flip through the grimoire and hastily find the reversal spell. Pressing the wand tip to the taut skin of Rivyr's forearm, I breathe in deep, concentrate and pull the gray toward me, the smoky color briefly clouding my vision as Rivyr's skin returns to a glistening marble white. We both turn and look to Za'ya, whose expression is full of conflict.

"Turn him back," Za'ya commands, her voice tight. "Show me you can do this many times."

I push the color back out, washing Rivyr in the steely hue once more. Then I turn him ivory and back to gray as Rivyr patiently waits, his eyes calm on Za'ya.

"Turn yourself back to Gardnerian green," Za'ya challenges me, her arms crossed before her.

"Um…well, the purple is a bit…stuck on me," I tell her,

feeling like I'm in a surreal dream. "My affinity lines latched onto it." Za'ya's brow lifts with some concern. "But gray seems to be easy."

Za'ya studies me for a moment, then turns to To'yir, and I can see the wheels of her sharp mind turning as she confers with the old woman in hushed Smaragdalfar. To'yir peers at me, her eyes narrowed in appraisal.

To'yir walks over to me and takes one of my hands in hers, studying the fastlines, running a coarse, emerald-patterned thumb over one of the black marks. I flinch at her touch, shame and despair flaring inside me as I'm reminded of my bond to Tobias. Despite my discomfort, To'yir holds on, nodding to herself, as if reading my life story in the lines.

She speaks to me in Smaragdalfar, pausing occasionally so Za'ya can translate.

"If they find you," Za'ya translates, "they will send you back to him, yes?"

Raw anger slashes through me, and I nod stiffly.

To'yir's wizened hand comes to rest on my shoulder. She looks intently at me as she talks.

"She tells you," Za'ya says, "light magery is a rare magic. If you do this thing for the Smaragdalfar, and your people find out, there will be a death warrant placed on your head by both the Gardnerians and the Alfsigr militaries. They will track you, with stronger magery than you have yet seen. And if they find you, they will question you and torture you. If you are lucky, they will kill you."

Her words are so final, and for a moment, I'm pinned by To'yir's unforgiving stare, forced to look the terrible danger of this in the eye. But then the image of the little Smaragdalfar girl clutching her doll fills my mind, followed by the terrified faces of the other children.

I return To'yir's savage look. "Is it true? Would the children have an easier time surviving if they looked Elfhollen?"

To'yir's intense expression doesn't waver. "Yes," she says in heavily accented Common Tongue.

My heart thumps hard in its chest. *This is what it means*, I realize. *This is what it means to truly be like Galliana, and fight for justice and freedom.*

"Sage." Ciaran is at my side now, his hand coming to the small of my back. "You don't have to do this unless you're sure."

I look up into his fiery green eyes. The shrill voice of my fear clamors out alarm bells and dire warning in the back of my mind, but the thought of the little girl in the wagon overrules it once more.

"I'm sure," I tell him, my voice full of finality. Like a line being stepped quietly over, the ground behind the line falling away into oblivion.

Ciaran looks momentarily overcome, then pulls me into a tight embrace, his lips pressing to my temple. He leans in close, his forehead to mine, his hands caressing my cheeks, and murmurs something in Smaragdalfar that is so impassioned, I understand his gratitude even without a translation. I look deep into his eyes, the rest of the world momentarily a haze, the two of us perfectly aligned.

Allied.

"Put the tip of your wand on this stone," Za'ya translates for To'yir. I step back from Ciaran and look to the old woman as she holds out a black, circular stone, its surface etched with an intricate, looping ward that glows a bright green. Carefully following To'yir's instructions, I press my wand to the stone as she pulls an emerald rune-stylus from her tunic pocket and touches its tip to the white wand.

"The stone will hold the reversal spell," Za'ya explains. "If you do this, Sagellyn, To'yir can remove this glamour once we come to safety."

I nod, feeling heartened.

"Now sound out the spell," Za'ya translates, and I comply, the stone's glowing green rune momentarily brightening to a golden green. To'yir pulls her rune-stylus away, looking satisfied, then pockets the stone and gives me a calculating smile. She gestures for me to accompany her as she starts for the hill.

I follow Za'ya and To'yir to the cave.

I glamour the refugees one at a time, changing their clothing to a stormy gray shade and giving them the false appearance of slate-colored skin, hair and eyes. As they approach me, each of the children takes in the sight of my new purple coloring with equal parts trepidation and fascination.

Za'ya brings Na'bee forward, and they both sit down before me. Za'ya's lip is trembling, her face tight, as if she's fighting back tears.

Na'bee looks to his mother with concern. "It is only a glamour, *Ma'mya*," he comforts her. "It will not change who we are. And it is only for a little while."

A hard, bitter laugh bursts from Za'ya as a single tear slides down her cheek. Her lips move, like she's wrestling with difficult thoughts, but then she takes a deep breath and her expression lightens. She smiles at Na'bee with bottomless affection and bares her forearm to me.

"Just do it, Sagellyn," she says, her expression turning brittle. "We will build a world where this will *never* be needed again."

I glamour Za'ya, then Na'bee. Za'ya looks momentarily devastated—not when she views her own gray arm, which she accepts with an almost aloof, removed curiosity, but when she takes in the sight of her gray-skinned son. Zeymir comes over and gently takes her hands, speaking softly to her. Za'ya swallows, refusing to look at him, then seems to gather herself. She gets up and walks off with Zeymir, who continues talking to her in low, soothing Smaragdalfar, one arm embracing Za'ya and his other hand on Na'bee's head, the child leaning against his father as if Zeymir is a tree standing steadfastly rooted in a whipping storm.

The hostile woman who jabbed me in the wagon comes forward, fury swimming in her eyes. She doesn't bother sitting down, but merely thrusts out her hand, like she's striking something. As the ashen color washes over her emerald skin, I feel like I'm committing a grave offense and aiding her at the same time.

When I finish, the woman pulls her arm away and glares at me as if I've burned her, then stalks away. Her reaction stings, but I try to understand her fury. No one should have to hide their true self to be safe.

The little girl with the doll, who I'm told is named Nil'ya, is one of the last to come forward. When I finish changing her coloring to gray, she turns her arm this way and that, eyes widening with surprise. Hesitantly, Nil'ya holds her doll out to me and asks me something in Smaragdalfar, her small voice barely a whisper. Despair tightens my gut as I realize what she wants me to do. I force a smile, place my wand on the doll's rough cloth and glamour the doll to a uniform storm gray.

"So, you're going with them?" I ask Wyla as we load packs of dense travel bread into the wagon.

They'll be leaving before nightfall, all of the refugees. No true chance to rest. Za'ya, Zeymir, Na'bee and Wyla are going with them, and my heart twists at the thought of losing them all.

Wyla pushes a small crate flush with another just beyond it and wipes her hands clean.

"Look at what you have done," Wyla says, perhaps sensing the dark turn of my thoughts. She flicks her hand toward the now-gray refugees sitting around the outdoor fire, eating a quick meal of black bread and cheese. "Before, the chances…" Wyla shakes her head and gives me a sober look. "Not so good." She tilts her head and clicks her tongue. "Now? Perhaps. Perhaps we make it."

There's a bustle of activity all around us. Kol is preparing the horses. Jules and Fyon have returned with an additional wagon and a pile of documents that Jules hands to Za'ya. The children are being bundled into blankets and led to the wagons, where they sit and wait with wide, expectant eyes.

Ciaran is loading crates of rune-weapons into the sides of the wagons. The two of us will be staying behind so that Ciaran can create more rune-weapons and prepare an underground armory for the Resistance here in the Western Realm. After that, we'll find a way to rescue my sisters so that we can all travel together to the Eastern Realm.

Rivyr's packing up his ivory mare for the journey, tying a saddlebag tight, his bow and quiver strapped to his back. He catches my eye, an arch smile lifting his lips, and abandons his task for the moment, coming over to me. He looks me up and down with exaggerated appreciation, one dark gray brow cocked. "I thought you were beautiful before," he says, "but I absolutely adore all this purple clinging to you."

I breathe out a resigned laugh. A quick intimacy has sprung up between us, and I'm surprised to realize that I don't want to see him go. "It's so odd to see you gray," I tell him, smiling. "Odder still to see you without so much jewelry…and glitter."

Rivyr shoots me a flirtatious look and laughs. "When you join me in Noi lands, you can glamour me into some spectacular rainbow-hued thing."

Another laugh bursts from me at the outrageous idea, and

Rivyr laughs, too, his gaze turning warm with affection. "I look forward to getting to know each other better, Sagellyn." He grins rakishly, but then his expression grows pensive. He reaches into his pocket and holds out his *Zalyn'or* necklace, the Alfsigr pendant catching a glint of the nearby firelight.

"I won't be needing this," he tells me with a defiant lift of his chin, glancing toward the refugees. "I rather like being a rebel." He looks back at me, his smile broadening, and I'm bolstered by it. "But *you*. Perhaps there may come a time when tamping down fear or some other emotion could be of some use."

I take it, watching it turn and gleam as it catches the firelight. I slide it in my pocket, struggling to contain my emotions. Everything is changing so fast.

Rivyr takes a lock of my violet hair in his storm-gray fingers. "I knew black was not your color, *ti'a*." I grin at this, and he breaks into a wider smile, still idly playing with my hair. "We are a couple of cultural outcasts, are we not?"

I nod, tearing up and laughing at the same time. "We are."

"It's good though, *ti'a'lin,* to leave it all behind." He leans in toward me and lightly touches his forehead to mine, gently pulling me close in the traditional Smaragdalfar farewell, his hands caressing the sides of my face. "You will save your sisters, Sagellyn. Of this, I am sure. And you and Ciaran…" He pulls back and shoots me a look full of wicked mischief as his knowing eyes dart to where Ciaran is loading the wagon. "Perhaps he will tag along?"

My cheeks flush at this, but I'm distracted by To'yir, who has appeared beside us. She looks up at Rivyr and launches into what sounds like firm direction in the Alfsigr tongue. He nods solemnly, pulling out his Alfsigr rune-stylus and showing it to her.

Little Nil'ya hides behind To'yir, the child peeking out at Rivyr with obvious fear. Noticing her distress, Rivyr lowers himself to the child's level and says a choppy phrase in Sma-ragdalfar as Ciaran joins us.

Nil'ya blinks at Rivyr, her brow knitting in confusion.

"*Silhe'lk* is 'frighten,'" Ciaran corrects Rivyr, forming the Smaragdalfar word deep in his throat, looking amused. "You said *sile'lk*." The words sound identical to my ears. "You just told her you're sorry for giving her a small fish."

Rivyr coughs out a sound of frustration, takes a deep breath and tries again. Nil'ya's eyes widen, and she looks to Ciaran, then To'yir. The old woman's mouth twitches into a grin.

"What did I say now?" Rivyr asks with a resigned sigh, rocking back on his heels.

"You are very sorry for giving her an old fish," Ciaran says evenly as he stands, arms crossed, fighting off his own smile.

Rivyr takes a deep breath and tries an entirely new phrase. The child stares at him for a moment, then lets out a small, bubbling giggle that she quickly squelches.

"What now?" Rivyr groans.

"You don't want to know," Ciaran says, and I wonder, not for the first time, at his fluent grasp of Smaragdalfar.

But the child is smiling now, peering shyly at Rivyr. The Elf pulls a small sack of sweets from his pocket, opens it and holds it out to Nil'ya. She eyes him with trepidation, but then her hand darts into the bag, withdrawing a candy. She pops the sweet into her mouth, her newly slate-gray eyes lighting up at the bright flavor. She grins widely at Rivyr.

Rivyr coughs out a laugh and seems quite overcome for a moment, tears glistening in his dark gray eyes. Then he looks to me, his own smile going as wide as the sky.

Na'bee runs over to me as I watch the other children climb into the hidden compartment of the largest wagon. I kneel down when he reaches me, and we throw our arms around each other.

"I'm so sorry, Na'bee," I tell him, my voice breaking. "I'm sorry you got hurt because of me."

He pulls back and gazes at me solemnly, his little hands firm on my shoulders. "I am a rune-warrior, Sagellyn Gaffney. It is a great *nis'vir* to protect you." He puts both hands on my cheeks, murmuring in Smaragdalfar, then presses his forehead to mine. He kisses my forehead and I kiss his in return.

"Be safe, Na'bee," I tell him, my heart wrenching.

His eyes brighten and he smiles. "I will see you in the dragon lands. And your sisters, too!"

A laugh bursts forth from me, Na'bee's enthusiasm momentarily making every last daunting thing seem possible. "My sisters will like you very much," I tell him, hope gaining some fragile ground in my chest.

I stand as Zeymir and Kol approach, Na'bee happily ensconcing himself between them.

Zeymir clasps my arm warmly. "We will meet again, Sagellyn," he says with a look of unflappable assurance that I want to hold onto and never let go. I thank him, and he kisses my head, murmuring farewell in Ishkart. Huge Kol extends his hand and grasps my forearm, which I assume is the Elfhollen way.

Wyla sidles up to Zeymir's side, leading a speckled stallion. She snaps her finger into the hilt of the rune-blade I have sheathed at my side—the blade she gave me.

"So, Light Mage," she says with a wry smile, glancing at the blade and the two wands pressed into the sheath next to it. "You are quite armed now." Her eyes glitter with approval. "It is better this way. Better than when we first met."

I nod and hold her stare, my chest knotting up over her leaving, but I don't move to hug her goodbye. I know that Wyla doesn't like being touched.

"It is a good first step," she tells me, grinning as she mounts her horse, "when you stop crying and start planning how to impale your enemies." She points at me with mock ferocity. "I want to see that Light Strike spell when we meet in Noi lands, Sagellyn Gaffney." She grins devilishly and snorts a laugh, and I can't help but smile back at her.

To'yir bids me farewell next. She pulls my head down to hers, pressing her forehead to mine, murmuring seriously in Smaragdalfar for a moment. "Be brave, Sagellyn," she says in halting Common Tongue. I bite at my lip and nod, and she pats my cheek and makes a clicking sound of approval.

And then Za'ya is before me, and my heart gives a hard twist, both of us tearing up.

She reaches in her tunic pocket and hands me her slim statue of the Smaragdalfar goddess, *Oo'na*—the statue from her altar.

"No," I say, waving the gift away, overwhelmed by the gesture. "I can't. It's too important to you."

She continues to hold it out insistently. "Which is why I am giving it to you, *ti'a*."

Touched by her kindness, I relent and take it from her, clasping my fist around it. Za'ya's hands come around to cup my fist, and I look up at her through a sheen of tears.

"*El'iyon sier'vir'en*, Sagellyn," Za'ya tells me, smiling. "Life is the Resistance, no? We resist, and we work. And we make a new world, hm?" I throw my arms around her, and she kisses my cheek, then wipes the tears from my eyes with her thumb. She pulls her forehead toward mine, her hand cupping the back of my head as she murmurs what sounds like a Smaragdalfar blessing, then kisses my forehead.

I take a shuddering breath as Za'ya and Ciaran help the last of the refugees into the secret compartment under the floorboard of the wagon, as I clutch at the statue of *Oo'na* like a talisman and pray to the Ancient One for their safety.

Little Nil'ya is one of the last to climb in, and I lift my hand to her in farewell. The child turns, clutching her gray doll, and gives me one last, long look before she disappears inside.

I watch them leave, Za'ya, Zeymir and Na'bee driving one wagon, To'yir, Fyon and Jules driving the other. Rivyr leads the caravan on his ivory mare and Wyla brings up the rear, hoisting her rune-blade to me in a final salute as the wagons turn and they're all swallowed up by the woods.

Tears streak down my face as I listen to the sounds of the horses fading to silence.

Ciaran's hand lightly touches my shoulder, and I turn. It's so quiet now, the only sound the crackling, spitting fire and gentle night sounds of the forest.

"We should go in, Sage," Ciaran tells me, looking up at the sky. "It's almost nightfall."

CHAPTER FOURTEEN:
Wards

I follow Ciaran into the common area at the mouth of the cave. The ghostly imprint of the crowd lingers—scattered mugs, crumbs coating the low table and stone counters. We make our way down a narrow corridor lit by glowing emerald runes. The air cools as we walk, filled with the smell of clean, water-washed stone.

There are runes suspended everywhere in the network of caves, marking the stone walls in glowing shades of green, gold and blue. Some are motionless, while others rotate lazily. Some are small as beetles, others large as millstones.

I follow Ciaran past a smithery built right into the cave. Long, broad iron pipes rise from the smith stoves through the cave ceiling to vent the heat. The flames of the three stoves are generated not from burning wood, but from rotating green runes, working against each other like gears with flames cupped in their center. Their blasting heat suffuses me as we pass.

There are three rune-swords lying on a table, breathtaking in their appearance. Their blades are made up of small emerald runes, all of the glowing marks rotating.

"What are those swords?" I ask Ciaran.

"Varg blades," he tells me. "The only blades that can slay demons. And they can only be wielded by Smaragdalfar."

There's another arching side entrance leading to what appears to be a rune-laboratory. Grimoires are scattered on tables and runic diagrams are printed in a careful hand on half-rolled pieces of parchment. Styluses of all shapes and sizes are scattered on every surface, and there are rows of glowing rune-stones on shelves around the room, again a mix of green, gold and blue. The blue runes are Noi runes—which means they must have contact with a Noi rune-sorceress. *Are they working with the Vu Trin soldiers?*

We pass multiple weapons caches, with swords and every type of bladed weapon imaginable jammed into large vaults in the rock, the rune-magery worked into the weapons glowing. They have a full weapons factory down here, I realize—and enough weapons to supply a sizable army.

We continue further into the caves until we come to a rune-curtain set into the wall.

Ciaran slides it open, and I step into a darkened, other-worldly space that's even more spectacular than his room back at the smithery.

The curtain falls shut behind us, and it's like I'm once again being enveloped in a constellation of runes. I circle around, taking in the spectacular runic designs on the dark tapestries, on the rug beneath my feet and suspended everywhere in the air like arrested raindrops.

Ciaran slumps his long, muscular form back against a tapestry-covered wall, multiple suspended runes passing right through him and raying out light, the green glow highlighting the hard planes of his face. He's quiet and constrained, but I can read it in his eyes—what he's held in check while saying goodbye to Zeymir and Za'ya and the others.

"You're worried for them, aren't you?" I ask with an uncomfortable sense of foreboding.

His dark expression doesn't budge. "The Alfsigr are very powerful, and the Zalyn'or necklaces give their hierarchy complete control. They have spies and allies all over the desert lands. If anyone even so much as suspects so many of them are glamoured Smaragdalfar…"

"Rivyr is with them," I remind him.

Ciaran nods stiffly, holding himself bowstring rigid. He gives me a poignant look, as if trying to convey all that he isn't telling me in his stricken gaze.

"Ciaran…" I pull him into an embrace, and his arms wrap tightly around me, his forehead falling to my shoulder.

"I'm tired of saying goodbye," Ciaran rasps out, clinging to me for a long moment, and I understand his anguish, my heart wrenching for him.

"I'm here," I attempt to reassure him. "You're not alone this time."

Eventually, his grip on me loosens, but his hands stay pressed to my back as he pivots his head against my shoulder, his lips brushing against the base of my neck. His warm breath hovers just above my skin as the tension between us changes, morphing from comfort to…something else. Something as charged as the runes.

"We're truly alone," Ciaran says in a low whisper, as if this moment between us is suspended and fragile as glass, my breath and his highlighted by the stillness of the cave as everything within me contracts into one gleaming shard of desire.

Ciaran presses his soft lips against my neck, making me shudder. He pulls back, his eyes glazed with a sudden want that heightens my awareness of his beauty—the startling green of his eyes, his red hair gleaming black in the verdant light.

"You're almost too beautiful to look at," he tells me, caressing a lock of my hair. I look down to see that my skin is shimmering a luminous violet, even in the green light, as if I'm lit up from within. He skims his finger along the skin at the edge of my tunic's collar, his touch making me shiver. "It's like you're coated in gem dust. You were beautiful before, but…this color is so lovely on you."

"My affinity is so drawn to purple." I give him a wry look. "The most forbidden of all the colors."

He smiles at this then brings his lips to the base of my neck and kisses me again. "I have an affinity for *you*." He trails kisses up my neck, my jaw, his lips now a fraction from mine. "*You're* my forbidden color."

I breathe out a delighted laugh which is enveloped in his kiss, a kiss that starts out sultry and lingering and soon takes a more heated turn, our self-control rapidly shredding as his tongue curls around mine. I caress his hard body, a bright thrill igniting all through my lines, our hands exploring familiar and then exciting, unfamiliar territory on each other, our breathing growing erratic as all the boundaries between us begin to fray.

"I want you," Ciaran tells me, his green eyes incandescent, his sorcery lighting up my lines and drawing me in. "I'd never even kissed anyone before you." His jaw shifts, as if he's having trouble finding the right words. "Everything has been a struggle. For *years*. And now…all I want…is to have you." He swallows, his eyes tightening. "And you're a fasted Gardnerian."

Ciaran steps back, blinking hard, as if breaking a spell. His whole body radiates a pent-up desire, and it makes me want him even more.

"We have to stop," he says.

"I know," I say, not wanting him to stop.

His eyes rake over me before he briefly closes them and shakes his head, his skin flushed. "The fastlines…it's not safe for you. And…there are more reasons than that to stop."

I know he's right, that we have to stop. And so I take a few steps back, smoothing down my clothes, trying to still my pounding heart.

Ciaran sits down on the bed—the only bed in the room. He looks at me, his eyes flickering with pent-up desire as he huffs out a hard breath and rubs the back of his neck. "I need to stay here now," he tells me, gesturing loosely around the room. "Now that it's nightfall, I can't leave. You have some freedom here, though, since the property and the caves are warded. Those wards will take care of any type of search your people could send out."

"But you have to stay here?" I ask, confused.

He nods, his expression abruptly turning guarded.

"Why are your rooms so heavily warded?" I ask, wanting answers to all the questions that have been building up inside me since we met. "And why do you suddenly need to hide yourself behind high-grade military wards?"

His jaw ticks as he holds my stare, his silence a wall against my words.

"You're all rune-sorcerers," I say, trying to work it out. "Za'ya. Na'bee. Zeymir. Wyla. And you. Yet you're the only one with a warded room. And not just warded—warded against a demon army."

Ciaran's gaze darkens. "How could you *possibly* know that?"

"I've studied military grimoires. Quite a few of them. I have a friend whose father ran a Mage Guard armory." I take a step toward him. "Ciaran. Please tell me what's going on."

But he just shakes his head. "I can't tell you, Sage. I want to, but I shouldn't. Truly. Not until we go east. In case…"

"In case what?"

Ciaran's expression grows pained. "In case they find us. It's safer if you don't know."

"Know what?"

He holds his silence.

Stubborn defiance bleeds into my voice. "I know you're smuggling refugees out of the sublands. I know you're smuggling weapons with battle runes on them. Demon-slaying runes. And I know you're building a huge armory down here, to arm the Smaragdalfar and maybe others in the Resistance. I know that you have rune-sorcery, even though you shouldn't, because you're a Kelt. I already know *all of this*, Ciaran. So why are you in hiding? What's hunting you?"

Ciaran's eyes are suddenly fierce, his mouth a tight, unyielding line.

"I've thrown my lot in with the Resistance," I say, matching his intensity. "There's no turning back for me." I hold up an arm that shimmers with a faint purple glow. "I don't even *look* Gardnerian anymore."

"You are Gardnerian." He says it tightly, as if he's struggling to force a boundary between us and failing. "You can glamour your color, but you *cannot* change that."

His words are a staggering blow, and a reminder of how trapped I still am because of what my people—my own parents—have done to me.

I rake my fingers through my tangled hair, feeling like the walls are closing in around me. "I need air," I tell him, futilely blinking back tears. "I can't be in here with you right now."

Ciaran rises, regret in his eyes. "Sage, I'm sorry…"

I shake my head, tears falling as I turn away and flee from the room, through the caves, through the common area. I burst out into the night, the damp air cool on my face.

I keep going, breaking into a run down the forest-edged road until my legs ache and my chest feels like it's full of cut glass. Until the rune-marked cave entrance is out of sight and I'm surrounded by darkness.

CHAPTER FIFTEEN:
Unwarded

I'm breathing hard as I lean down, my hands tight on my thighs, trying to slow my heavy breathing. There's an encroaching autumn chill to the air and an oppressive silence to the dark forest, and I'm overcome by a sense of painful isolation. My mind is heart-wrenchingly full of Ciaran, our rapid and deep connection, the balm of his presence. He's been a tether for me, keeping me from being completely lost to despair.

I pull in a hard breath, the truth slipping in, irrevocable.

I want him.

I don't care that I barely know him. I don't care that we're from completely different worlds. I want *him.*

A subtle vibration against my calf pulls my attention away from my turbulent thoughts. I rub my eyes and look down. *The wand.*

Then a streak of white catches my eye, and I glance up. There's a white bird in the tree directly in my line of sight, warning in its silver eyes. And then it's gone—the image such a quick flash that I blink hard and straighten, turning around to search for the bird…but nothing.

Just the gathering dark.

A chill creeps down my spine. I turn to face the direction

from which I came, and my eyes lock onto a glowing emerald ward set into a broad tree quite some ways back up the road. A bright flash of fear stabs through me.

I've gone too far—clear past the wards.

Filled with jagged alarm, I start for the ward at a fast clip, toward safety, until I'm back behind it. I breathe out a long sigh of relief, my breathing now close to a normal cadence.

The rune-ward flashes a fiery red and starts to spin, tendrils of dark shadow flowing out of it.

A stream of fear rushes into my heart. I wheel around, struggling to see into the dark shadows of the forest and down the road. I unsheathe my rune-knife, gripping the hilt tightly as I peer back in the direction of the cave. I'm too far down the curved road to make out the rune-marked door.

Something is watching me. I feel it with a sudden, terrible assurance that sets the hairs on the back of my neck prickling. I slowly turn to look back down the road, and my breath clogs in my throat.

There are two dark figures suddenly there, lit red by the whirling rune. Time seems to stretch as a feeling of unreality courses over me.

The council envoys. From all those years ago in Valgard. The men Gwynn told me were glamoured demons. Their forms shift to the two Keltic men who spotted me in Verpax City the night I fled my fasting, the men with the flash of red in their eyes. They were the same men...

Holy Ancient One. The truth hits me with brutal force. *The demons are real, and they know I have the Wand.*

Both men's eyes light up red as the taller man's mouth lifts in a vulpine smile. I flinch as his wrist flicks out and a net of glowing red lines fans out across the road, like a tide coming in. Terror rips through me as I turn and run, the lines pulsing around me, casting the woods in a blood-red glow.

A line makes contact with my ankle with a whip-like sting and coils tight around my leg. I cry out and pitch forward as my bound leg is roughly tugged backward. My elbows collide hard with the ground, my palms slamming down onto the dirt, my leg wrenched in my hip socket as I fall.

For a split second, I lay panting, crippled by the fear of what lies behind me. Then the binding on my ankle slackens.

The woods are silent, but I can feel their eyes on me.

I turn my head and flinch back with a terrified whimper.

Two demons float above the road, their powerful bodies slowly materializing from a cloud of glowing, burning red as the crimson lines of their rune-web pull in and disappear, save one—the one tied to me. Cruel faces made of fire leer at me, eyes simmering with vermilion flame, facial features flickering, spiraling shadow horns tendriling smoke.

Pyrr demons.

"Give us the White Wand, Light Mage," the tall demon demands in a voice that's multi-toned, as if sounded by a whole legion of demons.

The sound sends a palpable rumble through me, and the entire world tilts as I feel myself thrust into a legend. Into myth. Into the fate of the world. A fate I have sheathed at my side.

The White Wand.

With a rough cry, I hurl my rune-blade at the tall demon. To my shock, the blade actually hits it straight in the eye, emitting a burst of bright yellow flame.

Grinning, he reaches up, pulls it out and throws it down, impaling the ground. "Only varg blades can destroy us," the demon hisses, his mouth twisting into a snarl. "And only Smaragdalfar can wield them."

Heavy bootheels thud behind me and I whip my head around, panic exploding as I spot Ciaran rushing towards me.

"Stay down, Sage," he growls, wrathful eyes sweeping over the demons.

Everything Gwynn told me, everything she wrote so many years ago flashes desperately through my mind. *If they're glamoured, he won't be able to see what they are. Because he doesn't have the White Wand.*

"Ciaran! *No!*" I cry out as he strides closer. "They're not what you think!"

"They're *exactly* what I think," he snarls, eyes fixed on them.

Ciaran slows, thrusts both hands into his tunic pockets, pulls out two cylindrical rune-stones and flicks his wrists out in unison. Glowing, curved blades fly out from the stones, made up of countless runes of many sizes and shapes, all rotating and spitting a bright, crackling green.

The demons flick their taloned hands and throw out glowing scarlet swords nearly identical to Ciaran's, save their color and rune-markings.

"You seek to wield a varg blade, Kelt?" the tall one cruelly mocks.

With a growl that emanates from the base of his throat, Ciaran launches himself at the demons with berserker rage. A slash of green fire erupts as he sweeps his blade over both their swords with a deafening clang and an explosion of green and red sparks. I flinch back, the blades clanking powerfully against each other and moving so fast I can barely see them.

The taller demon falls back, murderous confusion in its fiery eyes, and the bindings around my ankle dissolve into black smoke. I hastily scuttle backward as Ciaran's blade slashes through the neck of the shorter demon. The demon's head bursts into a brighter ball of flames as it falls to the ground and rolls toward the trees, fire catching on the sleeve of Ciaran's tunic.

The tall demon lets loose a ground-shaking cacophony of

sound, its legs turning to smoke as it takes to the air, flies up and back, then loops back raptor-fast. Ciaran rears away, ducks the demon's whirling blade and slashes straight through the creature's middle. The demon explodes into bright-yellow flame with an earsplitting shriek, then smolders to the ground in a blackened heap.

Ciaran stands there for a brief moment, his back to me as flames rapidly consume his tunic. I cry out to him in alarm, but he seems oblivious and amazingly unaffected by the fire. Lines of slim golden chain tattoos come into view as his tunic falls apart, emerald runes attached to the gold loops, the design crisscrossing his entire chest. He's looking down at the slain demons, breathing hard, glowing green swords in his hands, the entire surrounding forest lit up green from the reflected rune-sword light.

I grasp at the tree behind me for support, my mind hurled headlong into confusion.

Ciaran rounds on me. "We have to get back to the caves. *Now.*"

He pulls the swords back into the rune-stones and stuffs them in his pants pockets, then tears off the remains of his flaming tunic and throws it to the ground. He comes over to me and takes hold of my arm. We rush back past the wards, back through the caves, back to the warded room, where all the runes are spinning and emitting snaking lines of dark shadow.

Ciaran pulls the curtain back into place so hard, I fear he'll rip it clear down.

"Why were they after you, Sage?" His green eyes are blazing with urgency. "Those weren't just any pyrr demons. They sent *varg* demons after you. Why are the Gardnerians sending elite demonic assassins after you?"

His words only barely register. "How…how are you wielding varg blades?" I force out, stunned. "I thought only Sma-ragdalfar can do that!"

"Sage," Ciaran insists, ignoring my question. "What do you *have*? What do you have that they want?"

My terror is gradually morphing into a wild confusion. "Why are those rune-chain tattoos all over you?"

"Tell me what you have, Sage!" he insists.

"It's the *Wand*!" I cry, his urgency breaking through my confusion. "They want the *Wand*! The stories Gwynn told me about it…" My head is spinning. I pull the Wand from its sheath and hold it up. "They've been stalking it for *years*…"

"Why *this* wand, Sage? There are many, many wands."

"It's not just *any* wand, Ciaran! It's *the* Wand! *Oo'na*'s shard! The tooth of *Zhilin*!" I tighten my grip on the Wand's spiral-ing handle. "This is it, Ciaran. The *White Wand*!"

His eyes widen. "Sage, that can't be. Those are just stories. Religious myths—"

"The myths are all *true*."

"But if they are…" He falls quiet for a moment, his gaze full of stunned horror.

I nod shakily, knowing where his thoughts have led him. "It means there's a dark tool. A Shadow Wand. Someone has awakened it. And it's stalking this one."

"Why would a shard of power…*the* shard of power…go to *you*?"

I know it, rock solid. "To hide. For all these years. To hide from the Shadow Wand."

Ciaran drops his outraged expression and goes completely still.

"How do you speak Smaragdalfar so fluently?" I press. "Enough to have an accent when you're tired? Enough to dream in it and curse?"

His eyes are suddenly blazing, his body rigid.

"Why aren't you burned from all that fire?" I take a deep breath and force my voice to be calmer. "What are you, Ciaran?"

"Not this," he says, his voice low and hard.

"Then what?" I touch a finger to one of the delicate chains tattooed all over his chest, criss-crossing him like a net. Small rune-discs are affixed all along each chain, imprinted with tiny Smaragdalfar runes that emit a faint, verdant glow. "What are these?" I breathe out, my head spinning with confusion.

"A runic glamour," he says.

Realization begins to sink in. "Show me what you're hiding."

He takes a deep breath, then slides a rune-stylus from his pocket and presses it to one of the chains, murmuring in Smaragdalfar. The design morphs from flat tattoos to three-dimensional chains and rune-discs before my eyes. Ciaran unhooks one chain and slides it off, his ears morphing to swift points. My breath catches tight in my throat, my hand flying up to cover my mouth.

His jaw rigid, his eyes locked on mine, Ciaran unhooks another chain, muscles flexing, and pulls it off. His hair darkens from dark red to darker hazel. He pauses, eyes storming.

"Show me," I insist, steeled.

He unhooks another chain and sets it on the bedside table. When he looks back up at me, his eyes are silver, with black pupils that are surprisingly slit, like dragon eyes.

My hand slides down off my mouth as I take this drastically altered Ciaran in, realization dawning.

Ciaran swallows and takes another chain off, his dark hazel hair turning a vivid green.

He takes another off and his skin takes on a subtle green hue. As he continues to remove the chains, faint geometric patterns appear across his arms, his chest, his face, and the light green of his skin moves toward a vibrant emerald.

Ciaran slides the last chain off and I watch, mesmerized, as his patterned skin explodes into a stunning sheen of emerald beauty. My eyes drink in the sight of him standing before me, a powerful Smaragdalfar Elf.

"Oh, Ciaran," I say breathlessly.

"That's not my name," he says, his voice impassioned.

"What is it?" I ask, heart thudding. But I know what it will be before he speaks. I know it deep inside me, all the pieces falling together.

It's his face, the face on the wanted posters.

"My name is Ra'Ven Za'Nor." All attempts to hide his thick accent fall away. "I'm the last surviving member of the Smaragdalfar royal line."

CHAPTER SIXTEEN:
Ra'Ven

I stare at Ciaran…*Ra'Ven*…stunned by his dramatic transformation.

Ra'Ven runs a hand through his spiked green hair, his riveting silver eyes honed on me. "I never imagined anyone could be in more danger than I am," he says, not bothering to conceal his prominent accent now.

"Do you think there's more of those…*things* after me?" I force out, both vertigo and the dazzling *green* of him sweeping me up, making me breathless.

Ra'Ven purses his lips—deep green lips that look almost black in the rune-light. His eyes cast around, taking in all the runes as their rotations slow. "No," he says, his muscular body still tensed, as if he's readied to fight. "I don't think there's more of them. They would be here already. And the runes wouldn't be slowing."

He gestures toward the Wand clutched in my hand. "If *that's* what we think it is, and they know of it, they would already be at our door." He swallows and looks me over, his expression softening as he reaches out to lightly touch my arm. "Are you all right?"

I force a few even breaths and nod, looking him over as well.

The shock of his beauty is an inescapable pull on my affinity lines—so many shades of green glinting all over the expanse of him. My light lines strain toward him, my wand hand tingling straight to my elbow.

"Your hand," Ra'Ven says, his mouth tilting up with a trace of amusement, a gratified spark in his silver eyes. "It's turned solid green."

A flush of heat stings at my cheeks as flashes of green edge my vision. "You're overwhelming." I glance away from him, momentarily abashed. "You're so...*beautifully* green. It's playing complete havoc with my affinity lines." I venture a glance back at him, overcome with renewed surprise at the sight of his true form. "Why are your pupils slitted?"

His eyes tighten. "Does it bother you?"

"No," I say quickly, sensing how easily I could wound him right now. "No. You're quite a bit different but...you're so beautiful, and...you're still you."

His lip twitches up, his eyes intent on me. "I have wyvern blood," he tells me. "Two generations back on my father's side. That's why the varg demons couldn't burn me." Ra'Ven takes in the confused knot of my brow. "My people have always had close ties with the wyvern shifters. We were closely allied once. They tried to free my people from the Alfsigr during the Realm War and failed. Most were murdered, and some are still imprisoned with us in the sublands."

"But if they're wyvern shifters," I say, surprised, "can't they shift to dragon and fight the Alfsigr?"

His expression hardens with indignation. "The Alfsigr place Elfin-steel bands around their wrists and ankles. Shifting would cripple them, so they are bound in human form."

"That's horrible." I massage my temples and hold his impassioned stare for a long moment, surrendering to the inconceivable impossibility of everything that's happened.

I close my eyes, waves of emotion overtaking me. "I need to sit down." I slump onto the edge of the bed and sit forward, my elbows on my knees, my head in my hands. Ciaran… *Ra'Ven*… takes a seat beside me.

Ra'Ven. Ruler of the Smaragdalfar. Za'ya's hope for a better future.

His hand comes hesitantly to my forearm, his fingers gently tracing down it. I sit up and let him take my hand in his, our fingers lacing together. He lifts my hand and kisses it, cupping it in both hands now, his eyes questioning—as if he's unsure where we stand, now that I know who he really is.

I'm both moved and calmed by his show of hope-filled affection.

"Ra'Ven." I savor the sound of his true name and the feel of his strong hand around mine. "I like your real name. It suits you."

His lips lift. "Like the purple suits you."

I smile at him, but his expression turns serious as he caresses my hand.

"What happened to you?" I ask, leaning against him, arm to arm, shoulder to shoulder. "I remember the wanted postings from back when I was thirteen. When I traveled with my family to Valgard, so many years ago." I hold up a fastmarked hand, bitterness rising. "For this."

A dark shadow passes over his expression. "My family was in hiding all my life, along with a small community of my people. We lived in the sublands of the Eastern desert. They were all killed by the Alfsigr when I was thirteen." He pauses, staring straight ahead at nothing, his jaw set tight as he holds onto me. "My parents had possession of that runic glamour." He gestures toward the pile of chains on the table. "It's the only glamour of its kind. It was meant for my father to use…our ruler. Our sovereign. But…" He forces the words out, his tone rough and hollow. "They used it to save me instead."

A knot forms in my throat as I hold onto him. "Oh, Ra'Ven. I'm so sorry."

His brow creases as he studies our clasped hands. "Before they were killed, my parents urged me to find the Resistance in Keltania. I fell in with some merchants traveling to Valgard and then from there to Keltania. It was very dangerous for me—I had a hard time holding onto the glamour fully. I was so young, and my sorcery wasn't strong enough. I'd hold it most of the day and then abruptly lose it."

"So you were spotted." It all starts to come together in my mind. "And they put up all those wanted postings."

He nods stiffly. "I was almost killed a number of times. I finally escaped into Verpacia, and was almost captured there as well. I fell into despair. One night, I just couldn't take it anymore. I was going to hurl myself off that same bridge I found you on."

"And then... Zeymir?"

"He found me." Ra'Ven is quiet for a long moment, as if struggling with his thoughts, his hand rigid in mine. I bring my still-green wand hand around our clasped hands and he takes a deep, quavering breath. "Za'ya and Zeymir took me in and found me shelter with a family in Keltania. A family active in the Resistance. When I turned fifteen and gained full control over my rune-sorcery, I came back here. To Verpacia. To apprentice as a smith with Za'ya and Zeymir."

"To make weapons for the Resistance?" I put in, the story now becoming clear.

He nods and gives me a look of resolve. "I seek to liberate my people from the Alfsigr. There is a part of our sublands in the east that is cut off from the Alfsigr holdings. I want to reclaim it." His tone becomes strident. "We're building an army, with the help of the Vu Trin. In a few weeks' time, a few other Smaragdalfar and some Vu Trin sorceresses will be converging here. I'm building our arsenal, to eventually fight the Alfsigr and the demons they use to keep us enslaved underground."

I reach around and pull the White Wand from its sheath and hold it up in front of us. "Perhaps this wants to be part of that arsenal."

Ra'Ven eyes the Wand with shrewd consideration. "If this is truly the *Eyil'lynorin*, then something even larger than the sublands is at stake." His gaze shifts back to me. "If the Shadow Wand has been released, then the coming fight won't just be for the sublands. It will be for the whole of Erthia."

I pull in a long, shaky breath. "So, what now?"

"We need to bring that Wand to Noi lands." His hand tightens around mine. "This changes *everything*. If that really is the *Eyil'lynorin*, and you're its bearer, you're going to need an army to help you protect the Wand."

CHAPTER SEVENTEEN:
Lines

Ra'Ven works in the smithery almost without ceasing, fabricating intricate varg blades to be wielded by Smaragdalfar freedom fighters. The runes around us remain blessedly stilled and static in color, no new searches cast over us.

Our affection for each other grows with each passing day—small touches, stolen kisses and then nights spent in each other's arms, although both of us are careful not to cross too many boundaries.

And I begin to experiment with my light magery.

I've discovered a portion of the caves close to the surface, with a ceiling partially open to the sky. I practice here, surrounded by Smaragdalfar runic grimoires and the spell book that Rivyr gave me, feeling like I own not only two wands, but my own piece of the sublands and a slice of the heavens above.

When I practice spells with the mahogany wand or try to use it as a rune-stylus, I'm unable to summon anything more than a small wash of purple over whatever piece of stone I set the wand's tip on. But when I use the White Wand, it's as if the Wand is drawing on my magic and wielding it for me. And soon, it's as if the Wand is gently and patiently teaching me how to be a Light Mage.

And my life lights up in a kaleidoscope of glorious, forbidden, rebellious color.

First, I learn how to Color Glamour one small section of the cave a deep, shimmering purple. Lit up by the dazzling color, my light magery ramps up, and soon I'm covering the cave's walls with every shade of purple—lilac, plum, violet and sparkling amethyst. Then I branch out, drawing huge swaths of every beautiful color all over the cave's walls, ceiling and floor. I touch my Wand's tip to all the stalactites and stalagmites, turning each one a different color, from marigold yellow to bright tangerine to midnight blue—my own dazzling stone garden.

I pull Ra'Ven from the smithery to show him my beautiful cave and the puffs of bright color I've suspended in the air like a rainbow of stars. He smiles and kisses me beneath the constellation of color I've created, reflections of every glorious hue flashing off his iridescent emerald skin.

I'm overcome with shock the first time I successfully use the Camouflage spell, first camouflaging my hand, then my whole body to perfectly blend in with the rose wall behind me, creating the illusion that I've completely disappeared.

Ra'Ven's silver eyes widen when I show him how I can make myself invisible this way, but then he grins mischievously and delights in finding me by touch alone, reeling me in to kiss me passionately, my camouflage inevitably washing over him as we both disappear into the colors of the wall behind us.

And I practice the Light Strike spell, the White Wand first teaching me how to carve slim lines into solid rock with hot, bright beams of white light, and then the shocking ability to blast a large hole straight into a wall of stone.

Soon, I realize as the awareness of my newfound power settles into me, *I'll be able to harness every last bit of my magic and become a true Light Mage.*

★ ★ ★

"What was it like," I ask Ra'Ven one night, my toes dipped in an underground hot spring deep inside the network of caves, "before the Alfsigr came to power?"

Ra'Ven is sitting back against the cave wall, ripples of green shimmering over his emerald skin. He's thrown three glowing rune-stones into the water, illuminating the entire spring with incandescent emerald. The submerged runes throw off lines of wavering green light that makes the entire cave seem underwater. One of Ra'Ven's long legs is splayed out straight, the other casually bent and tipped over to one side, his feet bare. His tunic is off, and I try not to stare at him too obviously as a decadent heat slides up my neck. I'm increasingly curious about his body—what's hidden under his clothes, the hard parts of him that remain a mystery. Instead, I focus on the water as he answers.

"I've only heard tales," Ra'Ven says. Steam fogs the luxuriously warm air. "Great cities hewn from cave rock. Subland waterways and ships. Expansive farms lit by lumenstone. Our own University. Huge markets. People from the sunlands would come to vacation there. Back before the Alfsigr War." His eyes darken. "The Alfsigr destroyed the cities and used demon creatures to establish control over us, to keep us prisoners underground. Their guilds took over our mines, our farms. Everything." An insurgent fire heats his gaze, and I see a bit of the Ra'Ven who took on the varg demons and struck them down. "We're going to rebuild them," he says with unflinching certainty. "The great cities of the sublands."

Ra'Ven pushes himself forward and slides his long body into the water, slipping completely under with a satisfied groan. His muscular frame is instantly transformed into a wavy, emerald blur. His head surfaces again close to me, his emerald hair dripping wet. He swims backward until his shoulders are up against the stone wall and gives me an inviting, half-lidded look. "You should come in."

My heart trips a few beats.

I slide into the hot water, the warmth a sultry caress. My loose golden tunic tries to float upward in small billows that I press down as the thin fabric of my pants floats around my legs. Ra'Ven reaches out to take my hand and gently tug me close. I float through the water, lost in the heat of his emerald gaze, until I'm pressed up against his slick chest, his full lips slightly parted and a fraction of an inch from mine.

Tension ignites between us as Ra'Ven smiles at me and pulls me in for a long, lingering kiss, our clothing rendered insubstantial by the water, the feel of so much of his skin so close to mine making my lines burn hot and bright.

I cling to him as our kissing rapidly grows in hunger, then becomes nearly molten.

Ra'Ven welcomes my new, feverish urgency as our bodies twine together in the water. As we kiss each other ravenously, he lets me feel the startling hardness of him, his body pressed against mine while I pull him relentlessly against me. It feels dangerous. Thrillingly dangerous.

A sharp sting races across my fastlines, like the tip of a pin being dragged along each line, and fear races through me.

I push myself away from Ra'Ven, breathing hard, a savage frustration flaring. Ripples of rune-light slide across the planes of his face and light up the silver in his now serious eyes, his own breathing erratic. "What happened?" he asks, his eyes flicking to the hands I'm wringing.

"The lines…they were starting to hurt."

He looks at me with heightened concern. "Are you alright?"

"I'm trapped," I rage, flexing my stinging hands. "They've trapped me. I don't get to love who I want to love."

Ra'Ven moves toward me in the water and takes my hands

in his, coaxing me to loosen my balled fists. "Does it hurt when I touch you?"

"No," I bite out, "not anymore."

His thumbs trace a slow, circular caress over my palms. "Sage, listen to me. You will find a way out of this, and it won't stop you from loving who you want to love."

"I wish I was fasted to you instead." My voice is ragged from wanting him. From wanting out of this fasting prison.

Ra'Ven shakes his head, his expression turning vehement as his touch stills. "No. You should not be fasted to anyone. You should own yourself."

The explosive mind-shifting boldness of what he's just said stuns me into silence. It's completely at odds with absolutely everything I've ever been told. I let out a quavering breath, overcome by the revolutionary idea.

Finally, I find my voice. "I love you, Ra'Ven."

He closes his eyes and inhales sharply. Then he opens them and looks deeply into mine, raw passion in his gaze. "*Ti'a'elon*. I love you, too."

Tears glistening in my vision, I pull one of my hands from his and hold it up. "There is a chance that I may never be free of this."

Ra'Ven catches my hand before I can withdraw it and presses it to his lips, his eyes blazing. "You will, *ti'a*. We will find a way, and you will."

An idea lights in my mind, stunning in its possibilities. "I'm going to use my magic to draw these lines off my hands."

Ra'Ven's expression turns cautionary. "Sage…be careful."

But I'm done being careful. I'm angry. And I want out of this cage.

Several days later, I approach Ra'Ven in the smithery as he sets a glowing, emerald rune into a varg blade he's fashioning.

He takes in my weighty expression and gives me a questioning look.

"I've lightened the lines," I tell him, excitement surging through me.

His silver eyes light with surprise, his gaze flicking down to the hands I have clasped tight against my chest. "The *fasting* lines?"

I nod and hold one of my hands out to him, a momentous thrum now in the air. Ra'Ven sets down his iron tongs and takes my hand in his.

My black fasting lines have faded to a dim gray.

"How did you do this?" he asks wonderingly.

I bite my lip, my heartbeat quickening. "I... I pushed the Light Strike spell into the lines."

"The *Light Strike* spell?"

"I held the Wand very loosely, which seems to dampen the power of the spell," I reassure him. "It did scare me at first. It lit the lines up and it hurt a bit. But then, after I ran it through the lines quite a few times...this."

He rubs his thumb along a line, as if trying to smudge it out, then looks back up at me. "Do you think you can break it fully?"

I nod, a heady anticipation sparking inside me. "Maybe." I hesitate as I gather up the courage to tell him something else, a flush heating my cheeks. "I found something with Za'ya's medicines. And I looked it up in her Apothecarium book." I've been through so much in such a short time, but I find being frank with him about this forbidden topic to be incredibly daunting.

"What is it, Sage?" he asks gently.

My blush turns searing. I pull my hand from his, reach into my pocket and retrieve a small vial containing dark strands root, then hand it to him, momentarily too flustered to speak.

Ra'Ven takes it from me and turns it over, reading the label, one green brow lifting. He looks up and studies me, as if trying to parse out the reason for my obvious difficulty talking to him about this.

"It's Sanjire root," he says calmly, as if this root that can prevent pregnancy is something known to him and quite ordinary, instead of something linked to the ultimate rebellion. An even bigger rebellion than my having set Za'ya's goddess statue by our bed, surrounded by small, bright orbs of color.

"I never knew about this," I say, struggling to speak about a topic that I was never allowed to speak of before.

"I suspect you didn't. It's illegal in Gardneria."

I hold his gaze, outrage rising because it's just one more way they kept me powerless. "I should have been told about this root."

"Yes, Sage. You should have been told about this." Ra'Ven is silent for a long moment as he considers me, what I'm offering up to him clear.

"Sage," he says with careful hesitation as he holds the bottle up slightly. "Even if we can now pair without worrying about this, we cannot risk breaking the fasting spell."

Rebellion spikes through me. "We won't have to. Because I'm going to destroy it."

He shakes his head. "Sage…"

"I do *not* want them to have this hold over me," I say, suddenly fierce. "*Any more.*" The troubled knit of his brow tamps down my intensity. "Ra'Ven," I try to reason, "perhaps it's all lies anyway."

"What is? The consequences of breaking a fasting?"

I nod.

He tilts his head quizzically. "You've never seen a broken fasting?"

"No. I've only heard tales of it. Just like I heard all sorts of tales about the Smaragdalfar, about the Ishkart. All of it lies or greatly distorted truth."

Ra'Ven considers this. "What if it is true, though? And what if we…" He gestures between us. "What if we give in to this, and it's all true?"

"What if it's not?"

He's silent for another long moment, considering, his gaze on me full of obvious temptation. "We'd have to be sure that you're safe," he insists.

"I know," I agree, but I'm already decided.

The risks be damned. They won't hold me prisoner any longer. I will love who I want to love.

"It's what I want, Ra'Ven," I tell him, my voice breaking. "I want to spell the lines away. And then I want *you*."

Two more days pass, and after pushing the Light Strike spell into my fastlines, honing the focus, doggedly sending it out through the spidery cage imprisoning my hands, over and over again…

The lines are finally gone.

I sit on a smooth piece of rock in my multi-colored cave, a small bonfire I've lit with a Light Strike spell crackling and spitting before me. The fire warms me as the temperature cools. The last of the day's sunlight streams in from the opening in the cave's roof and I sit there as late-day turns to twilight and twilight turns to night.

Stunned, I turn my hands over and over, waiting for the spell to reassert itself. But…nothing.

It's gone.

I'm free. I've done it. I've actually freed myself.

The enormity of what I've been through, what this spell put me through, swamps me like a ferocious storm. It all hits me anew—how I was forced into walking away from my family. From my people. My old world ripped to shreds.

All because of this spell.

And now it's gone. Suddenly…gone.

In a daze, I pull the bottle of Sanjire root from my pocket, unstopper it and eat a sliver of the bitter root. Then I rise and walk back to the rune-sheltered room I share with Ra'Ven.

Our bedroom is empty, the constellation of runes calm and still. I pull off my boots and my tunic and sit down on the bed, dressed only in my thin camisole and pants. I stare at my unmarked purple hands and wait.

Finally, Ra'Ven comes to find me.

"Sage?" he says, pausing at the bedroom's entrance as the curtain falls shut behind him, his eyes flicking over my partial undress.

"It's gone," I tell him, still dazed. I hold up my hands and turn them this way and that.

Ra'Ven pulls in a sharp breath, then quietly sits down next to me.

I'm outwardly calm, but inwardly too overcome to even react. "I'm free." I take a long, shuddering breath as Ra'Ven's arms wrap around me, pulling me in. I cling to him, feeling like I've weathered an overpowering, deadly storm.

He holds me for a long time. Then we wordlessly lay down on the bed and curl up around one another.

Ra'Ven presses his lips tenderly to my forehead. I reach up and press my palm against the center of his chest, his heartbeat steady and strong. At first, I touch him for comfort, for the way caressing him soothes and calms me. I slide my palm over his hard chest, his broad shoulder, his long arm and then, tentatively, just under his tunic and along his hard abdomen.

Ra'Ven lets out a small groan, and I pause, my fingertips

suspended on his skin as a sudden, hard rush of longing sparks through me. It's reflected in Ra'Ven's gaze, a gaze that has shifted from pure affection to something nocturnal and hungry.

I pull him into what starts as a gentle kiss, but quickly turns heated.

Fingers trembling, I unbutton my camisole and flex my shoulders to boldly shrug it off.

Ra'Ven's breath hitches. "Oh, Sage," he says, his eyes sliding over me.

He gently glides his fingers along the side of my breast, featherlight. I gasp and his eyes meet mine, unsure, but I shift and press my body against his hand. Emboldened, he trails his fingers over my curves, exploring, then pulls me in and closes the distance between us, bringing his mouth to mine. Our bodies are soon moving against each other in a surging rhythm, and I tug him on top of me as he presses his body hard against mine.

"We don't have to stop," I tell him, the words full of a burning desire to feel all of him. "And I've already taken the Sanjire root." We've spent so many nights tangled up around each other. Pushing up against the limits of the fasting. I feel like I know almost everything about him. Everything but what it would be like to have him inside me.

"Are you sure it's safe?" he asks hesitantly.

"Yes," I say, biting my lip with pent-up longing.

"I'll stop if you need me to, Sage."

I nod, the gesture cut off by his hard, deep kiss. Then Ra'Ven unfastens and discards the last of his clothing and mine.

His silken lips are on my neck, my collarbone. Everywhere. A delirious rush of heat burns away the last shred of hesitation as he strokes his body against mine and I arch up against him. We move as one, falling back into a deliriously perfect rhythm.

And then he pushes himself into me. All the way into me.

I gasp at the sensation and the brief, tight sting of it. My thighs tense against his as I hug him close. He feels so shockingly good.

Ra'Ven stops all movement, the muscles of his back rock-hard under my hands. "Sage," he asks, with careful, barely maintained control. He pulls back a fraction so he can look into my eyes. "Are you all right?"

I lift my hand from his back and look at it. *Nothing.* No lines. No pain.

"Yes," I tell him breathlessly. "Yes."

His hand comes up to caress the side of my face, his voice pitched low with desire. "Are you absolutely sure?"

"Yes. I'm sure."

He smiles and murmurs passionately in Smaragdalfar, and then his lips come down onto mine. And this time, we don't stop. We take each other without caution, no longer careful, claiming every last part of one another as our own.

CHAPTER EIGHTEEN:
Fire

That night my dreams are of comfort and happiness. Ra'Ven and I lie suspended in protective dark, white branches forming all around, supporting us.

And I'm free. Finally free.

Then, the comforting dream starts to give way.

There's an abrupt flash of black wings. A sudden explosion of fire. The wings flap, fanning the fire, heat lashing all around me. My sense of comfort and security shatters, singed to the ground by the mounting flames.

I wake with a start, the constellation of runes disorienting me. My heart is racing, sweat slick on my skin, my breathing harsh. Ra'Ven's arm is draped over me, his emerald skin catching the rune-light and reflecting brilliant emerald stars of light. I breathe in his masculine scent, trying to calm myself, pulling on the soothing green of him.

Then the nightmare slams back into me. A flash of wings explodes into the back of my mind as fire blooms in my center and ignites my affinity lines, all the color in my lines singed away to become white-hot.

I turn toward Ra'Ven in desperation. He's breathing languidly, seeming lost in a peaceful bliss, his body so cool against my fever-hot skin.

He opens his silver eyes and takes in my expression. "Sage, what's the matter?"

"I don't know," I say, consumed by the heat lashing through me, scared my affinity lines are in danger of bursting into actual flame.

Ra'Ven takes hold of my upper arm, his brow creasing. "You're so hot. Your skin…"

The flames leap higher and cloud my sight as the black wings explode back into my vision. Sweating and trembling, I sit up, clutching the blanket to my chest.

A prickling sting sparks to life on my hands, and I splay out my palms before me. My stomach constricts with panic.

The fastlines. They're faint, but they've returned. And they're not black.

They're red.

"Oh, no. *No*…" The sting rapidly becomes more pronounced, like a mild burn.

"Sage!" Ra'Ven is sitting up, his expression severe. "What can we do? How do we stop it?"

I shake my head, hot tears blurring my eyes, fear overtaking me. "I don't know." The sting morphs into a sharper pain, and I flex my fists, fire blasting through my affinity lines. I grab up my tunic and pants and throw them on with quivering hands as Ra'Ven quickly throws on his pants and grabs his rune-stylus.

"Give me your hands," Ra'Ven says. "I'll wrap a cooling rune around your skin."

I can barely hear him—my mind is caught up in a heated daze. I blink hard, trying to dampen the image of black wings that's warping my vision.

"Sage." I hear Ra'Ven somewhere in the back of my mind and am dimly aware of his cold hand around my upper arm.

I scramble for the White Wand and wince as I take it in hand, its spiraling white handle scraping against my fastlines like cut glass. I yank my arm away from Ra'Ven and start for the door.

Ra'Ven catches hold of me again. "Sage, wait—"

"*No!*" I say insistently. "There's *fire*. I can feel the fire building in me. It's too hot. I'll destroy everything in this cave…" Bright slashes of pain streak across my hands, and I cry out. I wrench my arm away from Ra'Ven again, stumble through the curtained doorway and break into a run through the cave's passages, through to the large common area, and burst outside.

I run, almost stumbling, through the chilly predawn air, down the hill toward the forest. The fire distorts my vision and ignites into an inferno threatening to consume me whole. I fall down on one knee before the broad trees, clutch the White Wand tight in my fist and throw my wand arm out as I desperately intone the Light Strike spell.

Golden fire burns through my lines and explodes from the Wand. I'm thrust backward, my tailbone slamming against a jutting root as fire explodes into the woods and ignites a stand of Blackwood Oaks.

Ra'Ven is down on his knees beside me, his form obscured by a veil of fire. He grabs my wrist hand, and I try to pull away from him, but he says something vehemently in Smaragdalfar and holds firm. He presses his stylus against my hand and attempts to draw a rune on my palm, the glowing green lines fading as fast as they're laid down.

"It won't set," he says in frustration. "The fasting spell's interfering with my rune-sorcery." He glances back at the inferno in the woods, the large trees rapidly being consumed by my fire.

Pain strafes through my hands and clear up my arms with a renewed force.

"No. Oh, Ancient One, *no!*" I stare at my hands, horrified

as the red fastlines crack open into gaping wounds and turn blood-red.

They're punishing me. Keeping me in their prison.

"Aughhh!" I cry out. The waves of slashing pain are astonishing, like someone flaying strips of my skin and then setting the wounds on fire. Stars burst in front of my eyes, explosion after explosion of horrible pain.

I fall back onto the dirt, writhing, my cheek pressed to the ground, gravel biting at my skin.

"I'll get help." Ra'Ven's tone is defiant, as if he's challenging the fasting. The fasting that's stronger than both of us. "I'll send for someone powerful enough to break this," he says through gritted teeth, but I can see the desperation in his eyes as the burning, torturous pain consumes me whole.

The world spins into a flaming spiral of agony.

And then it turns to black.

CHAPTER NINETEEN:
Vu Trin

I scream when I wake up, wishing I could chop my hands off to stop the pain. It's like spears are being thrust into my palms, clear through my arms. Again and again and again…

"Sage! They're trying to help you!" Ra'Ven's hands are clamped down on my arms as I thrash violently against his hold. Pain slashes my hands while waves of fire burn through me, dark wings suspended in my mind. Flapping, rhythmically…

I shriek, writhing, seized in the teeth of the nightmare. Flashes of Ra'Ven's devastated face come in and out of focus as the pain rides in on knifing waves.

I hate you! I rail at my people, at the Ancient One, as my hands are flayed and flayed and flayed again. I turn to Ra'Ven, delirious, the world blurring as my body burns. "I want *you*!" I sob to Ra'Ven, in defiance of my people's cruelty, hot tears coursing down my face.

"You have me, *ti'a'lin*," Ra'Ven says, his voice breaking. He lets loose with a stream of impassioned Smaragdalfar as he clings onto me.

Pain slices into my hands again, and I cry out in torment. And with fury. At this terrible, powerful, unforgiving spell.

There's a small break in the waves of agony and enough

focus returns for me to register that there's a gray-haired Noi woman standing beside Ra'Ven, a white dragon embroidered on her black tunic, a black metal circlet marked with glowing blue runes around her brow. Her brown, wizened face is round and kind-looking, and she's setting lines of rune-stones down on the table beside me.

Behind her stand three grim-faced Vu Trin soldiers, one a bent, white-haired crone with a long, rune-marked staff. The crone has a quiet air of unquestioned authority about her, and my pain-muddled mind marks her as someone powerful.

The other two soldiers are younger and hold themselves military straight. They have similar sharp features, coal-black eyes, brown skin and straight black hair arranged in looping coils. The slightly shorter and slimmer of the two young women is horribly burned on half her face, one of her ears partially melted, the top of it hidden by a black cloth tied around her head.

"Why are they here?" I cry out to Ra'Ven, alarmed by the presence of the Noi military.

"To help you, *ti'a'lin*," he says, desperation in his eyes as he holds onto me.

The white-haired sorceress with the rune-staff is watching me closely with a calm, unflappable gaze. I notice she's holding the White Wand in her other hand, and a covetous slash of yearning blasts through me at the sight of it.

My Wand.

The sorceress lifts my Wand and presses it against the glowing blue runes along her rune-staff as she closes her eyes and murmurs something that sounds like a chanted spell.

Rays of blue light burst out from the Wand, and everyone in the room flinches. The white-haired crone's eyes fly open, her gaze on me full of stunned amazement. "She is truly the bearer of the *Zhilin*."

"Two varg demons came for her," Ra'Ven tells the crone.

"Then the Shadow Wand has also awakened," she says to him, her voice rife with forewarning. The assembled sorceresses launch into low, urgent conversation in their language.

The fastlines continue to burn white-hot, and my back arcs with strained-to-the-point-of-breaking rigidity. The gray-haired, kind-faced woman beside Ra'Ven presses cool rune-stones against either side of my face, a buzzing energy flowing out from the stones and all through my affinity lines as the pain courses through my hands in rhythmic waves.

"I cannot break it," she says after a long moment, her accent heavy. "The spell is unforgivably strong." She removes the stones from my face and picks up two new ones. She brings them to my cheeks as well, and they're hard and cold as ice against my skin.

I gasp as blue light rays out from her hands and a cooling current flows through my arms, to my hands, both the pain and the terrible fire racing through me rapidly tamped down.

I struggle to catch my breath. "Who are you?"

"I am Sang Loi," the gray-haired woman tells me. "Rune-sorceress and healer of the Vu Trin."

"The fasting," I rasp out to her. "It's filling me with fire."

"No, *toiya*," she says with great compassion as she shakes her head. "The fire you have in you is not from the fasting spell. You are pregnant, *toiya*. And your baby is an Icaral."

The world tilts, threatening to cave in. "*No...*" I gasp.

"Yes, *toiya*. I can read the fire. I have seen the dark wings in it."

I cry out in agony as another wave of pain breaks through and threatens to undo me. Sang Loi sends more of her cooling sorcery into me, like icy water being poured straight through my affinity lines. I flex my fingers and whimper, the movement only making the pain spike again, like shards of glass gouging into my skin. I still my hands and struggle to take a deep breath.

Sang Loi pulls the rune-stones from my cheeks and carefully places one of them against my palm. I cry out at the explosion of pain, but it rapidly morphs into waves of cooling relief flowing into my hand and up my arm. I brace myself for the staggering pain as Sang Loi presses a rune-stone to my other palm, then secures both stones to my hands with long, black strips of cloth. Ra'Ven releases my arms, a tortured look on his face.

Another pulse of cold ripples through my hands, and the pain draws back a fraction, enough to stay my panic. I take a labored, shuddering breath.

"I can't be pregnant," I tell Sang Loi as fire races through my body. "We used sanjire root."

Sang Loi brushes back my hair with her fingers, the movement exceedingly gentle. "Sanjire root is light sensitive. You had a Light Strike spell coursing through your lines when you took the sanjire, and it suppressed the root's power."

For a moment I can't breathe.

She's wrong. I can't be pregnant. And with an Icaral!

"Sagellyn," Sang Loi says insistently, her eyes full of compassion. "Do not be frightened. This child is simply a child with wyvern blood, not a demon. Your people tell lies about Icarals. And this child could be the Long Awaited One. The Icaral of Prophecy."

The Great Icaral. Destined to fight the next Black Witch and destroy Gardneria.

I shake my head, panic overtaking me. "*No...*"

"Your child may be our only hope," she insists. "The Shadow Wand has risen. And your child will fight its evil power."

She's wrong. She's wrong, I inwardly rail, shaking my head back and forth. Icaral demons are made by dark forces. Shadow beasts of the Shadow Wand.

I scream as the pain cuts through her sorcery and knifes into me again, and I'm suddenly unable to focus on anything but the agony of it. Sang Loi urgently directs those around her in the Noi language as she hastily pulls a stylus and pushes up my sleeves. I writhe in agony, barely aware of Ra'Ven holding tight to my arms once more as Sang Loi draws runes all up my arms, their energy buzzing through me. But this time, her magery can't build a dam against the pain.

"Sage," Ra'Ven chokes out, guilt slashed across his face.

And then I'm screaming and spiraling down into a nightmare landscape of fire and dark wings and demons and rivers of blood. Dark spots burst into my vision, and I hear Ra'Ven somewhere in the distance calling my name, his voice distraught. His hands clinging to me. Far away as the abyss of darkness claims me.

CHAPTER TWENTY:
Prophecy

I'm lost in a sea of fire and nightmares. Demons made of crimson flame with spiraling shadow horns are searching, searching, searching for the Wand. Tracking me. But now they aren't just looking for the Wand.

They want my Icaral child, too.

Give him to us, they hiss through pointed teeth as I cower in the shadows of a destroyed Erthia. Blackened trees cover the land with branches that twist toward a blood-red sky. I shrink down in fright and watch as the demons' glowing, fiery forms pass by. Hunting for my child. Hunting for the Wand.

I run, darting around the dead forest, and hide behind a charred tree trunk when I hear another throng of demons approaching. And then, something new appears.

A young Gardnerian priest.

The bird emblazoned on his tunic is blindingly white in the gloom, his skin shimmering Gardnerian green.

"Find her," he tells the demonic horde, his voice low and elegant, his pale green eyes bright with controlled cruelty. "Find her and rip the child from her womb."

I pull myself down and in, struggling to breathe, wishing I still had a god to pray to. Tears stream hot down my face as terror grabs hold.

★ ★ ★

The nightmares break, and I'm left writhing in a feverish, half-conscious haze of pain. But I've an awareness of Ra'Ven there. Always there.

"I love you. I love you, Sage. *Tief'lia'lin…*"

Partial clarity breaks through the unbearable heat. The edges of him are distorted, cast off as blurred rays of light. There are tears in his eyes. I hear the distorted sound of a Vu Trin soldier sternly talking to him in her language, then Ra'Ven's fierce reply and refusal to budge.

He turns his tormented gaze back to me. "I'm so sorry," he rasps. His impassioned apology devolves into a stream of Smaragdalfar.

"Ra'Ven," I force out. Ra'Ven's shocked face comes into focus, even though he's wreathed in fire. Heat whips through me, along with an implacable rage. Rage against one, huge, deserving target.

My people. And this evil, unforgiving spell.

"You're not to blame for this," I grind out, my voice sounding as if it's coming from above. "*They* are. I'm going to make it to the Noi lands. And I will learn to use all of my power. And then I will come after this wandfasting spell. And I will *destroy* it."

Both his hands are on me now, cradling my fever-flushed cheeks, his face close but flickering, as if seen through flame.

"I will be in the Noi lands with you," he vows. "And I will promise myself to you in every way of every land."

And then there is nothing but fire and his voice struggling to compete with the roar of the flames. Something harsh said in Noi. Ra'Ven's lashing Smaragdalfar reply. His forehead pressed to mine.

"*Ti'a'lin. Ti'a'lin. Tief'lia'lin…*"

And then nothing but the fire.

★ ★ ★

When I finally come to again, I'm in another strange room, my hands bound and heavy, the pain tamped down to day-old burns.

Interlocking panels of wood above me form a geometric domed ceiling supported by dark rafters, the panels lacquered a deep crimson and carved with exquisite designs of white dragons. Amber glass orbs containing rune-flames are affixed to the walls, casting the room in a russet light.

I look down to find slim chains holding small, glowing crimson runes wrapped around each of my hands, so tight I can barely move my fingers. Shaken and flushed with fever, I push myself up on my elbows.

The old, round-faced Noi woman, Sang Loi, sits beside my bed. She clucks to me in the Noi language and slides her hand gently behind my back, helping me to sit up. I wince as the movement sets off new pain through my hands.

"Where am I?" I shakily ask her.

"We are in Amaz lands, *toiya*. In the military outpost we maintain here."

I look to her with surprise, my head spinning from the fever that's still rhythmically washing over me like a fiery tide. I glance at my hands and try to lift one, wincing at the cut-glass flare of pain, the rune-chains clinking against each other.

I look to Sang Loi, my lip trembling. "Where's Ra'Ven? I want to see him."

She pauses before answering. "*Toiya*, he is gone."

The center drops from inside me. "*Gone?* No…"

Sang Loi places a consoling hand on my arm. "He cannot be here, *toiya*. He fought to stay with you, but the Amaz will not allow a male to be here on their lands. And this is the only safe place for you now." Her expression darkens. "We are not the only ones who know of your Icaral child. The Gardnerians and the Alfsigr know, as do the peoples of the Ishkart lands."

Fear strafes through me. "How?"

"The trees read his image from the fire you cast at them, and they sent that knowledge out through the forests of both Realms. And now the seers of every race can read this image in their divinations." She looks to my belly significantly. "Wooden die-casters of Alfsigroth. Tree leaf readers, like myself. Stick soothsayers of the Ishkart lands. Earth-Mages of Gardneria. All know of this child. And all are searching."

I'm frozen, horrified.

"Be of strong heart, *toiya*," she staunchly assures me. "The *Zhilin*, or as you call it, the White Wand, has risen. It has risen to protect you. And to protect the Great Icaral."

A storm of confusion spins inside me. "Why would the Amazakaran agree to shelter a male baby?"

"The Amaz owe the Vu Trin a war debt. And we are asking for it to be repaid. It will be the only time the Amaz have ever allowed a male to exist on their territory." Sang Loi's expression turns sympathetic. "I am sorry, *toiya,* but they would not let Ra'Ven Za'Nor be here. Sheltering an adult male within their borders is too much for them to allow."

"Where is he?" I ask, my voice coarsened with misery.

"Headed for Noi lands. And after you give birth, you will join him there. The Amazakaran will give you shelter until we can create a runic portal to send you East. But building a portal that covers such a vast distance takes time, and the magic is complicated."

"I need to save my sisters first," I tell Sang Loi, a fierce desperation rising in me. "They're in terrible trouble…"

"You need to save *yourself*," Sang Loi cautions. "And the Child of Prophecy. And you need to save the *Zhilin*."

Distraught, I look to the Wand that lies peacefully on the bedside table. So quiet. So silent.

Help me, I silently plead to it. Pray to it. Since I have no one else left to pray to.

Please, help me.

I spend the next few months going in and out of the delirium of fever, losing myself to the oblivion of sleep for long stretches, the Wand nestled beside me. But slowly, the nightmares start to fade away.

A new dream comes in their place.

White branches wrap around me and multiply. Birds made of starlight take shape in their hollows, warding off the nightmares. And a new landscape forms in my mind—a lush, dark forest, the scent of loamy soil heavy on the air.

A figure arises in the heart of the forest. A young woman made of living branches, a serene smile on her lips. She reaches out her slender hand to me.

There is no fear in this dreamscape. No dead, blackened trees—only the sweet pulse of life. I pad across a bed of moss, the glow of Ironflowers suffusing the forest's verdant floor.

Then I reach out my unmarked hand and give the tree-woman the White Wand.

CHAPTER TWENTY-ONE:
Freedom

Time continues to pass, and I am there, but not there. I'm in a heated delirium of constant, mounting fever and inured pain, my dreams more real than my hazy reality.

"It is because you are carrying a dragon-child," Sang tells me during one of my rare moments of clarity as she pats down my brow with a cool cloth to quell the constant, burning fire. "You are not dragonkin yourself, so it will go hard for you, *toiya*."

The Wand brushes the back of my mind, and I turn toward its motionless presence on the table beside me. The gleaming, spiraling Wand is the one thing that's consistently clear in my vision, everything else fading in and out and obscured by a wavering fug of heat.

And it has started to speak to me.

In ceaseless, hushed tones, it murmurs in the back of my mind, just under my waking thoughts, like an incoherent, whispered song. Something familiar at the edges of its intonation...

But its meaning is lost, always lost, to the mindlessness of fever and the burning fire.

And then something shifts as the baby quickens inside me, rounding my belly. Fire whips through me and intensifies, winnowing away the old me. I've a strengthening sense of emergence as the flames inside me become less a battering inferno and more a torch kindled. The fire starts to fold itself into my affinity lines, its hot, golden threads weaving themselves through me, and then, where there was once only one strong affinity line inside me, there are now two.

Light...and fire.

And soon, what started as an assault to my body starts to feel like power rising.

I realize, stunned, as my blurred fog of heat starts a turn toward the blazing clarity of a star—I am becoming dragonkin.

Slowly, I rally. I'm still constantly feverish, but no longer bedridden and overwhelmed by the fire inside me. Instead, I'm gradually becoming strengthened by it. And I can use my hands now, thanks to the scarlet runes an Amaz healer has drawn in a glowing line up my forearms and the chains full of runes she's loosely affixed to my hands.

But even as I grow stronger and more consistently coherent, my longing to be with Ra'Ven grows and opens up an ever-widening rift inside of me. It rips my heart in half to be separated from him, and pains me even more to know, beyond a shadow of a doubt, that he's feeling the same way. And in the starkness of my despair, I realize even more fully what he means to me. And not just Ra'Ven—Za'ya and Zeymir, Wyla, Na'bee and even Rivyr. Every time I think of their faces, my heart constricts with an anguished yearning to be with all of them.

And all the refugees—little Nil'ya with her cloth doll, and the child with the lash-scar on her face, the whimpering little boy...where are they now? Are they safe? Will I ever see any of them again?

And will I ever make it to the Noi lands with my sisters?

Weighed down by the enormity of my situation, I begin to fall into the rhythm of the military outpost and the people I'm surrounded by. Waking in the predawn to the deep resonance of their large meditation bell, eating at rigidly set times, dousing the nighttime lights at the sight of the blue border runes flashing, signaling the start of the night guards' watch.

My midwife and near-constant companion, Sang Loi, seems to register my increasing slide into desolation and invites me to their predawn meditation one morning. Lured by curiosity and a remembrance of Za'ya's serene smile when meditating, I accept Sang's invitation to join them in their circular meditation hall. All of us face a statue of a white dragon that's wrapped around a central pillar, the carving flowing up onto the hall's roof, into a design of clouds and small graceful white birds.

At first, I find the silence difficult, as my mind explodes into a storm of conflict and a reflexive fear of religious condemnation for straying so far from the Ancient One. But Sang helps me to clear my mind by creating a suspended, calming rune for me to focus on, and more and more, I fall into their communal silence, thoughts of white birds and ivory branches and the woman made of tree limbs slowly taking the place of my tumultuous emotions.

And even though a dark whirlpool of sadness threatens to swallow me up at times, I begin to find solace here with the soldiers who are so quietly protective of me.

I eat with them, finding I've a taste for their delicate steamed breads paired with rich stews. I take tea with them, becoming used to tea flavored not with flowers and spice, but with the bold taste of grain toasted to the edge of burning. I start to pick up traces of their language. I learn to bathe up to my neck in deep, outdoor tubs fashioned from huge wooden barrels, with indigo cloth screens set up for privacy and a view of the stars overhead.

The military routine of their lives steadies me, and I wrap their regimented customs around myself, wanting their ways to be the better ways. Wanting them to be right about the child growing inside me. Not a reviled demon child at all, but a beautiful wyvern baby with a revered place in this world.

Evening falls, and I stare at the naked flame leaping above the flat rune-disc glowing blue beneath it. I've removed the amber glass orb from the rune-lamp on my bedside table, drawn to the fire. Increasingly drawn to *any* fire.

I want to consume the flames whole.

Flushed with desire, my finger strays toward the flame. Flirting with it. Sidling right up to its stinging heat. My fever-steeped affinity lines pull taut, entranced by the flame's rich, buttery gold hue.

I dot my finger into the flame and pull back, heart thudding. *No pain.*

The fire calls to me, its pull caressing my lines.

As if answering its playful dare, I touch the flame again, growing bolder. No pain again. Giddy with my discovery, I push my finger straight into the fire, the delicious warmth coating my skin like liquid butter.

"Ahhh…"

"Sagellyn!" Sang breathes out roughly as she looks up from her reading, astonished as she takes in the sight of my finger turning in the flame.

I look to Sang as surprised, overjoyed laughter wells up inside me, my palm now right on top of the flame.

"Oh, Sagellyn," she says wonderingly, her book now forgotten on her lap. "You are truly becoming part dragon."

Emboldened, Sang sets the book aside, gets up and pulls the room's tall, iron rune-brazier over to my bedside. Brandishing her stylus, she lights the runes marking the iron surface of its bowl-like interior, and a lusty flame rears up. She sends me a look crackling with possibility.

I slide one finger, then my whole hand into the fire, a delicious heat coursing over me. Then both hands, straight up to my forearms. I close my eyes and sigh with blessed relief as the fire singes away the pain of my broken fastlines.

"It's almost like I don't have fast-burns," I marvel, overcome, looking to Sang with bone-deep gratitude as tears well in my eyes.

Sang takes a deep breath and nods, seeming overcome herself as she gives a short laugh.

"What's happening to me?"

She shakes her head, looking confounded. "I do not know, *toiya*. I have never been midwife to a Light Mage carrying an Icaral child." We exchange a smile at the outrageous absurdity of the situation. "It would appear that your baby is giving you fire power. How that will manifest in you remains to be seen."

"I have fire lines now," I tell her. "Not just light lines. I can feel them blazing inside me."

A shimmering white in the rafters just above and behind Sang catches my eye, and I look up to find the now-familiar vision of three white birds perched there, their starlight bodies translucent. They blink out of sight as quickly as they appeared.

"I saw birds," I tell Sang, motioning toward the rafters with my gaze. "There. On the rafters. Can you see them?"

Sang squints at the rafters, then looks back to me, her expression suddenly serious. "No, *toiya*. Not today."

Not today. She's seen them before, then.

"What are they?" I ask her. "They're sewn on our priests' clothing—the Ancient One's bird."

"My people call them the *Ahnxils*, the Watchers. They are messengers of the Light. And they are clear to the *Vhion*—the holder of the *Zhilin*." Her expression grows somber. "They appear during times of great darkness, *toiya*."

I look down at the white bird pendant Za'ya gifted to me

and remember Gwynn's books. How we mocked the foreign religious stories so many years ago. A pang of remorse pulls at me, and a new resolve takes root to learn all I can about the other cultures and religions and magical systems of the realms, instead of dismissing and reviling everything foreign and unknown, like I was once taught to do.

"I want to learn all the runic systems," I tell Sang. "I want to join the Wyvernguard and learn everything I can do with my magic. I've already learned a few light spells."

Sang inclines her head, considering this. "You will have access to all the runic systems as a Light Mage, *toiya*, and that is a rare power. Only those rune-sorcerers with multiple bloodlines of rune-sorcerer ancestry will come close to rivaling your power."

"Do you think I'll have the power to break this spell?" I ask as I turn a fastmarked hand up in the fire. The minute I slide my hand slightly out of the flame, the pain starts to take hold yet again.

Sang takes a deep breath. "This fasting spell will be difficult to break, *toiya*. But you are a Light Mage, so perhaps, after many years of training, there could be some hope. Once fully trained, you will have the power to break many spells—and create new ones. Spells never seen before, because up until now, Gardnerian Mages have shunned the runic systems of other cultures. You will even be able to master Smaragdalfar runes, which means you will have demon-slaying powers."

An image of Ra'Ven striking down the varg demons fills my mind. His strong form effortlessly wielding the curved runeblades with lithe grace. My heart lurches at the thought of him, and I'm once again missing him with every fiber of my being. A powerful, aching desire flares to have his arms around me, to look into his star eyes and to be enveloped in his quiet understanding and love.

Ra'Ven. Will I ever see you again?

★ ★ ★

My mind is filled with Ra'Ven every night before I fall into sleep, but his beloved image doesn't stay as the deeper night closes in. Every night now, it fades, as do the peaceful dreams of the Tree and the Watchers and the young woman made of branches. These lovely images are less and less able to hold onto my mind as the tide of darkness comes sweeping back.

Demon shapes now ring the lush forest in my dreams that are morphing back into nightmares. The demons are massing and pressing in, growing in both power and numbers. They are sending red, flickering searchlight through the darkened woods. Coming closer…closer…ever closer as I cower back behind a tree.

And then they glide into view. Vulpine eyes stare right at me, vermilion swords in their hands as their voices scrape against my mind.

The Icaral is ours.

I wake with a start, coated in sweat, struggling to catch my breath, seized by terror. I reach down and touch my swollen belly, ignoring the sting of my fingers.

The edge of a small wing flaps inside me.

When my baby finally enters this world, they're hesitant to let me see him.

My Icaral child.

Sang has wrapped him in a dark blanket and is hugging him close, hiding his wings from sight as she eyes me apprehensively.

"Give him to me," I demand, my voice shaky. I'm propped up on my elbows, the sweat of a hard labor coating my back, my hair plastered to my head in wet tendrils, the pain of birth still reverberating through my body. "I want to hold him."

Sang and the row of Vu Trin sorceresses look to Chi Nam, their powerful rune-sorceress.

My gaze shifts to her as well. "He's just a baby," I rasp out. "Not a weapon. And he's my child. Not yours."

Chi Nam leans heavily on her rune-marked staff and gives me a grave, considering look, then motions to Sang with a quick nod. The healer folds the blanket back and places the small, warm bundle into my arms.

I gasp as soon as he comes into view.

His eyes are silvery green with round pupils, golden fire dancing in them. His skin is like Ra'Ven's, interlocking hexagonal shapes, but instead of flashing emerald, they glint a brilliant, overwhelmingly beautiful amethyst. Every shade of purple, like the new, intractable glimmer of my own skin. His hair is little tufts of Gardnerian black, and his delicate ears are ever-so-slightly pointed. Black wings, paper-thin, struggle to fan out from his back.

He squirms and gurgles, wraps his little hand around my finger and looks into my eyes, innocent and soft and new, with the helpless trust of a fledgling.

A stunned joy hits me like a glorious wave, quickly followed by a fierce desire to protect. Bolt after bolt of affection secures me to my child with just that one look as love swells powerfully in my heart.

"Fyn'ir," I tell them as I caress my child's tiny face, bursting into tears of relieved joy as he gazes trustingly up at me. "That's his name."

Smaragdalfar for *Freedom*.

"It is a beautiful name," Sang tells me, a tear streaking down her cheek, her face lit by a loving smile. She strokes my hair and kisses my head. Both Sang and I laugh and cry as happiness overtakes my heart.

My child. My precious, beautiful, sweet little winged child.

The White Wand stirs on the table beside me, sounding its

familiar, whispering call in the back of my mind, only more insistent and suddenly clear to me.

My eyes widen as I turn toward the Wand and cradle Fyn'ir protectively close.

A constellation of prismatic light bursts into view around the Wand's handle, whirling around the Wand as the White Tree starts to pulse in the back of my mind.

I look back into the eyes of my beloved Fyn'ir as realization crashes through me with the force of a gale storm. And I finally understand, with staggering clarity, what the Wand has been trying to tell me all this time.

A name. A ceaseless murmuring of one name. The next bearer of the White Wand—the protector of the *Zhilin*.

The most unlikely name of all.

Elloren Gardner.

CHAPTER TWENTY-TWO:
The Watchers

She comes to me that night.

The woman made of branches, made of wood, her form cloaked.

The forest around us is lush and fragrant, a blessed oasis. But I can feel malevolent forces pressing in around the green, living borders. The Shadow forces massing. Bringing the Void. The young, cloaked priest like a raptor, searching and searching...

The branch woman holds out her hand to me. Her branch legs flow down into the ground and fan out, rooting her to the forest floor. The Wand thrums against my hand and white birds made of light shimmer above.

A clutch of panic tightens my lines as her features become clear to me.

"No," I protest to the Wand, to the forest, to the Watchers in the trees. "There's been some mistake. You can't mean *her*. How can you possibly choose *her*? You chose *me*."

The forest and the birds remain silent and still, the branch woman's hand still extended.

"No." I step back and hold the Wand protectively close.

The branch woman pulls back her hood, and dread pools inside me. The Wand's choice is as clear as the Eastern Star.

Her face is the face of the Black Witch.

"The Wand has chosen a new bearer," I tell the sorceresses, setting the White Wand down on the large circular table before me.

The nine assembled sorceresses of the outpost's upper chain of command sit blinking at me with guarded surprise. Fyn'ir is sleeping contentedly, secured to my chest with a broad cloth. My love for my tiny, winged babe helps beat back my burgeoning sense of panic.

The demonic forces in my dreams are no longer massed around the lush forest. They're massed around my baby and me.

They're coming.

I take a deep breath to stay the sharp buzz of fear that crackles through me.

I glance up at the carving of the ivory dragon goddess, *Vo*, that flows over the entire ceiling. Compassionate *Vo*. Bearer of the White Tooth—the *Zhilin*. The Sacred Fang. The White Wand. Tiny white birds fly in necklacing patterns around the great dragon's form.

"The *Zhilin*, the White Wand," I tell them, "wants to go to Elloren Gardner."

Shock blasts through the room, only Chi Nam remaining silent, the crone-sorceress's eyes narrowing in on me, her rune-staff resting on the wall behind her. I can feel the force of her gaze from across the room. She has a bent back and relies heavily on her staff when she walks, and the lines of advanced age are deeply etched on her face, but it's clear she's their most powerful sorceress. I notice that even the young, strong soldiers—even the elite Kin Hoang soldiers and higher-ranking military—take on a deferential stance when faced with Chi Nam leaning rakishly on her rune-marked staff.

"It cannot be." Kam Vin's voice is sharp as cut glass. The young Vu Trin commander glares at me, her brow tight with incredulity. "You cannot mean the granddaughter of the Black Witch herself."

"It wants to go to her," I insist. "*Now.*"

"*Toiya,*" Sang says from where she sits beside me, laying a gentle hand on my arm. "The Wand escaped Gardneria. With your help. And now you are saying that it wants to go back to its captors?"

I turn to her, wanting to spring up and run toward Gardneria. Toward Elloren Gardner. Before the shadow things close in...

"No, Sang Loi," I insist, using her full name in this formal meeting, as is their custom. "Not back to the armory. Not to the Mage Council or to their military. To Elloren Gardner. To hide."

"Twenty years," Kam Vin insists, her tone hard, her eyes blazing, "the *Zhilin* lay in Gardnerian captivity. And now you believe the *Zhilin* wants to return to the same evil land that the Icaral of Prophecy will rise to destroy?"

I internally wince. *The Icaral of Prophecy.* They talk like this all the time, and I despise it. Like my Fyn'ir is a weapon, and not a child. Like he's a slave to the Prophecy.

I hug my son close. "The Shadow Wand has its sights set on Fyn'ir and me, and this place is becoming clearer and clearer to it," I vehemently insist. "The Shadow is coming. I have to get the *Zhilin* to Elloren Gardner *now.*"

Sang Loi is studying me very closely, still as a winter lake. I look to her in desperate appeal.

"If you place that Wand in the hands of *that family*—" Kam Vin's voice is like the lash of a whip. "—you potentially throw the *Zhilin* into the hands of the next Black Witch." She turns to Chi Nam, her rage barely restrained. "Are you forgetting what Elloren Gardner's grandmother did to my people? To my sister?"

I look to Ni Vin. The young soldier's expression is stoic and emotionless, as it always is. Half of Ni's face and body are burned beyond recognition. The hair and ear on one side of her head gone. Her hand turned to a melted stump. She has a black cloth wrapped around her head to conceal her disfigurement, but I've seen her bathing, seen the entirety of her devastating injuries.

I've also been on the receiving end of her small, quiet kindnesses.

Succulent fruit wordlessly set down in front of me with only a small, tight nod in response to my murmured thanks. Pragmatic help changing the baby's soiled cloths when the pain in my hands is too much to bear. I know that the day her body was melted, she lost her entire family, save Kam Vin. That she watched her whole village burn and ran with the few survivors, screaming, to the water, passing dying children clinging to mothers who were singed to the ground.

Sometimes I wonder if her trauma has washed most of her words away.

Kam Vin and Chi Nam break out into a low argument in the Noi language. Chi Nam seems to be calmly holding forth in consideration of my appeal, her palm placidly held out toward me.

I glance up at the intricate, raftered ceiling as three white birds flash in and out of view, white branches forming in the back of my mind like a bolstering scaffold, filling me with a heady sense of purpose. I rise to my feet and the sorceresses quiet, turning to me in question.

"They sent varg demons out after me," I remind them ominously, my voice quavering with emotion as I hug my baby close. "That was just the beginning. You don't understand what's coming."

"Why would the Wand want to leave a Light Mage?" Tu Jyn, leader of the deadly Kin Hoang, asks me with honest confusion. "To go to a powerless girl from a dangerous family?"

I struggle to form a coherent answer that will convey the full force of the Shadow to her. "I don't know."

Tu Jyn sits back with a lip-tightening frown. She looks to the other sorceresses. "It would have also seemed madness to believe the *Zhilin* could escape a Valgard armory via two teenaged Gardnerian girls." She glances at the gleaming Wand. "There are forces bigger than all of us at play here. It would be wise to follow the will of the *Zhilin*."

"But is this truly its will?" Kam Vin challenges. Once again, they break into low, impassioned conversation in the Noi language. Sang puts a steadying hand on my arm, offering comfort.

Chi Nam straightens, formally addressing the sorceresses. "*Vu Trin Noi'khin*. We will vote on this matter." She gestures toward a pile of polished black and indigo stones in the center of the table. "Who agrees that Sagellyn Gaffney should be allowed to follow what she believes is the true will of the *Zhilin*?" She holds up a black stone. "And who believes we should wait for our seers to have more guidance?" She holds up an indigo stone. "Remember, *Noi'khin*, that Sagellyn Gaffney stands before you not as a Gardnerian, but as a *Vhion*, a true guardian of the *Zhilin*."

Everyone is quiet for a long moment, the silence deafening.

Kam Vin is the first to move. She slides an indigo stone toward herself and glances around at the other sorceresses, harsh challenge in her eyes.

Sang Loi calmly pulls a black stone toward herself. Chi Nam chooses a black stone as well, followed by Tu Jyn, her lips pursed. I loosen a shaky breath of relief.

All the remaining sorceresses pick up indigo stones.

Hope chills and turns black in my chest.

CHAPTER TWENTY-THREE:
Escape

Sang comes to me in the darkness of predawn, a finger to her lips, warning me to be quiet, a small rune-lantern in her hand. I've been up all night, unable to sleep, wrestling with thoughts of leaving. Desperate to think of some way to escape a Vu Trin military outpost ringed with an unbreakable rune-barrier.

"I believe you," Sang whispers, glancing up toward the rafters. "About the Shadow forces coming for the child." Her gaze turns uncharacteristically fearful. "*Vo* sent a dream to me. And I saw the Shadow things."

I glance up to find three Watchers sitting on the rafters above, stunning in their ivory beauty. For a brief moment, they radiate light before promptly disappearing.

"I saw the *Anhxils* above me when I woke," Sang says, making an elaborate Noi blessing over her chest. "And I saw the face of your friend. She had the same face as the Black Witch. I know what you say to be true." She rises and holds a wizened hand out to me. "Come. And quickly. I'm going to help you."

My heart tight in my throat, I hastily dress and change Fyn'ir as Sang drapes Ra'Ven's rune-chains all over his little body. I watch as his violet-patterned skin morphs to a pale Keltic tone, the slight point to his ears rounding. I slide Rivyr's *Zalyn'or* over Fyn'ir's head, and he immediately stops fussing, his face turning blank and disquietingly emotionless as I pick him up gently and attach him to my body with a cloth sling.

"The necklace should keep him calm," I tell her.

I can't leave Fyn'ir here, even though it's risky to bring him with me. The Vu Trin have been kind to me, but I've no illusions regarding how they view my baby. He can't stay in a place where he's viewed as a weapon first and a child second, and I can't bear to be separated from him.

I sheath both my wands and my rune-blade at my waist, then follow Sang out to the stables. She has one of their finest black mares packed for my journey back to Halfix. We sneak out the back of the stable, and I watch as Sang presses her rune-stylus to one of the luminescent blue barrier runes that's suspended in the air at the edge of the woods. The floating rune snuffs out of existence, releases a puff of iridescent blue smoke into the air.

I follow Sang deep into the woods, down a narrow, twisting path, hugging Fyn'ir close to my chest, the blue light from Sang's lantern bobbing over us. The mare quietly trots beside us, Sang holding onto its lead.

Eventually we stop in a small clearing, and she looks to me. "Here's where we part, *toiya.*" Sang pulls her stylus and goes about marking two large adjacent trees with glowing sapphire wards, up and down the trunks. Then she fishes in her pocket and pulls out a black stone marked with a blue rune. She creakily lowers herself and presses the stone to the lowest trunk-ward and begins a low, monotone chant.

Blue fire catches and spreads in a crackling, static path along the lines of the runes, racing up the tree. The blue lightning jumps to the adjacent trunk and streaks down the runes along that tree's trunk to form a complete, chaotically illuminated arch.

I turn to Sang, astonished. "Are you building a portal?"

Her mouth lifts into a sly half smile.

"But…how?" I ask, bewildered. "I thought they took months to make?"

"They can," she assents. She pulls a flat, hexagonal black stone from her pocket marked with an intricate Noi rune. A fog of blue light encompasses the geometric stone. "This is a casting stone calibrated to a specific distance," she tells me. "I can use it to open up a receiving portal in the wilderness near Halfix."

I peer at the stone, trying to work it all out as my brow knits with confusion. "If you can cast portals, why couldn't you send Ra'Ven and me and Fyn'ir to Noi lands?"

"It's too far, *toiya*," she explains gently. "And these stones take many months to charge. But this one has enough rune-sorcery in it to reach northern Gardneria." Sang pulls a compass from her pocket, orients the brightest section of the rune-stone straight north and presses the rune-stone to the portal.

I flinch as a blinding flash of golden light explodes from the stone and sizzles around the entire portal, rays of blue lightning flickering out the sides. The air inside the portal begins to vibrate, like ripples on a lake, the forest image morphing and changing into another darkened landscape. I tighten the affinity lines around my eyes and brighten the nighttime scene. A small meadow appears before me through the portal entry, the dense forest beyond it leading up to the familiar peaks of the northeastern Caledonian Mountain range.

I stare in wonder.

Halfix.

"What is it your people say?" Sang asks, eyes twinkling with satisfaction. "I have the tricks up my sleeve."

"So, I just ride through?" I ask, breathless with awe at the fantastical distance spanned by the portal. "What then?"

She hands me the compass. "Ride west. You'll find the Northern Wayroad."

Which leads straight toward my isolated home in Halfix.

"It should only take you a few hours to get there," Sang tells me, taking Fyn'ir for a moment as I mount the mare, then handing my son back to me. "Tu Jyn will meet you there tomorrow at dawn. I will send her out after you. You will need the help of the Vu Trin after you give the *Zhilin* to Elloren Gardner."

I hug a now sleeping Fyn'ir close, my pulse hammering hard with anxious anticipation.

"Ride swiftly, *toiya*," Sang cautions with a glance back at the military outpost, warning in her eyes. "The Shadow is coming. Ride like the wind."

I urge the horse toward the portal and ride through.

CHAPTER TWENTY-FOUR:
Elloren Gardner

My heart twists as I peer through the trees and look down at my family's estate.

The estate is washed in the deep blue light of predawn, and for a moment, I'm a girl again. A young girl. Running through the flowers with Clover and Retta, innocent and trusting, desperately wanting to secure the favor of Father and Mother Eliss—an impossible game with impossibly high stakes.

I clumsily dismount and affix the reins to a tree inside the wilds. The White Wand in hand, I hug the edge of the forest, murmuring the spells to camouflage myself and Fyn'ir, blending into the woods until I come to the arching window of my sisters' bedroom. I murmur another spell and dissolve my camouflage, casting a Color Glamour over myself to temporarily turn my skin back to a green Gardnerian shimmer.

My heart pounds in my chest, and I look over my shoulder fearfully, craning an ear for any sign that we're being followed, unable to shake the feeling that Fyn'ir and I are being tracked by Shadow forces.

And that we're running out of time.

I look back at the windows of my sisters' bedroom, and

fierce outrage rises in me. There are new iron bars securing them shut. Imprisoning my sisters. Caging them like chattel.

I move closer and peer into the window.

My heart leaps in my chest when I see them. Retta is lying curled up in a ball in her bed, staring listlessly at nothing as her finger traces a design on the quilt beneath her. Clover is standing, talking to Retta. I take in the sight of her, and my outrage turns incendiary.

Clover's face is bruised and beaten, fury etched hard in her expression.

My determination renewed, I rap on the windowpane.

Clover's face jerks toward the window, then Retta's. Both my sisters' eyes go wide with a shock that momentarily freezes them in place.

And then Clover rushes to the window as Retta bursts into tears and follows her.

They wind open the windows as far as they'll go, the diamond-glass panes only opening a smidge before they bump up against the iron bars.

"Oh, Sage," Retta whispers, hiccupping from the ferocity of her tears, pushing her fingers out to meet mine. "We thought you were dead."

I touch Retta's fingers, then Clover's as I burst into tears as well, rebellious Clover letting her devastation show as her fingers cling to mine. Her entire bruised face tenses when she sees my fast-wounds, and she looks to me in abject horror.

"We don't have much time," I tell them, swallowing back my tears. "Pull on your boots and step away from the window."

Ignoring the slashes of angry pain riddling my hand, I tighten my grip on the Wand as Clover and Retta fall back. Clutching Fyn'ir tight to my chest underneath my cloak, I move away from the window and turn Fyn'ir aside so I can shield him with my body. Then I lift the White Wand and sound out the words to the Light Strike spell.

A beam of blindingly white light shoots from the Wand's tip and sizzles along the frame of the iron bars. The bars heat to a red glow that burns so hot, it scorches a black, smoking gouge clear around the window's Ironwood pane. Clover thrusts the edge of a book toward the iron bars, and they fall down to the grassy ground with a dull, weighty thump.

Clover winds the window open all the way and helps a whimpering Retta climb out to me. Gentle Retta hugs me tightly, sobbing, question coloring her gaze as she presses up against little Fyn'ir, who wiggles, still blessedly groggy and calmed by Rivyr's *Zalyn'or* necklace. Retta draws back and looks up at me with wide, worried eyes as Clover drops out of the window, her gaze darting around, fierce resolve on her angular, bruised face.

"I have a baby," I tell them both, firm assurance in my tone. "He's coming with us, too."

Retta hesitates, glancing at Fyn'ir's wrapped form, then nods with decision as she clutches at my cloak.

"You both need to hold onto me," I say, and Clover grabs hold of my cloak. "Don't let go." I pull out the Wand and murmur the camouflage spell, all of us immediately covered with the colors of the Ironwood forest before us.

We run until we're well inside the woods. Once we're clear of the house, I drop the camouflage, but keep myself washed in a Gardnerian green shimmer, the purple coursing just under my skin and straining to reassert itself.

"You've so much magic, Sage!" Clover marvels.

Retta looks to the Wand with awe, her mouth open, her face tear-streaked.

"Stay here and wait for me," I tell them. "I have one last thing to do. And don't be afraid if sorceresses come—"

"Sorceresses?" Retta cuts in fearfully.

I caress her shoulder, even though it burns my hand to do it. "You need to trust me. There are a lot of good people we've been told are bad, but they aren't. And they're going to help us. Now, you need to crouch down and just wait for a moment, all right?"

Clover shows no hesitation as she complies, her expression hard-bitten. Retta sends one long, grief-stricken look back toward the estate, and I can imagine the conflict raging in her mind.

Their home. Our parents. Our pets. Every last thing they own. Left behind.

"They won't let you stay there," I remind her grimly. "Even if you don't come with me. You know that. You'll have to leave for the Vasillis home." My gut heaves at the vile surname.

Retta's face twists in misery, but then she nods and takes a shaky breath, roughly wiping away her tears.

I camouflage Fyn'ir and myself anew, pull my hood over my head and follow the long line of trees toward Elloren Gardner's cottage.

The predawn light shifts to an ethereal blue, a low mist clinging to the ground. A Watcher flies by overhead, wings rustling, serene and graceful. Two more Watchers fly up ahead of me, toward a small patch of trees. They perch on branches, turn and set tranquil eyes on me.

Emboldened, I go to them and slide the White Wand into my cloak's inside pocket, then lean against the fence separating the two properties.

And I wait.

A few moments later, the third white bird flies back, perching between the two others above me.

Elloren Gardner, dressed in a night tunic thrown over a

skirt, tentatively comes into view. At first, she's not looking at me or the Watchers, but toward the wilds. Then she turns and freezes as she spots first the Watchers, then me, her eyes widening with fear.

"Elloren," I say, to halt her from bolting.

A shocked realization washes over her face. "Sage?" Warily, she makes her way toward me, her eyes darting to the Watchers above.

She sees them.

Fear rises as I glance toward the distant road, searching for the Shadow that I can feel closing in.

"Wh-where have you been?" Elloren stammers, her brow tight with concern. "Your parents have been looking *everywhere* for you…"

"Keep your voice down, Elloren." My eyes dart toward our estate, the road. *Hurry, Sage. Hurry.* Fyn'ir shifts under my cloak, and I hug him close.

"What's under your cloak?" Elloren asks, seeming bewildered.

I take a deep breath and lift my chin defiantly. "My son." *The Icaral of Prophecy.*

"You and Tobias have a son?"

"No," I spit out, revolted by my cursed fastmate's name, "he is *not* Tobias's."

Elloren winces, seeming alarmed by my flare of ire. "Do you need help, Sage?" she asks, clearly forcing herself to be calm, her voice measured and kind.

"I need to give you something." I reach into my cloak, clasp a shaking hand around the White Wand's spiraling handle and hold it out to her, pain flashing through my hand.

Elloren's head jerks back in horror at the sight of my bloody fastlines. "Holy Ancient One, what happened?"

Defiance roars through me as my face twists with bitterness.

"I did not honor my wandfasting." I look past her, toward her cottage, and glimpse an elegant carriage through the mist, the Mage Council *M* painted on its side.

Holy Ancient One, her aunt. Vyvian Damon. She must be here.

"Elloren." I push the Wand out toward her, desperate for her to take it. "*Please.* There's not a lot of time! I'm supposed to give it to you. It *wants* to go to you."

"What do you mean, it *wants* to go to me?" She eyes the Wand, brow tight, and doesn't move to take it. "Sage, where did you get this?"

"Just *take* it!" My heart is racing. *Vyvian Damon and her soldiers are already here. There's no more time.* "It's incredibly powerful. And you can't let *them* get it!"

Elloren is staring at me like I've come unhinged. "Who's *them*?"

"The Gardnerians!" I say, too loud. Wishing I could will her to understand.

She forces out a disbelieving breath. "Sage, *we're* Gardnerians."

Desperation rises. "*Please,*" I beg her. "*Please* take it."

"Oh, Sage," she says ruefully, shaking her head. "There's no reason for me to have a wand. I've no magic…"

Ancient One, she's stubborn!

"It doesn't matter! *They* want you to have it!" I gesture with the Wand toward the Watchers above us.

She glances at the Watchers and screws her face up in confusion. "The birds?"

"They're not just birds. They're *Watchers.* They appear during times of great darkness."

Pity washes over her face. It's clear she doesn't believe me.

"Sage, come inside with me," Elloren says, her voice low and kind. "We'll talk to my uncle…"

"No!" I vehemently counter, acutely aware of her powerful

aunt lurking somewhere in that cottage. "I told you, it only wants *you!* It's the *White Wand*, Elloren."

Pity flashes in her eyes once more. "Oh, Sage, that's a children's story."

Gods, Elloren.

"It's not just a story," I insist, teeth gritted. "You have to believe me. This is *the White Wand*." I thrust toward her again. *Take it, Elloren. Take it.*

And then, to my immense surprise and incredible relief...she does. She reaches out and takes the White Wand in hand. Then she slides it under her cloak, out of view, into an inside pocket.

The image of the Watchers blinks out of the back of my mind, and I know, without having to look, that they've vanished from the branches above.

Out of the corner of my eye, I see movement in the wilds— two black-clad Vu Trin on horseback. They quickly fade back into the woods.

Relief washes through me. *They're here. We've armed protection.*

Elloren is scanning the trees, her angular face tight with confusion.

"They're gone, Elloren." I grab hold of her arm, desperate to give her this one, last directive in a way she'll understand. And heed. "Keep it secret, Elloren! Promise me!"

"Okay," she agrees. "I promise." Her eyes are steeled, and this time she looks at me the way she once did, as a friend, the pity momentarily washed away. *Cultivate that steel,* I think. *You're going to need it, Elloren Gardner.*

I let out a deep sigh and release her. "Thank you," I tell her gratefully. I glance toward her aunt's carriage. "I have to go."

"Wait," she begs of me. "Don't go. Whatever's going on... I want to help you."

You can't help me. "They want my baby, Elloren," I tell her, my voice cracking.

"*Who* wants your baby?" she asks, her voice high-pitched with shock.

I roughly wipe away a stray, angry tear and look toward the Mage Council carriage again. "*They* do." I hug Fyn'ir close to my heart and glance back at my family's estate.

They'll never hold him, I rue. *My beautiful baby. My father will never smile at him and play with him and look at him with pride and love.*

"I wish…" I say distantly. "I wish I could explain to my family what's really going on. To make them *see*. But they *believe*." I turn back to her, my expression hardening. "The Council's coming for him, Elloren. They think he's evil. That's why your aunt's here."

"No, Sage," she says, shaking her head. "She's here to talk to me about wandfasting."

I shake my own head with vehemence. "*No*. They're coming for my baby. And I have to leave before they get here." I take a deep breath and hug Fyn'ir tight. It's time for us to go.

I'll never see my family's home again.

Za'ya's infinitely kind words reverberate in my mind. *Sometimes, you have to make a new home.*

And…it can be good, hmm? You must hold onto the faith of this.

Elloren's hand comes to rest gently on my arm. "You're imagining all this, Sage. There's no way anyone would want to hurt your baby."

Frustration momentarily rises inside me, along with a brief flash of envy for Elloren's benign, rosy view of things. It's going to be smashed to bits, I realize with crushing certainty, this naiveté of hers. "Goodbye, Elloren," I tell her, wondering if we'll ever set eyes on each other again. "Good luck."

I take one last look at Elloren Gardner, then turn and stride toward the wilds.

"Wait!" Elloren calls out after me, but I force myself to ignore her. It's up to her now. To unlearn everything she's ever been taught, so she can be like Galliana for us all.

When I reach my sisters, Tu Jyn and another sorceress, Kon Yi, are standing nearby, my horse and their two stallions tethered to trees. Retta and Clover rush to me, clinging to my skirts and regarding the sorceresses with open fear.

"You were right," Tu Jyn tells me soberly. "The Gardnerians came looking for you at our outpost not long after you left."

"How did they find me?" I ask, alarm spiking.

Tu Jyn shakes her head. "I do not know."

I glance down at my sisters, then give Tu Jyn a level stare. "I'm bringing them with me. I won't leave without them."

Tu Jyn smirks. "Well, then. They'll just have to come, won't they?"

"Oh, Tu," I breathe, tearing up. "*Khuy lon.*" *Thank you.*

I feel a small tug at the edge of my tunic. "Are they going to protect us?" Retta asks me in a small, cowed voice, eyeing the sorceresses with uncertainty.

"I'll protect you," I tell her, pulling the wand Rivyr gave me from its sheath. "I'm a Light Mage. A powerful one."

Both Retta and Clover look heartened by my bold declaration, and I'm heartened by the sight of their unmarked hands.

Your hands are going to stay that way, I vow.

I secure Fyn'ir under my cloak, his wings swaddled and hidden, my hands now free. Then Tu Jyn assists me as I mount my horse and Kon Yi guides my sisters up onto the sorceresses' own mares. The sorceresses gracefully throw the lines of star weapons affixed to their chests over their backs and pull themselves up to sit behind my sisters. Retta and Clover stare at me, wide-eyed and silent.

"Are you ready, Gardnerian?" Tu Jyn asks me with a wry smile, skinny Clover enveloped by her deadly black form.

Gardnerian.

I realize the word no longer fits me so cleanly. I'm Gardnerian, yes, but the word no longer tells the whole story of who I am. I'm no longer my people's idea of "pure" in any way.

But purity would mean no Fyn'ir. No Ra'Ven. No wand, and no power.

An unlikely smile tugs at my lips, and I realize, even though my hands burn as I grip the reins, even though I'm leaving everything I've ever known far behind for an uncertain future…

I never want to be pure again.

"I'm ready," I tell her. Tu Jyn throws a small rune-stone to the ground, a rune that will hide our tracks even from Fifth Division Trackers. The stone sends up a blue glow that briefly fans out into a crackling web of energy over the forest floor, as far as the eye can see, just as the first rays of pale-golden sunlight spear through the trees.

Tu Jyn holds up her hand, throws it down, and we're off, flashing through the forest, a blur of green coursing by me with thrilling speed as we ride back toward the land of the Amazakaran.

The perfect place to hide my son.

★ ★ ★ ★ ★

ACKNOWLEDGMENTS

First of all, thank you to my husband, Walter, for his unflinching and enthusiastic support. I love you.

To my epic daughters—Alex, Willow, Taylor and Schuyler—thank you for supporting me in this author thing and being so all-around great. I love you.

Love going out to my late mother, Mary Jane Sexton, and to my late close friend, Diane Dexter. In the moments that seemed most daunting, I remembered how much you both believed in me and this series. Your feisty legacy continues to inspire me.

Thank you to my mother-in-law, Gail Kamaras; my sister-in-law, Jessica Bowers; and Keith Marcum, for all your support. I love you guys.

A shout out to my brilliant author brother, Mr. Beanbag, for always being awesome and always being supportive of me. Love you.

Thanks also go out to my nephew, Noah, for your support and humor. You rock!

To authors Cam M. Sato and Kimberly Ann Hunt, my international writing group cohorts—thank you for sharing your incredible talent and friendship with me week after week. I feel privileged to be on this writing journey with you both.

Thank you to author/editor Dian Parker, for sharing your incredible talent with me, and to author Eva Gumprecht, for being an inspiration to the entire writing community of central Vermont.

Thank you to Liz Zundel for sharing your writing talent, and for your friendship. Love you, Liz. And thank you, Betty—much love going out to you.

Thank you, Suzanne. Your support has been everything.

A million thanks to my fellow authors at Inkyard Press. I'm not only star-struck by all of you and your talent, I'm also so grateful for your support and friendship.

To the authors of Utah (a new favorite place) and the librarians of Texas (I was told you all rock, and now I know the praise is spot-on)—I am so happy to know all of you. Thank you for all the support.

To YALSA and all the librarians who have supported me and my series—you are the definition of awesome.

Thank you to Jessie. And thank you to all of the many authors who have supported me throughout this journey. I feel so lucky to know you and to have the privilege of reading your phenomenal books!

Thanks going out to Lorraine for so much positive support. Love you, college roomie :)

Thank you to the Burlington Writers' Workshop and the 2017 debut group for all the support, and for sharing your endless talent and creativity with me.

Thank you, Mike Marcotte, for all the tech support with my website.

Thank you to local authors Rickey, Kane and Ryan, and to all the other Vermont authors (you are legion) who have been so supportive of me and my series. I'm so grateful to you all. Also, thank you to Vermont College of Fine Arts for all the support. You are a magical place of inspiration and talent and epic people.

Thank you to Dan and Bronwyn (I love you guys), and thank you, John, for your support and friendship.

To all the librarians at the Kellogg Hubbard Library for being so enthusiastic and supportive of my series—a giant thank-you. And thank you to librarian Loona, for all the support.

Thank you to all the bookstores that have been so enthusiastic about this series, including Phoenix Books in Burlington, Vermont; Bear Pond Books in Montpelier, Vermont; and Next Chapter Bookstore in Barre, Vermont. Also, thank you to the booksellers working in the YA section at the Burlington Barnes & Noble, for your boundless enthusiasm.

To all the bloggers and readers who have been so supportive of me online—you are all so fun and great. I'm enjoying being on this series journey with you all! Thank you for all the notes and letters and great ideas!

To my sensitivity beta readers: Thank you for making this book so much better with your insightful suggestions and inclusive vision. Any flaws that remain are completely my own.

Thank you to two of my favorite authors, Tamora Pierce and Robin Hobb, for your support and praise. I'll never be able to thank you enough.

Thank you to my phenomenally talented audio reader, Amy McFadden. And a huge thank-you to everyone at Inkyard Press and HarperCollins who have supported both me and this series. I can't believe I get to work with people of your caliber.

Thank you to Natashya Wilson, editorial director at Inkyard Press, for everything. And thank you to my phenomenal editor, Lauren Smulski, for making every one of my books miles better. Thanks also to Gabrielle Vicedomini, for her assistance and great attention to detail.

Thank you to Reka Rubin and Christine Tsai on Inkyard

Press's subrights team, for being such huge fans of The Black Witch Chronicles, and for your efforts to bring my books to readers all over the world.

Thank you to Shara Alexander, Laura Gianino, Siena Koncsol, Megan Beatie, Linette Kim, Evan Brown, Amy Jones, Bryn Collier, Aurora Ruiz, Krista Mitchell and everyone else in marketing and publicity who helped to promote this series.

To Kathleen Oudit and Mary Luna of Inkyard Press's talented art department—I can never thank you enough for my spectacular covers and maps.

Many thanks to the sales team for their support—and especially Gillian Wise, for your boundless enthusiasm for The Black Witch Chronicles.

A big thank-you to Inkyard Press's digital promoters/social media team: Eleanor Elliott, Larissa Walker, Monika Rola and Olivia Gissing.

And lastly, thank you to my wonderful agent, Carrie Hannigan, and to everyone else at the HSG Agency, for all your support and for believing in The Black Witch Chronicles for so many years. Much love going out to all of you.

*Turn the page for a glimpse at
the beginning of Elloren's adventures
with the White Wand in*
The Black Witch
by Laurie Forest.

Only from Inkyard Press!

CHAPTER ONE:
Halfix

"Take *that*, you stupid Icaral!"

I glance down with amusement at my young neighbors, a basket of freshly picked vegetables and herbs balanced on my hip, a slight near-autumn chill fighting to make itself known through the warm sunlight.

Emmet and Brennan Gaffney are six-year-old twins with the black hair, forest green eyes and faintly shimmering skin so prized by my people, the Gardnerian Mages.

The two boys pause from their noisy game and look up at me hopefully. They sit in the cool, sunlit grass, their toys scattered about.

All the traditional characters are there among the brightly painted wooden figures. The black-haired Gardnerian soldiers, their dark tunics marked with brilliant silver spheres, stand valiantly with wands or swords raised. The boys have lined the soldiers up on a wide, flat stone in military formation.

There are also the usual archvillains—the evil Icaral-demons with their glowing eyes, their faces contorted into wide, malicious grins, black wings stretched out to their full size in an effort to intimidate, fireballs in their fists. The boys have lined these up on a log and are attempting to launch rocks at them from the direction of the soldiers with a catapult they've fashioned from sticks and string.

There are assorted side characters, too: the beautiful Gardnerian maidens with their long black hair; wicked Lupine shapeshifters—half-human, half-wolf; green-scaled Snake Elves; and the mysterious Vu Trin sorceresses. They're characters from the storybooks and songs of my childhood, as familiar to me as the old patchwork quilt that lies on my bed.

"Why are you here?" I ask the boys, glancing down into the valley toward the Gaffneys' estate and sprawling plantation. Eliss Gaffney usually keeps the twins firmly near home.

"Momma won't stop crying." Emmet scowls and bangs the head of a wolf-creature into the ground.

"Don't tell!" Brennan chastises, his voice shrill. "Poppa'll whip you for it! He said not to tell!"

I'm not surprised by Brennan's fear. It's well-known that Mage Warren Gaffney's a hard man, feared by his fastmate and children. And the startling disappearance of his nineteen-year-old daughter, Sage, has made him even harder.

I look to the Gaffneys' estate again with well-worn concern. *Where are you, Sage?* I wonder unhappily. She's been gone without a trace for well over a year. *What could have possibly happened to you?*

I let out a troubled sigh and turn back to the boys. "It's all right," I say, trying to comfort them. "You can stay over here for a while. You can even stay for supper."

The boys brighten and appear more than a little relieved.

"Come play with us, Elloren," Brennan pleads as he playfully grabs at the edge of my tunic.

I chuckle and reach down to ruffle Brennan's hair. "Maybe later. I have to help make supper, you know that."

"We're defeating the Icarals!" Emmett exclaims. He throws a rock at one of the Icarals to demonstrate. The rock collides with the small demon and sends it spinning into the grass. "Wanna see if we can knock their wings off?"

I pick up the small figure and run my thumb across its unpainted base. Breathing in deep, I close my eyes and the image of a large tree with a dense crown, swooping branches and delicate white flowers fills my mind.

Frosted Hawthorne. Such elegant wood for a child's plaything.

I open my eyes, dissolving the image, focusing back in on the demon toy's orange eyes. I fight the urge to envision the tree once more, but I know better than to entertain this odd quirk of mine.

Often, if I close my eyes while holding a piece of wood, I can get the full sense of its source tree. With startling detail. I can see the tree's birthplace, smell the rich, loamy carpet beneath its roots, feel the sun dappling its outstretched leaves.

Of course, I've learned to keep these imaginings to myself.

A strange nature fixation like this smacks of Fae-blood, and Uncle Edwin has warned me to never speak of it. We Gardnerians are a pureblood race, free from the stain of the heathen races that surround us. And my family line has the strongest, purest Mage-blood of all.

But I often worry. If that's true, then why do I see these things?

"You should be more careful with your toys," I gently scold the boys as I shake off the lingering image of the tree and set the figure down.

The sound of the boys' grand battles recedes into the distance as I near the small cottage I share with Uncle Edwin and my two brothers. I peer across the broad field toward our horse stables and give a start.

A large, elegant carriage is parked there. The crest of the Mage Council, Gardneria's highest level of government, is artfully painted on its side—a golden *M* styled with graceful, looping calligraphy.

Four military guards, real-life versions of Emmet and Brennan's toys, sit eating some food. They're strapping soldiers, dressed in black tunics with silver spheres marking their chests, with wands and swords at their sides.

It has to be my aunt's carriage—it can't possibly be anyone else's. My aunt is a member of our ruling High Mage Council, and she always travels with an armed entourage.

A rush of excitement flashes through me, and I quicken my pace, wondering what on all of Erthia could have possibly brought my powerful aunt to remote Halfix, of all places.

I haven't seen her since I was five years old.

We lived near her back then, in Valgard, Gardneria's bustling port city and capital. But we hardly ever saw her.

One day, clear out of the blue, my aunt appeared in the front room of my uncle's violin shop.

"Have you had the children wandtested?" she inquired, her tone light, but her eyes sharp as ice.

I remember how I tried to hide behind Uncle Edwin, clinging to his tunic, mesmerized by the elegant creature before me.

"Of course, Vyvian," my uncle haltingly answered his sister. "Several times over."

I looked up at my uncle with confused surprise. I had no memory of being wandtested, even though I knew that all Gardnerian children were.

"And what did you find?" she asked probingly.

"Rafe and Elloren are powerless," he told her as he shifted slightly, cutting off my view of Aunt Vyvian, casting me in shadows. "But Trystan. The boy has some magic in him."

"Are you sure?"

"Yes, Vyvian, quite."

And that was when she began to visit with us.

Soon after, my uncle unexpectedly soured on city life. Without warning, he whisked my brothers and me away to where we now live. In tiny Halfix. At the very northeastern edge of Gardneria.

Right in the middle of nowhere.

As I round the corner of our cottage, I hear the sound of my name through the kitchen window and skid to a stop.

"Elloren is *not* a child anymore, Edwin." My aunt's voice drifts out.

I set my basket of vegetables and herbs on the ground and crouch low.

"She is too young for wandfasting," comes my uncle's attempt at a firm reply, a tremor of nervousness in his voice.

Wandfasting? My heart speeds up. I know that most Gardnerian girls my age are already wandfasted—magically bound to young men for life. But we're so isolated here, surrounded by the mountains. The only girl I know who's been fasted is Sage, and she's up and disappeared.

"Seventeen *is* the traditional age." My aunt sounds slightly exasperated.

"I don't care if it's the traditional age," my uncle persists, his tone gaining confidence. "It's still *too young*. She can't *possibly* know what she wants at this age. She's seen nothing of the world..."

"Because you *let* her see nothing of it."

My uncle makes a sound of protest but my aunt cuts him off. "No, Edwin. What happened to Sage Gaffney should be a wake-up call for all of us. Let me take Elloren under my wing. I'll introduce her to all the best young men. And after she is safely fasted to one of them, I'll apprentice her with the Mage Council. You *must* start to take her future seriously."

"I *do* take her future seriously, Vyvian, but she is still much too young to have it decided *for* her."

"Edwin." There's a note of challenge in my aunt's smooth voice. "You will force me to take matters into my own hands."

"You forget, Vyvian," my uncle counters, "that I am the eldest male of the family, and as such, I have the final say on all matters concerning Elloren, and when I am gone, it will be Rafe, not you, who will have the final say."

My eyebrows fly up at this. I can tell my uncle is treading on thin ice if he has decided to resort to *this* argument—an argument I know he doesn't actually agree with. He's always grousing about how unfair the Gardnerian power structure is toward women, and he's right. Few Gardnerian women have wand magic, my powerful grandmother being a rare exception. Almost all of our powerful Mages are men, our magic passing more easily along male lines. This makes our men the rulers in the home and over the land.

But Uncle Edwin thinks our people take this all too far: no wands for women, save with Council approval; ultimate control of a family always given to the eldest male; and our highest position in government, the office of High Mage, can only be held by a man. And there's my uncle's biggest issue by far—the wandfast-binding of our women at increasingly young ages.

"You will not be able to shelter her forever," my aunt insists. "What will happen when you are gone someday, and all the suitable men have already been wandfasted?"

"What *will* happen is that she will have the means to make her own way in the world."

My aunt laughs at this. Even her laugh is graceful. It makes me think of a pretty waterfall. I wish I could laugh like that. "And how, exactly, would she 'make her own way in the world?'"

"I've decided to send her to University."

I involuntarily suck in as much air as I can and hold it there, not able to breathe, too shocked to move. The pause in their conversation tells me that my aunt is probably having the same reaction.

Verpax University. With my brothers. In another country altogether. A dream I never imagined could actually come true.

"Send her there for *what*?" my aunt asks, horrified.

"To learn the apothecary trade."

A giddy, stunned joy wells up inside me. I've been begging Uncle Edwin for years to send me. Hungry for something more than our small library and homegrown herbs. Passionately envious of Trystan and Rafe, who get to study there.

Verpax University. In Verpacia's bustling capital city. With its apothecary laboratories and greenhouses. The fabled Gardnerian Athenaeum overflowing with books. Apothecary materials streaming into Verpacia's markets from East and West, the country a central trade route.

My mind spins with the exciting possibilities.

"Oh, come now, Vyvian," my uncle reasons. "Don't look so put out. The apothecary sciences are a respectable trade for women, and it suits Elloren's quiet, bookish nature more than the Mage Council ever could. Elloren loves her gardens, making medicines and so forth. She's quite good at it."

An uncomfortable silence ensues.

"You have left me with no alternative but to take a firm stand on this," my aunt says, her voice gone low and hard. "You realize that I cannot put one guilder toward Elloren's University tithe while she is unfasted."

"I expected as much," my uncle states coolly. "Which is why I have arranged for Elloren to pay her tithe through kitchen labor."

"This is *unheard of*!" my aunt exclaims. Her voice turns tight and angry. "You've raised these children like they're Keltic peasants," she snipes, "and frankly, Edwin, it's disgraceful. You've forgotten who we are. I have *never* heard of a Gardnerian girl, especially one of Elloren's standing, from such a distinguished family, laboring in a *kitchen*. That's work for Urisk, for Kelts, *not* for a girl such as Elloren. Her peers at University will be *shocked*."

I jump in fright as something large bumps into me. I turn as my older brother, Rafe, plops down by my side, grinning widely.

"Surprise you, sis?"

It's beyond me how someone so tall and strapping can move as quietly as a cat. I imagine his extraordinary stealth comes from all the time he spends wandering the wilds and hunting. He's clearly just back from a hunt, his bow and quiver slung over one shoulder, a dead goose hanging upside down over the other.

I shoot my brother a stern look and hold up a finger to shush him. Aunt Vyvian and Uncle Edwin have resumed their wand-fasting argument.

Rafe raises his eyebrows in curiosity, still smiling, and tilts his head toward the window. "Ah," he whispers, bumping his shoulder into mine in camaraderie. "They're talking about your romantic future."

"You missed the best part," I whisper back. "Earlier they were talking about how you would be my lord and master when Uncle Edwin is gone."

Rafe chuckles. "Yeah, and I'm going to start my iron-fisted rule by having you do all my chores for me. *Especially* dish-washing."

I roll my eyes at him.

"And I'm going to have you wandfasted to Gareth." He continues to bait me.

My eyes and mouth fly open. Gareth, our good friend since

childhood, is like a brother to me. I have no romantic interest in him whatsoever.

"What?" Rafe laughs. "You could do a lot worse, you know." Something just over my shoulder catches his eye, and his smile broadens. "Oh, look who's here. Hello, Gareth, Trystan."

Trystan and Gareth have rounded the cottage's corner and are approaching us. I catch Gareth's eye, and immediately he flushes scarlet and takes on a subdued, self-conscious expression.

I am mortified. He obviously heard Rafe teasing.

Gareth is a few years older than me at twenty, broad and sturdy with dark green eyes and black hair like the rest of us. But there's one notable difference: Gareth's black hair has a trace of silver highlights in it—very unusual in Gardnerians, and read by many as a sign of his less-than-pure blood. It's been the source of relentless teasing all throughout his life. "Mongrel," "Elfling" and "Fae-blood" are just a few of the names the other children called him. The son of a ship captain, Gareth stoically endured the teasing and often found solace with his father at sea. Or here, with us.

An uncomfortable flush heats my face. I love Gareth like a brother. But I certainly don't want to fast to him.

"What are you doing?" my younger brother, Trystan, asks, confused to see Rafe and me crouched down under the window.

"We're eavesdropping," Rafe whispers cheerfully.

"Why?"

"Ren here's about to be fasted off," Rafe answers.

"I am not," I counter, grimacing at Rafe, then look back up at Trystan, giddy happiness welling up. I break out into a grin. "But I *am* going to University."

Trystan cocks an eyebrow in surprise. "You're kidding."

"Nope," Rafe answers jovially.

Trystan eyes me with approval. I know my quiet, studious

younger brother loves the University. Trystan's the only one of us with magical power, but he's also a talented bowmaker and fletcher. At only sixteen years of age, he's already been pre-accepted into the Gardnerian Weapons Guild and apprenticed with the military.

"That's great, Ren," Trystan says. "We can eat meals together."

Rafe shushes Trystan with mock severity and motions toward the window.

Humoring us, Trystan bends his wiry frame and crouches down. Looking ill at ease, Gareth does the same.

"You're *wrong*, Edwin. You can't possibly send her to University without wandfasting her to someone first." My aunt's domineering tone is beginning to fray at the edges.

"Why?" my uncle challenges her. "Her brothers are unfasted. And Elloren's not a fool."

"Sage Gaffney wasn't a fool, either," my aunt cautions, her tone dark. "You know as well as I do that they let in all manner of unsuitable types: Kelts, Elfhollen...they even have two Icarals this year. Yes, Edwin, *Icarals*."

My eyes fly up at this. Icaral demons! Attending University? How could that even be possible? Keltic peasants and Elfhollen half-breeds are one thing, but Icarals! Alarmed, I look to Rafe, who simply shrugs.

"It's not surprising, really," my aunt comments, her voice disgusted. "The Verpacian Council is full of half-breeds. As is most of the University's hierarchy. They mandate an *absurd* level of integration, and, quite frankly, it's dangerous." She gives a frustrated sigh. "Marcus Vogel will clean up the situation once he's named High Mage."

"*If*, Vyvian," my uncle tersely counters. "Vogel may not win."

"Oh, he'll win," my aunt crows. "His support is growing."

"I really don't see how any of this pertains to Elloren," my uncle cuts in, uncharacteristically severe.

"It *pertains* to Elloren because the potential is there for her to be drawn into a *wildly* unsuitable romantic alliance, one that could destroy her future and reflect badly on the entire family. Now, if she was *wandfasted*, like almost all Gardnerian girls her age, she could safely attend University—"

"Vyvian," my uncle persists, "I've made up my mind about this. I'm not going to change it."

Silence.

"Very well." My aunt sighs with deep disapproval. "I can see you are quite decided at present, but at least let her spend the next week or so with me. It makes perfect sense, as Valgard is on the way from here to the University."

"All right," he capitulates wearily.

"Well," she says, her tone brightening, "I'm glad *that's* settled. Now, if my niece and nephews would kindly stop crouching under the window and come in and join us, it would be lovely to see everyone."

Gareth, Trystan and I give a small start.

Rafe turns to me, raises his eyebrows and grins.

CHAPTER TWO:
Aunt Vyvian

The Gaffney twins buzz past as I make my way into the kitchen, which is now full of friendly, boisterous noise.

My aunt stands with her back to me as she kisses Rafe on both cheeks in greeting. My uncle shakes hands with Gareth, and the twins are practically hanging from Trystan while holding up their toys for his inspection.

My aunt releases Rafe, stops admiring how tall he's become, and turns toward me in one fluid, graceful movement.

Her gaze lights on me and she freezes, her eyes gone wide as if she's come face-to-face with a ghost.

The room grows silent as everyone else turns their attention toward us, curious as to what's amiss. Only my uncle does not look confused—his expression grown oddly dark and worried.

"Elloren," Aunt Vyvian breathes, "you have grown into the absolute *image* of your grandmother."

It's a huge compliment, and I want to believe it. My grandmother was not only one of my people's most powerful Mages, she was also considered to be very beautiful.

"Thank you," I say shyly.

Her eyes wander down toward my plain, homespun clothing. If ever there was anyone who looks out of place in our tiny kitchen, it's my aunt. She stands there, studying me, amidst the battered wooden furniture, soup and stew pots simmering on our cookstove and bunches of drying herbs hanging from the ceiling.

She's like a fine painting hanging in a farmer's market stall.

I take in her stunning, black, form-fitting tunic that hangs over a long, dark skirt, the silk embroidered with delicate, curling vines. My aunt is the absolute epitome of what a Gardnerian woman is supposed to look like—waist-length black hair, deep green eyes and swirling black wandfasting lines marking her hands.

I'm suddenly acutely aware of the sad state of my own appearance. At seventeen, I'm tall and slender with the same black hair and forest green eyes of my aunt, but any resemblance ends there. I'm dressed in a shapeless brown woolen tunic and skirt, no makeup (I don't own any), my hair is tied into its usual messy bun and my face is all sharp, severe angles, not smooth, pretty lines like my aunt's.

My aunt sweeps forward and embraces me, obviously not as dismayed by my appearance as I am. She kisses both my cheeks and steps back, her hands still grasping my upper arms. "I just cannot *believe* how much you look like *her*," she says with awed admiration. Her eyes grow wistful. "I wish you could have gotten to know her, Elloren."

"I do, too," I tell her, warmed by my aunt's approval.

Aunt Vyvian's eyes glisten with emotion. "She was a *great* Mage. The finest *ever*. It's a heritage to be proud of."

My uncle begins scurrying around the kitchen, setting out teacups and plates, clunking them down on the table a little too loudly. He doesn't look at me as he fusses, and I'm confused by his odd behavior. Gareth stands rooted by the woodstove, his muscular arms crossed, watching my aunt and me intently.

"You must be tired after your trip," I say to my aunt, feeling nervous and thrilled to be in her lofty presence. "Why don't you sit down and rest? I'll get some biscuits to go with the tea."

Aunt Vyvian joins Rafe and Trystan at the table while I fetch the food, and Uncle Edwin pours tea for everyone.

"Elloren." My aunt pauses to sip at her tea. "I know you overheard my conversation with your uncle, and I'm glad you did. What do you think about being fasted before you go to University?"

"Now, Vyvian," my uncle cuts in, almost dropping the teapot, "there's no point in bringing this up. I told you my decision was final."

"Yes, yes, Edwin, but there's no harm in getting the girl's opinion, is there? What do you say, Elloren? You know that most of the young girls your age are already wandfasted, or about to be."

My cheeks grow warm. "I, um...we've never talked much about it." I envy Trystan and Rafe as they sit playing with the twins and their toys. Why isn't this conversation about Rafe? He's nineteen!

"Well—" my aunt shoots a disapproving look at my uncle "—it's high time you *did* discuss it. As you overheard, I'm taking you with me when I leave tomorrow. We'll spend the next few weeks together, and I'll tell you all about wandfasting and what I know about the University. We'll also get you a new wardrobe while we're in Valgard, and your brothers can meet up with us for a day or two. What do you say to that?"

Leaving tomorrow. For Valgard and the University! The thought of venturing out of isolated Halfix sends ripples of excitement through me. I glance at my uncle, who wears an uneasy look on his face, his lips tightly pursed.

"I'd like that very much, Aunt Vyvian," I answer politely, trying to keep my overwhelming excitement at bay.

Gareth shoots me a look of warning, and I cock my head at him questioningly.

My aunt narrows her eyes at Gareth. "Gareth," she says pleasantly, "I had the privilege of working with your father before he retired from his position as head of the Maritime Guild."

"He didn't retire," Gareth corrects, stiff challenge in his tone. "He was forced to resign."

The kitchen quiets, even the twins sensing the sudden tension in the air. My uncle catches Gareth's eye and slightly motions his head from side to side, as if in caution.

"Well," says my aunt, still smiling, "you certainly speak your mind very frankly. Perhaps talk of politics is best left to those of us who have finished our schooling."

"I have to be going," Gareth announces, his tone clipped. He turns to me. "Ren, I'll come by to see you when you're in Valgard. Maybe I can take you sailing."

My aunt is studying me closely. I blush, realizing what conclusion she must be forming in her mind about the nature of my relationship with Gareth. I don't want to respond too enthusiastically, to give the wrong impression. But I don't want to hurt Gareth's feelings, either.

"All right, I'll see you there," I tell Gareth, "but I might not have time for sailing."

Gareth throws a parting, resentful look at my aunt. "That's okay, Ren. Maybe I can bring you by to say hello to my family at least. I know my father would love to see you."

I glance over at my aunt. She's calmly sipping her tea, but the corner of her lip twitches at the mention of Gareth's father.

"I'd like that," I say cautiously. "I haven't seen him in a long time."

"Well, then," Gareth says, his face tense, "I'll be off."

Rafe gets up to see him out, the legs of his chair squeaking against the wooden floor as he pushes it from the table.

Trystan gets up, too, followed by my uncle and the twins, and all the males make their way out of the kitchen. I sit down, feeling self-conscious.

My aunt and I are alone.

She's tranquilly sipping her tea and studying me with sharp, intelligent eyes. "Gareth seems to take *quite* the interest in you, my dear," she muses.

My face grows hot again. "Oh no…it's not like that," I stammer. "He's just a friend."

My aunt leans forward and places her beautiful, alabaster hand on mine.

"You aren't a child anymore, Elloren. More and more, your future will be decided by the company you keep." She looks at me meaningfully then sits back, her expression lightening. "I am *so* glad your uncle has finally come to his senses and is letting you spend some time with me. I have a number of young men I am *very* eager for you to meet."

Later, after we have eaten supper, I make my way outside to bring the leftover scraps from dinner to the few pigs we keep. The days are getting shorter, the shadows longer, and a chill is steadily creeping in, the sun less and less able to fight it off.

Before, in the light of day, the idea of attending University seemed like an exciting adventure, but as the tide of night slowly sweeps in, I begin to feel apprehension coming in with it.

As eager as I am to see the wider world, there's a part of me that *likes* my quiet life here with my uncle, tending the gardens and the animals, making simple medicines, crafting violins, reading, sewing.

So quiet. So safe.

I peer out into the distance, past the garden where the twins were playing, past the Gaffneys' farmland and estate, past the sprawling wilderness, to the mountains beyond—mountains that loom in the distance and cast dark shadows over everything as the sun sets behind them.

And the forest—the wild forest.

I squint into the distance and make out the curious shapes of several large white birds flying in from the wilds. They're different from any birds I've ever seen before, with huge, fanning wings, so light they seem iridescent.

As I watch them, I'm overcome by a strange sense of foreboding, as if the earth is shifting beneath my feet.

I forget, for a moment, about the basket of pig slop I'm balancing on my hip, and some large vegetable remnants fall to the ground with a dull thud. I glance down and stoop to gather them back into the basket.

When I straighten again and look for the strange white birds, they're gone.

CHAPTER THREE:
Goodbyes

That night I'm in my quiet bedroom, softly illuminated by the gentle glow of the lantern on my desk. As I pack, my hand passes through a shadow, and I pause to look at it.

Like all Gardnerians, my skin shimmers faintly in the dark. It's the mark of the First Children, set down on us by the Ancient One above, marking us as the rightful owners of Erthia.

At least, that's what our holy book, *The Book of the Ancients*, tells us.

The traveling trunk Aunt Vyvian has brought for me lies open on the bed. It hits me that I've never been away from my uncle for more than a day, not since my brothers and I came to live with him when I was three, after my parents were killed in the Realm War.

It was a bloody conflict that raged for thirteen long years and ended with my grandmother's death in battle. But it was a necessary war, my beleaguered country relentlessly attacked and ransacked at the beginning of it. By the time it ended, Gardneria was allied with the Alfsigr Elves, ten times its original size, and the new, major power in the region.

All thanks to my grandmother, The Black Witch.

My father, Vale, was a highly ranked Gardnerian soldier, and my mother, Tessla, was visiting him when Keltic forces struck. They died together, and my uncle took us in soon after.

My little white cat, Isabel, jumps into my trunk and tries to pull a string from my old patchwork quilt. It's the quilt my mother made while pregnant with me, and it's linked to the only vivid memory I have of her. When I wrap myself in it, I can hear, faintly, the sound of my mother's voice singing me a lullaby, and almost feel her arms cradling me. No matter how bad a day I've had, just wrapping myself in this quilt can soothe me like nothing else.

It's as if she sewed her love right into the soft fabric.

Next to my trunk stands my apothecary kit, vials neatly stacked inside, tools secured, the medicines meticulously prepared. I've inherited this affinity for medicinal plants and herbs from my mother. She was a gifted apothecary, well-known for several creative tonics and elixirs that she developed.

Beside my apothecary supplies lies my violin, case open, its amber, lacquered wood reflecting the lantern light. I run my fingers along the violin's smooth surface.

I made this instrument, and there's no way I can part with it. I'm not *supposed* to know how to make violins, since women aren't allowed in the music crafter's Guilds. My uncle hesitated to teach me, but as time went on, he became increasingly aware of my natural talent and relented.

I love everything about violin-making. My hands have always been drawn to wood, soothed by it, and I can tell just by touching it what type it is, whether or not the tree was healthy, what kind of sound it will support. I can lose myself for hours on end carving, sanding, coaxing the raw wood into the graceful shapes of violin parts.

Sometimes we play together, my uncle and I, especially during the winter evenings by the light of the hearth.

A polite knock on the door frame breaks my reverie, and I turn to see my uncle standing in the open doorway.

"Am I disturbing you?" My uncle's face is gentle and softer than usual in the dim, warm light. His words, however, have a troubling edge of concern to them.

"No," I reply tentatively. "I'm just finishing packing."

"Can I come in?" he asks, hesitating. I nod and take a seat on my bed, which looks forlorn and foreign without its quilt. My uncle sits down next to me.

"I imagine you're feeling quite confused," he says. "Your aunt sent word a few months ago that she might be paying us a visit at some point, to discuss your future. So I started to make arrangements with the University. Just in case. I knew it was possible that she'd come for you someday, but I was hoping it wouldn't be for a few more years at least."

"Why?" I ask. I'm incredibly curious about why Aunt Vyvian has taken such a sudden interest in me—and why Uncle Edwin is so rattled by it.

My uncle wrings his clasped hands. "Because I *do not* believe what your aunt wants for your future is necessarily the best thing for you." He pauses and sighs deeply. "You know I love you and your brothers as much as if you were my own children."

I lean over onto his shoulder. His wool vest is scratchy. He puts his arm around me, and some of the stray hairs from his scraggly beard tickle my cheek.

"I've tried to shelter you, and protect you," he continues, "and I hope that your parents, if they were here, would understand why I've made the decisions that I have."

"I love you, too," I say, my voice cracking, my eyes filling with tears.

I've wanted to venture out for so long, but it's suddenly hitting me—I won't see my uncle or my loving home for a long time. Maybe not until spring.

"Well, now, what's this?" he asks, rubbing my shoulder to comfort me.

"It's just all so *fast*." I sniff back the tears. "I want to go, but… I'll miss you. And Isabel, too." Isabel, perhaps sensing my need for comfort, jumps onto my lap, purring and kneading me.

And I don't want you to be lonely with me gone.

"Oh, there now," my uncle says, as he hugs me tighter. "Don't cry. I'll take good care of Isabel, and you'll see her soon enough. You'll be back before you know it, with tales of all *sorts* of grand adventures."

I wipe at my tears and pull away to look up at him. I don't understand the urgency. He's always been so reluctant to let me go anywhere, always wanting to keep me here at home. Why has he made such a quick decision to finally let me go?

Perhaps seeing the questions in my eyes, my uncle lets out a deep sigh. "Your aunt can't force the issue of wandfasting as long as Rafe and I are here, but she *can* force the issue of schooling—unless I choose first. So I'm choosing. I've some contacts in the University's apothecary school, so it was no trouble finding you a spot there."

"Why don't you want me to apprentice at the High Mage Council with Aunt Vyvian?"

"It doesn't suit you," he explains with a shake of his head. "I want you to pursue something…" He hesitates a moment. "Something more *peaceful*."

He looks at me meaningfully, like he's trying to convey a secret hope and perhaps an unspoken danger, then he reaches down to pet Isabel, who pushes her head against him, purring contentedly.

I stare at him, confused by his odd emphasis.

"If they ask you," he says, focused in on the cat, "I've already wandtested you, and you have no magic."

"I know, but... I don't remember."

"It's not surprising," he says, absently, as he continues to stroke the cat. "You were very young, and it wasn't very memorable, as you have no magic."

Only Trystan has magic, unlike most Gardnerians, who have no magic, or weak magic at best. Trystan has *lots* of magic. And he's trained in weapon magic, which is particularly dangerous. But since my uncle won't allow wands or grimoires in the house, Trystan's never been able to show me what he can do.

Uncle Edwin's eyes meet mine, his expression darkening. "I want you to promise me, Elloren," he says, his tone uncharacteristically urgent. "Promise me that you won't leave school to apprentice with the Mage Council, no matter how much your aunt pressures you."

I don't understand why he's being so grave about this. I want to be an apothecary like my mother was, not apprenticed with our ruling council. I nod my head in agreement.

"And if something happens to me, you'll wait to wandfast to someone. You'll finish your education first."

"But nothing's going to happen to you."

"No, no, it's not," he says, reassuringly. "But promise me anyway."

A familiar worry mushrooms inside me. We all know that my uncle has been struggling with ill health for some time, prone to fatigue and problems with his joints and lungs. My brothers and I are loath to speak of this. He's been a parent to us for so long—the only parent we can really remember. The thought of losing him is too awful to think of.

"Okay," I say. "I promise. I'll wait."

Hearing these words, some of the tension leaves my uncle's face. He pats my shoulder approvingly and gets up, joints cracking as he stands. He pauses and puts his hand affectionately on my head. "Go to University," he says. "Learn the apothecary trade. Then come back to Halfix and practice your trade here."

Some of the creeping worry withdraws its cold hands.

That sounds just fine. And perhaps I'll meet a young man. I do want to be fasted, someday. Maybe, after I'm fasted, my fastmate and I could settle here in Halfix.

"All right," I agree, bolstered.

This is all sudden and unexpected, but it's exactly what I've wished for. Everything will work out for the best.

"Get some sleep," he tells me. "You've a long ride ahead of you tomorrow."

"Okay," I say. "I'll see you in the morning."

"Good night. Sleep well."

I watch him leave, his shy, friendly smile the last thing I see before he gently shuts the door.

CHAPTER FOUR:
The White Wand

I'm awakened by a sharp rapping at my window. I jerk up from my bed, look toward the window and am startled by the sight of an enormous white bird sitting on a branch outside, staring intently at me.

One of the birds I saw flying in from the mountains.

Its wings are so white against the blue light of predawn, they seem otherworldly.

I creep out of bed to see how close I can get to the bird before spooking it, but don't get far. As soon as I lose contact with the bed, the bird silently spreads its massive wings and flies out of sight. I rush to the window, fascinated.

There, I can still see it, staring fixedly at me, as if beckoning me to follow.

It's across the field, near the long fence that separates our property from the Gaffneys' estate.

I haphazardly dress and run outside, instantly consumed by the strange blue light that covers everything, transforming the familiar landscape into something ethereal.

The bird is still staring at me.

I walk toward it, the odd-colored scene making me feel like I'm in a dream.

I get quite close to the creature when it flies away again, past the garden, where the fence to my left disappears briefly into some dense bushes and trees.

I follow, feeling a thrill course through me, like I'm a child playing hide-and-seek. I round the corner to a small clearing then jump with fright and almost bolt in the opposite direction when I see what's there.

The white bird, along with two others, sits on a long tree branch. Directly below stands a spectral figure in a black cloak, its face hidden in the shadow of an overhanging hood.

"Elloren." The voice is familiar, halting me before I start to run.

Realization of who this is crashes through me.

"Sage?" I'm amazed and confused at the same time, my heart racing from the jolt of fear.

She stands, just beyond the fence. Sage Gaffney, our neighbor's eldest daughter.

Warily, I make my way toward her still figure, aware of the watchful birds above. As I get closer, I begin to make out her face in the blue light, her gaunt, terrified expression startling me. She was always a pleasant, healthy-looking girl, a University scholar and daughter of one of the wealthiest men in Gardneria. Her zealously religious family fasted her at thirteen to Tobias Vassilis, the son of a well-thought-of Gardnerian family. Sage had everything any Gardnerian girl could ever dream of.

But then she disappeared soon after starting University. Her family searched for her for over a year to no avail.

And yet here she is, as if risen from the dead.

"W-where have you been?" I stammer. "Your parents have been looking *everywhere* for you…"

"Keep your voice down, Elloren," she commands, her eyes fearful and darting around restlessly. She seems poised and prepared for escape, a large travel sack hanging from her back.

Something is moving beneath her cloak, something she's carrying.

"What's under your cloak?" I ask, bewildered.

"My son," she says with a defiant lift of her chin.

"You and Tobias have a son?"

"No," she corrects me, harshly, "he is *not* Tobias's." She says Tobias's name with such pure loathing, I wince. And she keeps the child hidden.

"Do you need help, Sage?" I keep my voice low, not wanting to spook her any more than she already is.

"I need to give you something," she whispers then reaches with a shaking hand for something hidden under her cloak. She pulls out a long, white wand that spirals up from an exquisitely carved handle, its tip so white it reminds me of the birds' wings. But my eyes are quickly drawn away from the wand to her hand.

It's covered with deep, bloody lash marks that continue up her wrist and disappear beneath the sleeve of her cloak.

I gasp in horror. "Holy Ancient One, what happened?"

Her eyes are briefly filled with despair before they harden again, a bitter smile forming on her mouth. "I did not honor my wandfasting," she whispers acidly.

I've heard tales of the harsh consequences of fast-breaking, but to *see* it...

"Elloren," she pleads, the look of terror returning. She pushes the wand out at me as if trying to will me to take it. "*Please.* There's not a lot of time! I'm supposed to give it to you. It *wants* to go to you."

"What do you mean, it *wants* to go to me?" I ask, confused. "Sage, where did you get this?"

"Just *take* it!" she insists. "It's incredibly powerful. And you can't let *them* get it!"

"Who's *them*?"

"The Gardnerians!"

I force out a disbelieving breath. "Sage, *we're* Gardnerians."

"*Please*," she begs. "*Please* take it."

"Oh, Sage," I say, shaking my head. "There's no reason for me to have a wand. I've no magic…"

"It doesn't matter! *They* want you to have it!" She gestures with the wand toward the tree above.

"The birds?"

"They're not just birds! They're *Watchers*. They appear during times of great darkness."

None of this makes any sense. "Sage, come inside with me." I try to sound as soothing as I can. "We'll talk to my uncle…"

"No!" she snarls, recoiling. "I told you, it only wants *you!*" Her expression turns desperate. "It's the *White Wand*, Elloren."

Pity flashes through me. "Oh, Sage, that's a children's story."

It's a religious myth, told to every Gardnerian child. Good versus Evil—the White Wand pitted against the Dark Wand. The White Wand, a pure force for good, coming to the aid of the oppressed and used in ancient, primordial battles against demonic forces. Against the power of the Dark Wand.

"It's not just a story," Sage counters, teeth gritted, her eyes gone wild. "You *have* to believe me. This is *the White Wand*." She lifts the wand again and thrusts it toward me.

She's mad, completely mad. But she's so agitated, and I want to calm her fears. Relenting, I reach out and take the wand.

The pale wood of the handle is smooth and cool to the touch, strangely devoid of any sense of its source tree. I slide it under my cloak and into a pocket.

Sage looks instantly relieved, like a heavy burden has been lifted.

Movement in the distance catches my eye, just inside where the wilds begin. Two dark figures on horseback are there and gone again so quickly, I wonder if it's a trick of the light. There are so many strange, dark shadows this time in the morning. I glance up and look for the white birds, and I have to blink twice to make sure I'm not seeing things.

They're gone. With no sound made in leaving. I spin around on my heels, searching for them. They're nowhere in sight.

"They're gone, Elloren," Sage says, her eyes once again apprehensively scanning around as if sensing some impending doom. She grasps my arm hard, her nails biting into my skin.

"Keep it secret, Elloren! Promise me!"

"Okay," I agree, wanting to reassure her. "I promise."

Sage lets out a deep sigh and releases me. "Thank you." She looks in the direction of my cottage. "I have to go."

"Wait," I beg of her. "Don't go. Whatever's going on... I want to help you."

She regards me mournfully as if I'm dauntingly naive. "They want my baby, Elloren," she says, her voice cracking, a tear spilling down her cheek.

Her baby? "*Who* wants your baby?"

Sage wipes her eyes with the back of her shaking, disfigured hand and casts a sidelong glance at my cottage. "*They* do!" She looks over her shoulder and gives her own home a pained look. "I wish... I wish I could explain to my family what's really going on. To make them *see*. But they *believe*." Her frown deepens, and she sets her gaze hard on me. "The Council's coming for him, Elloren. They think he's Evil. That's why your aunt's here."

"No, Sage," I insist. "She's here to talk to me about wand-fasting."

She shakes her head vehemently. "No. They're coming for my baby. And I have to leave before they get here." She looks away for a moment as if desperately trying to compose herself. She hides her hand back under her cloak and cradles the small bundle inside. I wonder why she won't let me see him.

I reach out to touch her arm. "You're imagining all this, Sage. There's no way anyone would want to hurt your baby."

She glares at me with angry frustration then shakes her head as if resigned to madness. "Goodbye, Elloren," she says as if she pities me. "Good luck."

"Wait…" I implore as she begins to walk along the fence line in the direction of the great wilderness. I follow her brisk pace, the fence separating us, leaning over it to reach her as she veers away, her back receding into the distance—a dark, ghostly figure making her way through the last of the morning mist.

The trees swallow her up into their darkness just as the sun rises, transforming the eerie blue dreamworld of early morning into the clear, sunlit world of day.

My fingers fumble under my cloak for the wand, half expecting it to be gone, expecting to find that I was sleepwalking and imagined all of this. But then I feel it—smooth and straight and very much real.

I rush back to the house, the sunlight steadily gaining strength.

Shaken, I'm desperate to find Uncle Edwin. Surely he'll know what to do.

As I round the trees, I'm surprised to see Aunt Vyvian standing in the doorway watching me, her expression unreadable.

A small wave of apprehension washes over me at the sight of her, and I immediately slow my pace, struggling to turn my expression blank, as if returning from an uneventful morning stroll. But my mind is a tumult.

Those marks on Sage's hands—they were so horrible. Maybe Sage is right. Maybe the Council is planning to take her baby away…

Aunt Vyvian tilts her head and eyes me thoughtfully as I approach. "Are you done packing?" she asks. "We're ready to go."

I stand awkwardly in front of her, not able to move forward

as she's blocking the doorway. "Yes, I'm done." I'm acutely aware of the wand, my hand involuntarily drawn to it.

My aunt's eyes flicker in the direction of the Gaffneys' farm. "Did you visit with Sage Gaffney?" Her face is open, welcoming me to confide in her.

Shock flashes through me. How does she know that Sage is here?

I glance back toward the wilds, my heart thumping against my chest.

Sage was right. Aunt Vyvian isn't just here for me. Clearly she's here for Sage, too. But surely she would never harm a baby?

Aunt Vyvian sighs. "It's all right, Elloren. I know she's here, and I realize it must be terribly upsetting to see her. She's... very troubled. We're trying to help her, but..." She shakes her head sadly. "How is she?" Her tone is one of maternal concern. Some of my tension lightens.

"She's terribly frightened." The words rush out. "The baby. She thinks someone wants to harm him. That someone from the Council is coming to take him away from her."

My aunt doesn't seem surprised by this. She fixes me with the type of look adults use when they are about to reveal to a child some unfortunate, troubling fact of life. "The Council *is* coming to take custody of her baby."

I blink in shocked surprise.

Aunt Vyvian lays a comforting hand on my shoulder. "The child is deformed, Elloren. It needs a physician's care, and much more."

"What's wrong with it?" I breathe, almost not wanting to know.

Aunt Vyvian searches my eyes, hesitant to tell me what I know will be something monstrous. "Elloren," she explains gravely, "Sage has given birth to an Icaral."

I recoil at the word. *No! It can't be.* It's too horrible to imagine. One of the Evil Winged Ones—like giving birth to a grotesque demon. No wonder Sage didn't let me see her child.

The dull thud of horses' hooves sounds in the distance, and I spot another Mage Council carriage rounding the hills and making its way down into the valley toward the Gaffneys' estate. It's followed by eight Gardnerian soldiers on horseback.

"Can the child be helped?" My voice comes out in a shocked whisper as I watch the carriage and the soldiers nearing the cottage.

"The Council will try, Elloren." My aunt reassures me. "Its wings will be removed and a Mage Priest will do everything he can to try and save the child's twisted soul." She pauses and looks at me inquisitively. "What else did Sage say to you?"

It's a simple enough question, but something stops me up short, some amorphous fear. And Sage has enough problems already.

Clearly she's stolen this wand. It can't possibly be the wand of myth that she imagines it to be, but it's obviously an expensive wand. Probably belonging to Tobias.

I'll wait until all this dies down and find a way to return it to him. And I don't mention that Sage has run off into the woods—I'm sure the Council will find her soon enough on their own anyway.

"She didn't say much else," I lie. "Only what I've told you."

My aunt nods in approval and lets out a small sigh. "Well then, enough of this. We've a big journey ahead of us."

I attempt a small, resigned smile in return and bury Sage's secret deep within, as well as my guilt in keeping it.